RIGHT PLACE WRONG TIME

A WELCOME TO MOONRIDGE NOVEL

AVERY ARUJO

WELCOME TO MOONRIDGE SERIES

Once Upon a Blue Moon
Date Night With Death
Right Place Wrong Time

A Note to Readers

This story explores a romantic relationship that includes emotional manipulation and abuse.

These elements are written intentionally and are part of the larger journey of one of the characters. They are not meant to be romanticized or endorsed, but to reflect how complicated and difficult certain relationships can be.

If these themes are sensitive for you, please take care while reading and feel free to step away at any point. Your comfort and well-being always come first.

If you or someone you know are currently experiencing any sort of abuse, or if this story brings up difficult feelings, support is available:

- **National Domestic Violence Hotline** (U.S.): 1-800-799-SAFE (7233) or thehotline.org
- **Love is Respect** (dating abuse, all genders): loveisrespect.org (call 866-331-9474 or text LOVEIS to 22522)
- **The Network/La Red** (TNLR): 24-hour confidential hotline for LGBTQ+ survivors (also inclusive of kink and poly communities): 617-742-4911 or 800-832-1901 | tnlr.org
- **The Trevor Project** (LGBTQ+ crisis support): thetrevorproject.org (call 1-866-488-7386 or text START to 678678)

With love,
Avery

Copyright © 2026 by Avery Arujo
Cover Design & Interior Design © 2026 Literally Everything Media
Cover fonts and elements licensed through Creative Fabrica & Envato Elements
Inside artwork and fonts licensed through Creative Fabrica

All rights reserved. No part of this publication may be reproduced, stored or transmitted in any form or by any means, electronic, mechanical, photocopying, recording, scanning, or otherwise without written permission from the publisher. It is illegal to copy this book, post it to a website, or distribute it by any other means without permission. Under no circumstances may any part of this work be used to train AI models.

This novel is entirely a work of fiction. The names, characters and incidents portrayed in it are the work of the author's imagination. Any resemblance to actual persons, living or dead, events or localities is entirely coincidental.

Avery Arujo asserts the moral right to be identified as the author of this work.

Designations used by companies to distinguish their products are often claimed as trademarks. All brand names and product names used in this book and on its cover are trade names, service marks, trademarks and registered trademarks of their respective owners. The publishers and the book are not associated with any product or vendor mentioned in this book. None of the companies referenced within the book have endorsed the book.

This book was written by the author and edited with the assistance of an editorial tool known as AutoCrit. This tool was used to identify grammar issues and stylistic inconsistencies. All final edits and creative decisions were made by the author. No generative AI was used to develop, create or rewrite content.

First edition
ISBN: 978-1-969289-12-5 (Hardcover)
ISBN: 978-1-969289-13-2 (Paperback)
ISBN: 978-1-969289-14-9 (KDP Paperback)

for boys who love boys

What's been happening in Moonridge...

Book 1: *Once Upon a Blue Moon*

When a love spell went wrong, witch Hazel Thornton accidentally swapped bodies with Blake Carter, the werewolf alpha she's hated since grade school. Forced to cooperate, the two uncovered old magic buried beneath Moonridge and learned that Bianca Mayweather, the town's resident fitness guru, was actually Ravena Blackwood, an exiled witch plotting to awaken something dark beneath the town.

With help from their friends, Hazel and Blake stopped Ravena and sealed her in the catacombs under the old mine. But as Moonridge began to heal, a black SUV appeared, watching, waiting, and reminding them that the fight was far from over.

Book 2: *Date Night With Death*

After the summer's werewolf chaos, Mina Cartwright's B&B is circling the drain. Her luck seems to change when the cast of *The Real Vampire Wives of Obsidian Hills* books a stay for the Halloween festival, but the real surprise arrives with Dex Grimm, a Reaper sent to collect Mina's dying soul.

While fighting his growing feelings for Mina, Dex uncovers the return of the Concord 13, a secret cult bent on tearing down the veil between life and death. Mina's soul is the key they need. On Halloween night, as the Concord's ritual unfolds, Vivienne St. James—one of the Vampire Wives—saves Mina by biting her, trapping her in a state between life and death and rendering her useless to the Concord.

The cult is beaten back for now, but they'll return to finish what they started.

LAST HALLOWEEN

CHAPTER ONE

Everett

The caramel apple booth smells like autumn used to when I was alive. Sugar and cinnamon and crisp October air. The smell takes me back to county fairs and endless nights. To harvest festivals and the promise of another year ahead. I breathe it in, trying to commit it to memory alongside everything else about tonight.

Calvin laughs at something the vendor says, his whole face lighting up, and the sound hits me square in the chest. I've got maybe three hours left with him. Three hours before I have to walk away from this and help tear the world apart.

"You want one?" Calvin turns to me, that smile I love spreading across his face. The one that makes me thankful I no longer have a working heart so I can't feel it breaking.

"Sure."

Calvin pays for both, handing me the apple.

I watch him lick caramel off his thumb, and think, *This. Remember this. The way he looks at you. The way he makes you feel.*

Because in a few hours, none of it will exist anymore.

Either the Concord succeeds and the world as we know it

ends, or they fail and I get dragged back to Skipper Lake. Either way, I'll never see Calvin again. Either way, what he and I had these last few days ends tonight.

"You okay?" Calvin puts his arm around me and squeezes my shoulder. I'll never get used to being touched again. That's what I've missed the most.

I paste on a smile. "Yeah. Just thinking how lucky I am. To be here. With you."

It's the truest thing I've said all week, and also the biggest lie. Because I'm not lucky. I'm a dead man walking through a borrowed moment, pretending I get to keep this.

God, I want to keep this.

"Come on." Calvin tugs me forward, threading his fingers through mine. "I want you to meet everyone. My brother, my friends. They're going to love you."

My throat goes tight. This is what I always longed for.

We weave through the festival crowds, past kids in costumes and teenagers making out behind the fortune teller's tent. The Haunted Halloween Festival is in full swing, everyone having the time of their lives, completely unaware that in a few hours, everything will change. That somewhere up at Whispering Falls, the Concord is preparing a ritual that'll split the veil between the living and the dead, ending life as all living beings know it.

The binding points are already activated. I did that. Walked through Moonridge touching each one, lighting them up like candles on a birthday cake and then kept them lit when the witches tried to extinguish them. All for a wish I never asked for, bound to a group I never wanted to join.

I should've said no when Calvin asked me to come tonight. Should've disappeared after our last morning run and spared him this. But I'm selfish and stupid and I wanted one more night. Wanted to pretend, just for a few hours, that I could have this kind of life.

"There they are!" Calvin waves enthusiastically at a group

gathered near the game booths. "Blake! Guys!"

My stomach, or what used to be my stomach, drops.

Blake looks just like his photos, only bigger. More intimidating. Next to him, a woman with curly auburn hair. Hazel. Her mother is the anchor holding the Concord together, and I wonder if she has any idea.

The others close in. I recognize La'Tasha, Dex, and Penny from last night—I'd followed them to the library basement, and watched them discover the Crucible Core. And there's Mina, the one the Concord actually sent me to get close to. Except I never did. Couldn't bring myself to use Calvin like that.

"Hey, guys!" Calvin's voice lifts with hope, like he's already decided they're going to accept me. The sound will haunt me for whatever eternity I have left. "I want you all to meet someone."

I straighten my jacket and paste on my best smile. The one I used to use at the auto shop when customers came in. Friendly but not too eager. Confident but approachable.

"This is Everett." Calvin's voice catches on my name, tender and proud, and something in me cracks.

"Calvin's told me so much about all of you." The words come out smooth enough, but I can hear the faint echo underneath. The sound of a voice that doesn't quite belong to the living world anymore.

Calvin stands close enough that our shoulders touch, and I try not to think about how I'll never feel this again.

"He's visiting for the festival," Calvin continues, "but I'm hoping he might stick around."

The naked hope in his voice kills me. Which is impressive considering I'm already dead.

I want to tell him the truth. That I can't stay. That in a few hours I'll be gone. That I've been lying from the start, even though none of what I feel is a lie. Every moment with him these last few days has been the most alive I've ever felt.

But I don't say any of that. I just smile and nod and pretend

I'm the kind of person who has endless amounts of time with him.

La'Tasha studies me, all casual curiosity. "What brought you to Moonridge, Everett?"

"The festival," I answer, keeping my tone easy. "I always loved it when I was a kid. Decided to visit again this year. Then I met this guy…"

Calvin ducks his head. "I thought I'd imagined him at first, when we collided during the race." Like running into me was the best accident of his life instead of the worst thing that could've happened to him.

This is torture. Standing here, pretending to be normal, watching Calvin look at me like I'm someone good. Someone worth introducing to his family.

Blake's studying me, shoulders squared, jaw tight. He's already deciding whether I'm good enough for his big brother. Fair enough. If I had a brother, I'd probably do the same. Except Blake doesn't know he should be protecting Calvin from me. From who I'm bound to. From what we're about to do.

Penny hasn't said anything yet. Just stands there, unnaturally still, fingers working at her cardigan sleeve. But her eyes keep darting between Calvin's face and mine, and there's something in her expression that makes me desperate to leave now.

She knows.

"He can't stay."

The words slice through the conversation like a blade through butter. Penny closes the distance between us, and the nervous, timid girl is gone.

Calvin's smile falters. "What are you talking about?"

No. No, no, no. Not yet. I need more time. Just a few more hours of pretending this could work.

"The Crucible Core. In the library." Penny's voice trembles but she keeps going, keeps destroying everything. "When I touched it, I saw every soul involved in the Concord's ritual." She advances, and I back up instinctively. "Including him. He's not just one of the ghosts fueling the ritual, though. He is a member. He's tied to the Skipper Lake binding point."

The world tilts sideways. Calvin's looking at me now, confusion shifting to something that might be hurt, and I want to sink through the ground and disappear.

Before I can explain, before I can find the words that might make this better, Penny lunges forward and grabs my wrist.

"Penny!" Calvin starts forward, but Blake holds him back.

"Look." Penny yanks my sleeve up.

The mark pulses with sickly green light. A spiral with thirteen points. The Concord's sigil, branded into what's left of my soul.

I jerk my arm back, panic flooding through me. The cool-guy mask cracks wide open, leaving me exposed and desperate. "I'm not... I didn't..."

But I am. And I did. And there's no way to explain that would make this okay.

My form flickers violently as I look at Calvin. At the hurt blooming across his face. At the betrayal in his eyes.

"I don't know what she's talking about." The lie tastes like ash, but I try anyway, reaching for Calvin's arm. My hand passes straight through.

My solidity wavers. The carefully maintained illusion flickers at the edges, and suddenly I'm transforming back into a ghost. Translucent and wrong and not belonging here.

"I swear, I've been fighting their control." The words tumble out. "I'm different. I'm bound to them. I don't want to be. I need help..."

"I don't understand." Calvin's voice comes out small. Broken.

"It means he's been using you to get closer to Mina." Blake steps in front of his brother, protective and furious.

"No!" My form flickers harder, transparency spreading up my arms. "It's not like that. I didn't want this. I was trapped—am trapped. I'm not willingly one of them. I can help you."

I'm begging now. Actually begging, which I swore I'd never

do again after Vince. But this is different. This is Calvin, and I'm watching everything good slip through my fingers.

"All of you. You have to believe me."

But Calvin refuses to look at me. He's looking at Blake, at Penny, at anyone but me.

It's over.

The tug starts then. That familiar pull around my middle, the rope yanking me back toward Whispering Falls. The Concord calling me home like the dog I am.

No. Not yet. I need more time to explain.

I turn to Penny, the only one who might understand. The only one who saw the Crucible Core.

"The basement," I force out as my edges dissolve. "The Core. Release it." The words rush out as the pull gets stronger. "Trust your instincts. Release it and you stop everything."

It's the only thing I can give them. The only way to sabotage the ritual. And maybe—just maybe—if they release all those trapped souls, I'll be free too.

I'm pulled away and I look at Calvin one last time. Try to memorize the exact shade of his eyes, the way his hair falls across his forehead, the shape of his mouth.

"I'm sorry," I whisper.

Then the ground trembles and the rope yanks hard, and I'm gone.

Ripped away from the festival lights and Calvin's heartbroken face.

Back to the dark.

Back to the Concord.

PRESENT DAY

CHAPTER TWO

Calvin

I inhale the last bite of pizza, hoping the cheese and carbs will soak up the four beers already invading my system.

"Happy Galentine's Day," Coco toasts, grabbing another slice and lifting it like a champagne flute. "To my favorite gals. Actual and honorary."

La'Tasha taps the neck of her bottle against Coco's slice. Penny raises her beer and Leo, half sprawled on a beanbag like his bones melted, gives a thumbs-up.

"Thanks for including us tonight," I say, tipping back the last of my beer. "Otherwise, I'd be sitting at home pretending it doesn't bother me that I'm alone on Valentine's Day. Again."

"Cupid can bite my ass." La'Tasha taps the table for emphasis and I raise a fist in solidarity.

"I've decided that Cupid's a fuckin' homophobe." I set my empty bottle on the coffee table with a thunk. "The guy won't throw a single arrow at the lone gay werewolf in town."

Leo grins from his sprawl. "I've got your arrow right here,

baby."

"Nobody wants your nasty little ding-a-ling." La'Tasha throws a pillow at him and he ducks, laughing.

Her apartment glows with amber lamplight and the chaos of personality. An orange sofa, a purple armchair, and a turquoise ottoman disappear under patterned pillows. Crystals catch the light from the window ledge while vines spill from hanging pots. Somewhere near the bookshelves, sandalwood and something earthy burn in a small dish, the scent curling through grease and tomato sauce.

Leo reaches over the pizza boxes and half-crushed chip bags. "Pass the ranch." His wrist clips an empty bottle and it rattles across the coffee table.

I slide the ranch his way. "You and your ranch obsession. And on pizza, of all things. That should be a crime."

"Says the guy who puts pineapple on his," Leo says, one eyebrow arching.

"Hey. Hawaiian pizza slaps, and anyone who says otherwise obviously has very poor taste."

Penny leans over the table and plucks another beer from the six-pack. For someone so tiny, she drinks like a champ. She pops the cap off, takes a long swallow, then says, "I saw Mina the other day. She looks like she's holding up okay."

Coco shifts on the loveseat, one leg hooked over the armrest. Her curly black hair spills from a messy bun on top of her head, star-shaped earrings flashing when she moves. "Yeah, she looks great. Has she said anything?" Coco asks. "You know… about being kinda dead but also not. Like, is she a vampire now or what?"

La'Tasha shakes her head. "She's still hanging in that in-between space. I tried to nudge the conversation last time I saw her, but she shut me down real quick. I think she's just enjoying her time."

I sink deeper into the couch cushions, beer cold against my palm. I can't imagine what Mina's going through. Standing between worlds, holding a choice nobody should have to make. If it were me, I know exactly what I would pick. Vampire werewolf sounds metal as hell.

"I'm just glad she and Dex are happy," Penny says, her features relaxing as she drifts into her own little romantic bubble. "I don't blame them for dragging this out as long as they can. Once Mina decides, he has to leave and go back to full-time Reaper duties. No more Moonridge."

"Oh, the perils of love," Coco sighs, throwing the back of her hand to her forehead like she's auditioning for a soap opera.

"It makes being single look not so bad, amiright?" I lift my empty bottle. "A toast to us. Moonridge's finest relationship disasters."

"Hey, speak for yourself." La'Tasha knocks her bottle against mine. "No disaster here. After the last jerk I dated, I am perfectly happy flying solo. Forever."

"Forever is a long time," Leo says.

"Not long enough to forget Kiran and his no-calling, no-texting, ghosting ass." La'Tasha peels at the edge of her beer label, little curls of paper gathering at her feet. "And when I say ghosting ass, I don't mean he was literally a ghost. No offense, Calvin." She winks. "Seriously, though. Men are trash."

"Gee, thanks," I say.

"Not you two. I like you…" She pats my knee. "Most of the time."

"I like you better as humans," Coco says. "Werewolves are cool and stuff, but it's really awkward when you walk around as wolves and I can see your buttholes."

Leo and I both freeze, eyes locking across the table.

"What about my butthole?" Leo asks. His voice cracks on the last word.

Coco shrugs. "We've all seen them. When you're in wolf form and your tails are all up, your little starfish are just *right* there."

Leo chokes on a laugh. "Coco, why are you staring at my

brown eye?"

"I'm not staring. It's just out there. And I'm not the only one who noticed." She jabs a finger at La'Tasha. "She said we should make the entire pack little rings with jewels that hang off the base of your tails so we don't have to look at them."

Oh. My. God. My friends have all been staring at my asshole. "What is wrong with you people?"

La'Tasha slides off the couch, laughing so hard her shoulders shake. "Coco, I swear, you need to stop saying the quiet part out loud. That conversation was supposed to stay between us."

I swat her with a pillow. "I'm never shifting again. Ever. Hope you're happy. You broke your favorite gay werewolf."

"Oh hush." She wipes tears from her cheeks. "You know I love you. But I am absolutely going to bedazzle you a bootyhole cover. Maybe add a tassel."

I groan into my hands. "So, anyway." I raise my voice over Leo's snickering. "Back to La'Tasha's very wise comment before…" I shake my head. "Yes, men *are* trash. Relationships *are* a nightmare."

"I've never been in love," Penny says.

We all stare at her in silence.

She blinks at us, cheeks beginning to flush. "What? I've dated. Sure. But love? That whole swept-off-your-feet, can't-eat, can't-sleep thing? Never happened. And I've never wanted to give my goodie bag to anyone." She giggle-burps. "At least not yet."

"Your goodie bag?" La'Tasha and I snort at the same time.

"What? There's nothing wrong with being a twenty-four-year-old virgin."

"There's nothing wrong with that at all, you little Puritan." La'Tasha pats her leg. "Just don't let your coochie seal itself up from disuse."

"Wait. Can that happen?" Coco asks.

We dissolve into laughter.

"Seriously, though." La'Tasha leans her elbows on her knees, label shreds scattered around her. "Do you *want* to be in love?"

Penny tilts her head, considering. "I don't know. Sometimes it sounds nice. Other times, looking at all the drama it causes…" She waves her hand, taking us all in. "I'm not sure it's worth it."

La'Tasha points at Penny like she's awarding her a prize. "Smart woman."

Coco twirls a curl around her finger like she's winding up a thought. "I've been in love a few times. Men, women, a snowman once. I just don't think I'm wired for one person. There are too many fun people on this planet."

Leo raises his beer. "Bisexuals for the win."

Coco shrugs. "I consider myself more fluid than bi. Life is a whole ice cream shop. Why would I pick one flavor when the samples are free?"

"That's one way to look at it," I say.

I grab another beer. With the TV off, the only sound is the faint hum of the fridge. Outside, snow falls past the windows in thick, steady sheets, blurring the streetlights and frosting the world in white. Winter has Moonridge in a chokehold this year. It won't let go.

"So, Leo." La'Tasha tips her chin at him. "What's the deal with you and Vivienne? You two still a thing?"

Leo shifts on the beanbag. His fingers tap a quick rhythm against his beer. "I wouldn't say we've ever been, like, a thing-thing. Just… interested. Very interested." He takes a swallow. "Her divorce is final now, so we can actually date without any mess, but we haven't seen each other. She's buried in press for the new season of Vampire Wives, plus all her fashion shows." He flicks his hand through the air, frustration tightening his jaw.

"You miss her?" Coco asks, softer now.

"Yeah." He takes another drink, jaw tight. "It's been months since I last saw her. Since the Halloween festival. We talk every day, but it's not the same."

Penny scrunches her nose in sympathy. "It's hard to get to

know someone that way."

"Tell me about it." Leo huffs a laugh. "Never thought I would be that guy refreshing social media to see if the woman I like posted a new thirst trap."

I lean over and pat his shoulder. "You're handling it better than most would. Dating a vampire celebrity sounds exhausting."

"How about you, Calvin?" Coco asks, turning those bright eyes on me. "How are you doing? Finally over that ghost dude?"

And there it is. The conversational land mine I've been tap-dancing around all night.

I set my beer bottle down with a thunk. "I'm fine."

Three pairs of witchy eyes plus one nosy werewolf stare at me.

"Seriously," I say. "I barely knew him. We hung out for, what, five days? Then we found out he was tied up in all that Concord crap and he vanished. I feel like an idiot for falling for it and putting Mina at risk, but otherwise I'm good. It would be pathetic to still be hung up on that, right?"

La'Tasha gives me a look. The kind that says she calls bullshit without saying a word.

I slump back into the couch and put my hands behind my head, the picture of unbothered. "What do you want me to say? Yes, I'm still messed up over my ex-fiancé leaving me five years ago, and it made me easy pickings when Everett showed up. I was excited to finally meet another gay guy I had something in common with." My throat tightens. I cross my arms and stare at a grease stain on the pizza box instead of their faces. "Then it turns out he's a literal ghost with ties to the same nightmare cult that tried to use my friend to crack open the veil."

"That's a very reasonable thing to be upset about," Penny says.

Jace's face flashes across my mind.

I shake my head. "Let's just say my breakup with Jace messed me up for a long time. I got real good at closing myself off. I was completely isolated. Then Everett shows up and suddenly I remember what hope feels like. That lasted maybe five minutes before everything went to shit."

"I still can't believe he was part of the Concord," Leo says.

"He swore he wasn't," I say. Everett's voice rings in my head. *I didn't choose this.* "But who knows."

"And you believe him?" La'Tasha asks.

"I want to." I huff out a humorless laugh. I stare at the condensation ring my bottle left on the table. "I can't tell if I miss him or if I just miss the idea of someone actually being interested in me. It was so effortless with him. We talked about everything. He seemed to be really into me. Wanted to know all about me and my friends. But then I wonder if all of that was simply because he was trying to get close to us to help the Concord." My chest squeezes tight. "But then another part of me keeps thinking, what if it *was* real? What if he really *was* forced to work with them?"

La'Tasha turns to me with a look that tells me she's not going to hold back. "Baby, you know I adore you, but I got to keep it real. A relationship with a ghost? Come on. Think about it. The man is dead. He doesn't even have a body. How is it even possible to be with him? Whatever you felt when he was here was probably Concord nonsense making him seem all touchable and broody. And if he really liked you like that, don't you think he would have shown up by now to explain? Or sent a sign? Something."

"I know." I drag a hand over my beard. "I know. But my brain won't drop it. I'm like a dog with a bone, except the bone is emotional baggage. And I'm a werewolf, so the metaphor fits a little too well."

"You know what you need?" Coco says. Her eyes light up. That look usually means the next idea will either fix my life or blow it up. "A cleansing ritual. We scrape all the Everett residue off you, make your aura all sparkly and fresh. Like a magical tune-up."

Leo snickers into his beer.

Coco continues. "The point is, you are energetically glued to Everett. We need to peel you free so you can move forward. Or sideways. Whatever direction feels right for you."

"Or," Penny says, sitting a little straighter, "we could contact Everett directly. Ask him what his deal was. You want answers, right? He's the only one who can give you what you need. All we need is La'Tasha's Ouija board."

La'Tasha chokes on her drink. "Girl, have you lost your damn mind? After what went down at the B&B? Mina and Dahlia got possessed, a whole Concord creeper tried to hitch a ride in Mina's brain. Absolutely not." She waves her bottle at me. "And what is a ritual going to do for you, really? You want a man. You need a real one. You can't have sex with a ghost. If the mission is to get you laid, we need someone with a pulse."

I bite back a laugh. "Getting laid is not the issue. I can handle that part."

Leo gives me a quick, knowing look. Years ago, we tried to make something happen between us. It didn't stick, but our friendship—and an occasional hookup—did.

But Penny's suggestion lodges in the back of my mind and refuses to move. Reaching out to Everett. Getting answers. It's not a bad idea.

"Actually," I say slowly, "that might work. The Ouija board, I mean. Just to get some answers. Closure."

La'Tasha stares at me like I've sprouted a dick on my forehead.

"You want to?" Penny asks, pushing her glasses up her nose.

"Why not? Three powerful witches in the room. You can protect me. Make it safe." I give them my best puppy dog eyes. "I just want to know if any of it was real. Or if I'm just that easy to manipulate. I need to know which kind of idiot I am."

La'Tasha chews her lip. She's totally about to cave.

"We could make it safe," Penny says.

"I have protection charms," Coco adds.

La'Tasha groans. "I can't believe I'm considering this. But if it'll make your petulant ass stop whining into your beer..."

"It will." It comes out too fast.

"Fine." She pushes herself to her feet and stretches. "We're doing this properly. No shortcuts. And nobody better tell Hazel. I don't need her riding my ass."

She disappears into her bedroom and comes back with an old Ouija board pressed to her chest. The wood looks worn, the letters slightly faded.

Coco hops up and starts pouring a line of salt and crushed lavender buds around the coffee table. The lavender's sharp, floral scent cuts through the pizza smell and makes the room feel smaller, like the walls just leaned in. Penny moves to a little desk shoved against the wall, opens a drawer, and pulls out a tiny bottle of dark ink and a thin brush. She returns to us and takes my wrist first. The ink is cool and thick against my skin as she paints a looping sigil along the inside of my arm. It tingles, almost like carbonated water on my nerves.

"What does it do?" I ask.

"Keeps the wrong things from getting in," she murmurs, moving to Leo next. Her hand stays steady, even though she's had more alcohol than me.

By the time she finishes, something crawls through the air and settles under my skin. Candle flames flicker where Coco has set them along the circle, wax pooling on mismatched saucers.

"Drink this." La'Tasha shoves a small cup into my hand. The liquid inside looks like watery diarrhea.

I sniff it and wrinkle my nose. "What is it?"

"Just a little something to open your third eye. Make you more receptive."

"You mean his brown eye—"

I almost choke on the drink.

"Leo, I'm about to rip that man-bun off your head and beat you with it." La'Tasha whacks him, and he dodges away, cackling.

I knock the cup back. The taste is better than the smell. It's sweet with a bite of something peppery that makes my throat tingle. A little buzz blooms behind my eyes, softer than the beer but heavier than caffeine.

We move to the floor, knees brushing, the Ouija board in the center of the salt and lavender ring. La'Tasha turns off the overhead light. Candlelight climbs the walls, painting everything in gold and shadow.

"Everyone put one finger on the board," Penny says. Her voice shifts into witch mode, calm and precise. "Light contact only. Calvin, both hands on the planchette."

I do as I'm told. The wooden pointer is smooth and cool, the little window in the middle hovering over the word "Hello."

"Now we open the connection," La'Tasha says. "Spirits of the veil, we seek peaceful communication with one who has passed. Everett… what was his last name again?"

"Bradshaw," I whisper.

"Everett Bradshaw," she continues. "If you can hear us, we invite you into our circle and ask you to speak through this board."

Silence settles. The only sounds are our breathing and the faint hiss of candle wicks. My knees ache already. I can't help but feel a little stupid. I'm sitting here resting my fingers on a triangle waiting for a dead man to text back.

"Maybe he's taking a dump," Leo mutters.

Coco snorts.

"Try again," I say, refusing to humor Leo.

La'Tasha repeats the invitation, words slow and careful. We wait. The planchette just sits there, heavy and still.

I'm about to tell them we can forget the whole thing when the air shifts. A thin chill brushes across the back of my neck. Goosebumps rise along my arms, prickling against the ink.

"Do you feel that?" I murmur.

Before anyone answers, the planchette moves. Just a slide at first, so small I wonder if one of us twitched. Then it glides, steady and sure, until the little window lands over YES.

"Holy shit," Leo breathes.

"Is this Everett?" Coco asks. Her voice stays even, but her eyes shine.

The planchette drifts away, then returns to YES.

My heart rolls behind my ribs. "Everett? Is it really you?"

YES.

H-I-C-A-L-V-I-N

My eyes sting. Of all the ways he could have started, he picked that. *Hi Calvin.* Like this is just a text thread that he's come back to.

I swallow. "I just need to ask you one thing. Did you…" My tongue feels thick. The words fight me. "Were you just using me to get to Mina?"

The planchette rockets to NO, so fast it almost slips from under my fingers.

My chest loosens a fraction. "I hope you mean that," I say. The words barely make it out.

The planchette creeps across the board again, letter by letter.

I-M-I-S-S-Y-O-U

The candles blur at the edges of my vision. Heat presses behind my eyes. The beer, the potion, the hit of seeing those letters, all of it swirls together.

"Are you really part of the Concord?" Penny asks, ever practical.

The pointer slides to YES.

My stomach drops.

The planchette continues to move, spelling out U-N-W-I-L-L-I-N-G

"You can't break free?" I ask.

NO.

"He says he can't break free," I say, even though they can all read.

"Do you want to be free?" Coco asks.

YES.

"Do you want to get naked with Calvin?" Leo blurts.

La'Tasha elbows him hard in the ribs. "What he means is, were your feelings for Calvin real?"

The planchette pauses, then sweeps across the board.

A-B-S-O-L-U-T-E-L-Y

The candle flames jump, bending sharply to one side. The hairs on the back of my neck stand straight up.

"I miss you too." The words scrape my throat. I force my fingers to stay steady against the planchette. "My feelings were real. Are real."

The planchette begins to circle, small tight loops, like it's pacing.

"Can we help you break free?" La'Tasha asks.

The pointer jerks to NO, then spells T-R-A-P-P-E-D

"There has to be a way." I lean forward. "Some kind of spell or ritual."

The planchette snaps to D, then A-N-G-E-R-O-U-S

"I don't care," I say. The alcohol burns warm in my veins. "We beat them once. We can do it again. I want to help you."

The temperature seems to drop. One of the candles gutters and dies, smoke curling toward the ceiling.

"Calvin," Penny says quietly, "maybe we should stop."

I ignore her. "Everett, please. Try to leave the lake. Let us help you. Come find me. I want to talk. Face to face."

The planchette slams to a stop. A sharp snap cracks the air, like an elastic breaking. Every candle goes dark at once, plunging the room into black.

"Shit." La'Tasha scrabbles along the wall for the switch.

The overhead light snaps on. My eyes sting at the sudden brightness. The salt circle is unbroken. Lavender buds dot the carpet. The board looks ordinary again, flat and harmless. The planchette rests where it stopped, cool under my fingertips.

"Well," Leo says after a beat. "That was anticlimactic."

"Why did you stop?" Coco asks me.

"I didn't." I pull my hands back. My skin buzzes, head swimming with magic potions and adrenaline. "It felt like the board just… shut off."

"We lost connection," La'Tasha says. She eyes the board like it might bite her. "You heard that pop. The energy was severed."

I sit back on my heels. Something inside me shifts, like a door opening. Hope, maybe. Or just the reckless courage that shows up when you're drunk and don't give a shit about repercussions.

"Maybe I set him free." A smile tugs at my mouth, small and satisfied. "Did I just free a trapped ghost?"

"Not just any ghost." La'Tasha narrows her eyes. "A ghost tied to the Concord."

"A ghost who wants me." I rest my forearms on my knees and meet her gaze.

"You are *so* drunk," she says, shaking her head.

"Probably." I shrug. "But I don't think I'm wrong."

"Calvin's going to get some ghost wiener," Leo says, and the room explodes into laughter.

"I think we're all drunk." La'Tasha stands and goes to the kitchen. "Who wants another beer?"

I lift a hand automatically. She presses a cold bottle into my palm.

"You better brace yourself, baby boy," she says. "If that ghost is really free, you might have invited trouble right to your doorstep."

She makes it sound like a joke, but something flickers in her eyes. Worry. Curiosity. Both?

I take a long pull from the bottle. Whatever I set in motion tonight is already moving. I can feel it under my skin—half fear of what might happen, half fuck it, we'll figure it out when it does. Or, maybe I'm imagining it. Maybe nothing will happen.

But for one hazy, beer-soaked moment, I'm going to let myself believe he's on his way back to me.

CHAPTER THREE

Calvin

Leo and I step out of La'Tasha's house into the cold February night, our boots sinking into the snow. My breath puffs out in quick clouds, each one drifting away like a smoke signal. The world tilts just enough to make the streetlights look like they're leaning in to watch us. My steps zigzag all over the sidewalk.

Behind us, the door creaks open again. Penny leans out, backlit by the lamp, arms folded.

"Text me when you get home!" she calls.

"Yes, Mom." I give her a sloppy salute, hand landing more on my ear than my forehead.

"I mean it, Calvin! It's Valentine's night. Weirdos are out!"

I walk backward down the icy sidewalk. "We are the weirdos. Big bad wolves, remember?"

La'Tasha laughs and Coco's giggle floats out after her before the door clicks shut.

Leo nudges me with his shoulder. "You're lucky she didn't send you home with a thermos of that swamp brew La'Tasha made."

"I already had two shots of it. Pretty sure I can taste colors now."

"Yeah, well, you were making eyes at the ceiling during the Ouija board thing, so I'm guessing it worked." He grins. "You really think Everett was there?"

I shrug, kicking at a snowbank. I lose my balance and Leo catches me before I fall on my ass. "Maybe. There was a ton of power in that room tonight."

Leo carries the last greasy box from tonight's binge under one arm. He flips it open, grabs a cold slice, and offers me one. I take it, because cold pizza is the best pizza.

We walk, laughing about Penny's "goodie bag" comment and strategizing how we can hold our tails while in wolf form to better hide our buttholes when we're around people. Somewhere between Maple and Cedar, Leo lets out a long, obnoxious fart that echoes off the quiet houses.

"Seriously?" I shoot him a look.

"What? I'm jet-propelled, baby. That was at least twelve feet of thrust. I'm trying to get us home faster."

"Pretty sure that's not how it works."

"Pretty sure it is." He forces another fart. "See? Almost home."

"Good thing because you're about to shit your pants by the sound of it."

We're still laughing when we hit his block. He slows in front of his place, snow dusting the hedges in front of the porch. "You good to walk the rest of the way? You've got, what, five more blocks?"

"Yeah." I give him a lazy wave. "If I vanish, tell people I died heroically fighting off a snow yeti."

"Nah. I'll say you stopped to pee and froze to death midstream still holding your wiener."

"Asshole," I yell as he walks up his sidewalk, flipping me the bird. "You're the worst best friend I've ever had!"

He grins over his shoulder and disappears inside, leaving me alone on the sidewalk.

The quiet hits hard after all of our noise. Snow falls through the cones of streetlight. I start walking, hands shoved deep into my jacket pockets, Everett's name still pacing in my head.

A gust hits, and snow skitters across my face. A prickle of wrongness creeps up my spine. I freeze.

I glance over my shoulder, expecting a late-night dog walker or one of Penny's mythical Valentine weirdos.

Nothing.

Just empty street, pale snow, and the yellow pools of light stretching into black.

"Hello?" My voice cracks through the silence.

No answer.

I pick up the pace.

The wind picks up with me, running along the curb in time with my steps. I spin around. Nothing but my own breath fogging the air. The street looks empty, but the air hums.

The snow swirls at the curb, and for a heartbeat it peels back, leaving a hollow shape. Shoulders. The suggestion of a head. Not solid. Not full. Just a cutout.

My skin prickles.

I turn away and walk faster. Another gust shoves at my back. By the time I reach my house, my pulse is racing and I'm breathing like I ran the whole way. I fumble my keys twice before getting my front door open, slam it shut, and lock it. The house is dead quiet.

I lean against the door.

"Get your shit together," I mutter.

I kick off my boots and hang up my jacket, then pad through the dark house to my bedroom. My bed waits, pillows piled high, sheets still rumpled from this morning. That's all the invitation I need.

I strip down to my boxer briefs and toss my clothes toward

the hamper. My jeans miss completely and land on my dresser, knocking over a framed photo. I pick it up, squinting in the dark. It's me and Blake as kids, both wearing hard hats too big for our heads. Dad's construction company opening, maybe twenty years back.

I set the photo back and flip on the night light by my door. I crawl into bed, pulling the blankets up to my chin. Sleep grabs me fast and drags me under.

***

THUMP.
My eyes snap open.
SCRAAAAPE.
It's coming from above me. From the attic. I sit up, suddenly wide awake. The digital clock on my nightstand reads 3:17 AM.
The witching hour. Great.
THUMP. THUMP.
Something is moving around in my attic. My first thought is raccoons. They've gotten in before, sneaky little masked bastards.
But what if it's something else? What if we let something nasty in with that Ouija board? La'Tasha did mention demons and possession. I don't have time to be possessed.
"Don't be a dumbass," I say out loud.
I get out of bed and head for the hallway.
I yank the cord and the pull-down attic stairs unfold with a creak, releasing a wash of cold air from the dark opening above. I click on the hallway light before climbing up into pitch blackness. The square of light from below barely helps as I fumble for the switch, heart hammering. The bare bulb flickers on, revealing my attic in all its dusty, cobweb-covered glory.

Nothing seems out of place at first. Then I spot it. A box has been knocked over near the far wall, its contents spilled across the wooden floor. I inch closer.

It's a box of my grandfather's things. Stuff that's been up here since before I inherited the place. Things I've never bothered to look through. In the center of the scattered items sits an old-fashioned radio that looks like it belongs in a museum. I crouch down and run my hand over the smooth wooden case. Something compels me to pick it up, and I'm surprised by its weight. I wonder if it still works? It would look great in my living room.

I tuck it under my arm and scan the rest of the attic. Nothing else seems disturbed. No holes in the roof or walls where an animal might've gotten in. I'll check for entry points tomorrow.

The radio feels warm against my side like it's just been used. Or maybe that's just all the beers from earlier affecting my nerves. I close the attic stairs, carry my grandfather's radio to my bedroom, and set it on top of my dresser. I love antiques. Tomorrow I'll see if I can get it to work. Right now, I'm done.

I crawl back into bed, pulling the covers up to my chin again. The night light glows. Everything is quiet. Normal.

With a crackle of static, the radio turns on.

I sit bolt upright. Music pours from the speaker, a slow, crooning love song from the 1950s. The song fills my bedroom with warbling strings and syrupy lyrics.

I crawl out of bed and turn the radio off, twisting the knob until it clicks. The music stops. I exhale and turn back toward my bed.

Click. The radio turns itself back on. The same song picks up right where it left off.

"Nope," I say, grabbing the radio. "Not happening."

I carry it down the hall to the living room and set it on the coffee table. I'm not getting any sleep with a possessed radio playing love songs in my bedroom all night.

I stumble back down the hall and faceplant in my bed.

I lie there thinking about all the weirdness since the Ouija board incident. I want to believe I set Everett free, but what if I have a poltergeist now?

I fall asleep and dream of ghosts trying to pull me into my TV.

***

My alarm blares at seven thirty, and I smack at my phone, missing twice before finally getting it. My mouth tastes like I've been sucking on cardboard, and my head throbs in perfect time with my heartbeat. I groan and roll onto my back. Last night comes back in pieces.

Beer. Pizza. Ouija board. Footsteps in the snow. The radio that played by itself.

I sit up too quickly and immediately regret it as the room spins like a carnival ride.

"Never again," I lie to myself.

I shuffle out of bed and head toward the kitchen for water. The living room looks normal. My grandfather's old radio sits on the coffee table, silent. I give it a wide berth as I pass.

"Stay off." I point a finger at it. "I'm not above smashing you with a hammer."

After downing two aspirin and a full glass of water, I check my phone. Two texts from Blake about a job site we need to visit today, one from La'Tasha making sure I got home safe, and three from Leo. The last one simply reads: **DID THE GHOST BOOTY CALL HAPPEN??**

I roll my eyes and type back: **Yep. And now I'm pregnant. Thanks for asking.**

Work. I need to focus on work. Today, Blake and I have to check progress on the Wilson renovation, then meet with a potential new client about building a sunroom before starting to tackle a renovation project at Ravena's old wellness store.

I head to the bathroom, shedding my skivvies and turning

the shower as hot as it will go. Steam quickly fills the small space as I step under the spray, water pounding against my shoulders. Everett's messages keep playing on repeat.

I miss you.

The feelings were real.

I lean my forehead against the tile, letting the water run down my back. We did that séance to reach him. To help him. And something answered. The noises in the attic last night, the radio playing old love songs at two in the morning...

It has to be him. Right?

But if it is Everett, why can't I see him? Why can't he just appear and talk to me like a normal ghost? Well, as normal as ghosts get. La'Tasha said the Ouija board opened a door, that we gave him permission to cross over from wherever he was stuck. So why is he hiding?

Unless he can't control it.

Or maybe it's not him at all.

I don't know why this keeps eating at me, but what if something else came through? What if the Concord sent something to fuck with me, to make me think Everett's here when really it's just them playing games? They've done worse. Way worse.

I rinse off, trying to scrub away the knot of anxiety in my chest, then turn the water off. The silence feels too loud. I step out of the shower, grabbing a towel from the rack, and start drying off. The bathroom mirror is fogged from the steam.

Except...

My breath catches in my throat.

A perfect heart appears in the mirror's condensation.

"What the hell?" I whisper.

Wait.

"Leo?"

He's fucking with me. Has to be. He has a key. He pops by sometimes without warning. And he was giving me shit about trying to contact Everett.

I wrap my towel around my waist and step out of the bathroom to an empty hallway. "Come on, Leo. I know you're here."

Still no answer. I cross the living room and peer out the window. My truck is the only vehicle in the driveway.

My pulse stutters. If it isn't Leo, then the list of possibilities gets a whole lot shorter. A colder thought pushes in. The one that's been sitting under my skin ever since the Ouija board.

"Everett?" I say, softer. "If you're here, please show yourself. I'm not mad. I just want to talk."

Nothing answers. Just the hum of the bathroom fan and the drip of the faucet. The air behind me shifts, cool against the back of my neck.

I whirl around. Just an empty room.

I hurry back to my bedroom, get dressed, and then check the house. Living room, kitchen, spare bedroom. I open closets, check behind furniture, test window locks. Nothing out of place. The heart on my bathroom mirror is gone now. Like it was never there in the first place.

The attic is my last stop. I pull down the stairs and climb up, scanning the space in the bright morning light filtering through the small window. The box that held the radio is still knocked over, its contents scattered. I kneel to put everything back and notice something I missed last night.

A photo album has fallen open, displaying a black and white picture of my grandfather, Sam Carter, as a young man. He's standing with a group of friends, all of them dressed in 1950s clothing. I pick up the album for a closer look. My grandfather has his arm thrown around another guy, both of them laughing at something outside the frame. Two more boys crowd in close. And in the distance is a red convertible, the one still in the garage. Standing next to it is...

My stomach drops.

"No way."

I remove the picture and hold it toward the attic window,

squinting in the weak morning light. The photo is grainy, the details blurred by age and poor focus. But the more I stare, the more certain I become.

Medium height. Swimmer's build.

That's Everett. It has to be.

He has the same way of standing, weight shifted to one side like he's half-ready to bolt.

If that's really him in this photo with my grandfather, that means... what? That Everett knew my family?

A horn honks from the driveway, sharp and impatient.

"Shit." I glance at the window. Blake's truck idles in the driveway, exhaust puffing white in the cold air.

I take the picture and climb down from the attic. The stairs fold back up with a soft click. I set the photograph on the kitchen table. I'll look at it later, when my head's clearer. I grab my jacket off the back of the chair and scoop up my keys. I make it three steps toward the door before I stop, hand hovering near the doorknob.

I glance around the living room one last time.

"Everett?" I say it softer this time, like I'm testing the name out. "If you're here... And I really hope you are..." I glance around the empty room. "The radio thing was a little creepy. And the heart on the mirror was... I don't know. Sweet? But also a little invasive. Maybe give me some bathroom privacy?"

The air stays still. No answer. No cold breeze or moving shadows.

"Look, I have to go to work. But if you really made it here, if you're actually in my house right now..." I swallow hard. "Stay. Please. We'll figure this out when I get back. I want to talk to you. For real this time."

A honk comes from outside, long and annoyed.

I take one last look around the living room, half expecting to see him standing there. But there's nothing. Just my couch, and that damn radio sitting silent on the coffee table.

I lock up and jog to Blake's truck, yanking the passenger door open.

"You look like shit," Blake says as I climb in.

"Good morning to you, too."

He pulls away from the curb, already launching into something about the Wilson job and timeline issues. I nod along, making the right noises at the right times, but my mind stays pinned to the house behind us.

I glance at the side mirror.

For a split second, I swear I see a figure standing in my living room window. Blonde hair. Pale face. Watching me leave.

I blink.

Nothing. Just the morning sun glinting off the glass.

Chapter Four

Calvin

I sneeze for the third time in five minutes as another dust cloud erupts. This place is a health hazard, which is ironic considering what it used to sell. Dusty rows of vitamins, herbal teas, and protein shakes stand abandoned, their labels curling at the edges. The grime makes everything, including the shelves, look like it's been here for centuries.

The problem is, none of this stuff is harmless. Renovating *Bianca's Health & Wellness* is like cleaning out a cursed pantry. Every drawer we open, every crate we haul from the back room feels like it's one mistake away from biting us. According to Hazel, every bottle and powder had been infused with Ravena Blackwood's blood. People thought they were buying energy boosters and immunity tonics. What they really bought was a mind-control starter pack. This place is filled with so much tainted junk, we can't just toss it into a dumpster and call it a day. The witches have to burn it all in ritual fire just to be safe.

Blake tosses me a bandana from his back pocket. "You know

there's such a thing as a dust mask, right?"

Leo snorts. "Like you'd catch him covering up that pretty face." He winks, then fumbles the tape measure and trips over a box of expired protein shakes. The box bursts open, spilling mint green bottles that roll across the floor in every direction.

"Smooth," I say. "You're always so graceful."

"Hey, that's why you keep me around." He bends to gather the bottles, knocking over his own coffee cup in the process.

Mason, our newest hire, stands a little apart, jaw tight. His eyes flick over the shelves lined with dusty teas and powders. He edges back.

"I don't like it here," he says finally, low and tense. "I can still hear her in my head. It's like she never left." He stares at the dusty shelves, shoulders hunched like he's bracing for an attack.

I pat him on the shoulder. "Hang in there, Mas. We'll get this crap out of here by tomorrow and then it'll be just another empty building in need of renovation."

Blake slaps his hands together before removing his gloves. "We have three months to transform this dump into a clothing boutique. The client wants a retail space up front, design studio in back, offices upstairs, storage in the basement."

"And they're paying double for the rush job," I add with a grin. "My kind of client."

"The cleanup crew will be here tomorrow to clear out the rest of the inventory so Hazel and the witches can dispose of it. We'll start demo the day after," Blake says, already heading for the door. "Calvin, you good to finish the walk-through and mark everything that needs to go?"

"Yeah, no problem." I unfold the blueprints on the dusty counter. "Go handle the Miller quote."

Mason drifts after Blake, his gaze scanning the room even as they head out. Leo stops at the door. "Don't get possessed by any leftover witch vibes."

"Very funny," I call after him, but he's already gone, laughing as the bell over the door jingles.

And then I'm alone. Just me and whatever energy Ravena left behind in this place. I try to focus on the blueprints, but the hair on my arms stands up. The air is too thick, too quiet. After last night's haunted radio nonsense, it hits a little too close.

"Stop freaking out," I mutter to myself, grabbing my tape measure.

I walk the space, measuring and marking with spray chalk. The client wants walls knocked down, new display areas built, a fitting room where the old herb shelves used to be. Standard renovation work. Pretty straightforward.

Except every time I pass the rear wall, a draft sneaks along the back of my neck like the building is breathing cold air down my collar.

I shake it off and try to focus on square footage and load-bearing walls, but my mind keeps drifting back to that heart on my mirror. To Everett—or whomever it was—reaching out through the Ouija board.

I miss you.

Was it really him doing all that stuff last night? The music, the noises in the attic, the heart traced in the steam?

Or did I bring something else home with me?

The metal stairs groan under my boots as I make my way down to the basement. Each step echoes, sharp and hollow, until I hit the concrete floor. My flashlight cuts across rows of steel shelving stacked with abandoned crates, boxes of bottled supplements, and dusty jars of powders that look more like lab experiments than anything meant for human consumption. Clipboards hang from nails, order forms yellowed with age, as if the staff walked out mid-shift and never came back.

I guess they kind of did.

I sweep the beam wider. A door at the far end catches the light. It's black, barely visible, and tucked behind a stack of pallets. As I move closer, I notice strange symbols have been carved deep into the wood, twisting and curling in a language I don't recognize. This room isn't on the blueprint.

"What the hell were you up to, Ravena?" I whisper. I shove the pallets aside and approach the door. I try the handle. Locked. My fingers brush over the markings, and a pulse shudders through the wood, hot and alive. I snatch my hand back.

My phone buzzes in my pocket, making me jump. It's a text from La'Tasha.

Dinner at Raven & Rye tonight? 7pm?

I tap out a quick reply.

Count me in. Need alcohol after today.

She responds with: **You didn't get enough last night? =) See you in a bit.**

I pocket my phone and circle back to the door. Part of me wants to grab a crowbar from upstairs and pry it open right now. The other, smarter part, which sounds suspiciously like Blake, is screaming that messing with witch doors is a horrible idea.

"Just finish the walk-through," I tell myself. "Mark everything for demo and get the fuck out."

I plug my earbuds in and crank up my early 2000s playlist. The familiar opening notes of my favorite childhood song blast through my ears, and I can't help but grin.

The first time I heard this song, Blake and I were riding bikes around Moonridge. Mom had just bought me my first MP3 player, and I blasted this on repeat, convinced I was the coolest kid alive.

Before Jace. Before Everett. Back when my biggest problem was whether Mom would find out it was me and not Blake who ate all the cookies.

I'm back at the black door before I realize it, the handle gleaming in the beam of my flashlight. I reach out, not really expecting anything to happen, but this time the door pops open.

I hesitate. The door swings in on silent hinges, revealing darkness beyond. I fumble for a light switch, but can't find one. I step inside, and the door slams shut behind me. The world tilts. My stomach drops. Light explodes around me, and when my vision clears, I'm standing in a building that opens up to Main Street.

But not the Main Street of today.

The buildings are wrong. Where the Enchanted Bean coffee shop should be, there's a neon-lit video rental store, posters for movies from twenty years ago plastered across the windows. The yoga studio is a beauty supply shop with wigs on faceless mannequins. I turn and look at the building I just exited. The sign for Bianca's Health & Wellness is gone. Now it's just a warehouse with boarded-up windows, like it's been forgotten by time.

"What the actual hell?" I whisper, turning in a slow circle.

The cars parked along the curb are boxy sedans and minivans with faded bumper stickers. The streetlamps are the old wrought-iron kind the town swapped out ten years ago. And the people...

A kid rockets past me on a silver bike, earbuds plugged deep in his ears, head bobbing to a tinny beat. His skinny arms and floppy haircut make my chest seize.

No. Impossible.

It's me. Thirteen-year-old me, gangly and awkward, lost in his own world.

"What in the..." The words trail off as my younger self swings around at the corner and pedals straight toward me. "Oh, this is not happening."

I step into his path, half testing, half daring the universe to prove me wrong.

We collide. He topples sideways, the bike skidding out from under him. He hits the pavement with a grunt, then scrambles up, brushing gravel off his jeans.

"Sorry!" He pulls his earbuds out and leaves them draped over his shoulders. "I wasn't paying attention."

His eyes meet mine directly. He can see me.

"My fault too," I say. "You okay?"

"Yeah." He squints. "Do I know you?"

Before I can answer, another bike careens up. Dirty-blonde hair. Freckles. A glare that could cut glass. Blake at nine.

"You good, Cal?" he barks, planting a foot and steadying the bike with his knee. "I saw you wipe out."

"I'm fine," Mini-me grumbles, brushing dirt off his shorts.

Blake's attention snaps to me. He scans me head to toe. "Who are you?" His chin juts toward me.

"New in town. Passing through."

"Passing through where?" Blake's eyes narrow to slits. "Through our neighborhood? You look like a creepy guy who says he's passing through and then steals kids."

Typical Blake, but I can't help feeling offended. I look like a creeper?

Mini-me snorts. "Dude, he's not stealing me."

"Yet," Blake says. He still hasn't blinked. "You don't even know his name."

"Carter," I say, because my brain refuses to invent anything better.

Mini-me studies my face, curious rather than afraid. "Hey, that's our last name."

"Funny," I say. Am I somehow fucking up the future by talking to past me? I should probably get out of here.

"Don't tell him our name, dummy," Blake says. "Come on. We have to go. Mom made spaghetti."

He reaches out and flicks a pebble from little Calvin's back tire.

"Nice earphones," Mini-me says, suddenly friendly. "Mine always get tangled."

"Yours are classic," I say. I touch my own ear. Wireless. Sleeker. Same brand, different century.

Blake squints, suspicious as always. "We're going," he declares. "C'mon, Cal. Race me. Whoever loses has to do all the chores for a week."

Mini-me mounts his bike and pushes off, but looks back once. "See you around," he calls with a wave.

"Maybe," I say.

I jog back toward the warehouse, blood racing, lungs tight.

I've stepped straight into 2005 and I talked to myself as a kid. What if I've already changed something? What if I said the wrong thing, or left some ripple that cascades forward and breaks everything?

My chest constricts. I run faster.

Shit. What if I can't get back?

The thought makes my gut twist. What if the doorway closed? What if it only worked that once? What if I'm stuck here and it hurts the younger me and—

Stop. Focus.

I turn the corner and the warehouse comes into view, its corrugated walls streaked with rust and old rain. I stumble through the entrance, my breath coming too quick. The hallway stretches ahead.

Which one? Which one did I come through?

I try the first door. Locked. The second. A storage room, nothing but shadows and dust. My heart hammers against my ribs as I move to the third.

Come on. Come on.

The fourth door creaks open. Inside, it's pitch black except for a faint glow coming from the back. A doorway, outlined in swirling, colorful light.

Relief nearly drops me to my knees.

I sprint toward it, praying it leads back to my time. As I get closer, I can see through to the other side. The basement of Bianca's shop. My present.

I dive through the doorway, the world shifting again beneath my feet. I land on the concrete floor of the basement, the black door slamming shut behind me.

For a second, I just lie there, gasping for breath. Then I start laughing. I just time traveled. The group is not going to believe this.

My fingers fly across my phone screen.

ME: **Don't go to Raven & Rye. Come to Bianca's old shop ASAP. Found something INSANE. Like, beyond ghost boyfriend insane.**

I add a string of exclamation points because this situation deserves nothing less.

LA'TASHA: **Should I be worried or excited?**

ME: **BOTH!!! Bring everyone. Trust me.**

I pocket my phone and pace the length of the basement, my footsteps echoing off the concrete walls. A time travel door. An actual, working, honest-to-god time travel door. The possibilities make my head spin faster than that whirlwind trip to the past.

What if we could all go? Just take a field trip to the 80s. Maybe see a concert. Win the lottery. Accidentally prevent our own births.

Hmm. Maybe it's not such a great idea.

I circle back to the black door, once again tracing the symbols with my fingertips. No power pulses this time. The door feels ordinary, just old wood. Maybe there's a trick to it. Maybe it only works at certain times. Maybe I hallucinated the whole thing.

No. I crashed into my thirteen-year-old self. I have a bruise forming on my hip to prove it. I saw Blake and me as kids. That was real.

The tinkling of the bell above the lobby door snaps me out of my thoughts. Voices call my name, footsteps thundering down the stairs.

La'Tasha descends into the basement. "This better be good, Carter. I'm so hungry my stomach is about to eat its damn self."

Penny follows, adjusting her glasses. "Is this about a ghost? Please tell me it's not about a ghost. I'm all ghosted out this month."

"It's not about a ghost," I promise as Leo and Coco squeeze

past them into the basement.

"Hot date?" Leo asks, wiggling his eyebrows. "Did Everett fully materialize? Is he corporeal now? Can you finally get your ghost groove on?"

I throw a dusty rag at his face. "It's way better than that. And weirder. So much weirder."

Coco circles slowly, her curls bouncing as she takes in the basement. "I'm getting weird vibes down here. Ravena energy."

"Forget Ravena," I say, waving them all closer. "You guys. I found a time travel door."

The four of them stare at me. Penny's eyebrows shoot up so high they practically disappear into her hairline.

"A what now?" La'Tasha asks.

"A time travel door. Right here." I point to the black door with its strange symbols. "I opened it earlier and stepped through into Moonridge twenty years ago. I saw myself as a kid. I saw Blake, too. It was real."

Leo coughs into his fist. "Riiiiight."

"I'm serious." I grab his arm, pulling him toward the door. "Listen. The door was locked when I first found it. Then something shifted and it just fell open. I stepped through looking for a light switch, and boom, I was standing on Main Street two decades ago."

"Time travel," Penny says slowly, like she's testing the words. "That would require a very specific spell structure. One I'm not sure exists."

"Or a very active imagination," La'Tasha adds, though her tone is gentle.

"I know what I saw," I insist, moving to the door. "Here, I'll show you."

Please work. Please work. Don't make me look like an idiot.

I grasp the handle and twist. Nothing happens. I try again, harder this time. The door doesn't budge.

"It's locked," I say, frowning. "It wasn't locked when I came back through."

Leo pats my shoulder. "Sure, buddy. The magical time door locked itself."

"It did work," I insist, running my hands along the frame. "I swear it worked. I'm not making this up."

Coco stands beside me, pressing her palm flat against the door. "I do feel something. But it's faint. Like an echo."

"See?" I practically shout. "Coco feels it."

"Coco is cold. She's probably just shivering," La'Tasha jokes.

I lean against the door, defeated. "I'm not making this up. I'm not hallucinating. I went back in time."

Leo places a hand on my shoulder. "Look, I believe you believe it happened. But maybe it was more like a vision. Some leftover witch magic from Ravena playing tricks with all of our heads last summer."

"Or," Coco suggests, waggling her fingers, "your ghost boyfriend is getting creative. Giving you glimpses of the past."

I hadn't considered that. Could Everett be behind this? But why show me my own childhood? And how would he access that kind of power?

"I know what I experienced," I say, pushing myself off the door. "And I'm going to prove it to you all."

"Can you prove it over dinner?" Leo asks, rubbing his stomach. "Because I'm starving, and Raven & Rye has that pulled pork special on Saturdays."

"I could eat," Coco agrees, already heading for the stairs. "Plus, they have those giant milkshakes. I need at least two after coming down to this creepy basement for nothing. No offense, Calvin."

My shoulders drop, and I take a deep breath. "Fine. Food first, time travel later."

"That's the spirit," La'Tasha says, linking her arm through mine as we climb the stairs. "For what it's worth, weirder things have happened in Moonridge."

"Exactly," I say, my posture straightening. "So why is time travel so hard to believe? We literally almost had a ghost apocalypse three months ago. Time travel is barely a footnote at this point."

Leo holds the shop door open. "Maybe it's not impossible. But if we're time traveling, I'm bringing a sports almanac." He winks.

"Of course that would be your plan," La'Tasha says, rolling her eyes.

We step outside into the evening air and lock up. Leo's still obsessing over the pulled pork at Raven and Rye, Penny's deciding between two cocktails, and La'Tasha and Coco keep trading looks that turn into sudden laughter. I hear them, but none of it lands. My mind is stuck on that black door. What I saw. What I felt.

I'm coming back tomorrow with crowbars and bolt cutters if I have to. That door opened once. It will open again.

And next time, I'm bringing witnesses.

CHAPTER FIVE

Calvin

I take a sip of my beer as Leo leans across the sticky table, his eyes wide with disbelief. "So you're telling me your place is actually haunted now? Like, for real?"

The restaurant hums around us, packed with regulars. La'Tasha raises an eyebrow, stirring her martini, while Penny adjusts her glasses and leans in closer. Coco bounces in her seat, like she's about to drag the rest of the story out of me if I don't hurry up.

"I'm not saying it's haunted," I clarify, wiping beer foam from my mustache. "I'm just saying weird shit happened all night last night, and I'm running out of rational explanations."

"Like what?" Penny asks, already frowning like she's trying to logic it out.

I set my mug down and count off on my fingers. "One, footsteps following me home last night. Two, noises in the attic that led me to my grandfather's old radio. Three, that same radio turning itself on and playing 1950s love songs. And four," I pause for dramatic effect, "a perfect heart drawn on my bathroom mirror while I was in the shower this morning."

"Holy crap," Leo whispers. "Ghost booty call totally happened."

"Not exactly a booty call. More like… ghost flirting? Ghost signals? I don't know the terminology here."

La'Tasha leans forward, resting her elbows on the table, her dark eyes serious. "And you think it's Everett?"

"Who else would it be?" I shrug, tearing at the edge of my napkin. "It's not like I have a harem of ghosts lining up at my door. Just the one."

Penny pushes her glasses up her nose. "The question is, why can't you see him? If he's strong enough to draw on mirrors and turn on radios, why not materialize visually?"

"Maybe he's trying," I say, running a finger along the edge of my beer mug. "Maybe he's forbidden. Maybe there's some weird Concord magic that prevents it."

"Possibly," Penny says, thinking. "They must have some type of hold over him. When I released the Crucible Core last fall, ghosts under Concord power were released. I'm surprised he wasn't."

"Or maybe he was, but he hasn't made himself known because he was afraid," Coco points out.

Afraid? Of me? What would he have to be afraid of? That I'd reject him? I guess that's fair. I *was* angry.

La'Tasha shakes her head. "I just feel like if it was him, he'd make himself known. You told him you wanted to see him. You basically forgave him." She levels me with a look. "Why would he be afraid to show himself? This is really suspicious to me."

The waitress arrives with our food, plates piled high with Raven & Rye's famous loaded fries and burgers the size of my head. The conversation pauses as we arrange ketchup, napkins, and extra plates. My stomach growls. Haunted house or not, I'm starving.

"So what's your plan?" Leo asks through a mouthful of fries.

"Ghost exorcism or ghost romance? Because one is definitely more fun than the other."

"Neither yet," I admit, picking up my burger. "I don't even know for sure it's him. But I really hope it is, which probably makes me an idiot."

La'Tasha sets her fork down with a clink. "Please be careful. Everett was with the Concord. We know that for a fact. And we don't know what kind of hold they have over him."

Forks pause midair. Everyone stares at me.

"He said he was unwilling." My voice softens. "That he was trapped."

Even as I say it, I wonder if I'm just hearing what I want to hear.

"And maybe that's true," La'Tasha says, her tone gentler. "But things have been quiet since we stopped their ritual. Too quiet. I don't think the Concord would simply give up and go away. What if this is their way back in?"

Coco nods solemnly. "Ghost boyfriends are super romantic until they're actually evil coven spies."

"Thanks for that," I mutter. "Great for my mental health."

"Happy to help."

We forget about my alleged haunting and stuff our faces. Forks clatter. Fries disappear from the middle of the table. Leo steals one of Penny's onion rings and gets smacked for it. The food dwindles, drinks empty.

"Look," Penny says, checking her watch. "Not to cut this short, but the movie starts in twenty minutes. Mason's saving seats."

Leo perks up. "That new horror flick? I'm in." He glances at me apologetically. "Sorry, dude. Rain check on ghost hunting?"

"No problem." I wave them off. "Go enjoy your fake ghosts while I deal with my possibly real one."

Coco stands, gathering her colorful purse. "Coming, Tash?"

La'Tasha shakes her head. "Think I'll pass. I'm not really in the mood for fake blood and jump scares." She raises her martini. "One more drink with Calvin, then home to my trash TV."

The three of them say their goodbyes, leaving La'Tasha and me alone with half-eaten food and too many empty glasses.

"You didn't have to stay," I tell her as the waitress clears away the others' plates.

"Please." She snorts. "Like I'd miss a chance to hear more about your paranormal romance." Her smile softens. "Besides, you look like you need to talk. Like, really talk."

I signal for another round. "That obvious, huh?"

"You forget I've known you since we were kids. Even back when witches and wolves supposedly hated each other, I always liked you." She drums her fingers against her empty glass. "I know when something's bugging you."

The waitress brings fresh drinks, and I take a long sip of my beer. La'Tasha waits.

"I think Jace broke something in me," I admit, shredding a napkin to keep my hands busy. "Not just my heart. My ability to trust. To hope. God, that sounds dramatic. But it's true." I catch a drop of condensation on my beer mug and run it between my fingers. "And then Everett came along, and for the first time in five years, I felt that spark again. That possibility."

"And now?" La'Tasha asks softly.

"Now I'm talking to empty rooms and getting excited about hearts on bathroom mirrors." I laugh, but it sounds hollow. "I've officially lost it. This is rock bottom."

La'Tasha reaches across the table and pats my hand.

"I didn't know he was dead when I met him. Had no idea I was falling for a ghost. I know there's no way we can be together, but…" I take a breath. "I want to love again. I want to stop being afraid." I grab my beer. "Sorry, that got heavy."

La'Tasha leans closer. "I get it. Love is scary enough without adding ghosts to the mix."

"Speaking from experience?" I ask, genuinely surprised. La'Tasha never talks about this stuff.

She takes a long sip of her fresh martini, then traces the rim of her glass with her finger. "Actually, yeah." She sits back. "Three years ago, I was at a family reunion in the Caribbean, and I met a guy—Kiran—at a beach party. There was this instant attraction, you know? Like magnets. Like our souls knew each other. It sounds so cliché, but our eyes locked and that was that. He approached me and we instantly fell into easy conversation."

"I had no idea you were ever seriously involved with anyone," I say.

"It was only a month." She shrugs. "We spent every minute together. It was intense. Magical, literally. I told him I was a witch, and turns out he was half human, half Solari."

"Solari?" I whistle low. "Aren't they super rare?"

"Exactly why I thought it was perfect." She smiles sadly, her fingers still caressing her glass. "Someone who'd understand my magical side. We made plans. He was supposed to visit Moonridge."

I can guess where this is going. "But he didn't."

"Called a few times after I got home. Always had an excuse why he couldn't visit yet. Then the calls got less frequent. Eventually, they stopped completely." She finishes her drink in one smooth motion. "Totally ghosted, as the kids say."

"I'm sorry," I say, reaching across to squeeze her hand. "That really sucks."

"Ancient history," she says. Her jaw tightens. "My point is, I get it. The wanting to try again thing. Sometimes I think about tracking him down."

"Why don't you?" I ask. "You're a powerful witch. Finding one guy should be easy."

She laughs. "Says the man mooning over a literal ghost."

"Fair point." I grin. "But seriously, if you still have feelings for him, why not look for him?"

"I think I'm afraid of what I'll find."

I nod. I certainly get that.

"Plus he's a tropical guy. Loves the sun and beach. Obviously. Me? I'm a four seasons a year type of girl."

"Have you ever thought about leaving Moonridge?" I ask. "See who or what else is out there?"

She shrugs. "Yeah, but… I can't."

"Why not?"

She takes a deep breath. "Because this is home. My family's legacy is here. We were one of the founding families. Ten generations of Morehouse witches have protected this town. The rest of my family has bailed. If I leave too, that'll be the end of our legacy. It just feels wrong." She shrugs and shakes her head. "I'm not willing to do that. This is where I belong."

We both go quiet, thinking about this weird little town that has its hooks in us. She tilts her head. "Could you leave? Really leave? I mean for good?"

I tried leaving once. I missed Moonridge the entire time. I'd have come back sooner than I did had I not met Jace. Coming back felt right.

"No," I admit. "I couldn't."

My friends are my family. Crazy, but family nonetheless.

"Then you understand." She smiles, softer now.

"Hey, at least your guy is corporeal," I point out. "Mine's one step above a puff of smoke."

She laughs. "We're quite the pair, aren't we?"

"To the perpetually single," I say, raising my glass.

"May we find peace," she responds, clinking her glass against mine. "Or at least really good sex."

I nearly spit out my drink.

We spend the next hour eating cold fries and talking about everything else. Whether we think Vivienne and Leo will ever see each other again. Whether we think Blake will propose to Hazel. Whether Mina will decide to fully transform into a vampire. Anything but ghosts and lost loves.

But in the back of my mind, I keep seeing that heart on my

mirror. Hearing that old radio play. And wondering if Everett is watching right now, trying to reach me from the other side.

We pay the bill and linger a few extra minutes. Eventually, La'Tasha drains the last sip of her drink and gives me that look that says, "Let's get the fuck out of here."

The February air hits us as we step outside. At least the snow has stopped. Stars poke through gaps in the clouds overhead, and our breath creates little ghost clouds that vanish. La'Tasha places her purple earmuffs over her ears as we start the walk back to our respective homes.

"Thanks for staying," I say, jamming my hands into my jacket pockets. "I needed that more than I realized."

"What are friends for if not drinking and trauma bonding?" She links her arm through mine.

"Still, I appreciate it. And thanks for not thinking I'm crazy about the whole ghost thing."

"Oh, I definitely think you're crazy," she teases. "Just not about this. After what we've seen in this town? A haunting is nothing."

We walk in comfortable silence for a block, our footsteps crunching on patches of leftover snow. Moonridge at night always looks picture perfect. Old buildings with their pretend Victorian details. Lampposts glowing and storefronts quiet behind frosty glass.

"You know what's weird?" I say, kicking at a small piece of ice. "Part of me is terrified of actually seeing Everett again. What if he's not what I remember? Or, what if he is what I remember, but we have nothing to say to each other?"

La'Tasha chuckles. "So normal relationship fears, just with a supernatural twist."

"Exactly," I laugh. "Dating is hard enough when both people are alive. Man, I really know how to pick 'em."

We turn onto Maple Street where the massive Victorian that houses Moonridge Bed & Breakfast rises against the night sky. Light glows from several windows. A couple sits on the wraparound porch, bundled in blankets, steam rising from their mugs.

It's good to see the place busy again. The Real Vampire Wives' social media posts seem to have done their job. Tourists are back, and the episodes haven't even aired yet. Once they do, this place will be booked solid for months.

La'Tasha stops suddenly, her grip on my arm tightening. "Wait a minute."

"What?" I follow her gaze to the B&B. "You see something?"

"Not something. Someone." She points to a first-floor window where a tall figure stands silhouetted against the light. "Dex."

I squint at the window. "What about him?"

La'Tasha turns to me. "Calvin, Dex is a Grim Reaper."

"Yeah, I know. Hard to forget that little detail." I shudder, remembering how I felt when I first learned the truth about the quiet, intense man who'd come to town and fallen for Mina. "Not gonna lie. He still freaks me the hell out."

"But think about it." She rocks forward on her feet. "He's been attracting ghosts to Moonridge ever since he arrived. His whole thing is guiding souls, right? He literally walks between worlds. He deals with ghosts. It's his whole personality."

My back straightens. "You think he could help with Everett?"

She nods. "I think he might be able to help manifest Everett's presence. Make it easier for you two to communicate."

I step closer to her. "That's... actually brilliant."

"I know," she grins. "I'm very smart."

"But would he help?" I ask, my shoulders sagging. "Dex isn't exactly pro-Everett, and I don't quite know how to read him."

"He's a decent guy. Weird, but decent. Mina's changed him. And he owes us after we helped save her." La'Tasha starts walking again, tugging me along. "Besides, he's still looking into the Concord. I bet he'd jump at the chance to speak with one of their members. It's a win-win."

I consider this as we pass beneath a streetlight. If anyone could help bridge the gap between me and Everett, it would be

Dex. Maybe I can finally get my answers.

"It's worth a shot," I decide. "I'll talk to him tomorrow."

"*We'll* talk to him tomorrow," La'Tasha corrects. "No offense, but your negotiation skills suck. You need backup."

I laugh, nudging her with my shoulder. "None taken. You're absolutely right. I'd probably just stammer and make it weird."

We pass the town square. The trees are wrapped in those little white lights the town refuses to take down until April. The gazebo's empty, crusted with frost like everything else tonight.

"There's something else," I say, slowing my pace. "I want to try the door again."

La'Tasha stops walking. "The time travel door? Calvin…"

"I know what I saw, Tash." I turn to face her, shoving my hands in my pockets. "It was real. And I need someone to witness it. Someone who will believe me."

She studies my face, searching for something. Maybe sincerity. Maybe sanity. "You're really serious about this, aren't you?"

"Dead serious." I meet her gaze. "Will you help me? Be my witness?"

La'Tasha sighs, her breath clouding between us. "You realize if this works, it's a massive magical discovery, right? Time travel isn't supposed to be possible, even with magic."

"All the more reason to check it out," I press. "Think about it. If Ravena had this technology or spell or whatever it is, we need to understand it. The Concord could use it against us."

That gets her.

"Fine," she says. "But we do this properly. Protected."

"Deal." A stupidly big grin stretches across my face. "Meet me at the shop at nine tomorrow morning?"

"Make it ten," she counters. "Some of us need beauty sleep. I promise to bring breakfast."

We reach the corner where our paths diverge.

"Nine thirty," I counter.

"Deal." She adjusts her hat one last time. "But if we get stuck in 2005 or whatever, I'm blaming you."

"If we get stuck in 2005, you can say 'I told you so' forever," I promise.

La'Tasha laughs and gives me a quick hug before heading down her street. "Tomorrow's going to be interesting," she calls over her shoulder.

I stand at the corner watching her go, my fingers drumming against my thighs. Tomorrow I might finally get some answers.

Or tomorrow I might make a complete fool of myself.

Either way, La'Tasha is right. It's definitely going to be interesting.

CHAPTER SIX

Everett

I shove my hand through the front door. Easy. My whole arm follows, then my shoulder. One foot crosses the threshold, then the other. Almost there. Almost—

The invisible wall slams into my chest and hurls me backward through the coat rack. The impact sends shockwaves through what little form I have, leaving me dizzy and weak on the living room floor.

"Son of a bitch."

I thought leaving Skipper Lake meant freedom. Turns out I just traded one prison for another. Now I'm stuck haunting the house of the guy I've mooned over for months, and for some reason I can't even step outside. I had more freedom at the lake.

Just last night I'd been hovering over Skipper Lake like I always do—not much else to do when you're a ghost bound to the Concord. I'd watched a couple glide across the frozen water, her red mittens flashing against his black coat as they twirled. Snow drifted down in wide spirals, each flake catching moonlight before disappearing into the ice. Another proposal. Another Valentine's Day. Not that it mattered. Marriage, futures, forever in love—none of it was something I'd ever have.

She'd accepted, and they packed up their skates, knocked snow off their tires, and drove away. I hung there over the ice, watching dark swallow their taillights. They had a real future ahead. Something I'd always hoped for.

I'd stared down the empty stretch of asphalt toward town, wondering what Calvin was doing. Wishing that proposal on the ice had been between him and me. Not that it could ever happen. I'm dead, he's not, and he never wants to see me again. I hurt him, and he'll never forgive me.

I know this because after the botched Concord ritual last fall, something had shifted with the barrier. My binding to the lake loosened and I found I had more freedom. I could actually drift down to Moonridge, something I'd never been able to do before. So I went. I needed to see him.

At first it felt like freedom. I watched him at The Howling Moon laughing with his friends, or through the window of the coffee shop nursing a cup gone cold while families passed by on the sidewalk. It lifted something in me every time I saw him smile, but it also twisted the knife. Things had been so easy between us, even if forever was impossible. Then one night I overheard him tell his friends my betrayal hurt worse than his ex-fiancé's, and I knew I could never see him again. I stopped going after that. No point haunting someone who hates you.

But then last night, as I was about to spend another evening wallowing in self-pity, a sound slid across the ice. A voice like someone talking through water. Calvin. Looking for me. He asked me to come find him.

So, of course I did.

And now I'm stuck in his house and he doesn't even know I'm here.

I drift to the window, watching afternoon sun creep across the hardwood floors. This place hit me in the chest the moment I followed Calvin through the door last night. What are the chances he lives in the last place I called home?

I take in details I was too disoriented to notice before. The built-in bookshelves still flank the fireplace, unchanged after all these years. The wide archway that used to separate the dining room from the kitchen is gone now, opened up into one sprawling space that would've seemed impossibly modern in my day. The window seat is the same, though the cushions are new.

I drift closer to the mantel where a few framed photographs sit. Most are recent—Calvin and his brother Blake with arms slung around each other's shoulders, grinning at the camera. Blake appears in another photo, mid-laugh, his witch girlfriend tucked against his side.

Then I see it. An older photograph in a silver frame showing two young boys standing on either side of an elderly woman on the porch of this very house. She has her arms around both of them, her smile warm and familiar in a way that makes something ache in my chest.

I lean closer, studying her face. The shape of her eyes. That smile.

It's Lois. Holy hell. Lois Randall.

I'd only met her once, when she came home from studying abroad for Christmas. She'd breezed in like sunshine, hugged her parents, then sat with me at the kitchen table and asked about my life like she actually cared about the answer. Same warmth as Earl and Viola. Same way of making you feel like you mattered. She even wrote me letters after she left.

I stare at the photograph. She aged beautifully, and lived a long life by the looks of it. And those boys... I float back to the recent photos. Same dark hair. Same smile. Calvin even has Lois's eyes.

He's Lois's grandson.

Which means this house stayed in the Randall family all these years. Earl and Viola's house, passed down to their daughter, and now to her grandchildren.

My chest tightens even though I don't breathe anymore. This was the first place I ever felt safe. The first place anyone cared whether I came home at night. It feels right that the house is Calvin's now.

I'm about to drift away when another photograph catches my eye, tucked behind the others. I concentrate, making my hand solid enough to shift it forward. Two teenage boys—Blake and Calvin again, older now, definitely in their teens—stand on either side of an old man. He has his hands on their shoulders, his grin wide and proud. He's aged, hair gone white, face lined, but I'd know him anywhere.

Sam Carter.

Of course. Why didn't I pick that up before? Calvin Carter. He'd told me his last name. I'd wondered in the back of my mind if he was related to Sam somehow. Extended family, maybe. But no. Calvin and Blake are Sam Carter's grandsons.

Does he know who Sam really was? What he was?

This is all very overwhelming. I drift toward the door, needing space. I'd love to just hang out on the porch where I used to sit and play guitar. Maybe I can at least do that.

I can't.

The barrier seizes me, yanks me back, and dumps me on my ass in the hallway of this too-quiet house.

"To hell with this bunk."

I drift back through the living room, trying to shake off the disorientation. My gaze snags on the dining room table where a black and white photograph sits next to a stack of books. I'd found it in the attic last night, tucked in an old album. Me at twenty-seven, leaning against my red convertible while Sam Carter and his friends joked around in the background.

I remember that day. We were at the lake, like we often were, with Sam and his werewolf buddies. And Vince.

Seeing my own face staring back at me twists something in my chest. That kid thought he'd finally found somewhere safe.

Somewhere he could love who he wanted without getting killed for it. He was wrong.

I was just a shifter kid from Georgia with more nerves than sense, trying to find somewhere I could be myself. Then I met Vince, and that was my first mistake. He was kind at first, broken in ways that made me think we were the same. Something haunted his eyes when he talked about his family, about the world that had turned its back on him. Two outcasts who'd finally found each other. Or so I thought. He talked about the life we deserved, how the world wasn't kind to two men in love, how he knew people who could make all our dreams come true.

He promised me forever, then made me a ghost.

And not even a proper ghost. I screwed up in life and couldn't even do death right. They bound me to the lake, invisible unless the Concord needed me to haunt someone or cause an accident on the mountain road. I can't choose when to appear or who to scare. They pull my strings and I dance. No bleeding walls. No ominous whispers. Just a glorified tool that shows up when called, does what's needed, then fades back into nothing.

It's surreal, looking at that boy I used to be. All that hope in his eyes. All that belief that life was finally opening up for him. I don't know how he ever turned into whatever I am now. A jaded ghost. The "Drowned Man of Skipper Lake."

And the stories aren't even right. Folks whisper about the man who jumped, the man who couldn't take it anymore. No one knows the truth.

I drag my gaze from the photo and look around Calvin's living room. I shouldn't be here like this. But somehow Calvin reached right through the veil and broke whatever kept me bound to the lake.

And now I'm here—not free, exactly, just trapped in a different way. Close enough to watch him moving through the space but not close enough to answer him. Closer to him than I've been in months, yet somehow further away.

I float over to where Calvin left my old Philco radio on the side table. Just looking at it knocks me back. Summer afternoons at the shop with Earl, learning how these things worked. That was a lifetime ago. Literally.

"Let's see if I can rig you into something useful."

The thing doesn't need a wall socket, not for me. I proved that last night when I got it belting out The Platters. Ghosts don't run on current. We *are* current. The trick is aiming my energy like a beam instead of flooding the circuits. Music's easy, just coaxing the tubes awake. But talking through it? That's a whole other dance. I need the radio to pick me up like a broadcast tower, tune my voice into a frequency Calvin can hear.

I push my hand inside the chassis, brushing through dust, finding the familiar bones. Tubes, resistors, coils. I feed some of my energy into the tuning dial, then the speaker. A low hum shivers out, then dies.

"Closer. Work it out, buddy. Like fixing a busted carburetor."

I remember Mr. Randall showing me how a signal rides a carrier wave, how the coil pulls voices out of thin air. Maybe I can be the signal.

I pour energy into the coil, picturing my words riding the wave. "Calvin," I whisper, shaping the sound inside my chest. The radio buzzes, lets out a garbled syllable that almost sounds like a name before collapsing into static. The effort leaves me gasping, my energy wavering like heat shimmer.

I drift back, waiting until the dizziness fades. Then I try again.

The afternoon turns into a grind of trial and error. Short bursts, rest, try again. Sometimes the speaker just coughs static. Sometimes I get a hum, a syllable half-formed. Enough to make me think this might actually work, even if each attempt drains me further. But I keep pushing.

By mid-afternoon, I can make the Philco hold my voice for three full seconds. Warped, shaky, but mine. Not enough, but definitely closer. By the time night settles in, I feel thin as mist, barely here at all. I need to rest. If I can get Calvin to notice the picture, he'll think of me, and that should spark enough energy for me to push through.

Here's hoping.

The hours crawl. Eight o'clock. Nine. I pace from window to window until finally, at half past ten, a shadow appears and footsteps crunch up the walk. He looks bone-tired, shoulders sagging.

He comes in with the day's mail tucked under his arm and walks right through me, the impact shredding what little there is of me like smoke pulled apart. His keys hit the end table with a dull clatter before he shuffles the envelopes, frowning at bills and junk.

He looks around the room and shrugs out of his jacket, hanging it neatly by the door. His movements are tense. Careful. Like he's waiting for something to jump out at him. He pauses in the hallway, staring toward the bathroom. His jaw works like he's trying to decide something. Then he shakes his head and heads that direction, flicking on lights as he goes.

Guilt twists in my gut. I didn't mean to scare him. Last night might've been a bit much. The thumping around in the attic while I searched for photos probably didn't help. And getting the Philco to play "Only You" at two in the morning seemed romantic at the time, but in hindsight, maybe a little creepy. Poor guy seems terrified.

I start to follow him then remember he asked for privacy. I'll give it to him. I'm not that desperate. Yet.

The toilet flushes, water runs in the sink.

When Calvin emerges, he's shirtless, his jeans unbuttoned and riding low on his hips. My energy flickers involuntarily, drawn to the sight. His chest is broad, dusted with dark hair that narrows to a trail disappearing beneath his waistband. A small tattoo of a crescent moon marks his left shoulder.

"That's not fair," I whisper, my mission forgotten. "Showing me that when I can't even run my hands over it."

He pads to the kitchen in bare feet, fills a glass with water, and drinks it in long gulps. A drop escapes, sliding down his chin to his chest. I watch its path, mesmerized.

Focus, Everett. The photo. The radio.

He exits the kitchen, still looking unsettled, glancing over his shoulder like he expects to see something. Someone.

This is it. If I can just get his attention, make him understand it really is me, maybe he'll stop being so afraid.

I concentrate hard, directing all my energy at the photograph on the dining room table. With a final push, I send it flying across the wood floor. It slides to a stop at his feet.

Calvin freezes. Stares down at the photo like it might bite him. For a long moment, he doesn't move, just stands there with his chest rising and falling. Then he glances around the room, searching the shadows before crouching down to pick it up.

"Everett?" His voice cracks on my name.

Now's my chance. Maybe my only chance.

I fix on the radio, scraping together what little power remains. If I can just get a word through. One word.

I push every ounce of energy I have into the radio, my awareness flickering wildly with the effort. The dial turns. Static fills the room, loud enough to make Calvin jump and spin toward the sound.

"Not this again," he mutters, moving toward the radio with cautious steps.

I focus on the sound waves, on shaping them into words. It's like trying to swim through mud. Everything's fighting me. I push harder.

"Calvin," I force out, the word crackling like fire through decades-old speakers.

He freezes mid-step, the photo still clutched in his hand. His knuckles go white around the edges. "Everett? Is that you?"

"Yes," I say, the word hissing with static. "It's me."

Calvin spins in a slow circle, his head tilting as he searches the empty room. "Where are you? I can't see you."

"Here. Near you." The effort drains me. I'm fading with every word, but I hold on.

He approaches the radio cautiously, like it might bite, then sits heavily on the couch. He turns the device so it faces him, his hands shaking as he stares at the speaker grille.

"Why can I hear you now? What changed?"

I pull myself together for a longer explanation, feeling my consciousness fragment with the effort. "You called me. I came. But now I'm... tethered to your house. Can't leave."

Calvin's face brightens, then his brow furrows with worry. He scratches his forehead. "You mean you're trapped here?"

"Different kind of prison," I manage. "But... closer to you."

He leans forward, elbows on his knees. "I can barely hear you. Are you... okay? I mean, as okay as you can be?"

I laugh, the sound distorting through the radio speakers. "For a dead guy, I guess I'm okay."

The worry lines deepen around his eyes. "The Concord. What really happened to you? Why? How?"

This is the hard part. The ugly truth I never wanted to share. But maybe this will finally convince him I'm not the villain he might think I am.

"They killed me," I say, letting the words hang in the static-filled air. "I was a sacrifice."

Calvin goes very still. "What do you mean, a sacrifice?"

The memories surface, sharp as knives, but I push through them. "I was young. Stupid. Trusted the wrong person. Someone who said they loved me. But they just wanted power. They used me to get it."

Calvin's eyes soften. He shakes his head in disbelief.

The radio crackles with my emotion. "The Concord wanted a shifter to complete their circle. They said I was special, but I was just raw material for their ritual. They murdered me. Tied my soul to Skipper Lake to power their magic."

Calvin's face goes pale, his hands clenching into fists. "Jesus, Everett. You were murdered."

"I never wanted to be part of them," I continue, needing him to understand this above all else. "Never chose any of it. They tricked me, used me, then bound me to that damn lake for eternity."

For a long moment, Calvin stares at the radio. His shoulders drop.

He shakes his head slowly. "It makes sense now. Why you held back. Why you always looked like you were carrying two different weights." He runs a finger along the edge of the radio. "For a while I wondered if you'd chosen them. If what you felt for me was just part of their trap."

"Never." I force the word through, sharp as I can make it. "You were the only real thing I had in almost seventy years. You made me feel alive again."

Calvin's mouth twists. "I hate what they did to you."

"Not your fault." Static buzzes around my words as the connection frays. "You gave me a few days of happiness. I'm grateful for that, even if it makes moving on harder. Thank you for the hope."

He leans closer. "Hope?"

"That maybe somehow I'd be able to come back to life. But we both know that's not possible. I'm dead. No spell can fix that, no matter how badly we want it."

He closes his eyes, shoulders sagging. "I know." His voice is raw. "Fuck, I wish things were different."

The room goes still, broken only by the hiss of the radio. I ache to touch him, to take his hand, but the gulf between us is too wide.

"I'm tired, Calvin," I admit. "Decades of being bound, used. I want to rest. To move on."

He raises his head. "Then maybe that's what I can do. Help

you break whatever's still tying you to them. Help you move on. So you can find peace."

The connection is weakening rapidly now, my voice growing faint. "I just want you to know... The feelings were reciprocated. You didn't develop a crush on a monster. Just a man who was too trusting for his own good. Wrong place, wrong time. I'm sorry I can't be more for you."

Calvin lets out a breath. "I never doubted my feelings. But knowing you didn't choose this... it helps."

"Good," I whisper. "That's all I—"

The radio squeals with feedback, a harsh sound that makes Calvin wince and cover his ears. Something is wrong. This feels like interference.

"Everett?" Calvin calls over the static. "What's happening?"

I try to respond, but something else is here now. A presence that makes my energy recoil. Cold. Ancient. Angry.

Static roars up, swallowing my voice whole. Calvin twists the radio dials, again and again, but it's no use. Whatever this is, it's cutting me off from him.

The presence presses closer, and I catch a whisper of familiar evil. The Concord. I think they've found me.

"Calvin!" I manage to force out one last word before the connection snaps completely.

The radio goes silent. I slump beside the couch, my essence fragmenting, barely visible even to myself. Calvin can't see me, can't hear me, can't feel me when I try to brush my hand across his back.

But worse, I can still feel that presence lingering at the edges of my consciousness. Watching. Waiting.

I cower, expecting to be snapped back to Skipper Lake at any moment, but my tether to this place holds.

Calvin fiddles with the radio for another ten minutes, turning dials, adjusting the antenna, even slapping the side like that ever fixed anything. Finally, he gives up with a frustrated sigh.

"We'll find a way," he promises the silent radio. "We'll figure this out."

He picks up the photo again, studying my face. "I'm sorry you had to go through all that," he whispers. "Fucking Concord assholes."

Eventually, he heads to his bedroom, taking the radio and my photo with him. He places both on his nightstand before stripping down and climbing into bed. The night light stays on, casting shadows over his troubled face.

I watch him from the doorway, not wanting to intrude but unable to look away. He falls asleep with one hand stretched toward the radio.

Maybe he's reaching for me.

Tough break, us meeting like this on opposite sides of the grave. Trust the universe to drag us across the line between life and death, dangle a chance at something real, then snatch it away. But at least now he knows the truth. I'm not a villain who chose evil. I'm just a man who was used and discarded, trying to find peace after decades of torment.

So here I am, haunting the house of a man I can't have, wanting him from a distance he can't cross. Some ghosts stick around because of unfinished business. Maybe my unfinished business is learning to let go, and helping Calvin learn to move on. Or maybe I'm just making excuses to stay near him a little longer.

I drift to the window, looking out at the night sky, but my attention keeps returning to that lingering presence. I can't help but think the Concord knows where I am now. They likely know I've broken free of the lake's binding, even if I'm still trapped in this house.

I turn back to watch Calvin sleep, memorizing the rise and fall of his chest, the way his dark lashes rest against his cheeks, the slight part of his lips. If I cross over, at least I'll take this with me. At least I'll have known, for a brief moment, what it felt like to be seen. To be heard. To matter to someone.

But first we have to deal with the Concord. They'll come calling soon enough.

CHAPTER SEVEN

Calvin

I shift my weight from foot to foot, checking my watch for the fifth time in as many minutes. The dusty reception area of Ravena's old shop feels colder this morning, like the walls know we're up to something. I know I'm here to meet La'Tasha to look at the black door in the basement. What it means. Where it leads. But my mind keeps drifting to Everett instead. At least now I know it's really him in my house, but what the hell happened last night? One minute we were talking through the radio, the next he was just… gone. Cut off mid-sentence like something yanked him away.

Fifteen minutes later, La'Tasha bustles through the front door with two steaming cups and a paper bag that smells like sweet heaven in the form of maple bars.

She hands me a coffee. "You're early."

"Just didn't want you to think I chickened out. Or that I made the whole thing up." I take a grateful sip. Perfect. Strong enough to wake the dead. Which might come in handy later with Everett.

La'Tasha pulls a maple-glazed donut from the bag and passes it to me. "So we're doing this? Hunting for your magical time travel door at nine in the morning?"

"Nine thirty," I correct, frosting already smeared on my fingers. "And yes. Thanks for coming."

She shrugs, but I can see the curiosity. "Like I'd miss this. Either you've discovered something world-changing or you're having a mental breakdown. Whatever the case, I expect quality entertainment."

"Your support means everything." I bat my eyes at her, then drop the bomb. "By the way, Everett contacted me last night."

La'Tasha freezes mid-coffee sip. "Wait, what?"

I tell her everything while we work through our pastries. The radio crackling to life. Everett's voice, static-filled but unmistakably him. How they killed him in 1958 and bound his soul to Skipper Lake.

La'Tasha's mouth falls open. "He was *sacrificed*?"

"Yeah." The word sits heavy between us. "I can't even imagine."

"Jesus Christ." She sets her pastry down, appetite apparently gone. "Calvin, that's... I mean, I knew the Concord was evil, but that's a whole different level. So he was trapped at the lake and now he's trapped in your house?"

"Can't leave. Can't make himself visible. Just stuck there."

She stares at me for a long moment, processing. "Okay. Okay, so we definitely need to talk to Dex about this. Maybe he can help." She glances toward the stairs leading to the basement. "But we came here to look at the time travel situation, and we should probably do that before your brother shows up and complicates things."

She's not wrong.

We head down to the basement, our steps echoing. Everything looks exactly as it did yesterday. Cold concrete floor. Dusty shelves lined with Ravena's leftover witch junk. And at the far end, the black door with its strange symbols.

La'Tasha runs her fingers over the symbols etched into the wood. "These are old. Like, really old. Some I recognize from ancient binding spells."

My stomach tightens. "Binding what exactly?"

"Not what. Where." She taps one particularly intricate symbol with her fingernail. "This binds a place to another place. Or maybe a time to another time. Or maybe both?" She steps back, hands on her hips. "Okay, hotshot. Show me how this works."

I step forward and grab the handle. It's cool and solid in my hand. Definitely locked.

"Last time it just fell open," I explain, giving it a hopeful push. Nothing happens. "Then I went through looking for a light switch."

"Were you doing anything special? Saying magic words? Blood sacrifice? Doing the hokey pokey?"

I shake my head, dragging my memory back over the day. "I was listening to music. Had my earbuds in." I pull them from my pocket. "Not sure if that matters, but..."

La'Tasha gestures for me to put them in. "So put them in. Play the same song."

I slip the earbuds in and scroll through my phone. The familiar opening notes fill my ears. I close my eyes, then try the handle again. Still nothing.

"Maybe add some special effects?" La'Tasha suggests. "Jazz hands? Little soft shoe?"

"Very funny." I pull the earbuds out. "I don't get it. It worked before."

She taps her chin. "What were you thinking about when it happened? Were you focused on anything specific?"

I think back. "The song... it reminded me of being a kid. Blake and I used to ride bikes around town while listening to it. I was thinking about how simple life was back then."

"So you were thinking about the past while listening to a

song that connects you to a specific memory." La'Tasha's eyes light up. "Maybe the portal responds to emotional connections to the past. The music helps trigger the memory, and the door opens to that exact time."

It makes a weird kind of sense. "Worth a shot."

I put the earbuds back in and restart the song. This time, I close my eyes and focus. I picture thirteen-year-old me on my silver bike, wind in my hair, not a care in the world. Summer 2005. The freedom of childhood. The warmth of the sun. Blake racing ahead of me.

The air tingles against my skin. I open my eyes and reach for the handle.

It's unlocked. I give it a twist and the door swings open.

"Holy shit," La'Tasha whispers, stumbling backward against the wall. "It actually worked."

I push the door open, my heart hammering. "Told you. See? I'm not crazy."

The door opens to reveal darkness beyond. La'Tasha inches closer, her hands trembling as she peers over my shoulder.

"What now?" she asks, her voice barely above a whisper.

"Now I go through and hope I don't get stuck in 2005." I take a deep breath, steadying myself. "If I'm not back in five minutes, call the time police."

Before she can argue, I step through the doorway. Reality tilts sideways and my stomach lurches like I'm on a roller coaster. Light explodes around me, and suddenly I'm standing before the door looking out on Main Street again.

Same scene as before. The old video store. The weird mannequins in bad wigs. Kids on bikes weaving through sparse traffic. I glance at the rotating bank sign on the corner of the street. It reads:

July 17, 2005. 5:26 PM. 89 degrees. Have a nice day.

I did it. Again. Holy shit, this is amazing.

A familiar silver bike zooms past. Mini-Me, bobbing his

head to what I know is the same song playing in my earbuds right now. He turns the corner without noticing me this time, Blake close behind.

Part of me wants to follow them and watch my childhood unfold from the outside. That feels like a fast track to time-travel-induced therapy bills, though, so no thanks. And La'Tasha is waiting. I need to get back and show her it works.

I turn and head back to where the portal should be. I find it behind the same door deep within the old warehouse. I step through, and the world spins again. The door pops open and La'Tasha's face comes into focus, her eyes wide. She reaches out and grabs my arm with both hands.

"You disappeared," she says. "You literally vanished right in front of me. I tried to step through after you, but the door locked."

"How long was I gone?"

"A little over five minutes." She releases my arm but keeps staring. "Calvin, this is incredible. This breaks every rule of magic I know."

"Your turn." I hand her my earbuds. "Think of a memory. Something strong. A time you'd want to revisit."

She wrinkles her nose. "I'll use my own, thanks. I don't want your nasty ear germs," she says with a smirk.

She scrolls through her phone, selects a song, and puts her earbuds in. Her eyes close, face relaxing as the music takes her someplace I can't see. She reaches for the door, but nothing happens.

"It's not working." She tries the handle again.

"Try again. Really lose yourself in the memory. Something you loved. Something you miss." My stomach clenches. What if it only works for me?

La'Tasha's expression softens. Her shoulders drop. She tries once more, fingers brushing the handle. It falls open. She looks at me, her eyes bright with unshed tears.

"See you soon," she whispers, and steps through.

The door swings shut behind her, the lock clicking automatically.

I wait, pacing the length of the basement. One minute. Five. Ten.

At fifteen minutes, I start to worry. At twenty, I am wearing a groove in the concrete floor. At thirty, I am about to break the door down when I hear footsteps on the stairs.

"Calvin? You here already?" Blake's voice echoes through the basement. "Thought we said eleven for demo day."

"Umm… yep…," I call back, eyes still fixed on the door. Shit. Where is La'Tasha? "Just checking some things first."

Blake appears at the bottom of the stairs, tool belt already strapped around his waist, hard hat in hand. "What things? And why do you look like you farted in church?"

Before I can answer, the black door swings open.

La'Tasha steps through, her eyes red-rimmed and glistening. She looks dazed. She clutches something in her closed fist.

"It worked," she whispers. "It really worked."

Blake looks between us. His hard hat slips in his grip. "What worked? What's going on?"

La'Tasha wipes her eyes with her free hand, then opens her fist to reveal a small gardenia. Her mouth opens. Closes. Opens again. No words come out. She just stands there, staring at the flower trembling in her palm. Then finally, "I saw my grandmother. I was there, too. I was six years old, helping her work in the garden." She holds up the flower. "I couldn't stop watching. I couldn't believe it. I picked this and brought it back with me just to see what would happen."

Blake stares at the flower. "I don't understand."

"It's a time portal. Show him," La'Tasha tells me, still cradling the flower.

He scoffs. "Bullshit."

"He won't believe it until he sees it. Have him try."

I hesitate and then pass my earbuds to Blake. "Think of a

memory. Something you'd like to see again. Then think of a song that helps remind you of that memory."

"This is ridiculous," he mutters, but he takes the earbuds anyway. I catch the tremor in his fingers.

"The memory has to match the song. You have to be very specific." I coach him. "Something you'd love to see again."

This has to work. Now that he knows, I need it to work so we can prove it to Hazel.

He scrolls through my phone with a skeptical frown. Finally, he selects a song and puts the earbuds in. His eyes close. The harsh lines around his eyes soften. After a moment, the lock clicks open.

He twists the handle and the door swings open to swirling light.

"No way," he whispers, staring at the open door, frozen.

"Yes way," I reply. "Go see for yourself."

He hesitates, his hand hovering over the doorframe. His jaw sets. He steps through. The door closes behind him with a soft click.

La'Tasha and I exchange looks. We wait in silence, barely breathing.

Exactly eleven minutes later, the door opens. Blake stumbles through, face drained of color, staring at nothing. His hands shake so badly he drops his hard hat. It clatters on the concrete floor like a gunshot.

"We need to call Hazel," he says, voice thin. "Right now. And nobody uses this thing again until we know what we're dealing with."

I've never seen Blake look so shaken.

"Hey," I start, stepping toward him. "What did you see?"

He shakes his head hard, backing away from the door. "We need to get Hazel over here."

La'Tasha gently touches his arm. "Are you okay?"

"No. I'm really not."

She pulls out her phone, thumbs moving quickly. "I'll text her and ask her to come quick."

Blake sits heavily on an overturned crate, elbows on his knees, hands pressed to his forehead. He keeps his gaze fixed on the floor, as far from the door as he can get without leaving the room.

None of us touch the door while we wait for Hazel. La'Tasha stands near the portal, the gardenia now tucked behind her ear. I lean against a support beam, trying not to look as anxious as I feel.

Footsteps echo on the stairs above us, quick and light. Hazel appears a moment later, her curly auburn hair wild and her cheeks flushed. She carries a leather satchel that probably contains enough magical supplies to level a city block.

"This better be good," she says, slightly out of breath, one hand pressed to her side. "I left three potions simmering and told a customer I had a family emergency. I left Coco in charge. You know how that usually goes."

I wince. Coco running the shop alone is never a good sign. She'll be lucky if the apothecary is still there when she gets back.

Blake pushes to his feet and points to the black door. His hand is still unsteady. "You're gonna want to check out that door."

Hazel's whole demeanor shifts. She moves toward it, steps measured and careful. Her hand hovers over the symbols without touching them, and I swear I can see a faint glow emanating from her fingertips.

"These are old," she whispers, echoing La'Tasha's earlier assessment. "Pre-colonial, maybe older. The magic is…" She pauses, her eyes widening. "Powerful. Interesting. And very much active."

"It's a time travel portal," I blurt out, unable to contain myself any longer. "We all went through it. We all saw the past."

Hazel's head snaps toward me so fast I hear her neck crack. "That's impossible."

"That's what I said," Blake adds. His voice sounds scraped raw.

"It's real," La'Tasha says. "I didn't believe Calvin either when he told me, but I literally watched him disappear behind the door, and then I tried it myself. I went back to 2006. It's some sort of portal, but I don't know what kind."

"Wait, *you* tried?" Hazel focuses on La'Tasha. "Tash, seriously? You of all people should know better."

La'Tasha's face flashes with annoyance. "I can hold my own, Hazel."

"Still, you should have checked with me first."

Hazel's gaze cuts to the gardenia behind La'Tasha's ear. "Tell me that is not from the past."

La'Tasha plucks it free and holds it out. Hazel takes it carefully, eyes narrowing as she studies the petals. The flower looks fresh, no wilting, no browning at the edges.

"This should not be possible," Hazel murmurs. She brushes a thumb along one petal. A faint shimmer ripples over it, then fades. "Matter crossing timelines without disintegrating. Do you know how many laws of magic this breaks?"

"Enough to make you yell at us some more?" I ask.

Hazel ignores me and kneels in front of the door, her satchel open beside her. She sets the gardenia beside her tools. She lights a bundle of herbs and runs them over herself, chanting. She rubs some oil on her hands and then pulls out what looks like a compass made of silver and bone. She sprinkles herbs on the threshold while muttering something under her breath. The herbs glow briefly with blue-white light, then turn to ash.

"I'm guessing this is some type of temporal magic," she confirms, sitting back on her heels. "But if it's really a time travel door, it could unravel reality if it's not handled properly. Tell me exactly what happened. Every detail."

We take turns explaining. I start with yesterday and my first trip through. La'Tasha describes how we figured out the connection between music, memory, and the time travel trigger. Blake just nods along, arms crossed tight over his chest, his shoulders rigid.

"And you're sure you traveled to the exact times and places you were thinking about?" Hazel asks, picking up a pendulum and holding it in front of the door. It immediately begins spinning in rapid circles.

"One hundred percent," La'Tasha confirms. "I was back at my childhood home in 2006. I saw my grandmother. She's been gone fifteen years, but there she was, alive and gardening and singing to herself like she always did. And she was real." Her voice catches.

"And you?" Hazel asks Blake, her voice gentler now.

Blake's whole body tenses. "A time when I was a kid. It was real." His hands start trembling again, and he shoves them deep into his pockets.

Hazel's shoulders loosen a fraction. "Did you interact with anyone? Talk to them? Touch anything? Change anything?"

La'Tasha shakes her head. "I just stood behind the treeline and watched my grandmother talk to younger me."

Blake shakes his head too, eyes fixed on some point on the floor.

All eyes turn to me. I squirm under their collective gaze.

"I might have bumped into thirteen-year-old me the first time," I admit. "And talked to him. And mini-Blake."

"Calvin!" She drops the pendulum in her bag. "What were you thinking?"

"I wasn't. It just happened. How was I supposed to know I'd literally run into myself?" I throw my hands up. "I was disoriented."

Hazel stands and begins pacing, finger tapping at her chin. "If you changed something significant in the past, the present would be affected. But how would we know? We'd have no memory of the original timeline." She stops and stares at me. "Did anything feel different when you came back? Any sense of wrongness?"

I think back to yesterday, searching for any changes, any sense that something was off. "No. Everything seemed normal."

"And do either of you remember meeting adult Calvin when you were kids?" she asks Blake and me.

Blake shakes his head slowly. "No. But that was a long time ago." He pauses, his brow furrowing. "But I do remember you having nightmares about meeting someone who looked like you in your dreams."

"I don't remember any nightmares." The hair on my arms stands up. If I don't remember, what else might have changed without me knowing?

"Dude." Blake looks at me sideways. "Everything gave you nightmares, so…"

Hazel stops pacing and looks between us. "Maybe the timeline protects itself. Minor changes get absorbed, rationalized away. But the subconscious would remember. Your thirteen-year-old mind must have processed the encounter as a dream to maintain temporal stability."

"So I didn't break anything?" I ask, relief flooding through me.

"Doesn't seem like it. But that doesn't mean you couldn't. This kind of magic is dangerous, Calvin. Really dangerous." She turns back to Blake. "Remember the night we broke into Ravena's office last summer? We sensed something powerful below us. This must have been what we felt."

Blake nods.

"So this is Ravena's doing?" La'Tasha asks. "Or the Concord's?"

Hazel traces one of the symbols with her fingertip. It flashes under her touch, almost as if it's connecting with her. "It's Concord magic, for sure. The magical signature is almost identical to the ones that were on the bindings around town back in October. But why? What would they gain from a time travel door?" She looks up at us. "And more importantly, why did they leave it here after we locked up Ravena?"

The question hangs in the air.

"Maybe they wanted to change something in the past," Blake

says quietly. "Undo a failure. Set up something in the future. Maybe they're still using it?"

"Or maybe they're planning to use it to escape if their plans go wrong," La'Tasha adds, adjusting her glasses.

I snap my fingers. "What if Everett knows about this? He was part of the Concord, right? Maybe he's seen this door before."

"Everett?" Hazel arches a brow. "The ghost who nearly got Mina killed?"

"He was forced into it," I say, probably too quickly. My face heats up. "He didn't have a choice. He told me through the radio. Said the Concord murdered him, bound him to the lake. He was sacrificed. They've used his death to power their spells for decades."

Both Hazel and Blake stare at me. Hazel's eyes narrow.

"Through the radio?" Hazel repeats slowly, like she is testing the words for sense. "What do you mean?"

Blake lets out a short, flat breath. "That's not something you hear every day."

I cross my arms. "Look, I know how it sounds, but it's true. I spoke to him last night. He told me he was sacrificed."

Blake leans forward, elbows on his knees again. "Sacrificed. For what?"

"I don't know all the details," I admit. "But he never chose to be one of them. They tricked him, killed him, then chained his soul. He was a victim, not a traitor."

Blake studies me. "And you believe him?"

"Yes," I answer without hesitation. "I do. And I know that sounds crazy, but it's the truth. And if he was stuck in their operations for nearly seventy years, he might know about this portal. Maybe even what they could be using it for."

La'Tasha tips her chin. "Calvin's right. Everett might have information we need. But how do we reach him?"

Hazel narrows her eyes at me. "Wait. How did you even get in touch with him in the first place?"

"I..." My throat goes dry. I glance at the others, fumbling. "It's complicated."

La'Tasha folds her arms. "I gave him a hand. It was safely monitored."

Hazel's gaze snaps to her. "You what?"

"Relax," La'Tasha says, all smooth confidence. "Penny, Coco, and I set up a safe channel. Protective wards, containment circles, the works. Calvin's not about to get possessed by a vengeful spirit."

"That's not the point," Hazel fires back. "You did this behind my back? Without even telling me? You're messing with the Concord and you know that's dangerous."

"I didn't realize I had to get your permission for every little thing I do," La'Tasha shoots back, one brow arched in challenge.

Hazel's shoulders go rigid. La'Tasha plants her feet and refuses to look away.

I need to step in before we find ourselves in the middle of a witch-off.

"Look, I needed closure... and maybe that was selfish, but" I hold up my hands. "What we need to focus on right now is this door."

"Calvin's right," La'Tasha says after a beat, still watching Hazel. "Everett might have information we need. You said the radio helped you contact him?"

"It was brief and it was spotty. But I think maybe we should ask Dex," I say. "If anyone can help us talk to Everett directly, it's him."

"But... you have to tell Mina," Hazel says. "She might not like this. Everett played a part in almost getting her killed."

"Unwillingly," I interrupt. "He was a victim too, Hazel. How many times do I have to say it?"

Hazel holds up a hand and closes her eyes for a second. I have obviously worked her last nerve. She speaks slowly, deliberately. "She deserves to know. I won't keep this from her. And we need to prepare for Concord interference."

"So we'll invite Dex and Mina over, then we'll contact your ghost and be done with this?" Blake asks. His voice is tired, like he's worked a full day already and he just got here.

"Something like that," I confirm. "So, my place tonight. I'll order pizza."

"Pizza with the Reaper," La'Tasha snorts. "Sounds like a bad horror movie."

Hazel stands, brushing dust from her jeans. "No one uses this thing again until we know more." She looks at both La'Tasha and me. "I'm serious. The magic feels stable for now, but time travel has consequences we can't predict. We need to know what the implications are. Promise me, Calvin. No more trips to the past until we understand what we're dealing with."

"I promise," I say, and mean it. The last thing I want to do is accidentally erase myself from existence. Or Everett.

"I'll call Dex and Mina," I offer, already planning what to say. *Hey, want to come over and help me chat with my ghost crush who might know about a secret time travel door and a murderous cult?*

"I'll come prepared to fight back against the Concord in case they show up," Hazel says, gathering her magical supplies.

"And I'll bring wine," La'Tasha adds. "Lots of it. We might need it."

Blake picks up his hard hat from where he dropped it, turning it over in his hands. "I'll be there. If Everett has information about the Concord, we need to hear it." He heads up the stairs without looking back at the door. "Come on, Cal. We've got shit to do upstairs."

Blake leads the way. I can't stop myself from glancing back at the door one last time.

If Dex can do what we hope he can do, I might get to see Everett again. Not just his voice crackling through static, but actually *see* him. Face to face. The thought makes my chest ache.

But then I remember. I promised to help him move on. To find peace.

Which means tonight could be another hello and a final goodbye, all at once.

CHAPTER EIGHT

Everett

I float near Calvin as he buzzes around the living room, straightening cushions, picking up stray magazines and worrying over pizza toppings.

"Hawaiian for me. Pepperoni for everyone else. Maybe a veggie just in case?" He pauses mid-reach for a dropped sock, phone in hand. Then he looks up, scanning the room like he might actually spot me. "Everett? You're still here, right?" His voice softens. "People are coming over tonight. Dex is coming. He's the Reaper dude I was telling you about. He might be able to help you."

Help me? As in free me from the Concord? The thought is almost too overwhelming.

"So, six large pizzas," Calvin continues, thumbs flying across his phone screen. "Figure we'll need at least that much. The Grim Reaper probably has a killer appetite, right?" He snorts at his own joke.

I laugh too, though he can't hear me. His jokes are real groaners, but they get me every time.

"So here's the plan," Calvin says, tossing his phone onto the couch and moving to straighten a stack of magazines. "First, we need to figure out what that weird door in Ravena's old basement is all about. We need to know if the Concord built it and what for."

He rubs his head, leaving his hair sticking up in front. I want to smooth it down. Feel the texture between my fingers.

"Hazel nearly had a stroke when she found out we'd used it. And Blake..." Calvin pauses. His mouth tightens. His gaze drops to the floor. "Blake saw something through that door that really upset him."

I follow him to the kitchen where he starts washing a few stray dishes in the sink. Water splashes over his hands, soaking the front of his shirt. He doesn't seem to notice.

"If anyone knows what the Concord was planning with that door, it's you. Or at least I hope you do," he says, scrubbing a coffee mug. "Maybe they mentioned something while you were... you know... trapped and all that."

I press my lips together. If only I could tell him now, instead of waiting for the whole gang to arrive. The Concord kept me in the dark about most things, and apparently, I didn't need to know about this specific doorway. I was their puppet, their bait. Not their confidant. I'd heard rumblings about time travel and possible manipulation, but no specifics.

Calvin dries his hands on a dish towel and leans against the counter, his eyes scanning the room like he might catch a glimpse of me. For a second, his gaze passes right through where I stand. I freeze, waiting.

Nothing.

"The second part," he continues, "is that I might actually get to see you again." His smile is small, private. Just for me. "Like, really see you. Talk to you. If Dex can do what La'Tasha thinks he can."

I move closer, hope flickering through me. Last night's radio conversation nearly tore me apart, but if this works? If I can actually see him, talk to him without static between us? It's almost too much to wish for.

"I've missed you," Calvin admits, staring at his hands. "Which is stupid because we barely knew each other. I know it was only five days, but it felt like…"

"More," I finish, though he can't hear me. Not stupid at all. It felt like more to me too. Like finding something I didn't know I was missing until it was right in front of me.

Calvin pushes off from the counter and moves back to the living room, plumping cushions that don't need plumping. "And then there's the third part," he says, his voice steady but quieter. "Dex might be able to help you cross over. For good."

Cross over. Be free. Find peace. It's what I've wanted for years. So why does the thought make my chest ache?

"I know it's not what I want," Calvin admits, sitting heavily on the couch. "Ideally we could bring you back to life, but I know that's not possible. This is the best I can do for you. You deserve freedom. Peace."

I sit beside him, wishing he could feel the dip in the cushions. "It's not what I want either," I whisper uselessly. What I want is impossible. I want to be alive again. I want to feel the sun on my skin. Feel air in my lungs. I want Calvin's hand in mine. To finally experience real love.

"You didn't choose any of this," Calvin continues, staring at the floor. "You didn't choose the Concord. You didn't choose to die. Maybe now you finally get to choose what happens next."

Something inside me gives way. A tightness I've carried for nearly seventy years finally loosens. All this time I've been a prisoner, a tool with no choices, no freedom. Calvin wants to help set me free. Even if it means losing me forever.

It's an act of selflessness I've never had directed at me before. I almost don't know what to do with it. But at least I get to feel this before I go. Something close to love. It's more than I ever had when I was alive.

I reach out, focusing all my energy into my fingertips. For

just a second, I manage to disturb the air enough to ruffle his hair. The barest touch.

He freezes, his eyes going wide. "Everett?" he whispers. "Was that you?"

I do it again, this time managing to make the papers on the coffee table flutter.

Calvin laughs. His eyes glisten. "Hi, handsome."

I wish I could tell him everything now. About the Concord. About the door. About how the thought of crossing over fills me with both longing and dread.

Instead, I watch him smile at nothing. And I think about what peace really means. I've wanted it for so long. So why does it feel like I'm giving up the only good thing I've ever had?

"They'll be here soon," Calvin says, checking his watch. "And then we'll finally get to talk. For real this time."

For the first time in decades, I have something to look forward to. And something to fear losing. Funny how hope and heartbreak always come in the same breath for me.

La'Tasha arrives first, bustling through the front door with two bottles of wine. Her bracelets jingle as she shrugs off her coat and starts talking before the door even shuts. I hover by the bookshelf, watching them.

"You're early," Calvin says, taking the wine from her hands. "I'm still freaking out about all this."

"Better early than ghosted," La'Tasha jokes, then winces. "Sorry. Poor choice of words."

I laugh despite myself. At least someone around here has a sense of humor about the whole dead coulda-been-boyfriend situation.

They move to the kitchen where Calvin fumbles with a corkscrew. La'Tasha leans against the counter, pushing her sleeves up, bracelets chiming.

"So," Calvin starts, wrestling with the cork, "what was the deal with you and Hazel today? I felt like I walked into the middle of something."

La'Tasha's jaw tightens, and she picks at her nail polish. "It's nothing new. Just the same old power struggle. Hazel thinks because she inherited the apothecary and leadership over the coven, she gets final say on everything magical in Moonridge."

"And you disagree?" Calvin asks, finally freeing the cork with a satisfying pop.

"Not necessarily. I respect her authority, but she goes overboard. She always has. Anytime she feels out of control she tightens down." She accepts the glass Calvin hands her, her grip tight around the stem.

"Lately she acts like I need her permission to do anything magical." She takes a long drink. "And it's been rubbing me the wrong way."

Calvin nods slowly, letting her talk.

"My family helped found Moonridge." She swirls the wine in her glass. "I have roots here older than hers. Sometimes I think she forgets I'm not some amateur who needs babysitting. That I'm more than her errand girl and right-hand witch."

I drift closer, fascinated by this peek behind the witch curtain. The Concord had whispered about divisions among the Moonridge witches. They had planned to exploit them someday.

"She seemed pretty pissed about the Ouija board thing," Calvin observes.

"Because she wasn't involved." La'Tasha takes a large gulp of wine, her eyes flashing. "Don't get me wrong, I love Hazel. She's like family. But sometimes she forgets she's not the only witch in town. And sometimes I wonder if she would rather keep it that way."

Calvin nods slowly. "I get that. Blake's the same way about the pack sometimes."

A knock at the door cuts their conversation short. La'Tasha drains half her glass in one gulp, her shoulders squaring. "To be continued," she says.

Calvin opens the door to reveal Blake, Hazel, Mina, and a tall, imposing man I recognize as Dex. The air in the room shifts instantly. It grows heavier, charged with something that makes my ghostly form vibrate like a plucked string.

"Thanks for coming," Calvin says, ushering them inside. "Pizza should be here soon."

I can't take my eyes off Dex. There's something ancient about him, something that sees right through the veil of life and death. His presence pulls at me, like gravity but softer. His eyes scan the room and stop exactly where I'm floating. He sees me. The sensation is like being dunked in ice water and fire all at once.

"You have a visitor," Dex states, his voice deep and calm.

Calvin's head whips around, eyes searching frantically. "Everett? Can you see him?"

Dex nods once, studying me. "By the bookshelf. Blond. Dressed like he stepped out of a Buddy Holly concert."

"Hey," I protest, looking down at my clothes. "This was sharp as a tack in my day."

No one reacts. They still can't hear me.

The doorbell rings again. Calvin moves to answer it, wallet already in hand. A young guy with a stack of pizza boxes stands on the porch.

"Big party tonight?" the guy asks, shifting his weight from foot to foot. He pokes his head in and waves.

"Thanks, buddy." Calvin hands over some cash. "Keep the change."

As Calvin turns back with the pizzas, he gasps. The boxes slip from his hands, landing with a soft thud on the floor. His face goes white, then flushes.

"Everett," he whispers, eyes wide and fixed directly on me.

I look down at myself, shocked to discover my shape has solidified. I'm still translucent, like I'm made of colored glass, but I'm visible.

"Hi," I say, and my voice bounces off the walls, startling me.

Hazel and La'Tasha gasp. Mina's hands fly to her mouth, her eyes going impossibly wide.

Only Dex seems unbothered, crouching to gather the fallen pizza boxes with a sort of bored grace. "This all seems very dramatic," he says. "Isn't this exactly what you were hoping for?"

Calvin takes a shaky step toward me, hand outstretched. His fingers meet my arm, sliding through with the faintest drag, like moving through cold honey. His breath catches at the contact.

"You're really here," he says, awe making his voice crack.

"I've been here the whole time," I answer, though my voice falters under the weight of six pairs of eyes. "Just couldn't get your attention very well."

Calvin's face lights up. "By the way, the heart on the mirror?"

I nod, a sheepish smile tugging at my lips. "All me. Sorry about the shower thing. I didn't look. Much."

Calvin laughs, a startled sound that cuts through the charged air.

Mina's eyes grow cold. She takes a sharp step forward, her body rigid. "I nearly died because of him."

The laughter dies at once. Every head swivels toward her.

She advances another step, her fists clenched and trembling. "He lured me to the Concord. Don't you all remember?" Her voice rises, Scottish accent even more pronounced. "If they hadn't done what they did, I wouldn't be like this. Stuck between human and vampire because of them. Because of him."

I face her fully, my form flickering with shame. "Mina, I'm sorry. I never wanted to hurt you. I never wanted to hurt anyone. They forced me. They've controlled me since 1958."

"Controlled?" Hazel asks. Her tone is clinical. She leans forward, eyes sharp, like she's cataloguing every detail for future reference.

"They killed me," I say, the words scraping out with a bitterness that has never dulled. "Then bound my spirit to Skipper Lake. I've been their puppet ever since."

The room goes quiet except for the sound of Mina's harsh breathing. Even Dex looks up from straightening the pizza boxes, his dark eyes steady on me. Blake sits stiffly, jaw tight, like he would rather be anywhere but here.

Mina shakes her head violently, pacing now, her movements sharp. "Convenient story." Her voice wavers, but her glare does not. "And you expect me to just believe you? After everything that happened?"

I can't meet her eyes.

"No. I expect you to hate me. I would hate me too."

Mina's fingers twitch, but she lets me go on.

"But I tried. Honest. At the falls. You saw it." I force myself to look at her. "That wasn't Concord triumph in my face."

She flinches, barely.

"It was me trying to warn you. Trying to apologize." I exhale, voice low. "You have to believe me."

Silence sits between us.

"I'm no one to them. Just a cog. I stand in their circle because I have to."

Mina's eyes narrow, searching mine.

"If I could have done anything to stop them, I would have."

She nods, her voice dropping to barely above a whisper. "That night. Your eyes. You did seem… bothered. Conflicted."

My shape solidifies slightly as the tension eases. "I'm not one of them. At least not by choice."

Her shoulders sag, though her gaze stays guarded. She wraps her arms around herself. "I'll leave it be. For now. For Calvin. But if you think I'm going to trust you…"

Calvin clears his throat, stepping between us. "Maybe we should all have some pizza. Nobody can yell while they're chewing."

The line earns him a groan from Blake, low and tired, but it breaks the tension. Chairs scrape as everyone shuffles to sit. Mina keeps her distance but no longer looks ready to bolt.

I hover near Calvin, not quite sitting, not quite standing, the attention of the room pressing on me heavier than any shackle. After seventy years of being invisible, I've never felt more exposed.

"What do you know about the door in Ravena's basement?" Hazel asks. "Is it Concord magic?"

I focus, trying to remember any whispers or plans I might have overheard during my decades of servitude. "I'm not high ranking in their organization. I was just a tool, so they didn't share much with me. But I know they've tried to manipulate time before."

"For what purpose?" Dex asks, his dark eyes fixed on me with an intensity that suggests he already knows more than he's letting on.

"To bring back powerful members who died. To change outcomes that didn't favor them. To reach into other realities where magic works differently." I shrug helplessly. "They've had limited success from what I gathered. But if that door is on Ravena's property, it's likely connected to them. The Concord has been planning something big for decades. I don't know what, exactly, but it's something that requires more power than they've ever wielded before."

Blake leans forward, pizza forgotten in his hand. "If you're supposedly bound to Skipper Lake, why are you here now?"

Calvin jumps in. "That's my fault. We did a Ouija board thing at La'Tasha's. I invited him to haunt me instead. I was drunk and didn't think it would actually work."

"But it did," La'Tasha says with a knowing look.

"What's interesting is that he's tethered to this specific house," Hazel points out. "Why here?"

I smile. "I think it's because I lived here before I died. Back in the fifties. Your maternal grandparents were the Randalls, right?" I ask Calvin and Blake.

They both nod, looking stunned. Calvin's mouth falls open slightly.

"Mr. Randall gave me a room in exchange for helping at his auto shop. They were good people. Kind. They didn't care that I was…" I pause, still not used to saying it openly even in this more accepting time. "They didn't care that I preferred men. Not many people were that accepting back then."

Calvin's eyes widen, his whole body going still. "You lived in my house?" His voice is barely above a whisper. "Here?"

"Small world," I say, though that doesn't begin to cover it. Of all the houses in Moonridge.

Blake sets down his pizza, staring at me with something like acceptance. "Wow."

Warmth spreads through me. "Some of the happiest memories of my life were in this house. The Randalls treated me like family. They were very kind."

Calvin looks around the room with new eyes. "You were here. In my room. In our kitchen. You walked these same halls."

"Every day for almost a year," I say softly. "Until the Concord got me."

The realization settles over him and a small smile plays at his lips.

"Wait," Blake interjects, his voice cutting through the moment. "If your tether to the lake is broken, does that mean your connection to the Concord could be broken too?"

Hope flickers through me. My form shimmers. "Maybe. I don't know. I still feel tethered, but since you all got here, it shifted." I glance at Dex. "Like I'm being drawn somewhere else now."

"The other side," Dex confirms with a slight nod. "Your spirit wants to move on. It has been held back for far too long. The pull you're feeling is death calling you home."

"So you could help him cross over?" Calvin asks, his voice tight with something caught between hope and grief. "Completely free him from the Concord?"

"I believe so," Dex replies, studying me. "The question is whether he's ready. And whether crossing over is what he truly wants."

All eyes turn to me, waiting for my answer. What *do* I want? To be free, yes. To stay, also yes.

Both.

Neither.

The silence stretches until I realize they're all still waiting.

"I want to be free," I say finally, the words feeling both true and incomplete. I can't have everything I want. I can't be alive again and I can't have Calvin, but I can be free of the Concord and the lake. I can move on.

Mina shifts in her seat. Her shoulders loosen. "You deserve that. I'm sorry I came for you earlier. Even though what happened was traumatic for me, one good thing came from all of it. I've gained some time. My tumor's gone. I'm not fully a vampire, but I'm not dying tomorrow either." She looks at me directly, meeting my eyes for the first time tonight. "Time is precious when you think you've run out of it. You deserve to be able to choose, just like I was able to do."

I nod, understanding completely. "Time is exactly what I thought I'd never have again. But here I am."

"Here you are," Calvin echoes softly, his hand hovering near mine, not quite touching but close enough that I can pretend to feel his warmth.

Time. The living waste it. The dead would do anything for one more minute. And here I am with a little more of it. Maybe enough for a proper goodbye this time.

For now, that's enough.

CHAPTER NINE

Calvin

I can't stop staring at Everett. He's sitting here in my living room, slightly see-through but definitely here, sneaking smiles my way.

I scoot closer, drawn to him now that I can actually see him sitting beside me. If I squint and ignore the way I can see my bookshelf through his torso, it's almost like he's really alive.

"So," Blake says, clearing his throat and gesturing with his pizza slice. "You lived in this house? In the fifties?"

"Sure did." Everett nods, glancing around the room with a soft smile. "Your grandfather gave me a job fixing cars and a room to sleep in. He was a good man."

"That's wild," I say, scooting closer to the edge of my seat, wiping my greasy fingers on the napkin in my lap. "Did you work on the red Chevy convertible that's still in the garage?"

"The fifty-two Styleline? That was *my* car. You have my car?" Everett's form brightens, edges sharpening, color deepening. "I helped rebuild the transmission. Mr. Randall taught me the fine points of restoration, and then he handed me the keys and said it was mine."

"It still runs," I tell him, grinning. "Blake and I take it out sometimes on nice days."

La'Tasha perks up. "You mean that gorgeous red thing? I love riding in that car."

Hazel tips her head, studying Everett. "So you likely knew my family back then as well. And La'Tasha's."

Everett's smile turns a little wistful. "I did, yeah. Both sides, actually. Moonridge was even smaller then. Everybody knew everybody." He chuckles under his breath. "Your grandmother Agnes was a little spitfire."

Hazel huffs a laugh. "That tracks."

"I'll never forget the Skipper Lake Labor Day Jamboree," Everett goes on. "I'd only been in town a couple of weeks. They had vendors, pie contests, some terrible rockabilly band. Your grandmother Agnes cheated at the pie contest, by the way."

La'Tasha slaps a hand over her heart. "Excuse you. Agnes Thornton was a saint."

"Sure," Everett says. "A saint who glamored the judges to make sure her blueberry pie won."

Hazel sits up straighter. "Wait. She did what?"

He lifts his hands in surrender. "I know what I saw."

La'Tasha leans in, bracelets clinking as she props her elbows on the table. "What about my grandma? You said you knew her too."

"Bea Morehouse." Everett smiles wider. "You think Agnes was a spitfire. She had nothing on Bea. They didn't like each other much if I remember. I knew her brother Ronald well. Nice guy. And your great grandma Esther was the bee's knees."

La'Tasha's eyes fill with tears.

Everyone is caught up in Everett's tales of 1950s Moonridge. Only Dex stays apart, sitting back in his chair, hands folded in his lap, eyes fixed on Everett like he's waiting for a bell to ring.

We keep talking, swapping stories and questions, and the longer it goes on, the more my skin buzzes. Everett laughing with my friends. Everett talking about our grandparents like it's the most normal thing in the world.

And it dawns on me. I'm not just interested in him. I'm not just attracted to him. I'm smitten.

With a ghost.

Of course I am.

The impossibility of my situation makes my stomach want to turn itself inside out. I set down my pizza, suddenly unable to swallow. Everett watches me with those sad blue eyes, like he knows exactly what I'm thinking. Maybe he does. Maybe that's his super ghost power—seeing through idiots who fall for people they can't keep.

"So," I say. My voice comes out rough. I clear my throat and try again. "You said you might be able to help Everett cross over. For good."

Dex nods. "I believe so. It seems his spirit's no longer bound to the lake, but it's still tethered to this plane. With the right push, he could move on to what's next."

"And what's next?" Everett asks, his form shimmering a little as he shifts in his chair. "Pearly gates? Endless void? Reincarnation as a squirrel?"

He's making jokes. Of course he is. And I'm over here trying not to fall apart.

"I cannot say," Dex replies, his deep voice oddly gentle. "That knowledge isn't mine to share, even if I wanted to. But I can tell you it isn't an end. It's a transition."

Everett nods slowly, eyes fixed somewhere past the wall, hands clasped together. "A transition," he repeats. "That sounds nice. Better than being stuck, anyway."

"Is that what you want?" Dex asks, leaning forward. "To cross over? Now?"

The room goes quiet. My heart pounds so loud I'm pretty

sure everyone can hear it. I hold my breath. My fists clench until my knuckles ache.

Everett lets out a long, thin sigh. "What I want," he says, "is to be alive again. To breathe. To touch things. People. A chance to really fall in love…" His eyes flick to me for half a second. My pulse stutters. "But that's not possible. My body's been gone for too long. Even a necromancer couldn't bring me back."

"I'm sorry," I whisper. It feels useless, but it's all I've got.

"It's not your fault," Everett says with a sad smile. His outline flickers, edges going soft, then pulling tight again. "And hey, being free of that lake's already more than I ever hoped for. The Concord held me there for far too long."

"About the Concord," Hazel cuts in, setting her plate aside and pulling out her notebook. "You said you're one of their thirteen members, right? Even if unwillingly?"

Everett nods. His smile fades and his shoulders draw in. "They need thirteen. Always thirteen. It's a sacred number in their magic. If I cross over, they'll have to find a replacement. That could buy you all some time."

"Time for what?" Blake asks, leaning forward, pizza crusts lined up on the plate in front of him.

"To figure out what they're planning next. To stop them." Everett's form grows more solid. His voice comes out stronger. "They're going to try to rip open the veil again. They're trying to bring something or someone big into this world. I don't know who exactly. I wasn't important enough to have that information."

La'Tasha shifts in her seat. "So us freeing you from the lake and then helping you cross over might actually weaken them?"

"Yes," Everett says. "They lose access to one of their power sources. They have to recruit and bind someone new. That takes work. Time. Once I'm gone, they won't be able to channel their power."

Gone.

My stomach twists. I study his face instead, memorizing the

crinkle at the corners of his eyes when he concentrates, the small scar on his chin I somehow missed until now.

"So," Dex says, dark eyes steady on Everett. "Do you wish to cross over now?"

Everett hesitates, gaze drifting to me again. I try to smile like I'm the picture of supportive maturity. Judging by the way my cheeks fight me, I probably just look constipated.

"Yes. As much as I hate to say it, there's no other option for me. It's time," Everett says.

"Actually," I blurt, words tumbling out before my brain can stop them. "My birthday's this Friday. Just four days away. Maybe you could stick around for a few more days? I mean, if you wanted to…"

"And celebrate with you?" His whole face lights up. "I'd like that very much."

It's a tiny thing on paper. In my chest it feels huge. Four more days with him. Four more days before he's gone.

"Birthday boy's turning the big three-four," Blake announces, throwing an arm around my shoulders and nearly knocking me off my chair. "We're having a party. There'll be cake. And booze. Lots of booze."

I'm absolutely going to need the booze.

"I've never seen a modern birthday party," Everett says.

"Well, prepare to be amazed," La'Tasha says with a grin. Her gaze flicks to Hazel, a spark of challenge there. "I go all out for birthdays."

"I can help you cross whenever you're ready," Dex tells Everett. "There's no rush."

"Thank you," Everett says. He looks at Dex, then at me, then away. His form flickers again, like a light trying to decide if it's staying on. "I really do want to stop the Concord, and I won't stay long, but I'd like to…" His voice trails off. "To celebrate with Calvin and then say a proper goodbye."

The word goodbye hits hard. I shove it into a mental closet

and stack boxes on top of it. Four more days. I've got four more days with him. Future Calvin can deal with the crater afterward.

Everett smiles, but then his image suddenly wavers, like someone's adjusting the opacity on a photograph. His mouth moves, but the sound comes out garbled, like he's underwater.

"Everett?" I bolt upright. "What's happening?"

"I don't…" His voice cuts in and out. "Something's pulling… can't…"

Mina goes rigid. Her head snaps toward the window. "Does anyone else hear that?" she whispers. Color drains from her face.

"Hear what?" Blake's already on his feet, muscles tensed for a fight.

"Voices," Mina says, wrapping her arms around herself. "Like they're coming from somewhere far away." She grabs Dex's arm. "The whispering. It's back."

Dex stands so fast his chair crashes to the floor. "The Mortician," he says, voice hard as stone. His body's already starting to change, skin dulling, shoulders widening. "He's found us."

"Who's the Mortician?" I ask. Panic claws up my throat. Everett's form flickers like a candle in a draft.

"Concord," Everett manages. The word echoes, distorted. "Collects souls. Ghosts. Uses them for power. He's my… boss."

Everett lets out a sharp cry. His form yanks toward the window like an invisible hook caught him by the chest. His face twists, every line straining against whatever has him. "No!"

"Everett!" I lunge for him. My hands pass straight through, grabbing nothing but cold air. "Fight it! Stay with us!"

"Calvin," he says, voice thin and frayed. His gaze locks with mine, clear and desperate. "Find me at the lake. I'll try to…"

With a sound like air being sucked from the room, Everett vanishes. All that remains is a faint wisp of cold air where he stood.

"No!" I spin, scanning every corner like he might be hiding behind a lamp. "Everett!"

"Outside," Dex barks. His body finishes the shift, big and gray and terrible. A massive scythe appears in his hand, blade gleaming with otherworldly light. "Now."

We rush to the front door and spill onto my porch.

Three massive creatures stand in my front yard, positioned in a triangle formation like they're preparing for battle. They're like nothing I've ever seen. Seven or eight feet tall, their bodies a horrific mixture of bone and sinew held together by rusted wire and rotting leather. Their skulls hang at impossible angles, connected by metal pins that gleam wetly in the moonlight. Pale fire burns in their empty eye sockets, casting sickly light across my lawn, making the shadows dance.

"Graveborn," Dex says. "They won't go easily."

Holy fuck. These things are huge.

"Get back inside," Dex orders Mina, his voice no longer human but something deeper, more primal. "They want you too."

"Like hell," Mina says, but she steps back toward the doorway, her hands clenching into fists. "Be careful."

Blake's already transforming beside me, his body contorting as fur sprouts along his arms and his face elongates into a snout. I feel the familiar pull of the moon in my blood, the beast inside me clawing to get out. I let it come, my body shifting fast. Bones crack and reform. Fur bursts through skin. The change hurts, but right now I don't care.

La'Tasha and Hazel take positions on either side of the porch, their hands already moving in complex patterns. The air around them shimmers with building power, but I notice something different about La'Tasha. Her stance is wider, more confident, and there's electricity literally crackling between her fingers.

"Calvin, Blake, take the one on the right," Dex commands, his scythe glinting in the moonlight. "Witches, the left. I'll handle the center."

The nearest Graveborn tilts its head, bones creaking like ancient doors. It makes a sound like wind through dead trees, and then it charges with surprising speed for something held together with wire and malice.

The battle erupts with stunning violence. Blake and I leap from the porch simultaneously, our werewolf forms giving us strength and agility no human could match. I slam into the right Graveborn, using my momentum to drive it backward, my claws tearing into its patchwork flesh. It smells like grave dirt and old blood. Like death took a shit and left it to rot. I almost gag.

The creature swings a massive arm, catching me in the chest and sending me flying across the yard. I crash into my truck with a sound like thunder, denting the door and shattering the passenger window. My ribs crack on impact, but the wolf's healing is already kicking in, bones knitting themselves back together. I shake off the glass and charge back into the fray, rage fueling my attack.

Blake circles the Graveborn with predatory grace, darting in to slash at its legs with surgical precision before dancing away from its grasping hands. We work together like we've done this before. Quick strikes from opposite sides. The thing spins between us, confused.

Meanwhile, Dex is a blur of motion, his scythe cutting through the central Graveborn like it's made of paper. Each strike severs another bone or wire, sending pieces flying across the yard, yet the creature keeps coming, reassembling itself even as Dex tears it apart with methodical efficiency.

On the left side of the yard, Hazel unleashes her magic in careful, controlled bursts. Her spells manifest as glowing sigils that burn the air, precisely targeted strikes that sear through the Graveborn's bindings. But La'Tasha…

Holy shit.

La'Tasha rises at least three feet off the ground, her eyes blazing with white light so bright it's hard to look at directly. The air around her crackles with electricity, and her hair floats around her head like she's underwater. Power radiates from her in waves that I can feel even in my wolf form, making my fur stand on end.

"La'Tasha!" Hazel shouts, backing away.

With a shout that shakes the windows of my house, La'Tasha throws her hands forward, and lightning explodes from her fingertips, striking the Graveborn dead center. The bolt is easily three times the size of any natural lightning, blue-white and crackling with power that makes the air itself scream.

The monster shrieks, a sound like metal being torn apart. But it doesn't fall. It keeps coming, reaching for La'Tasha with skeletal fingers, its pale fire flaring brighter.

"Behind you!" I try to shout, but it comes out as a growl in my wolf form.

La'Tasha spins in mid-air just as the Graveborn I'm fighting hurls a chunk of my mailbox at her. She deflects it with a casual wave of her hand, sending it crashing into the creature's skull with enough force to shatter concrete. The impact destroys its jaw, pale fire spilling from the wound like lava.

I seize the moment, leaping onto the Graveborn's back and driving my claws deep into what passes for its spine. My teeth find the spot where rusty wire connects skull to vertebrae, and I bite down with all my strength, tasting metal and decay. The wire snaps with a sound like a guitar string breaking. The head topples forward, hanging by a few strands of leather and sinew.

Blake darts in low, his claws ripping through the creature's legs with surgical precision. It falls like a tree, still grabbing for us with bony hands that spark when they hit the concrete.

Across the yard, Dex makes a complicated gesture with his free hand, symbols appearing in the air around his fingers before sinking into his opponent. His Graveborn freezes mid-lunge, then begins to crumble from within, as if something essential is being pulled out of it. Within seconds, it collapses into a pile of bones and tattered leather, the pale fire in its skull winking out like a candle.

"The head!" Dex shouts to us, his voice carrying absolute authority. "Destroy the skull completely!"

I don't need to be told twice. I slam my paw down on the Graveborn's skull, putting all my werewolf strength behind it. The bone cracks like an eggshell, then crumbles completely. The pale fire spills out, hissing where it touches the grass before fading to nothing.

La'Tasha's power reaches a crescendo that makes my teeth ache. Thunder booms directly above us, though the sky was clear moments ago. Storm clouds gather with impossible speed, swirling in a tight spiral directly over her position. A lightning bolt the size of a telephone pole explodes from the clouds, striking her outstretched hands before she directs it into the final Graveborn.

The monster lights up from the inside. Bones glow white-hot, lines of light racing through its skeleton. It jerks violently as Hazel throws one last spell. The energy hits its skull and the bone fractures with a clean, high crack. The head crumbles to dust. The pale fire snuffs out.

Silence hits fast and hard. The only sounds left are our harsh breathing and the faint sizzle of burnt grass. The storm above us unravels, clouds thinning and vanishing until the sky is clear again. Ozone stings my nose.

I shift back to human, wincing as bones rearrange and fur slides back under skin. Cold air slaps every inch of me. Blake shifts too. Blood trickles from a cut on his forehead, then slows, then stops as the skin knits. By the time he wipes it away with the back of his hand, there's only a pink line left.

"What," I pant, leaning against my dented truck, "the actual hell was that?"

Dex's scythe fades from his hand as his form settles back to normal. His eyes stay hard as he scans the street. "The Concord's hunters. They came for Everett."

"And they got him." My voice sounds scraped out and thin. "They took him back."

"To the lake?" Hazel steps over the scattered bones as they begin to crumble. I glance around the yard. The Graveborn remains are disintegrating into ash, gray powder lifting and dispersing in the breeze until nothing remains.

"Most likely," Dex says, brushing dust from his sleeves. "The Mortician will want to re-establish the binding as quickly as possible."

I stare at the empty space where Everett vanished. Anger and helplessness churn in my gut. I want to punch something until my knuckles split. "We have to get him back."

"We will," La'Tasha says. She drifts back down to the ground, the glow in her eyes fading. Every line of her body screams exhaustion, but she's still standing tall.

Hazel stares at La'Tasha like she's never seen her before. "Where did that power come from? I've never seen you do anything like that before. I didn't even know you could do that... floaty thing."

La'Tasha shrugs, brushing grass from her jeans like it's no big deal, but there's steel in her voice when she speaks. "It's always been there. I've just never unleashed it before."

"How did you..." Blake says, still a little dazed. "That was... I don't even know what that was."

"That was La'Tasha Morehouse not holding back anymore," she says. She meets Hazel's gaze without flinching.

"La'Tasha," Hazel says slowly, choosing each word, "why didn't you tell me? We could have..."

"Could have what?" La'Tasha's eyes flash. "I love you, Hazel, but you've never trusted me to show my true strength."

"That's not..." Hazel starts.

La'Tasha lifts a hand. "We can argue about witch politics later. Right now, we've got a friend to save."

"Agreed," Dex says. He turns his gaze on me, something ancient moving behind his eyes. "We need to find and then free Everett. Permanently."

I nod, jaw tight. I promised Everett I'd help set him free. That's exactly what I'm going to do.

Even if it rips my heart out.

CHAPTER TEN

Calvin

I drop another nail for the third time in ten minutes.

"Fuck," I mutter, watching it bounce across the floor. The hammer dangles uselessly from my hand as I stare at the crooked mess I've made of this simple patch job. Blake would laugh his ass off if he saw this. Master carpenter Calvin Carter, defeated by a two-by-four and some basic framing. I haven't slept more than three hours a night since the Graveborn showed up, and it shows. My eyes burn. My muscles ache. And inside my chest, it feels like someone scooped everything out and left me running on empty.

"That looks like absolute garbage," Blake says, appearing next to me. "You trying to make modern art over here?"

I roll my eyes. "Thanks for the vote of confidence."

"Just telling it like it is." He leans against the wall, watching me. "What's going on with you? You've been out of it for days."

"I'm fine." I pull the crooked nails out and tosses them into my tool belt.

"Uh huh. Totally believe you." Blake runs his thumb across his bottom lip, not breaking eye contact. "You went up to the lake again last night, didn't you?"

I focus on the wall in front of me. My jaw tightens. I've been at Skipper Lake every night since they took Everett. I've spent hours calling his name into the dark and getting nothing back.

"What if they're hurting him?" I finally ask. The words crack on the way out.

Blake's shoulders loosen, and he moves closer. "Cal, you know we want to help him. But we need a plan. Running off alone is just asking for trouble."

"I just need to contact him. To know he's okay. La'Tasha won't do another séance," I say, bitterness creeping into my voice as I set down my hammer. "Hazel's got her spooked about the Concord."

"With good reason." Blake gives me a pointed look. "Those Graveborn assholes nearly killed us in your front yard, remember?"

How could I forget? My truck still has the dent from where the Graveborn threw me into it. My mailbox is still scattered across the lawn. And somewhere out there, Everett is trapped again, possibly in worse condition than before. Those Concord fuckers took him. The thought makes my hands shake, and I have to grip the hammer tighter to steady them.

An idea forms in my head. The door.

I put my hammer down. "I have an idea. We can use the door. It can take us back to things we've already experienced. I could just travel back to that night a few days ago and make Everett cross over before the Concord get to him."

He places a hand against my chest. "Don't even think about it."

"But it could work."

His jaw tightens and he runs a hand over his head. "Do not use that door again."

"Dude, what did you see?"

He takes a deep breath. "I tried to go back to see if I could catch a glimpse of Mom. I didn't plan right and I landed on the night she crashed. I watched it happen."

I place the hammer on the counter beside me. "Oh, shit..."

He shakes his head. "You see that portal as a way to fix things. I get it. But it can rip you open too."

The sound of whistling echoes across the construction site, growing louder as Leo approaches. He's got that manic look he gets when he thinks he has a great idea.

"You two look like someone shit in your coffee. Cheer up, it's almost your birthday, you hairy beast!" Leo calls out, spreading his arms wide in greeting. His enthusiasm propels him forward faster than his coordination can handle, and he trips spectacularly over a stack of two-by-fours we left near the doorway.

"Smooth entrance," Blake snorts.

"I meant to do that," Leo says, brushing sawdust off his jacket with wounded dignity. "It's called making an entrance."

"It's called being a hazard," I mutter, but I can't help the tiny smile that tugs at my lips despite everything.

Leo picks up a scattered wrench and tosses it back into the toolbox, then claps my shoulder with enough force to make me stagger. "You're wound too tight. You need to celebrate. Get your mind off ghost boyfriend for one night."

I shrug his hand off, my jaw tightening. "Don't call him that."

He's not my boyfriend. He can't be. And that's the whole goddamn problem.

Leo's face falls, and he backs up with his hands raised. "Sorry. Bad joke."

I look away, guilt twisting in my stomach. I rub my face with both hands, trying to scrub away the exhaustion and frustration.

"Look," I say, my voice rough around the edges. "I know it's stupid, okay? I know I can't actually be with him. He's dead. But I hate that he's stuck at the lake for eternity doing their bidding. I want to find a way to set him free so he can move on. He deserves that."

Blake pats me on the back. "It's not stupid. You care about him. The circumstances are just... complicated."

"I do care about him." I swallow hard, my throat feeling raw. "And I feel responsible. If I hadn't asked him to stick around for my stupid birthday party, Dex could've helped him cross over before they showed up. He'd be free right now."

The words burn my lips. He wanted to stay longer, and I encouraged him. Because I was selfish. Because I wanted more time with him.

"You couldn't have known," Blake says.

Leo checks his watch. "Not to interrupt the brooding session, but it's almost three. Blake, didn't you say we need to meet with the Wilsons about their sun room at 3:30?"

Blake nods, though his eyes stay fixed on my face. "Yeah. We should get over there."

Leo turns to me before he leaves, his face lighting up. "Pre-birthday margaritas tonight? I'm thinking Casa de Loco at seven. We can drink and eat and put all of our troubles to rest."

"I don't know," I hedge, already thinking about another trip to the lake, but my voice lacks conviction.

"Come on," Leo pleads, knocking my water bottle off the counter. He immediately starts wiping up the mess. "One night of fun. We'll drink too much, tell embarrassing stories about you, and then end the night at my place playing games and being stupid."

I look at their hopeful faces. I don't have the energy to keep saying no. "Fine. But I need to go home first. Shower. Maybe grab a nap."

"Sold!" Leo claps his hands together, apparently forgetting he's still holding wet paper towels, which immediately splatter water everywhere. "Seven o'clock. Don't be late or I'll send La'Tasha to hunt you down."

"Yeah, yeah," I mutter, but I can't help the tiny smile that tugs at my lips again.

Twenty minutes later, the site is deserted. Blake and Leo drove off together, and the rest of the crew scattered to their afternoon plans. And me?

I'm standing in front of the portal again.

The carved symbols stare back. I know I promised Hazel I wouldn't use it again, but desperate times call for desperate measures. She'll understand.

Maybe.

But the thought takes shape. If I try hard enough, then maybe... Maybe I don't need to go back to the other night. Maybe I can go back even further. Back to 1958. Warn him. Convince him to leave Moonridge before the sacrifice happens. Give him the chance to live a full life.

A hollow spot opens in my chest. That means I'll never meet him.

But I can't be selfish. He deserves to live.

I pull out my phone and scroll through my music library until I find the song he played through the radio that night. The song my grandmother used to sing while baking cookies.

I put my earbuds in and close my eyes. I picture my house as it might've been in the 1950s. I imagine Everett there, young and alive, working on cars with my great-grandfather. I focus on that image so hard my head hurts, letting the doo-wop melody fill my mind, trying to push myself further back than I've ever gone before.

The lock clicks.

My eyes snap open, heart racing as I push the handle down. The door swings open to darkness rippling with tiny points of light, moving like they're caught in an unseen current. I step through without hesitation, my stomach lurching as the world spins around me like a carnival ride.

When everything stops moving, I'm standing looking out on Main Street again, but something's off. I definitely went further than 2005. The storefronts are familiar yet different. Where The Enchanted Bean now stands, there's a video rental store and the yoga studio is a hardware store. That hasn't been there since before I was a teen. I definitely went back further this time. I spot a newspaper stand and rush over, my heart sinking as I read the date. February 20, 1997. Not far enough.

"You've got to be kidding me," I mutter, staring at the date. Instead of traveling back to the 50s, I've landed on the day before my fifth birthday. Again, I'm limited to times I actually existed. It's like the portal won't take me back before I was born.

A familiar laugh catches my attention. I turn and see my grandmother, her silver hair gleaming in the afternoon sun, holding the hand of a tiny boy with messy dark hair.

It's me.

Mini-me skips beside her, chattering non-stop as she leads him toward Scoops, the old ice-cream shop.

"Since tomorrow's your birthday," she's saying, "you get to have ice cream today too."

I steady myself against the newspaper stand. I remember this. Every year, the day before our respective birthdays, Grandma would take Blake and me for ice cream to celebrate our "last day" at that age. It was our little secret. Something just between us.

I watch as they disappear into the shop. Grandma's been gone for twelve years now. Seeing her again, even like this, makes my vision blur and my throat close up.

And that isn't what I came for. I need to go back further. I need to find a way to reach Everett before the Concord sacrificed him.

I return to the warehouse and step back through the door, emerging in the basement. I try again, focusing harder on the 1950s, on Everett, pouring all my desperation into the image. It opens, but this time I end up in 2001. Then 1998. Then 2010. Never the 1950s. Never Everett's time. Never before I was born.

The limitation becomes clear. I can only travel to times I

existed. The portal responds to my memories, my experiences. And I have no memories of the 1950s. No connection to that time.

After my sixth attempt, I'm ready to put my fist through the door. Then my phone buzzes. Who the hell is calling me? Don't they know I only answer texts?

La'Tasha.

"Hello?" I answer.

"Where are you?" La'Tasha's voice has that no-nonsense edge. "Everyone's here waiting. It's 7:15."

"Sorry, I lost track of time," I say, eyeing the door with growing resentment. "Maybe I should skip tonight. I'm not really in the mood."

"Calvin Carter," she says, her voice dropping dangerously low, "if you're trying to contact Everett alone, stop right now. It's dangerous, and you know it. Besides, I might have an idea that could help."

My heart skips, and I straighten up. "What kind of idea?"

"Get your butt over here and find out. I have a margarita with your name on it." She hangs up before I can argue.

I stare at the black door, tempted to try just one more time. But La'Tasha's words echo in my head. She might've found something to help Everett. That's worth more than my wild goose chase through time.

With a sigh, I pocket my phone and head for the stairs. My time traveling adventures will have to wait. For now.

***

I push open the door to Casa de Loco and the wall of noise punches me in the face. The place is packed, every table full, the bar crammed with people shouting drink orders. Through the crowd, I spot my friends in our usual corner booth. They've already got a pitcher of margaritas and plates of nachos, chips and salsa on the table. La'Tasha catches my eye and waves me over.

"Look who decided to join us," Leo announces as I slide into the booth next to La'Tasha, my movements sluggish. "The birthday boy himself."

"It's not my birthday yet," I grumble, reaching for the chips with hands that aren't entirely steady. My hand freezes midway when I see the look on La'Tasha's face. "What?"

"Where were you really?" she asks, her dark eyes boring into me.

"I told you, I lost track of time." I shove a chip into my mouth, avoiding her gaze as I chew.

"And that had nothing to do with a certain magical door we all promised not to mess with?"

The table goes quiet. I take a long sip of my drink, the tart lime and tequila burning pleasantly down my throat, buying myself time to figure out how much to admit.

"Fine," I admit, setting the glass down with a loud thunk. "I tried the portal again. Happy?"

"Calvin!" Penny looks shocked, her glasses slipping down her nose. "Hazel specifically said—"

"I know what Hazel said." I grab another handful of chips, more to have something to do with my hands than from actual hunger. "But Everett is trapped, and no one seems to give a shit but me."

La'Tasha leans closer. "That's not true. We've been working on it."

"What exactly have you been working on?" I ask. "Because from where I'm sitting, it looks like everyone's just moved on. Everett's gone, too bad, let's all get back to our normal lives."

Blake taps my foot with his under the table. "That's not fair and you know it."

I deflate. "Sorry. I'm just… I feel useless."

"Well, stop feeling useless," La'Tasha says, leaning forward. "Because we might have a plan."

My head snaps up. "What kind of plan?"

"The kind that involves understanding exactly what that portal is and what the Concord wants with it." She glances around the table, then continues. "Coco, Penny, and I convinced Hazel to check out the door tomorrow morning. Maybe we can finally get some answers and decide on next steps."

"You what?" I nearly choke on my margarita. "But Hazel was so against anyone going near it again."

"She still is," Penny chimes in, adjusting her glasses. Her voice is firm. "But she also knows we need to understand what we're dealing with. The door isn't just going to disappear on its own."

"And," Coco adds, her voice dropping, "we may have pointed out that if she doesn't help us figure it out, you're likely to keep trying on your own. We need to keep you safe."

I wince. "Using me as the bad example? Low blow."

"But effective," La'Tasha says with a smirk. "Blake already gave us permission to be on the premises tomorrow morning."

I look at my brother, who shrugs. "Better to have Hazel supervising than you messing around alone and potentially erasing yourself from existence."

"So what's the plan?" I ask. "Are we trying to use the door to find Everett?"

Coco and Penny exchange glances.

"Not exactly," Penny says carefully. "Hazel asked me to research how to seal it shut. Permanently."

"What? No!" I slam my hand on the table, making the glasses jump. Several people turn to stare. I force myself to lower my voice. "You can't seal it. That thing could be our only way to help him."

"Or it could be exactly what the Concord wants us to think," Penny counters. "Think about it, Calvin. Why would they leave something so powerful just sitting in a basement if it wasn't part of their plan? It seems like bait to me."

"She's right," Leo says as he gestures with a chip, flipping salsa across the table.

"Leo!" Coco exclaims, jumping up and grabbing napkins.

"Sorry! Sorry!" Leo scrambles to help clean up, somehow managing to knock over his own drink in the process.

"Just… sit still," Blake says, moving Leo's hands away from the spreading mess. "Let us handle this."

"What if it's a trap?" Leo continues his argument while everyone else cleans around him, apparently oblivious to the chaos he's caused.

I run my hand over my face. "But what if it's not? What if it's our only chance to find Everett in the past, before the Concord got to him? Or to understand how they're using him now?"

"That's exactly why we're checking it out first," La'Tasha says, dabbing at the salsa stains with a wet napkin. "We need to know what this thing is capable of before we decide what to do with it."

"And what about Everett?" I press, my voice rising. "Are we just giving up on him?"

"Of course not," Blake says firmly, his eyes meeting mine. "But rushing in half-cocked isn't going to help him. We need a real plan."

I want to argue more, but I know they're right. Still, the thought of sealing it makes my stomach churn.

"What if sealing it means losing him to the Concord forever?" I ask.

La'Tasha opens her mouth, then closes it. Blake stares at the ground.

Great. Just great.

"Fine." I swallow hard. "What time tomorrow?"

"Nine AM," La'Tasha answers. "Just promise me you'll let Hazel lead, okay? No cowboy stuff."

"Fine." I drain half my margarita in one go. "Nine it is."

"Now that that's settled," Leo says, still dabbing ineffectively at the mess he's made, "let's talk birthday plans. I'm thinking karaoke at my place after dinner tomorrow?"

The conversation shifts to birthday plans and my mind drifts.

If Hazel seals the door shut, we lose any chance of using it to help Everett. But if the Concord is using it somehow, leaving it open could put all of us in danger.

"Hey," Blake says quietly, leaning closer while the others debate song choices for karaoke. "We'll find another way to help him. I promise."

I nod, not trusting myself to speak. I want to believe him.

Hazel walks in and everyone moves over to make a seat for her next to Blake. They all fall into easy, casual conversation while that small voice in the back of my mind whispers that maybe I should try the door one more time before Hazel seals it forever.

Just one more time.

What could it hurt?

Everything, probably. But maybe, just maybe, it could save him too.

CHAPTER ELEVEN

Everett

I wake up to darkness and the smell of wet stone. Where am I? I try to move my hands but metal bites into my wrists. The contact burns. Not like fire, but like ice that cuts deep, in that special way only demon-forged restraints can. The shackles squeeze around what passes for my wrists, and it feels like my essence is being scraped raw. This is just swell. I've been downgraded from lake ghost to dungeon wall ornament.

A slow drip echoes somewhere behind me. Over and over. Driving me crazy already. I stare into the darkness, forcing my eyes to adjust. It hurts, which is ridiculous because technically I shouldn't feel anything. But I do. The demon cuffs make sure of that. The shadows peel back and the room takes shape. Stone walls slick with moisture. Iron bars straight out of a Vincent Price movie.

I go rigid. I know this place.

The ceiling arches low, the stones the same uneven gray, the same dank atmosphere pressing in. A chamber built for one purpose: breaking spirits.

The Concord's binding room. The place where they sealed

me to their will after they murdered me.

The last thing I remember is Calvin's living room. Warm light, the smell of pizza, laughter. For the first time in decades I almost felt real. For a moment I let myself believe I could have that. Stupid.

And then chaos erupted.

I was ripped from the room and the attack came. Graveborn tearing through the night, stinking of rot and blood. Calvin shifted before my eyes, brown fur erupting as bones snapped and reshaped. He was terrifying and beautiful, a massive wolf ripping through monsters. Blake was there too, the brothers fighting as one, while La'Tasha and Hazel lit the sky with magic.

Hands held me tight, yanking me backward, my form stretching like smoke in the wind. And then that voice, colder than the grave.

"Time to come home, boy."

The Mortician.

I struggled, shape flickering between solid and translucent, but it was useless. Then The Collector appeared beside him, raised their hands, and pain tore through me. Like someone reached inside and twisted everything that made me me into something else.

The last thing I saw was Calvin, in wolf form, breaking free from a Graveborn's grip. Darkness swallowed me whole, and when I woke up, I was here. Back in hell, alone again.

"Hello?" My voice bounces back at me. The shackles flare with pain, ice shooting up my arms. I grit my teeth.

Funny thing about being a ghost. You'd think nothing could hurt you anymore. The Concord proved me wrong. The binding rune they carved into me still aches.

I try to shift positions but my shoulders scream in protest. The chains have left me in an awkward slouch against the wall, spirit-form cramping in ways I'd forgotten were possible. How long have I been here? Hours? Days? Hard to tell when every second drags.

The floor beneath me radiates cold that seeps into what passes for my bones. I struggle to stand, chains clanking, but my cuffs are anchored to the wall. Three feet of movement in any direction is all I have. Just enough slack to mock me, but not enough to do anything useful. Smart cookies, these Concord creeps. They've had ages to work out the kinks in their torture routine. They know what they're doing.

I test the bonds again, instinctively pulling back as the metal flares with sickly green light. Each symbol etched into the surface responds to my touch, and I recognize them now. Binding runes. The same marks they burned into me during that first binding. They've locked me down completely.

Footsteps approach down the corridor outside my cell. Two hooded figures walk past, deep in conversation. They don't notice me watching.

"The binding is holding," one says, voice low and gravelly. "He can't leave the cell, can't contact the surface."

I lean toward the bars, ignoring the pain in my shoulders. I need to hear this.

"Good," replies the other, a woman with a crisp, cold voice. A shiver runs through my form. "If we'd lost him, our plan would have fallen apart." She pauses, and I catch the cruel smile in her voice. "The Spring Equinox is our next target. If we hit at the right time, this will be catastrophic to Moonridge. We'll finally be able to make up for the setback we experienced during Samhain."

My form flickers, a cold jolt running through me. Are they going to try to complete the ritual during the spring equinox? But how? Did they find a new key? What about the Crucible Core? Penny released it.

Their voices fade as they continue down the corridor. A heavy door clangs shut somewhere in the distance, the sound echoing off stone walls.

I might actually lose it down here. I want to scream, to rage against these restraints until my voice gives out. Instead, I bite back the sound, jaw clenching so hard my teeth ache. If I'd just let Dex help me cross, we wouldn't be in this mess now. The Concord would have lost a member. I chose to stay so I could have a few more days with Calvin, and now I won't even get that.

Please let him be safe.

I can't shake the memory of his wolf form, powerful and fierce. I brought this danger to his door. Why does my very existence always put everyone I care about at risk?

I have to get out of here. Not just for me, but for him. For all of them. Whatever the Concord is planning, it's bad. End-of-the-world bad. Reality-breaking bad.

But maybe I *can* do something.

There are twelve more Concord members out there, most of them evil, but I know there are at least four others who are prisoners like me. If I can reach them... Well, wouldn't that be something? Using the Concord's own chains to strangle them.

CHAPTER TWELVE

Calvin

I arrive at the construction site an hour early, my hands trembling as I fumble with the keys. The third cup of coffee before I left was a mistake, but I need something to keep me functional. Two hours of sleep isn't cutting it. My eyes feel like sandpaper, and when I catch my reflection in the window, I look like roadkill.

Back in the basement, the portal mocks me from the shadows. Last night I promised everyone I wouldn't try using it again without supervision. I've kept that promise.

Barely.

My fingers drum against my thigh. Every instinct screams to try again, even though I know it won't work. It won't take me to 1958. It won't take me to Everett. Not directly, anyway. But there has to be a way to use it to help him. There has to be.

I pace the length of the basement, checking my watch every few minutes like time might suddenly decide to sprint ahead. My boots echo on the concrete floor. The sound makes the place feel even emptier.

My phone buzzes with a text from La'Tasha:

On our way. Stopping for coffee and pastries.

I reply with a thumbs-up emoji and pocket my phone, then immediately pull it out again to check the time. The construction site is quiet this morning and should stay that way for a few more hours. Everyone's working on an emergency deck repair at the Cahills' this morning. Everyone except me. I'm trying to save a ghost.

What even is my life?

I sit on an overturned bucket and close my eyes, remembering how it felt to see him in my living room. Transparent but present. Smiling at me with those sad blue eyes. Telling stories about my grandfather. About this town. About a life cut short by the Concord. God, I miss him. Which is pathetic, but there it is.

Footsteps clatter on the stairs above. La'Tasha enters first, balancing a drink carrier in one hand and a bag of what smells like maple bars in the other. Hazel follows behind her, a leather satchel slung over her shoulder. Her green eyes scan the basement.

"Morning, sunshine," La'Tasha says, handing me a coffee. "You look like you slept in a dumpster. At least you don't smell that way, too."

"Thanks," I reply, accepting the cup gratefully. The warmth of the cup grounds me. "Love the honesty. Really brightens my day."

"You're welcome." She grins and passes me a maple bar, but her smile is tight around the edges. "Eat something. We don't need 'cranky ass' Calvin. We need 'get shit done' Calvin."

Hazel slides by us and approaches the black door, her movements slow and deliberate. She holds her hands up near the surface without touching, and I see her fingers tremble. "It feels different today," she says, not turning around. "More... active."

"Active how?" I ask, setting down my coffee with unsteady hands. It looks the same to me. Black wood. Strange symbols. Ordinary doorknob.

"The magic is stirring," she explains, running her fingers over the carvings without quite touching them. Her voice carries a note of fear. My stomach knots. "Like it's been used recently." Her eyes flick to me accusingly.

"Not by me," I say, holding up my hands. "I swear. I did not break the rules."

At least not this time.

She studies my face for a long moment, then nods reluctantly. "Let's get started. The sooner we understand this thing, the sooner we can decide what to do with it."

La'Tasha sets her coffee cup and the rest of the pastries on a shelf. "So what's the plan? More tripping through time?"

"Information gathering," Hazel corrects, pulling a small notebook from her satchel. "I want to know exactly where you both went when you used it. Every detail."

La'Tasha and I exchange glances. I gesture for her to go first and she rolls her eyes. The tension between them is obvious even though they're doing their best to act like they're still inseparable besties.

"I went back to 2006," La'Tasha says, perching on the edge of the table and wrapping her arms around herself. "I was nine. My grandmother was gardening behind our old house on Willow Lane." Her voice catches on the word "grandmother". Hazel's gaze lifts from the page, her lips quirking into a faint, gentle curve. "I watched her teach little me how to plant gardenias. It had to be sometime in April or May because she had her spring butterfly flag hanging on the porch—the one she put up every April."

"You both mentioned listening to music when you went through. What were you listening to?" Hazel asks, her pen hovering over the notebook.

"A song Grandma used to sing while she worked." La'Tasha's voice grows thick with memory, and she blinks rapidly. "I picked one of the flowers while I was there and brought it back. I wanted to see if it would make the journey, and it did. It wilted at the same rate a normal flower would wilt."

Hazel nods and writes this down. "And you, Calvin?"

I clear my throat and focus on the first time I entered. "I went back to summer 2005. I was listening to a playlist of songs that reminded me of being a kid. I was thinking about riding bikes with Blake. The door took me right to that day. I saw mini-me zooming down Main Street, past the old video store."

"Both times, the same place?" Hazel confirms, looking up from her notes.

"Yeah. Same song, same memory, same destination." I take a sip of coffee to buy myself time, then set the cup down with a slight rattle. "But yesterday I tried something different."

La'Tasha's head snaps up. Her right eyebrow sneaks above the rim of her glasses. "What did you do?"

"I knew you'd be pissed, but what was I supposed to do? Just sit here?" I lift my hands. "Nothing dangerous. I just... I tried to reach Everett."

"Calvin," Hazel sighs, pinching the bridge of her nose. "We talked about this."

"I know, I know. But I had to try." I set my coffee down and start pacing again. "I listened to a song from the fifties. The same one Everett played through my radio. I focused as hard as I could on him, on the fifties, on what my house may have looked like back when he lived here."

"And?" La'Tasha prompts, her voice softer now.

"And nothing. I couldn't go back before I was born. I tried six different times. It always took me to random years in my lifetime instead." I shrug. "The song was one my grandma used to sing and I always ended up somewhere with her. It's like the door only responds to our actual memories, places and times we've lived through." I slump against the wall.

Hazel taps her pen against her notebook, the sound sharp in the quiet basement. "That's a significant limitation. It suggests the portal can't be used to change history before our existence."

"Which means it's useless for finding Everett in the past," I add. The finality of it sits heavy in my throat.

La'Tasha finishes her muffin and brushes crumbs from her hands. "Let me try something." She pulls out her phone and earbuds with determined movements. "I want to see if I can go somewhere specific."

"Where?" Hazel asks, and I catch the note of worry creeping into her voice.

"The Caribbean. Five years ago." La'Tasha's expression darkens, and she looks away from both of us. "I want to find out why Kiran ghosted me."

She says his name like it still hurts.

"Are you sure that's a good idea?" Hazel asks.

"No," La'Tasha admits. "But I need to know. I need to know if I was just some vacation fling, or if something actually happened to him." She pauses, her hands clenching around her phone. "It's been five years, and I still wonder if I wasn't good enough, or if he found someone better. Or maybe he just never really cared at all."

Hazel takes a step closer. "La'Tasha…"

"I know it's stupid," La'Tasha continues, looking up with determined eyes. "But he was the first person I cared about in a long time. He accepted me. And then he just… disappeared."

"That's not stupid," Hazel says firmly, closing her notebook. "But promise me you won't change anything significant. Just observe."

"Yes, mother." La'Tasha rolls her eyes but smiles. She puts in her earbuds, scrolls through her phone, and closes her eyes. Her lips move silently.

After a minute, she tries the handle. Nothing happens. She frowns, her shoulders sagging, then switches songs and tries again. Still locked. After a third attempt, she pulls out the earbuds with a frustrated sigh.

"It's not working," she says. "I was thinking about our hotel in St. Lucia, the exact spot where I last saw him. I tried three different songs we listened to on that trip."

"Interesting," Hazel murmurs, making more notes. "Try somewhere in Moonridge."

La'Tasha puts the earbuds back in and thinks for a minute. Her face lights up with a mischievous grin. She picks a song from her music library and closes her eyes, swaying to whatever she's hearing. When she reaches for the handle this time, it opens smoothly.

"Jackpot," she says, and steps through. The door closes behind her with a soft click.

Hazel and I wait in silence. I finish my maple bar and start on a second one, trying not to watch the clock. My leg won't stop bouncing, and I catch myself checking my phone every thirty seconds. Twenty minutes later, the door swings open and La'Tasha stumbles out, doubled over with laughter.

"What's so funny?" I ask. My shoulders finally loosen when I see her back in one piece.

She wipes tears from her eyes, giggling. "Junior prom. 2013." She looks at Hazel, who suddenly turns pink and looks away. "Remember what we did?"

"Oh god," Hazel groans, covering her face with her hands. "Everything about that night was a disaster. I tried to give Jenny Whitaker a makeover and turned her green."

"And then at the prom?" La'Tasha's laughter bubbles up again, and Hazel follows. "Neither of us had dates, so we went together. We tried to spike the punch with that hair growth potion."

"But we mixed it wrong," Hazel continues, wiping tears from her eyes. "Everyone's hair fell out instead. Principal Wilson's toupee was the only bit of hair left in the room."

"And Lettie Gordon's face when Bobby Landers' eyebrows disappeared," La'Tasha howls, reaching out to grab Hazel's arm. "I thought she was going to pass out."

They collapse into giggles together, and the tightness behind my ribs eases. At least something's getting fixed today.

"You have to see it," La'Tasha says, grabbing Hazel's hand without hesitation. "Come with me."

"Can you both go through together?" I ask.

"I'd assume so since it's a shared memory. Only one way to find out, I guess." La'Tasha offers an earbud to Hazel. "Ready for a trip down memory lane?"

Hazel hesitates, looking down at their joined hands, then takes the earbud. "This is potentially dangerous."

"We'll be fine. We won't interact with anyone. I'll cloak us so no one sees us," La'Tasha offers her a grin. "Come on, live a little."

They stand shoulder to shoulder, sharing the earbuds. La'Tasha scrolls to the song, and they both close their eyes. Their faces go distant, eyes unfocused. La'Tasha reaches for the door, and it opens.

"See you soon," Hazel says to me, squeezing La'Tasha's hand, and then they're gone.

Alone again, I finish my coffee and start another round of pacing. Their friendship is complicated, I can see that much. Maybe like siblings who love each other but also drive each other crazy.

I think of Blake and me. Yes, he's our alpha, but I've never been good at following anyone's advice, especially my younger brother.

Thirty minutes later, the door opens again. Hazel and La'Tasha spill out, arms linked, both laughing so hard they can barely stand.

"Principal Wilson's face," Hazel gasps, leaning into La'Tasha for support. "I'd forgotten how purple he turned!"

"And Miss Abernathy," La'Tasha adds, setting them off again. "Remember how she kept patting her head like she couldn't believe her bun was gone?"

I smile watching them. Their laughter is infectious. I also know what a prude Miss Abernathy was, so it makes it even funnier.

"So you can both go through together," I observe. "That's useful information."

"Very useful," Hazel agrees, composing herself and straightening her clothes, though she keeps one hand on La'Tasha's arm. "It means we could potentially send teams through if necessary."

Send teams through? So she's not going to seal it?

La'Tasha pulls out her phone again, her expression growing thoughtful. "Let me try for the Caribbean one more time. Just to be sure."

She repeats her earlier attempt, trying different songs, different memories. But the door remains firmly closed.

"I think we have our answer," Hazel says gently. "The portal only works within Moonridge. And only to places and times we've personally experienced."

"That's actually good news." Part of me feels relieved that my earlier failures weren't just personal inadequacy. "It means no one can get lost in ancient Rome or something. The boundaries are limited."

"But it also means the Concord must be using it for something specifically related to Moonridge's past," Hazel points out, her mouth flattening. "Something that happened during the lifetime of whoever built this."

The room goes quiet.

The basement door opens above us, and footsteps clatter down the stairs. Penny appears first, her arms full of books and papers, her glasses askew. Coco follows, her face barely visible behind a fluffy purple scarf.

"Sorry we're late," Penny says, adjusting her glasses. "But I think I found something important."

We clear space on the nearby table, and Penny spreads out her papers carefully. Diagrams. Old texts. Printouts of what look like physics equations.

"So," she begins, her hands moving rapidly as she organizes

her materials. "This is definitely a time portal, but it's not just any portal."

Coco nods enthusiastically. "It's super rare. Like, basically theoretical until now."

"In simple terms," Penny continues, "it needs specific information to work. The reason you've been able to travel to memories is because you lived those moments. That information is encoded in your brain, so the door knows exactly where to drop you."

"Like GPS coordinates for time?" I suggest.

"Exactly." Penny adjusts her glasses, warming to the topic. "Not to get too nerdy, but it's a history-anchored temporal doorway. Your memories are the map. Without them, the door has no destination." She pauses, chewing her bottom lip. "Though theoretically, if you fed it enough historical, factual, concrete information about a specific time and place—dates, names, events, locations—it might be able to construct coordinates even without a personal memory. Like giving it enough data points to triangulate a destination."

Wait, could I?

Holy shit. It might work.

"The door also appears to be coded to Moonridge specifically," Penny adds. "So no traveling outside of Moonridge, past or present. You're geographically locked to this area."

"That explains why I couldn't go to St. Lucia," La'Tasha says, catching on.

"Right. And you have to enter this specific portal to exit it," Penny adds, shuffling through her papers.

Hazel leans forward, studying Penny's diagrams with intense concentration. "What about the time differential? When La'Tasha and I were inside for almost an hour, how much time passed out here?"

"About thirty minutes," I answer. "I was keeping track."

Penny nods, and the lines around her mouth deepen. "That matches my calculations. Time moves at half the rate here as in the portal. So two days inside equates to one day here."

"So what could the Concord be trying to do?" Hazel asks, voicing the question we're all thinking.

Penny sighs, her shoulders sagging. "That's the part I haven't figured out yet. I also haven't been able to find a way to shut it down. The magic is too old, too complex."

I straighten a little. If they can't shut it down... Maybe there's still hope.

"What about sealing it?" Hazel asks. "Magical barriers?"

"We could try," Penny says. "But I don't know how effective it would be against Concord-level magic that we don't completely understand."

Hazel thinks for a moment, tapping her pen against her notebook, the sound sharp and rhythmic. "We need to put up magical barriers at minimum. Something that will alert us if anyone crosses the threshold."

"Like a magical doorbell?" Coco asks, leaning forward.

"Exactly like that," Hazel confirms. "An alarm system that will ping one of us if anyone comes near this thing."

"We should also double up on the building's security," La'Tasha suggests. "Change any codes Ravena might have used. Make sure none of her Concord buddies can just walk in and out as they please."

"Good thinking," I agree. "Blake and I can install new locks today. Maybe even cameras."

"And I'll keep researching," Penny promises, gathering her papers. "There has to be a way to deactivate it, or at least understand what the Concord wants with it."

Hazel stands. "Alright. We secure the portal today. La'Tasha, help me set up the magical barriers. Coco, assist Penny with her research. Calvin, get those new locks and security in place."

Everyone nods.

"What about Everett?" I ask, unable to keep the question inside any longer. My voice cracks on his name. "How does this help him?"

Hazel's eyes warm, and she moves closer to me. "I don't know yet. But understanding the Concord's tools is the first step to understanding their weaknesses. If we know what they're after, we might find a way to get to it first. We have to keep Moonridge's safety in mind first. Then we'll help Everett."

"And we *will* stop them," La'Tasha adds, her jaw set, fingers flexing like she's ready to call another lightning storm. "We're not giving up on him."

I nod. It's not the rescue mission I was hoping for, but it's something. Better than sitting around doing nothing while Everett's trapped god knows where.

As the others start organizing their tasks, I move back to the black door. I run my hand over the ancient symbols and wonder if maybe there are other portals, other ways to reach him. Maybe there's something buried in Moonridge's twisted history that we haven't found yet. A way back to him.

CHAPTER THIRTEEN

Calvin

I stare at the German chocolate cake sitting in front of me as everyone finishes singing the world's most off-key rendition of "Happy Birthday." Leo's enthusiasm makes up for his complete lack of musical talent, and Mina's pitch-perfect harmony somehow makes everyone else sound worse by comparison.

I lick the frosting off my fork, wondering how I managed to reach this age without figuring out how to not fall for unavailable men. Dead men, specifically.

"Make a wish!" Coco jumps up, nearly knocking over Blake's beer in her excitement.

I force a smile, lean forward, and blow out all the candles in one breath. Everyone cheers.

"What did you wish for?" Leo asks, already cutting the cake into uneven slices.

"He can't tell you," Penny says, adjusting her glasses. "Then it won't come true."

"I wished for a better singing group next year," I lie, accepting the first slice of cake from Leo. The truth is, I wished for Everett. To see him again. To know he's okay. Shocker.

I glance away from Blake's knowing look.

"So," La'Tasha says, spearing a bite of cake and gesturing with her fork, "who's ready for game night? I call dibs on not being paired with Leo for charades. Last time he broke Mina's lamp."

"I said I was sorry. Sometimes I over-commit to my craft!" Leo protests, waving his fork enthusiastically and sending a bit of chocolate frosting flying across the table. It lands on Dex's immaculate shirt collar. He looks down at it with mild disgust but says nothing.

"You were a disaster," Mina corrects with a fond smile.

The conversation continues around me, everyone laughing and planning the night ahead. I push cake around my plate. All I can think about is Everett at that lake. Alone. Suffering. While I'm here eating cake.

"Earth to Calvin," Blake says, nudging me with his elbow. "We're paying the bill. Ready to head out?"

"Yeah, sorry." I pull out my wallet, but Hazel waves me off with both hands.

"Birthday boy doesn't pay," she says firmly, already reaching for her purse. "House rules."

Outside the restaurant, the night air hits my face with a welcome chill. Stars speckle the sky above Moonridge, bright and clear against the darkness. Our breath clouds in front of us as we huddle on the sidewalk, everyone talking over each other about transportation logistics.

"My place is just a few blocks from here," Leo says, jingling his keys enthusiastically. "We can walk if everyone's up for it."

"Or we could drive," Blake counters, eyeing Hazel's impractical but very cute heels.

"I can manage," Hazel insists, but wobbles when she steps off the curb.

We end up splitting into two groups. Blake drives Hazel,

Penny, and Coco in his truck while Leo, La'Tasha, Mina, Dex, and I walk. The cool air feels good.

"You okay?" La'Tasha asks quietly, falling into step beside me while the others walk ahead. "You've been a million miles away all night."

"Just thinking," I reply, shoving my hands deeper into my pockets.

"About our spectral friend?" she guesses, her voice gentle.

I nod, my throat tight. Pathetic.

"We'll figure something out," she promises, squeezing my arm. "We always do."

Leo's house is exactly what you'd expect from a guy who regularly destroys things by accident. Everything is either secondhand, super sturdy, or easily replaceable. No glass coffee tables. No fragile vases. Just comfortable furniture that's seen better days and walls covered in movie posters and pack photos.

"Welcome to Chateau Leo!" he announces, flipping on lights and immediately tripping over his own shoe. He catches himself against the wall, narrowly avoiding taking out a floor lamp. "Drinks in the kitchen, games in the living room, karaoke machine already set up."

"I'll get the drinks," Mina offers, heading for the kitchen with Dex trailing silently behind her.

I sink into Leo's oversized couch. All of this is catching up to me. The time travel. The Graveborn attack. Losing Everett. Not sleeping. Pretending I'm fine when I'm absolutely not. My shoulders sag and my eyes start to droop.

Leo plops down beside me, the couch dipping under his weight. "Birthday boy looks like someone shit in his shower," he says. "What can we do to cheer you up? Karaoke? Charades? Strip poker?"

Blake, coming in the door with the others, snorts. "Nobody wants to see that, Leo."

"Speak for yourself," Leo replies with an exaggerated wink

that makes Penny giggle.

"We've already seen all that," Coco says. "Multiple times."

I shake my head, managing a small smile. "I appreciate all this, guys. Really. I'm just... tired. And worried."

"About?" Leo prompts, leaning forward.

"Everett." I say his name quietly. "I just want to know he's okay. Even if he's still stuck at the lake, even if I can't be with him or help him cross over yet. I just need to know he's not suffering."

The room goes quiet. Blake and Hazel exchange looks that I can't quite read. La'Tasha sits on my other side, her hand finding my shoulder in silent support.

"We could go check," Blake says suddenly.

All heads turn toward him.

"What?" Hazel asks.

"We could go to Skipper Lake," Blake clarifies. "Right now. Dex could help bring Everett out if he's there. We could build a bonfire, maybe even try to help him cross over. It's Cal's birthday. Let's give him what he really wants."

I sit up straighter, hope flaring in my chest. "Could we?"

"We can try," Blake says, turning to face me fully.

"Absolutely not," Hazel cuts in, shaking her head while moving to stand beside Blake. "The Concord could be watching. After what happened at Calvin's house, we'd be walking into a potential trap."

"So we come prepared," La'Tasha counters, rising to her feet as well. "We handled those Graveborn once. We can do it again if necessary."

"I could help with that." Dex's voice carries from the kitchen doorway, making heads turn. He steps into the room. "If Everett's at the lake, I should be able to make him visible. Let you talk to him, at least." His jaw tightens. "But helping him cross over? That's a different story. If he's been bound again, I won't have the power to free him."

Hazel opens her mouth to object again, but Blake gently

takes her arm and leads her toward the hallway. I can't hear what they're saying, but I can see Blake's earnest expression, his hands moving as he makes his case. Hazel's shoulders remain rigid, then relax.

They return to the group, and Hazel sighs deeply, her shoulders dropping. "Fine. We can go. But," she holds up one finger, "everyone needs to be on high alert. If The Mortician or any other Concord member shows up with Graveborn, we could have another fight on our hands. Is everyone prepared for that?"

Leo jumps up, nearly knocking over an end table. "I'll bring marshmallows! And hot dogs! And my portable speaker! And..."

"Just the marshmallows and hot dogs," Blake interrupts with a grin. "Let's try to keep a low profile."

"And I need to go home and change. This isn't exactly skirts and strappy heels at the lake weather," Hazel says.

I look around at my friends. My throat constricts, and I have to swallow hard before I can speak.

"Thanks, guys," I manage, my voice coming out rougher than I'd meant. "This means a lot."

"That's what family's for," Mina says, and everyone nods in agreement.

Family. How did I get so lucky?

***

Skipper Lake looks different at night. And not good different. It feels wrong. Like something's watching us from under the ice. The lake stretches black and still under the nearly full moon, reflecting pinpricks of starlight.

Leo dumps an armful of firewood onto the ground with a clatter that echoes through the surrounding woods. Blake winces and shoots him a look.

"Sorry," Leo whispers dramatically, then proceeds to create even more noise as he arranges the wood in what I think is supposed to be a teepee structure but looks more like a wobbly pile of wooden blocks.

"Let me," Blake says, moving Leo aside and rebuilding the pile. Within minutes, he has a perfect fire going, the flames casting dancing shadows across our faces and warming the cool night air.

Hazel paces the edge of our little gathering, her eyes constantly scanning the tree line. "Everyone try to look casual," she instructs. "If the Concord is watching, we don't want them to know why we're really here."

"Yes, because nothing says 'casual hangout' like constantly looking over your shoulder like you're waiting for the police to jump out at any minute," La'Tasha remarks, rolling her eyes while she stakes out a spot near the fire.

"I think we look perfectly normal," Leo declares, stabbing three marshmallows onto a stick and immediately holding them so close that they burst into flames. "Oops." He blows frantically, sending flaming marshmallow bits flying.

Penny ducks just in time to avoid taking molten sugar to the face. "Your definition of normal concerns me."

"Anyone want a s'more that's crispy on the outside and gooey on the inside?" Coco offers, holding up her perfectly golden marshmallow with pride.

"Sounds exactly like the state of my life," I mutter, but accept the s'more anyway. The sweetness hits my tongue as I try to quiet the nervousness buzzing through my veins.

Dex stands apart from the group, his tall form unnaturally still as he stares out at the forest.

La'Tasha catches my eye and tilts her head toward the lake. I nod and stand up, brushing crumbs from my jeans.

"We're going to take a walk," La'Tasha announces, pulling me away from the others. Dex follows silently, like a shadow detaching itself from the night. Hazel watches us go but stays with the others.

The three of us move away from the firelight, the darkness swallowing us as we approach the lake's edge. The temperature drops the closer we get. My skin prickles with more than just the chill.

"Now what?" I ask, my voice sounding too loud in the quiet night.

"We call to him," Dex whispers. "You should do it, Calvin. He will respond to you most strongly."

I swallow hard, my mouth dry. What am I supposed to say? *Everett, if you're there, please pick up?* Like he's just stepped away from the phone?

"Everett?" I try, my voice catching. I clear my throat and try again, louder. "Everett, it's Calvin. Can you hear me?"

Nothing. Just the distant crackle of the bonfire behind us.

"Keep trying," La'Tasha encourages, her hand warm on my back. "He might need time to respond if he's bound again."

"Everett!" I call, louder this time, my voice carrying across the darkness. "Please, if you can hear me, give us a sign. Anything."

Still nothing. My shoulders slump. Of course it didn't work. Why would anything work?

"Let's try the dock," La'Tasha suggests, already moving toward the wooden structure extending into the lake.

The dock creaks under our weight, old boards protesting as we walk to the end. I sit down, letting my legs dangle over the edge, my boots just inches above the black ice. La'Tasha sits beside me while Dex remains standing, his eyes scanning the space before us.

"Everett," I try once more, softer now, more intimate. Like a prayer. "I just want to know you're okay. Please. Show yourself."

At first, I think it's just the wind when I hear it. A whisper so faint it might be my imagination.

"...Calvin..."

I jerk upright, scanning the lake. "Did you hear that?"

La'Tasha nods, her eyes wide. "Look." She points at a spot

directly in front of us.

A shimmer appears above the surface, like moonlight through warped glass. It wavers, then begins to take shape. First a suggestion of shoulders, then the outline of a head. So faint I have to squint to make it out in the darkness.

"Everett?" My heart hammers against my ribs.

The shimmer becomes more defined. Blonde hair. The curve of a jaw. Blue eyes that glow faintly in the darkness. It's him, but wrong somehow. Like looking at a photo that's been left in the sun too long, all the colors bleached and faded.

"Calvin," Everett's voice is barely audible, like a radio picking up a distant station. His shape flickers, fading in and out of visibility. "You shouldn't... be here."

"We came to check on you," I say, leaning forward so far La'Tasha grabs the back of my jacket to keep me from falling off the dock. "Are you okay? What did they do to you?"

"Not... okay." His form wavers, almost disappearing before solidifying again. Pain etches every translucent feature. "They've... bound me tighter. Using... my energy."

"For what?" La'Tasha asks.

"Attack," Everett manages, his face contorted. "The equinox. They're planning... something big."

I go dizzy. "What kind of attack? Where?"

"Don't know." Everett flickers violently. "They've locked us down... whatever they're planning can't be good."

Dex steps forward, his eyes beginning to glow with an otherworldly light. "I'm going to take a closer look," he announces, and before anyone can respond, his body goes rigid, blurring at the edges like reality bends around him.

La'Tasha and I exchange glances but stay silent. Dex's face goes blank, his eyes unfocused as he stares at something we can't see, his head tilting. After a minute, he snaps back to himself with a small gasp.

"I can see him clearly now," Dex says, his voice tight. "He's bound with Concord hellfire and demon shackles. They've weakened his spirit considerably."

"Can you break the shackles?" I ask, my voice cracking. "Help him cross over?"

Dex shakes his head. "There's nothing I can do against those bindings. It would take stronger magic than mine to break them."

I look back at Everett's fading form, my hands clenching into fists. "Hold tight," I tell him. "I have a plan."

I haven't been able to get it to work yet, but I'll keep trying until I can.

"Calvin," Everett's voice comes stronger for just a moment, his eyes fixing directly on mine. "Be careful. Don't do anything stupid."

"I won't," I say, though I know it's not true. What I have cooking in my head is beyond stupid.

His shape flickers one last time, his mouth moving to form words I can't hear, and then he's gone.

"We need to get back to the others," La'Tasha says, pulling on my arm. "Tell them what we learned."

I nod, but can't tear my eyes away from the spot where Everett disappeared.

We have less than four weeks before those assholes attack again.

As we approach the others, Hazel immediately stands, her eyes searching our faces. "Well? Did you find him?"

"We did," La'Tasha confirms, dropping onto a log with a heavy sigh. "He's not in good shape."

Leo stops mid-marshmallow roast, the flaming sugar forgotten on his stick. "Is he okay? Wait, stupid question. Of course he's not okay if he's a ghost."

"He's worse than before," I say, sitting down hard on the nearest log. "The Concord has him bound with something Dex called hellfire and demon shackles."

"Oh! That's not good," Penny whispers, her eyes wide behind

her glasses as she closes the book she'd been reading.

"It gets worse," Dex adds, remaining standing at the edge of our circle. "The bindings are draining his energy at an accelerated rate."

"For what purpose?" Hazel asks.

"They're planning an attack," I tell them. "Spring equinox. Everett doesn't know the details, but they're using his energy to power something big."

Blake swears under his breath, his hand finding Hazel's shoulder. "Do we know where? What kind of attack?"

I shake my head. My jaw clenches. "He couldn't tell us much. They've locked him down tight. But it's clear they need his power for whatever they're planning."

Coco hugs herself, looking small in her oversized sweater. "So what do we do? How do we stop them?"

The fire crackles in the silence that follows, sparks dancing upward into the night sky. The threat sits between us. Penny's fingers worry the edge of her notebook. Mina stares into the fire. Leo's marshmallow droops and burns.

"I have an idea," I say finally, my heart pounding. "And it involves the time portal."

Hazel's eyebrows shoot up her forehead. "Excuse me?"

"Hear me out," I continue. "Penny said the portal can take you wherever you want to go if you feed it enough information, right? So we'll feed it a shit-ton of information from 1958 and I can use it to go back and stop Everett from being sacrificed in the first place."

"Calvin, that's…" Blake starts, but I cut him off with a wave of my hand.

"If Everett is never sacrificed, never bound to the lake, then the Concord loses a member. It's the only way to save him. The only way that makes sense. Everett said they always need thirteen, right? Without him, they'd be weakened. Maybe enough to stop whatever they're planning."

"You're talking about changing history," Hazel says slowly. "Altering events that happened almost seventy years ago."

"Events that should never have happened in the first place," I counter. Heat boils in my gut. "The Concord murdered him, Hazel. They cut his throat and bound his spirit. They've used him for decades. Why shouldn't we try to stop that?"

"Because we have no idea what the consequences would be," Blake says firmly. He stands up, towering over the rest of us. "You could change everything. The entire timeline. You could erase people from existence, including yourself."

"But we've already established the timeline has protections," I argue, looking to La'Tasha. "Remember what happened when I bumped into mini-me? It got incorporated as a dream. The timeline protects itself."

"From small changes," Hazel emphasizes, rising to her feet as well, hands on her hips. "We don't know how it reacts to larger events like stopping someone from being murdered."

"But it's the right thing to do," I insist, standing up. The flames cast strange shadows across all our faces. "Even if we can't save him now, we could stop it at the source. We could give him the life he deserved."

"I think it might be possible," La'Tasha says, earning a sharp look from Hazel. "From what we've observed so far, the portal does seem to have some built-in safeguards, and I did a little research of my own. It does appear all it needs is enough information to send it to the correct spot. It doesn't have to be a memory."

"And the research I've been doing suggests a theory," Penny adds, pushing her glasses up her nose while rifling through her ever-present notebook. "As long as you have a tether to this world and know where you entered the timeline, you should be able to get back. The portal seems to remember its travelers."

"Should be able to? Seems to?" Blake repeats, throwing his hands up. "Are you hearing yourselves? We're betting Calvin's entire existence on theories about a magical door we barely understand."

"I'm willing to take that risk," I say firmly, meeting his eyes across the fire.

"Well, I'm not willing to let you," Blake responds, crossing his arms. The firelight catches the determination in his eyes. "What if you get stuck in 1958? What if you change things so drastically that you never exist? What if the Concord in 1958 realizes what you're doing and kills you too?"

I stand my ground, squaring my shoulders. "Then at least I tried."

"This is insane," Hazel throws up her hands. "We're talking about time travel like it's just a harmless thing we do every day."

"Only on Tuesdays and Thursdays," Leo jokes, then immediately shrinks back when everyone glares at him. "Sorry."

Mina finally speaks up. "What about alternatives? Could we maybe find another way to break Everett's bindings without potentially changing history?"

"Good thought, but that's next to impossible," Dex says. "The bindings the Concord uses are ancient and powerful. Breaking them would require either significant collective power or knowledge we don't currently possess."

"And we don't know where to find the Concord or what they even have planned," Blake insists. "We need to research. Prepare. We can't just jump through a magic door into the past and hope for the best."

"In less than four weeks?" I challenge, stepping closer to him. "You think we can find a solution in less than a month when Dex, who knows the most about the Concord, doesn't even know how to break these bindings? And what are we going to research exactly when we don't know what to look for?"

Blake and I stare at each other, neither willing to back down.

"I forbid it." There it is. The alpha card. "As pack leader I refuse to let you do this. It's too dangerous. We'll find another way."

"I agree," Hazel adds, stepping up beside him and taking his hand. "As head of the coven, I can't allow this kind of reckless magical tampering. The portal stays closed until we understand it better."

I take a deep breath and bite back my response. The lines have been drawn. Authority over desperation.

Or so they think.

"Fine," I say.

Across the fire, La'Tasha raises an eyebrow and gives me the slightest nod. She knows I have no intention of obeying the rules.

The conversation shifts to other potential solutions, everyone throwing out ideas that sound increasingly far-fetched. Research avenues to explore. Spells to try. Ways to strengthen our defenses. I nod and contribute where I have to, but my mind is elsewhere.

Sometimes asking permission just gets you told no.

So maybe I stop asking for permission.

As we pack up to leave, dousing the fire and gathering our things, La'Tasha falls into step beside me. She bumps her shoulder against mine once, a silent question.

I curl my fingers around my car keys in my pocket and answer with a nod.

CHAPTER FOURTEEN

Calvin

I slam my hammer down on the last nail, the blow echoing through the empty construction site like a gunshot. Everyone else left an hour ago, eager to start their weekend, but here I am, still fussing with things that don't need fussing with. Anything to keep me from thinking about the door in the basement. The door that could take me back to save Everett. The door that my brother and Hazel have forbidden me to use. Like I'm some kid who can't be trusted with a box of matches.

"You're still here?" Blake's voice startles me. I nearly drop my hammer on my foot. He stands in the doorway, keys jingling in his hand, eyebrows raised.

"Just finishing up." I shove the hammer into my tool belt. "Didn't want to leave things half done before the weekend."

Blake's eyes narrow. "Uh huh. And this has nothing to do with a certain magical door in the basement?"

"Can't a guy just take pride in his work?" I force a smile.

Blake closes the distance, his voice dropping to that serious alpha tone that grates my last nerve. "I need you to promise me you won't try the door again. Hazel set up magical barriers. She'll know immediately if someone tries to use it, and I don't want to hear about it."

"Yeah, I know all about Hazel's magical surveillance system." I can't keep the bitterness out of my voice.

"It's for your own protection." Blake's hand lands on my shoulder, heavy and warm. "We'll find another way to help Everett. One that doesn't involve you traveling through time and potentially fucking up everyone's lives."

I shrug off his hand. "Yeah, I got it. No time travel for Calvin."

"I mean it," he says, his eyes boring into mine. "Promise me."

"I promise I won't trip Hazel's magical alarm system," I say carefully, meeting his gaze without flinching. Not exactly what he asked for, but close enough that I don't feel like I'm completely lying to my brother's face.

He studies me for a long moment, then sighs. "Good enough, I guess. Want to grab dinner? I'm meeting Hazel at Midnight Stack. I know how much you love breakfast for dinner."

"Rain check. I've got some stuff to do at home." Like figuring out how to save Everett without causing a magical SWAT team to take me out.

"Suit yourself." Blake hesitates at the door, his hand on the frame. "I meant what I said. We'll find another way to help him."

"Sure we will," I mutter as he leaves. In a month. With no plan. No problem.

The door clicks shut behind him, and I'm alone again with my thoughts and the basement below.

I sit on an overturned bucket and drop my head into my hands. I want to crawl out of my skin. I know my idea might work, if they'd just cooperate instead of putting up roadblocks.

Sure, I don't have a concrete plan. And I don't know how to find Everett in 1958 or how to stop the Concord from killing him. Hell, I don't even know if I could return to the present once

I went back that far. But sitting here doing nothing while Everett suffers feels worse than any risk I might take.

I stand and pace the room, my boots scuffing the dusty floor. The basement door pulls at me. *Just go down and look*, a voice in my head whispers. *You don't have to use it. Just check it out.*

But I know myself. Looking would lead to touching, and touching would lead to trying, and then Hazel would know, and she'd probably have me banished from this work site. Any chance I had of helping Everett would vanish.

"Screw this," I mutter, grabbing my jacket. I need to get out of here before I do something stupid. I'll go home, take a hot shower, and maybe actually sleep for more than three hours. Tomorrow I'll figure out a better plan.

I'm halfway to my truck when a familiar voice calls my name. I turn. La'Tasha strolls across the lot with what looks like a rolled map in her right hand. She has her big-ass bag of magic slung over her shoulder which can only mean one thing. She means business.

"Fancy meeting you here," she says, smiling like we're about to get up to some shit.

"What are you doing?" I ask, glancing around to make sure Blake hasn't doubled back.

"Looking for you, obviously." She shifts the map to her other hand. "We need to talk."

"About what?"

La'Tasha's gaze flicks back toward the building. "About your time-traveling ghost-saving plan. You still want to do it, right?"

My pulse jumps and rattles my throat. Is she offering to help? "You know I do. But Hazel put up magical barriers."

"I know." La'Tasha's smile turns smug. "I helped her design them."

"You what?"

"Which means," she continues, ignoring my outburst, "I know exactly how to bypass them without triggering any alarms."

I stare at her. "You're serious?"

"You know I am." She holds up her bag of magic supplies. "I came prepared. We've got planning to do."

"But why?" I ask, my voice cracking. "You could get in serious trouble for this. Hazel trusts you."

La'Tasha rolls her eyes and sets down her bag. "You know what I'm tired of? Research. Meetings. Sitting around studying maps and drawing circles while we debate the safest way to handle the Concord." Her jaw tightens. "We've been doing the same song and dance anytime a threat rears its head. We study them, ward against them, react to their moves. Meanwhile, they keep getting stronger."

I nod. "You want to go on the offensive."

"Damn right I do." Her eyes flash. "It's what we should have been doing all along. They need thirteen members to operate at full power. If we can save Everett, or take out another member, we weaken them significantly. Maybe enough to stop whatever they're planning for next month."

"And if we fail?"

"Then we fail trying instead of failing while sitting on our asses and wringing our hands." She picks up the bag again, her jaw set. "The stakes are too high for half-ass measures anymore. Sometimes you have to take the big risks to get the big rewards."

Ten minutes later we're back inside and La'Tasha has her photocopied map tacked to the wall. Moonridge circa 1958 spreads before us in faded lines and careful labels.

"If we're doing this, we're doing it right." She taps the map with a red marker. "Tonight."

"Tonight?" The word catches in my throat. I cough. "That's... soon."

"It's Friday. You've got the weekend off." She gives me a look. "Two days here means four days back then. More than enough time to find Everett and convince him to come back with you."

"Wait." My hands go still. "Bring him back? I thought we

were stopping the Concord from killing him."

"We will. But if you leave him there, that only delays his death." La'Tasha pulls several photocopied newspaper clippings from her bag. She smooths one out on the table. "The smarter play is to pull him out of that timeline entirely and bring him to ours."

I lean over the article. The headline swims into focus:

Local Man Found Dead at Skipper Lake.

Below it, a grainy photo of a red convertible, driver's door hanging open. My stomach lurches.

"June 25, 1958," I read aloud. The date blurs. "He'd been missing three days before they found the car."

"Which means we go back before June 22nd." La'Tasha circles a date on a pocket calendar. "June 18th. Four days before he was reported missing. Enough time for you to find him and build enough trust that he'll believe your insane story."

"Four days." A laugh escapes me. It sounds unhinged. "Can the portal even bring someone forward? He won't age seventy years the second he steps through?"

La'Tasha shakes her head and pulls out her notebook, pages covered in equations and diagrams. "You didn't regress when you went back, did you?"

"No."

"And that flower I picked in the past? It didn't wilt the moment I returned." She flips to a page marked with sticky notes. "Lasted a couple of days, like any cut flower. The portal preserves the physical state of whatever passes through it."

She spreads her hands over the map. "If you bring him through, he'll still be twenty-seven. He'll get to live a full life." She says it quieter. "With you. And we can protect him from the Concord."

Everett. Alive. Here.

Not a ghost.

My hands tremble. I grip the edge of the table.

"So what's the plan?" My voice comes out steadier than I feel.

La'Tasha hands me a copy of a second clipping. I take it from her carefully, hands shaking.

Missing: Everett James Bradshaw, age 27.

Another photo. Everett in a white t-shirt, leaning against a car, grinning at the camera like he owned the world.

"According to county records, he worked here." She taps a spot on the map labeled Randall's Auto Repair. "Your grandfather's shop. And he rented a room in their house." Her finger moves to another mark.

I stare at the address. "My house."

"Exactly." She pulls out a red marker and starts circling locations. "He stayed with and worked for your great-grandfather. Visit that area and you're guaranteed to cross paths with him."

"But I can't just show up and—what—knock on the door?" My voice pitches up. "Hey, Great-Grandpa Earl, don't freak out, but I'm your great-grandson from the future.'"

"Obviously don't do that." La'Tasha caps the marker. "You'll need a cover story. A reason to be in Moonridge. A reason to need a job." She pauses, then meets my eyes. "But Calvin? When you find him, you can't just blurt out the truth. Get to know him first. Build trust. Then tell him about the Concord."

"And if he thinks I'm insane?"

La'Tasha reaches into her bag again and pulls out two more photocopied articles. Current ones. She sets them on the table. The top headline reads: *Moonridge Celebrates 200th Anniversary.*

"Show him this. Dates, details, things that haven't happened yet." She taps them. "Nothing says 'believe me' like proof of the future. I've also included the two articles about his death. If the first one doesn't grab his attention, these will."

I pick up the papers. They feel too light. Too flimsy to be carrying the weight of Everett's life.

"Right." I set them down carefully. I cross my arms and breathe deep. "This is completely insane."

"Here's to taking chances." La'Tasha grins. "But first, we need to get you looking the part. You can't show up in 1958 wearing jeans with holes in them and a super hero t-shirt. You'll need to cut your hair, and the beard has to go."

I run a hand over my face. "I haven't been without a beard in over ten years. Or had short hair. I'm not going to recognize myself."

"It just doesn't fit the style of the time. You're too early for the hippie movement." She stands up and offers me a hand, her grip firm when I take it. "Come on. We need to get moving."

"Now? As in right now?"

"Yes, now. We've got just a few hours to turn you into someone who'll blend in in 1958." She hands me my jacket. "Thrift stores first. We need Levi's, plain white t-shirts, maybe a leather jacket if we can find one cheap enough. The more authentic the better." La'Tasha removes the map from the wall and rolls it up. "While you're doing that, I'll work on creating a backstory for you. People will know you're not from around there. We need a solid cover story."

We walk to our vehicles. My hands shake as I fumble with my keys.

"You'll need to brush up on 1950s culture too," La'Tasha says as she unlocks her car. "Music, slang, current events. You need to blend in."

"Right. Because nothing says 'I belong here' like a guy who doesn't know who the president is." My stomach twists with nerves. "What if I mess up? What if I say or do something that changes history?"

"Stop worrying so much. We've been through this," she says, her voice gentle but firm. "As long as you don't do anything drastic like assassinate someone in power or start a war, you should be fine."

"That wasn't on my to-do list, but thanks for the tip." I fidget with my keys, the metal slipping in my sweaty palms. "What if

I can't find him? Moonridge was different back then."

"Moonridge isn't that big. It was even smaller then. And that's what the map is for." She taps my forehead with it. "And you know where he lived…"

"Why are you really helping me? I mean, beyond the strategic stuff. Hazel would lose her shit if she knew."

La'Tasha's smile fades, and she leans against her car. "Because I'm tired of playing it safe while people suffer. Because Everett deserves a chance at life. And because…" She pauses, her eyes meeting mine. "Because I've seen how you look when you talk about him. You deserve a chance to be happy, too."

I have to look away. If I can bring Everett back. If I get a chance to know him, not as a ghost I caught glimpses of, but as a real person.

In the past.

And then it dawns on me. I'm going to see younger versions of my relatives, too. My breath catches. My great-grandparents who owned my house, who I only know through faded photographs and my grandmother's stories. And my grandparents would likely be teenagers then, or close to.

"Calvin?" La'Tasha's voice is concerned. "You okay?"

"Yeah, just… I realized I may get to see my great-grandparents. Alive. Young." My throat closes up. "People I only know from photos."

La'Tasha's gaze turns warm. "That's going to be hard. But remember why you're there. You can't get distracted by family reunions."

"Right." My stomach churns at the thought. "Stay focused. Find Everett, convince him I'm not crazy, bring him back through the portal. Easy peasy."

"Meet me at your place in two hours," La'Tasha says, breaking the moment. "Pick up whatever vintage clothes you find. We'll go through them together and figure out the rest of your plan then."

I nod. She gives me a quick hug, then slides into her SUV

and drives away, leaving me standing in the parking lot with my head spinning.

***

Two hours later, I barely recognize myself in the mirror. Clean-shaven. Short hair. The barber completely went to town with his scissors. I've been trimmed, primped and pomaded to the point that I look ten years younger. Not bad.

I've pulled together enough vintage clothing to get me through a week—just in case it takes longer than four days. I've got several white T-shirts and managed to find three pairs of jeans that might work if I roll up the cuffs, a couple of button-down shirts that smell like mothballs, and a couple pairs of shoes that should pass. I also managed to find a leather jacket in one of the trunks in my attic. It's seen better days, but it'll work. The only place I'm lacking in vintage clothing is in the underwear department. What did underwear even look like back then? I suppose it doesn't matter. I don't expect anyone to see me in my skivvies. Easy enough to hide.

La'Tasha arrives with a stack of books about the 1950s. We spread everything out on my living room floor like we're planning a heist, which I guess we kind of are. She settles on the rug and starts arranging papers and maps across the coffee table. We rehash everything we covered earlier multiple times to orient me to the timeline.

"He was last seen at Skipper Lake on June 21, 1958. Summer Solstice."

"So I need to find him before that date and convince him to come back with me." I pick up one of the shirts to place in the rucksack I'll take with me. I run my fingers over the worn fabric. It's soft from countless washings. "How exactly am I supposed to do that? Four days isn't a lot of time to get someone to trust you."

"Maybe ease into it a bit. You have to remember, he doesn't know you yet, and you don't know who he was back then. You're going in blind. Live by my golden rule. Trust no one." She looks me dead in the eye. "Build trust. Then, when the time is right, tell him the truth."

"And if he thinks I'm insane?"

"You'll have copies of the newspaper articles. Two of them cover his death specifically. Nothing says 'believe me' like a look at your future. Or... death."

"Right. Good call." I nod.

"Speaking of the portal," La'Tasha wipes her hands and pulls out another notebook, this one filled with diagrams and symbols. "We'll need to go at midnight. I can get us past the detection shield Hazel put up, but it'll be late enough that she should be fast asleep by then. She won't be prowling around. I have a feeling she doesn't trust you."

"You think?"

"We'll be fine. I'll cast a cloaking spell that should hide our magical signatures from the detection spell she put on the door."

"Should?" I raise an eyebrow, my voice tight.

"Will," she corrects herself, meeting my gaze steadily. "Definitely will. I'm very good at what I do."

We spend the next several hours going over every detail. La'Tasha quizzes me on 1950s trivia. Who's the president? Dwight D. Eisenhower. What's a popular song? "Rock Around the Clock" by Bill Haley & His Comets. How much does a gallon of gas cost? About 23 cents. What can't you talk about in polite company? Anything to do with sex, politics, or my true identity as a time traveler.

By eleven PM, my brain feels scrambled, but I'm as ready as I can be considering what little time we've had to cram. I've packed a rucksack with essentials: clothes, a toothbrush, deodorant, a small first aid kit, and a few other items La'Tasha insisted I bring. She confiscated my phone. I can't take any modern tech that might raise questions.

"You ready for this?" La'Tasha asks as we load the last of our supplies into her SUV.

"Not even a little bit," I admit, zipping up my grandfather's leather jacket. It smells like dust and old cologne and memories that were never mine. "But I'm doing it anyway."

She gives me a quick hug, fierce and brief.

"That's the spirit." She starts the car and puts it in reverse. "For what it's worth, I think you're doing the right thing."

"Let's hope the timeline agrees with you."

We drive to the construction site in silence. Her hands are steady on the steering wheel, but I can see the tension in her shoulders. Outside, the night is clear, stars scattered across the sky. A good night for time travel, if there is such a thing.

La'Tasha parks a block away, and we walk the rest of the distance, keeping to the shadows. The old building looms dark and silent, no sign of anyone watching.

"Remember the plan," La'Tasha whispers as the lock clicks and she pushes the door open. "And one more thing."

"Yeah?"

"Be careful." Her eyes are serious in the darkness. "The past is a different world. People thought differently, behaved differently. Remember that."

"I will." I follow her inside, my heart hammering against my ribs.

We make our way to the basement door. I feel like every step might trigger some magical alarm. The door to the basement creaks open, revealing the stairs that lead down to the time portal.

La'Tasha begins a whispered incantation, her hands moving in complex patterns. The air around us feels charged. Blue light shimmers around her fingers, then spreads outward in a dome that encompasses both of us.

"Cloaking spell," she explains as we descend the stairs.

The basement is dark and cool, smelling of dust and old wood.

The black door stands at the far end, its ancient symbols somehow darker than the darkness surrounding them. My mouth goes dry at the sight of it, and I have to wipe my palms on my jeans.

"You ready?" La'Tasha asks, her hand on my arm.

"No," I admit, my voice barely above a whisper. "But I'm doing it anyway."

She nods, then reaches into her bag and pulls out a small silver pendant on a chain. "Wear this. It's a tether. If my research is right, this will link us and ensure that you can find your way back here. I'll be wearing one as well. We'll be bound to one another. It should also provide a level of protection. Not much, but it might help if you run into magical trouble."

I slip it over my head, tucking it under my shirt. The metal is warm from her touch. "Thanks."

"Now, we need to feed the portal." She places my old radio—the one that used to belong to Everett—on a small table next to the door. She also places a couple of actual newspapers from Moonridge in 1958, a stack of old letters I found in the attic written by my great-grandmother, and a photo album.

She turns on the radio and twists the dial. Nothing but static. The sound prickles over my skin.

"Let's give it something to work with." She speaks like this is just another spell. She places her hand on the door and starts to read headlines from the newspaper aloud. The radio sputters, catching half-formed sounds before dissolving again into white noise.

My pulse thuds in my ears.

She keeps reading. Headlines. Weather reports. Obituaries. The static shifts, weaving around her words like it's listening. A man's voice blips in for a second, then vanishes. Another few lines, and music begins to thread through, thin and warbling, like it's leaking from another room.

I take a step closer.

The voice returns, this time holding. "Good evening, Moonridge…" Tinny, distorted, but real. The date and time follow—"it's 4:15 PM on June 18th"—and then music swells until it's clear, bright, and unmistakably alive.

The symbols on the door blaze to life.

This didn't happen before. Sweat gathers at the back of my neck. In a few minutes, I'll be in 1958. A different time. A different world.

Or I might fail spectacularly and get stuck in the past forever.

Before I can talk myself out of it, the door clicks open.

"You've got this," La'Tasha says, squeezing my shoulder. "Remember. Starting tomorrow, you have four days. Find him. Bring him home."

I nod. I don't trust myself to speak. My throat's too tight. She steps forward and hugs me, grounding me.

The song Everett played through my radio that night begins to bleed from the speakers. I close my eyes, focus on Everett's name, the photos, the map of Moonridge burned into my mind. I pull the door open, revealing not the wall behind it but a swirling vortex of light and color. I take a deep breath, give La'Tasha one last look, and step through.

CHAPTER FIFTEEN

Everett

It's been several days since The Collector dragged me back to Skipper Lake. I'm trapped here with nothing but snowflakes and memories I can't escape. I've been released from the dungeon and my energy has returned, but the leash around me has tightened. I can wander as far as the shoreline, but no farther. Every attempt to slip into the trees or toward the road slams me with a jolt that rattles whatever counts as my bones. It hurts like the dickens and steals a little more hope each time.

Tonight, I drift above the glassy surface of the frozen lake. Moonlight highlights the snow and ice. All is quiet except for the occasional hoot of an owl.

Headlights slash through the darkness. My form perks up, edges solidifying. Could it be Calvin? He hasn't been back since I saw him two nights ago.

Hopefully he brought Dex with him. Now that they've let me drift again, maybe I can connect with him, if even for a moment. Just to let him know that I'm doing better even though the threat still looms.

The vehicle stops at the edge of the parking lot. My hope

deflates. Not Calvin's truck. Of course it isn't. This one's a smaller, sleeker SUV. Two figures emerge and I strain to see them in the dim light. The first is a woman with braids piled high on her head: La'Tasha. Beside her stands Dex, the Grim Reaper himself, looking very mysterious in his all-black wardrobe.

They walk toward the dock, snow crunching beneath their feet.

"You sure about this?" La'Tasha's words carry across the water. "Because the Concord has eyes everywhere, and I didn't drive all the way out here to fight more of those demon monsters."

Dex speaks, smooth as black ice. "You said you needed to speak with him. This is the only way I know how."

I glide closer to the dock, careful to stay within my boundaries. No need to hit the barrier and alert The Collector.

La'Tasha stops at the dock's edge. She raises both hands, fingers tracing patterns in the air. The words she speaks aren't English, or any language I recognize. Magic words. Witch words.

And then she and Dex vanish. Gone like someone wiped them clean off the page of reality.

What the hell? Did The Collector snatch them? Are there more Concord members hiding in the trees?

"Hello?" My voice sounds thin and hollow against the snow and ice. "La'Tasha? Dex?"

"We're still here." Dex's voice comes from where they'd stood moments before. "You just can't see us."

I glide in, but reality wrinkles, like it can't agree on what I'm seeing. Or not seeing in this case. "What gives?"

La'Tasha laughs. "Cloaking spell, honey. The Concord won't sense us unless one of them trips over my invisible foot. We need to talk to you, and we can't risk them overhearing."

"Color me impressed." I hover as close as my boundaries allow. "Though I'm not sure how much help I'll be. They've got me on a pretty tight leash these days."

"We can see that." Dex's voice carries that usual gruff, academic thing he has going on. "But we need information only you can provide."

"What about Calvin?" I ask. "Is he okay?"

A pause stretches too long. Clothes rustle. Someone shifts their stance on the dock.

"Calvin's gone." La'Tasha pauses. "Temporarily. I helped him use the portal that we found to travel back to 1958. He's going to save you."

If I had a body, I think I would have collapsed. "He what?"

"We found a way to use the portal in the basement of that building he's renovating." La'Tasha's words tumble faster, invisible but electric. "Calvin got this crazy idea that he could go back and save you before the Concord sacrificed you."

Calvin went back in time. To save me. Before I was murdered. Before I became this.

"That's impossible." But even as I say it, I want it to be true.

"Apparently not." Dex's voice carries a faint edge that fits the absurdity. "The door seems capable of taking people to specific points in the past with the right instructions. Not just within their lifetime. They found a workaround."

"If he's successful, you won't be tied to the Concord anymore." La'Tasha shifts closer. A pebble skitters across the wood. "You won't be a ghost. You'll have a chance at a real life. And if it all works out the way I think it will, the Concord will be weakened because they will be down a member and whatever they're planning for the end of this month will fail."

A real life. A chance to breathe again. Feel sunshine on my skin. Taste food, drink soda, dance, sing.

Love.

"He's really doing this for me?" My form wavers. He traveled through time to save my life?

"But wait, if he saves me in 1958, I never become a ghost. Which means Calvin never meets me. Which means he has no reason to go back. Which means I do die, which means…"

"Time is more flexible than you might think." Dex cuts me off with a low chuckle.

La'Tasha speaks, closer now. "After Calvin left I realized that if he saves you, you'll no longer have Concord information from over the years that could help us." A pause. "We need to know about their weaknesses. Anything you can tell us that might help if Calvin succeeds and they come looking for a replacement."

A tight, cold pressure closes around me. My awareness flickers.

The Scribe.

The thought freezes me solid.

"But The Scribe... he's there."

"Who?" La'Tasha asks. "Is that bad?"

"Bad?" I let out a hollow laugh. "It's worse than bad. It's dangerous. The Scribe can rewrite history. If he finds out Calvin is there to upset their plan, he could erase him from existence entirely. Prevent him from being born. He'll be gone. Like he never existed at all."

Silence follows. Then La'Tasha releases a sharp breath. "Shit. We should have talked to you first. Before sending him back."

"He doesn't know to watch for him. To protect himself." My voice snaps before I rein it in. "Look, I'm sorry. It's just... he's in danger. Real danger."

"He knew there would be risks." Dex speaks evenly, steady as a stone in a stream. "He chose to take them anyway."

"For me." The words scrape out of me. "He risked everything for me."

"That's what love does." La'Tasha says it plainly, letting the truth sit there.

Love. The word catches me off guard. Is that what this is? We barely know each other. But maybe that doesn't matter.

"Are there others in the Concord like you? Bound against their will?" Dex asks.

I nod instinctively. "Yes. There are four others. Brother Ash,

The Painted Lady, The Neon Revenant, and The Oracle of Chains. All of us trapped. All of us wanting out."

"Can you contact them?" La'Tasha asks. "Without the other Concord members knowing? If we can connect with them, maybe we can use them to our advantage."

"I'm one step ahead of you. I've been thinking about this for days. I've been planning to reach out to them, but until today I've been under lock and key. I can send messages through water. It's how the four of us communicate. The Concord isn't always watching."

"We need them to be ready." La'Tasha's words come out quick and clipped. "If Calvin succeeds, there will be a moment of weakness. A crack in their armor. If your allies are prepared, they might be able to break free too."

Hope flares inside me. Not just for me, but for all of us trapped in the Concord's web. "I'll try to reach them tonight. Tell them to be ready."

"Is there a way they can contact us? If Calvin is successful and he is able to bring you forward with him, you'll no longer be connected to the Concord and we'll lose our inside man. We need to be able to connect with the others somehow. We need to be able to help them."

I think about each of my fellow prisoners. Their abilities. Their connections to the world. "Look for signs. Esme works through paintings. Images that shift, words hidden in brushstrokes. Brother Ash speaks through fire."

"Fire?" La'Tasha asks.

"Yes. Candle flames dancing when there's no wind. Campfires forming shapes." I continue down the list. "Adrian uses electricity. Flickering lights, neon signs spelling messages. And Seraphine…" I pause. "Dreams and weather. Wind and thunder."

"We'll watch for them." La'Tasha says.

"Thank you…" I hesitate, then push forward. "For doing this for me. When I was alive… no one would have done what you are doing for me now. I was so alone. I can't thank you enough."

There's so much more I want to say. Thank you for remembering me. For thinking I'm worth saving.

"Hopefully, the next time we see you, you'll be running through that door with Calvin." La'Tasha says. "We should go. The spell won't last much longer, and we don't want to draw attention."

"Thank you, Everett." Dex adds.

I hear their footsteps retreating. The dock creaks under their invisible weight. Car doors open and close. An engine starts. Headlights flash once, like a final goodbye. Then they're gone, leaving me alone with the lake and the stars and a dangerous, beautiful hope burning in my empty chest.

I don't waste time. I float to the center of the lake and sink until I'm hovering just above the surface. The black water gleams inches below the ice. I place my hands on the surface, feeling the cool resistance. I may not have a body, but I can still interact with water. Part of my binding. Part of my curse. But for once, I can use it for something good.

I push my consciousness down through frozen layers and into liquid darkness. It spreads like ink, carrying fragments of thought. Images instead of words: Calvin. The door. La'Tasha. Rebellion. Freedom.

Be ready, I send. *If this works, we'll have our chance.*

The lake carries my message away, following the underground streams and rivers that connect to other bodies of water. To the abandoned asylum where Esme sits. To the old church where Brother Ash is bound. To the neon-lit bar that holds Adrian. To the mines where Seraphine, the most powerful of all of us, is locked up.

I wait for what feels like hours, though time moves differently for the dead. Finally, responses trickle back through the water. Not words. Feelings. Acknowledgment. Agreement.

Hope.

They're ready. We're ready.

Now it's all up to Calvin.

I look up at the stars, wondering if he's seeing them right now, in a time before I died. Before everything went wrong.

"Be careful." I whisper to the night. "Come back to me."

The wind whips around me, carrying my words away like a prayer.

1958

CHAPTER SIXTEEN

Calvin

I plunge through the portal, half convinced I'll just end up somewhere in the '90s dressed like someone from the '50s. My pulse hammers as the world twists, stretches, and folds. Colors blur like wet paint. Sounds fade then swell like a badly tuned radio. This didn't happen before. It's taking much longer than it did the other times I tried this.

Then everything stops.

Nausea churns through me in waves, my stomach still catching up.

Well that's new.

I focus on breathing through my nose. I dig my fingernails into my palms, the sharp pressure anchoring me.

Focus, Calvin. You can freak out later. Right now, you need to remember every single detail so you can find your way back.

I drag in a breath and scan the space around me. It appears I'm in a shed. It's dark, dusty, and full of cobwebs. Shelves sag under the weight of large boxes. Thin beams of sunlight slice through the slats. Dust motes dance in the light.

I press a hand against a wooden beam to steady myself, the rough surface grounding me in this new reality. When the world stops spinning, I peek through a gap in the wooden planks. Outside is an alley I don't recognize, backing up to a brick wall. Interesting. All the other times it dumped me out facing Main Street.

The door creaks when I push it open, making me wince. But no one comes running. The alley is empty except for a mangy cat that gives me a disinterested glance before slinking away. I step out, my boots crunching on gravel. The air is thick with summer heat, nothing like the February I just left.

Holy shit. I think I actually did it.

Only one way to be sure. I hoist my backpack over my shoulder and pick up my duffel bag. I edge down the alley, committing every detail to memory. I take a forced right down another alley. After a few more feet it spits me out onto a street that can only be Main. So it dumped me out behind the building this time instead of in front of it. Interesting.

I blink against the late afternoon sun. Main Street sprawls out in either direction, looking wider and more open than usual. It takes me a second to process it. The way the town seems to breathe around me. I stand there feeling exposed, clutching my bags like a drifter who just rolled off a freight train, trying to make sense of the view without looking like I'm having a stroke.

The geography is right—I know these bones—but the skin of the town is completely different. No potholes. No faded paint. The asphalt gleams black as oil, white parking lines crisp and unbroken.

Storefronts glow with fresh paint and polished windows. Signs hang straight, colors bright and unfaded. The sidewalk runs smooth beneath my feet, unmarred by the occasional tree-root buckles I know.

Museum-worthy cars cruise past at leisurely speeds, their

chrome flashing in the sun like jewelry. A Chevy Bel Air and a Thunderbird convertible with the top down glide by, purring, powerful and new.

A truck rumbles past, its engine deep and throaty. The exhaust smell is sharp and chemical, causing me to cough. I'm breathing in what's probably pure lead. Who needs lungs anyway?

A woman pushes a baby carriage past me, wheels squeaking. The carriage is massive, built like a small car with springs and chrome accents. The woman nods at me as she passes, and I nod back, trying not to stare at her dress with its impossible waist and thin belt.

Men in fedoras and suits stride down the sidewalk despite the heat. A paperboy on a bicycle weaves through pedestrians, yelling about something called the Explorer 1 satellite.

We did it.

My mouth hangs open like a tourist. I probably look suspicious as hell.

I turn down Main and head toward Briarwood. The street layout stays the same, but the buildings have changed. I make note of the building the shed was behind. It's a hardware store with a hand-painted sign announcing Hillman's Housewares. Through the window I can see displays of toasters and blenders that look like props from a retro sci-fi movie. In my time this is the Once Upon a Tome bookstore.

On the other side of the street is a park that doesn't exist in the future. Children spin on a merry-go-round in the center, their laughter carrying across the street. Metal screeches against metal as they push it faster, faster, until the whole thing becomes a blur of summer clothes and flailing limbs. A boy flies off the edge, tumbles into the dirt, and gets right back up, grinning.

A woman walking by gives me a strange look. I realize I've been standing here staring like an idiot. I force myself to keep moving, trying to look like I belong here. Not sure it's working.

I walk to the end of the block and then turn the corner onto

Briarwood and pause when I see The Blue Moon Apothecary.

The structure is the same, but the ivy that blankets it in my time is just beginning to climb. The sign above the door is hand-painted with stars and moons. Flowers in window boxes spill over the sides, bright and cheerful in the summer sun. The colors vibrate in the sunlight, purples and whites and pinks so bright they almost hurt to look at.

The door to the apothecary stands open, propped with a brass doorstop shaped like a cat. Cool air drifts out, carrying scents of dried herbs and spices. Through the doorway, I catch a glimpse of shelves lined with glass bottles and ceramic jars.

A middle-aged man carrying a small paper bag emerges. He tips his hat to someone inside, calls out a cheerful "Good day, Mrs. Thornton," and continues down the street. Mrs. Thornton. Hazel's great-grandmother? Another piece of the past clicking into place.

Across the street, where the Midnight Stack restaurant should be, stands a building with a neon sign announcing Moonridge Diner. Outside, carhops on roller skates weave between parked cars, taking orders and delivering food on trays. I watch mesmerized until the sound of footsteps catches my ear.

Two young women pause across the street in front of the diner, bags in hand, talking in low voices. Air stutters in my lungs. One of them is unmistakably Agnes Thornton. But not the gray-haired, wise elder I once knew. A young woman barely out of her teens. She's tiny and fierce-looking even now. She wears a sleeveless button-front blouse tucked into high-waisted pedal pushers in pale yellow and white canvas sneakers. Her dark red hair is pulled back in a ponytail.

The young raven-haired woman with her wears a black scoop-neck top tucked into a high-waisted pencil skirt in cherry red. She turns so I can see her face, and my stomach falls out of my ass.

Ravena.

I want to run. This Ravena doesn't know me. But seeing her

hawkish face behind those red cat-eye glasses sends a prickle of heat over my skin.

They begin to cross the street, and I kneel down and pretend to tie my boot. I can't help but eavesdrop on their conversation.

"...I told her I don't want it." Agnes's words come clipped. "I'm not ready to spend my whole life running that store and playing the part of head witch of Moonridge."

Ravena lets out a low laugh. "Not ready, or not willing?"

"I want to travel," Agnes says. "Maybe attend college overseas like Lois Randall. There's a whole world out there beyond Moonridge."

"You'd leave all this behind?" Ravena's voice drips sugar, her eyes staying flat and hard. "Your family, your power?"

"It's what everyone expects me to want," Agnes says. "Stay in Moonridge. Take over as Virtus Suprema. Run the coven because that's what the women in my family have always done. I want more."

"But we need you," Ravena says, her voice lacking conviction. They pause outside the apothecary, less than ten feet from me.

"You could always do it. My mother likes you better than me anyway."

Ravena's smile stretches too wide, too polished. "Don't be silly," she says. "Your mother loves you. And the position is rightfully yours."

Her words land like a promise I know she plans to break.

That's when Ravena's head tilts, eyes narrowing as she studies me. "Are you okay over there? You've been crouched down for a long time."

I stand so fast I nearly lose my balance. My heart feels like it's trying to kick out of my chest.

"I, uh..." My voice cracks like I'm thirteen. "Just tying my boot lace."

Get it together, dummy.

"And I'm kind of lost. New in town."

"I could tell." Agnes studies me. "You look like you've never seen people before."

"Where are you from?" Ravena asks, voice like honey though I can't help but taste the vinegar at the edges.

"Michigan," I say, clinging to the backstory La'Tasha and I built. "Just arrived in town. Looking for work."

I'm a horrible liar and the words seem to hit the air wrong, but they don't seem to notice.

Agnes tilts her head, frowning. "Are you sure we haven't met? You seem… familiar somehow."

Oh crap. I stretch my mouth into what I hope passes for a casual smile. "Pretty sure I'd remember meeting you."

Agnes stares through me. The moment stretches a beat too long before she turns to Ravena. "We should probably get going. Mother wants those herbs before dinner."

Ravena lingers, still watching me. "Maybe we'll see you around," she says.

"Yeah," I say. My tongue feels thick. "But first, maybe you can help me. I'm looking for a place to stay. Maybe a job."

"The Moonridge Inn up on Maple Street usually has rooms," Ravena offers. "As for jobs, I think Mr. Randall's auto shop was looking for help. He put a sign in the window yesterday. And the diner is always looking for bus boys and car hops."

The auto shop, huh? How convenient. That would definitely get me closer to Everett.

"Thanks." The word comes out thin. "I'll check them out."

Agnes's eyes narrow again. "There's something about you. Something urgent. It's like you have a tangled thread around your heart. Are you sure you're okay?"

A chill licks the back of my neck. How do I respond to that?

I glance away, toward the apothecary. "It's complicated."

Ravena rolls her eyes. "Don't mind her. She's always seeing things."

"Well, have a good night," Agnes says, giving me a quick

wave as they walk up the apothecary steps. "See you around."

They continue up the steps, heads bent together in conversation. Two women who have no idea what's coming. That one will give everything to protect the town. That the other will try to destroy it.

I force myself forward, shaking off the weight of their futures. La'Tasha's map crinkles in my pocket as I make a left onto Overlook Street. Auto shop on the right, she'd said. Half a block past Town Square at Overlook and Elm.

And there it is. Randall Auto Repair.

The building is smaller than I expected, but neat and well-maintained. There are two gas pumps out front and three bays to the right of the main entrance. My steps slow as I take it in.

A car sits in the largest bay with its hood up. All I can see of the person working on it are a pair of legs in oil-stained coveralls.

The hood slams shut with a definitive clang. He turns and I gasp when I see his face.

Everett.

The world narrows to just him.

He slams the hood shut and pats it twice, satisfied. He grabs a rag from his back pocket and drags it across his forehead, wiping away the sweat. He unzips his coveralls and drops the top so it hangs around his waist. Even from across the street I can see the way his shirt clings to his frame. He's lean and wiry, several inches shorter than me, maybe 5'10" to my 6'2", and something about that hits me sideways. I could pull him against my chest. He'd fit perfectly there, tucked under my chin. I can almost feel it—the weight of him in my arms, the warmth of his body pressed to mine. Long nights on the couch, his head on my shoulder. Morning light filtering through curtains while we're still tangled together.

God, what I wouldn't give.

He reaches for a soda bottle sitting on the workbench, tips his head back, and takes a long drink. His throat works as he swallows. Blonde hair falls across his forehead when he lowers the bottle, and he swipes it back.

It's really him. Alive in a way I've never seen him before.

He glances toward the street.

Our eyes meet.

For a moment, neither of us moves. Something flickers across his face. Curiosity maybe, or concern. The look you give a stranger who's been watching you too long.

Because that's what I am to him. A stranger. He has no idea who I am. No memory of me, of us, of anything that hasn't happened yet.

Then he smiles. Shy, uncertain. He raises his hand in a small wave.

I wave back, my arm on autopilot. I should go over. Introduce myself. Instead I stay rooted to the sidewalk, tongue glued to the roof of my mouth. Not yet. I need to get my bearings.

I force my legs to move. I need distance from the shop, so I look the other way and move quickly, refusing to glance back to see if he's watching me.

I turn the corner onto Maple and my shoulders finally drop. I make my way to the end of the street and the long, circular drive leading to what's now known as The Moonridge Inn. The B&B sits where it always has, though it looks much different. The paint runs yellow instead of blue. The porch is crowded with rocking chairs and hanging ferns. A hand-painted sign proclaims "Vacancy" in flowing script.

Perfect.

The screen door creaks as I push it open. A plump woman with kind eyes looks up from behind a small desk, her face brightening with a welcoming smile. It takes me by surprise because I'm expecting to see Mina, but she hasn't even been born yet.

"Well, hello there, young man! How can I help you?"

I put on my most charming smile. "Hi, ma'am. Just arrived in town. Name's Calvin… Mitchell. I noticed the vacancy sign out front. I'll be here for a few days and could use a nice place to stay." The false name feels strange on my tongue, but using my real surname seems too risky. Especially since Carters have lived in Moonridge since it was settled.

"We've got a lovely room on the second floor available." She reaches for a large book. "How long will you be staying with us?"

Four days. That's all I have. Four days to save Everett.

"Not sure yet." I keep my voice casual. "I'm looking to relocate. Thought I might look for work while I'm here and see if it feels like the right fit for me."

I unconsciously reach for my phone to check the time before remembering where I am. When I am. I cover by patting my pocket like I'm looking for my wallet.

She beams. "Well, you've come to the right place. Moonridge is just the sweetest little town. I'm sure you'll want to stay."

If only she knew.

"I'll take the room." I pull out the cash La'Tasha helped glamour to look like period-appropriate bills. They feel wrong in my hands. Too thick. Too textured. I hand them over, trying not to look at them too closely, hoping the glamour holds.

As she handles the paperwork, I glance out the window at the summer evening beyond. The mission starts now. Tomorrow, I'll go back to the auto shop. I'll introduce myself to Everett for real. I'll start building the trust I need to eventually tell him the truth.

"Welcome to Moonridge, Mr. Mitchell. My name is Loretta. Loretta Fredericks. I hope you enjoy your stay."

"I'm sure I will."

I smile and take the key.

Here we go.

CHAPTER SEVENTEEN

Everett

The strawberry milkshake sweats on the counter while I drag my straw through the melting whipped cream. The diner buzzes with Wednesday night noise; silverware clinks, the jukebox croons, and Betty's gum snaps from across the way as she refills coffee.

I'm not sure why I stopped in tonight. Probably needed a break from Vince and whatever mood he's in today. Or maybe I just wanted five minutes where I didn't have to be anyone but myself.

Then the bell above the door jingles, and being alone is the last thing on my mind.

It's him. The guy from earlier. Tall, broad shoulders. Dark hair. Strong jaw. White T-shirt stretched across his chest in a way that makes my heart slam against my ribs.

He turns to scan the diner, and I get a perfect view of what might be the finest backside I've ever seen. Those Levi's are doing the Lord's work.

My eyes drop back to my milkshake. I sneak another glance. Something about him pricks at my senses. The way he moves, confident but cautious, all coiled awareness. The slight flare of his nostrils as he takes in scents. Werewolf. Has to be. But not from any pack I know around here.

He turns, and our eyes lock. My stomach lurches. He smiles, easy as anything, and I look away again, eyes back on the whipped cream melting in my glass.

The next thing I know he's walking toward me. Straight toward me, purposeful and direct. I hunch over the milkshake, fingers tight around the cold glass.

"Mind if I take this seat?" He points to the empty stool next to mine.

His voice is deep and warm. I grab my milkshake so I have something to do with my hands. "Sure thing."

"Thanks." He slides onto the stool, and his scent hits me. Definitely werewolf, threaded with soap and fresh-cut pine.

Betty swoops in, coffeepot in hand. "What can I get you, handsome?"

"Coffee and whatever pie smells so good."

Betty beams at him. "Apple. Just baked it this afternoon." She winks before hurrying off.

He turns to me, extends his hand. "I'm Calvin. Calvin Mitchell."

I wipe my palm on my jeans, then take his hand. His grip is firm, warm. His hands are surprisingly soft and clean for a wolf. I wince at the grease stains on mine. "Everett Bradshaw."

"Nice to meet you, Everett." The way he says my name makes something flutter in my chest. "I think I saw you working at the garage today?"

I shrug. "Possibly. I'm a mechanic at Randall Auto Repair." I take a sip of my milkshake so I have something to do. My knee bounces under the counter as the conversation lags.

I clear my throat. "You new in town? Don't think I've seen you around before."

"Just got into Moonridge today. I'm from Michigan originally." His coffee arrives, and he adds a splash of cream. "Left home looking for a fresh start, you know? Heard good things about this place."

"Moonridge is alright. Small, but it grows on you." Like fungus sometimes, but it's better than where I came from.

Betty appears with a plate of apple pie, setting it in front of Calvin with a warm smile. "Here you go, hon. Still warm from the oven." She refills my water glass without asking and bustles away.

Calvin picks up his fork, cutting into the pie. Steam rises from the filling. "I'm hoping to find work. Maybe a place to settle for a while." He takes a bite, his eyes closing briefly. When he looks at me again, it feels like he touches my soul. His eyes are brown, deep and steady. "Been a bit of a drifter, but I'm getting tired of moving around."

I know that feeling too well. I lean forward, elbows on the counter. "The garage might be hiring. Mr. Randall mentioned needing another pair of hands if you know anything about cars."

"Really? That's..." His smile sparks across his whole face, bright and sudden. "That would be perfect. I'm actually very good with cars. And construction."

I've always struggled with small talk, but I want to keep this conversation going. I don't want him to get bored and walk off. But I also can't sound like I've been thinking about him since this afternoon... even though I have. That spark when our eyes met hit me so hard I almost chased him down right then, desperate to learn everything about him.

"What made you pick Moonridge?" I finally ask.

He shrugs. "Heard it was a good town. Peaceful. Thought it might be a place I could finally stay put for a while." He takes a bite of pie. "What about you? How long have you been here?"

"About ten months now. Came here last August."

"Family here?"

I shake my head. "No family. Not anymore. Just me."

"Same here," he says quietly.

The door jingles again. My grip tightens on the milkshake glass. Part of the wolf pack strides in, with Vince right in the middle even though he's not a wolf. He just likes to act like one. Sam Carter, just home from college, leads the group, his leather jacket gleaming under the fluorescent lights. He spots me and waves. I wave back.

"Friends of yours?" he asks.

"Something like that."

The pack descends before I can say more. Voices overlap, shoulders bump mine. Sam claps me on the shoulder. "Everett! Thought you were busy tonight?"

"Just grabbing a quick bite."

Vince's stare finds me. Heat crawls up the side of my neck. He doesn't say anything, but his jaw clenches tight enough to crack teeth.

Sam notices Calvin and extends his hand. "Sam Carter. A friend of Everett's."

"Calvin Mitchell." Calvin shakes Sam's hand. His gaze flicks over the group, taking them in one by one. "I'm new in town."

"Where you from, Mitchell?" Vince rolls a toothpick between his teeth, each word clipped.

"Michigan originally. Been traveling around a bit."

Vince cuts his eyes toward me, toothpick angled like a warning. "This guy bothering you, Ev?"

"Not at all." The answer jumps out of me. "We were talking."

Sam leans against the counter, arms crossed. "You got a certain smell about you. Wolf, right?"

Calvin doesn't even flinch. "Good nose. Yeah, I am."

The pack trades looks. Sam straightens, shoulders back like he has to be taller than everyone else. "What pack?"

"No pack." Calvin matches his posture. Not aggressive, not backing down either. "I was adopted. Never knew my real family. Didn't have my first shift until I was twenty-two. Been on my own for a few years now."

"Late bloomer, huh?" Sam's mouth twists. "Looking to join up with someone?"

"Maybe. If I find the right fit. Not sure how long I'll be in town."

"We've got pretty strict rules about who runs with our pack." Sam tilts his head, studying Calvin. "Not just any stray can walk in."

I wince. Calvin just nods. "Understood." He turns to me. "Are you part of the pack?"

"I'm not a werewolf." I drum my fingers on the counter. "I'm a hybrid shifter. Can change into different animals. People too, if I know them well enough."

Stop talking.

Calvin's eyebrows lift. "Really? That's impressive."

"The pack was kind enough to let me hang around." I leave out the part about rolling into town with a duffel bag and nowhere else to land after exhausting ten other towns over the last nine years. Vince stepped in and provided what I needed. The rest of them saw a quiet guy with a Southern accent and figured that was the whole story.

"Shifters are rare." Sam gives me a quick grin. "Everett's special."

Vince steps forward, pulls out his wallet, and slaps some cash on the counter. "That should cover your shake." His mouth tightens around the words. "How about we get out of here."

I glance at the milkshake, more melted than anything now, then at Calvin, who watches Vince with sharp, measuring eyes. I could tell Vince I'm staying. I could stay here, keep talking, pretend this night belongs to me.

I slide off the stool instead. "Nice to meet you, Calvin." I clear my throat. "Maybe I'll see you around the garage."

"I hope so." The answer comes quick, no hesitation, and my heart flips. "I'll swing by tomorrow, check on that job."

I smile before I can stop it.

Vince's hand finds the small of my back, fingers pressing just a little too firm as he steers me toward the door. I offer Calvin a smile and a nod, then let myself be guided outside. I shouldn't look back.

I look back anyway.

Calvin is still watching me, expression unreadable in the diner light.

Vince stays silent. The set of his shoulders and the tight pull of his mouth say enough. He spits out his toothpick and immediately reaches for a cigarette. I trail him to his car and climb in. The cool night air brushes my cheeks before the door shuts me in with the smell of stale smoke and Vince's too-strong cologne.

He yanks the driver's side door open and slams it shut after climbing in. The engine growls to life.

"So." Vince finally speaks as we pull away from the curb. "Want to tell me why you were cozying up to that drifter?"

"I wasn't cozying up to anyone." I stare out the window at the darkened storefronts of Main Street sliding by. My fingers worry at a loose thread on the seat. "He sat next to me and we talked. That's it."

Vince snorts. "You think I'm stupid? I saw how you were looking at him. You're attracted to him. You want him because he's a wolf, don't ya? I know how you crave guys with power. You don't have a use for unlit like me."

How was I looking at him? I have no idea. Whatever Vince saw, though, I'll pay for it.

"He's new in town." I keep my focus on what's happening behind the window. "I was being friendly."

"Friendly." The word comes out like a pit he wants me to fall into. His knuckles whiten on the steering wheel. "Is he like us?"

"I…" Is he? "I don't know. I don't think so."

"So you didn't tell him about us being queer?"

Us. The version of us that only exists where no one can see.

"Why would I? It's no one's business. And there's nothing

to tell." I mutter it, watching the town lights thin out. Trees take over, taller and darker, the road narrowing. I know where we're headed now. Skipper Lake. Our usual spot.

The paved road gives way to dirt. The car bounces over potholes, jostling us together then apart. Each bump rattles my teeth. My hands curl into fists in my lap. When we reach the clearing, Vince cuts the engine and the headlights. Darkness pours in. Through the windshield, a slice of moonlight glints on the water.

Vince turns to me in the dark. I can't see his face clearly, but his gaze drags over me. The hairs on my arms lift.

"So this Calvin guy." His voice has a soft edge that makes my stomach knot. "What did you two talk about?"

"Nothing much. He's from Michigan. Looking for work." I shrug. "I told him Mr. Randall might be hiring."

"So he'll be at the garage."

"Maybe."

Vince shifts closer on the bench seat. His hand lands on my thigh. "And you'd like that, wouldn't you?" His fingers tighten.

I swallow. "He seemed nice."

"Nice." His grip bruises. "And what am I?"

"You're you." The words scrape on the way out. "My... fella."

He laughs once, low and empty. "You're a terrible liar, Ev."

His fingers slide up to my cheek, rough palm against my skin. I flinch before I can stop myself.

"Why are you so jumpy?" He stares at me with eyes so dark they swallow the moonlight. A lock of hair curls across his forehead as he runs his thumb over my bottom lip. He leans in, his mouth finding mine in the dark. The kiss is rough, all teeth and force. His stubble scrapes my skin as he moves to my neck, biting hard enough to make me wince. I let him.

I always let him.

His hands push under my shirt, cold against my warm skin. "You like this stranger? This Calvin?"

"I just met him." I gasp as his teeth find my earlobe.

His breath is hot against my ear. "But you want him."

I don't answer. My throat locks around the truth I can't hand him. Vince takes my silence as enough. His grip tightens. His teeth sink harder. He yanks me closer, dragging me against him.

"You know what I want." He whispers at my ear. "Shift."

His fingers dig into my hips.

"Please, Vince." The words scrape out thin. "Not tonight."

"Yes, tonight. Don't pretend you're too good for this now."

I'm not too good. I'm just tired. Tired of being anyone except myself whenever he touches me.

His mouth crashes against mine again, hands roaming, claiming. My body goes heavy. My jaw clenches.

"Who do you want me to be tonight?" I ask, the fight slipping out of me.

"Sam," he says without hesitation.

Of course it's Sam. It always is.

I knew Vince had a thing for him the first time I saw them together. The way Vince leaned in whenever Sam spoke, hanging on every word like it was gospel. How his whole face lit up when Sam asked him to go somewhere with him. And the flip side—how his jaw would tighten when Sam bragged about some girl he was chasing, or worse, when he'd openly flirt with women right in front of us. That sharp, bitter edge that would creep into Vince's voice.

It wasn't subtle. At least not to me.

Vince wants Sam. But Sam's into women, and Vince can't compete with that.

With my shifting ability, he can almost have him.

I drag in a breath and look past Vince to the faint shimmer of the lake through the window. Heat gathers under my skin, prickling, restless. My features loosen, edges blurring. I picture Sam Carter. His square jaw. Dark hair. The cleft in his chin. The way his eyes crinkle when he laughs.

The change rushes through me in a sick, smooth wave. Bone

and skin slide into new shapes. It feels like being wiped away, layer by layer. The glass in front of us catches a ghost of reflection; Sam's face stares back where mine should be.

I look away.

Vince's eyes gleam in the dark. "Perfect." He immediately grows hard beneath me as his hands roam over arms that aren't mine, placing kisses across a jawline I borrowed.

He pulls off my shirt and I fix my gaze on the lake. Moonlight skips across the surface in thin broken lines. Crickets sing in the trees. The glass fogs with our breath. Vince whispers Sam's name against my borrowed throat.

Calvin's face flashes in my mind. His smile. The steady way he listened. The way he looked at me like I was someone worth seeing.

Something Vince has never done.

CHAPTER EIGHTEEN

Calvin

I sit up and the bed protests with the creak of real springs instead of memory foam. The disorientation only lasts a few seconds before reality crashes in. La'Tasha's pendant lies warm and heavy against my skin—my only connection to home. To the time I need to get back to as quickly as possible.

The floorboards are cold beneath my bare feet as I cross to the tiny mint-green bathroom and shock myself awake with a splash of cold water to the face. I brush my teeth with the weird-tasting toothpaste I bought yesterday, and meet my own bare-faced reflection in the mirror.

"You got this."

After a quick shower, I pull on a plain white T-shirt, jeans with the cuffs rolled just right, white socks, black boots, and my leather jacket. I look like I belong. Now if I can just act like it.

I study my reflection, smooth my pomaded hair, and practice a casual smile that doesn't look like I'm about to rob the place. The smell of bacon and coffee drifts up from downstairs and my stomach complains like I skipped three meals. I pocket the small wad of La'Tasha-glamored cash and head down to eat.

Sunlight pours into the dining room and gives the yellow wallpaper a soft glow. White tablecloths brighten the space and give it that tidy late-1950s charm. A few guests sit scattered at the tables. Mrs. Fredericks moves among them, coffee pot in hand, chatting with them like they're old friends.

"Good morning, young man!" She beams when she sees me. "Sleep well?"

I sit at the empty table by the window. "Yes, ma'am. Thank you."

"Coffee?" She starts to pour before I answer.

"Please." The cup is delicate, nothing like the chunky mugs I'm used to. The brew is a little weak, but hot and welcome. I almost ask for almond milk before catching myself. That doesn't exist yet. Neither does oat milk. Or half the things I normally eat. Another reminder to watch myself.

"Breakfast is flapjacks and bacon today." She beams at me. "Orange juice fresh-squeezed. My husband picked the oranges from our tree out back just this morning."

"Sounds great."

While she heads back to the kitchen, I sip my coffee and watch the room. An older couple sits at the far table, both reading sections of a newspaper. The headlines are all events I vaguely remember from history class. A young woman sits alone at another table, writing in a small notebook. She glances up, catches me looking, and offers a small smile before returning to her writing.

Mrs. Fredericks returns with a plate piled high with pancakes and bacon. The food is incredible. Real butter, real maple syrup, and thick-cut bacon greasy enough to clog my arteries. By the time she comes back to check on me, the plate is bare.

"My goodness, you were hungry!" Mrs. Fredericks laughs as she refills my coffee. "Strong man like you needs his strength, I guess."

I smile and nod. "That totally slapped. Thank you."

"Slapped?" The look on her face makes me realize my blunder. "You young folks sure do have a funny way with words."

"Pardon me. I meant it was delicious. Thank you."

Keep the 2020s slang in check, dipshit.

"What brings you to Moonridge?" She gathers my plates and silverware. "Just passing through, you said?"

I nod, sticking to my cover story. "Not sure how long I'll be staying. Looking for work, though. I'm good with my hands. Carpentry, auto repair. Whatever needs doing."

"Well, you're in luck. The hardware store on Main is hiring, and Earl Randall's looking for help at his auto shop." She leans forward. "His son Jeff is off gallivanting somewhere with his motorcycle gang. Hasn't been home in months. And with their daughter Lois studying abroad, poor Earl and Viola are stuck here. They can't visit her because he can't leave the garage."

My heart drops a little when I realize I likely won't get a chance to meet my grandmother or great-uncle while I'm here.

"I'll check out the garage. Thanks for the tip."

"You know we have our big Fourth of July celebration coming up in a few weeks. Definitely don't want to miss that if you're still in town." She pulls a rag from her apron and wipes down the next table. "Parade down Main Street, carnival in the park, fireworks and dancing under the stars. The whole town turns out."

"Sounds fun."

"Oh, it's the highlight of the year." Mrs. Fredericks's eyes light up as she talks, her hands never stopping their work. "We always have all kinds of home crafts and produce and the witches always sell their remedies and tonics. If anything ails you, the Thorntons can fix you right up at the apothecary. Best herbal teas in three counties."

"I'll remember that."

"And the Randalls sponsor the pie-eating contest every year. Viola makes the best cherry pie you ever tasted." She moves to another table, straightening already-straight napkins. "And the local wolves always sponsor some kind of ropes course for the kids."

"Anything else I should know about Moonridge? I want to fit in, you know?"

"Well, let's see." She pours herself a cup of coffee and settles into the chair across from me like she's about to give me all the gossip. "There's the Moonridge Women's Club over on Juniper. They organize every bake sale, parade, and scandal this town's cooked up since '32, and they know everyone's business before it happens." She grins. "Moonridge folks are friendly. And a little nosy."

She takes another sip of her coffee. "Moonridge Diner on Main, makes the best milkshakes you'll ever taste. Flo Bailey runs it with her sister Betty. Great women, though Betty has a few screws loose if you know what I mean. They're open until ten most nights, midnight on Fridays and Saturdays. Good place to meet people." She winks. "Lots of pretty girls come through there."

I force a smile. If she only knew…

"Any people or places I should stay away from?" Any clues she can give me into who's shady and who's not will be helpful.

She pauses just long enough to make sure I'm listening, then lowers her voice. "Now, Skipper Lake… that's an interesting place. It's frequented by the local werewolf pack. They've kind of claimed it as theirs, but the teens like to go up there and raise hell—pardon my language—now and then. It's mostly harmless, but lately folks've been whispering about odd things out there. Some kids claimed to see people in long robes wandering around after midnight. It's not the witches because they tend to prefer Amethyst Beach on the other side of town. Kids also claim to have seen phantom smoke and fires. There one minute and gone the next. And the lights." She shakes her head. "Strange colors moving across the sky. Not stars. Not lightning. Something else entirely. Sheriff says it's just the kids causing mischief, but between you and me, I think there might be something going on up there. I'd stay away if I were you."

"Skipper Lake," I repeat, fingers tightening around my cup. "Thanks for the tip."

"Well." She pats my hand and stands, gathering her coffee cup. "I'll let you go on and see about that job. Tell Earl I sent you. He's a good man, fair employer. He'll treat you right."

I push back from the table, thank Mrs. Fredericks, and step outside into the bright June sunshine.

Maple Street stretches before me, impossibly new and old at the same time. I walk toward town center, head down, trying not to stare. Kids race past on bicycles, playing cards clothespinned to the spokes. The sound is like tiny motorcycles.

I stop at the intersection of Cedar Drive and Main. There's my house. Except it's not mine yet. Won't be for decades.

The bones are the same: the porch, the basic structure, the little sapling that will become my massive oak. No sage green paint, no garden beds, no sign of my life here yet. My great-grandparents are behind those walls right now, living their day with no idea their great-grandson is standing outside, staring like a creep.

"Hey, Michigan! Good morning!"

I drag my gaze away from the house and find Agnes Thornton waving at me from across the street. She looks fresh and pretty in a green sundress, her red hair pulled back with a matching ribbon.

I cross to meet her. "Morning."

"Settling in all right?" She smiles.

"As much as I can." I stuff my hands in my pockets.

"I'm sorry. I forgot your actual name. I'm Agnes."

I take the hand she offers. "Calvin. Pleasure to meet you. Again."

"Likewise." I see hints of Hazel in her smile. "What are you up to this morning?"

"Just headed to the garage to see about that job."

"Oh, Earl's looking for help, that's for sure." She nods toward the house I was just staring at. "That's where he lives, actually."

I point at my future home. "Right there?"

"Yes, with his wife Viola. Their daughter, Lois, is overseas so she's not here now, and who knows where their older son Jeff is, but they rent a spare room to Everett Bradshaw. He works at the garage, too."

A car engine growls behind us. A sleek white Chrysler pulls up to the curb in front of the Randall house. The passenger door opens and Everett climbs out.

Every nerve in my body snaps awake.

He wears yesterday's clothes, wrinkled now. His hair is mussed, and even from here I can see the dark circles under his eyes. He looks exhausted. Haunted. His shoulders curve inward, like he's trying to take up less space.

Vince says something to him, and Everett's whole body flinches. He nods, his shoulders slumping further. He turns and walks into the house without looking back, steps heavy. Each movement seems to cost him something.

Vince watches him go, his expression impossible to read. Something flickers across his face. Possession? Satisfaction? Then he drives off with a squeal of tires that makes Agnes shake her head.

"That poor boy," Agnes says softly.

"Everett?"

Agnes nods. "People say he's... you know. Different." She gives me a significant look. "And that's fine in Moonridge. We're not like other towns. But Vince Franelli... He's something else." Her expression darkens.

"What about him?"

"Vince thinks he's fooling everyone, but we all know he likes men too. I mean he's twenty-four and never had a girlfriend." She shakes her head. "He just has to be extra careful because his father is rich as sin and would disown him if he learned it was true. Vince wouldn't be able to live without daddy's money. I can't say for sure, but I get the feeling he doesn't treat Everett well."

"What do you know about him? Everett, I mean."

"Not a lot. Nice enough fella," Agnes says. "He showed up about ten months ago. Keeps to himself mostly. Friendly enough when you talk to him, but there's a weight around him I can feel."

"What do you mean?"

She taps her temple. "I can sense things. Feelings. Not thoughts, just... emotions. And his are all tied up in knots. Like a tangled ball of yarn that can't be undone."

"Anything else I should know about him?"

"What are you, some sort of detective or something?"

I chuckle and shake my head. "No, I met him yesterday. He seems like a nice guy. And I get what you mean about Vince. He seemed controlling. I find him a little suspicious."

"Vince is drawn to people with special abilities. He's unlit."

"Unlit?" Never heard that term before. Must be a 1950s thing.

She waves her hand in front of her face and laughs. "Sorry. It's what we call humans with no powers around here."

I smile. "I like it."

"But he thinks he's tough." Agnes sniffs. "Runs with Sam Randall's pack. They let him hang around because he buys them things, I think." She narrows her eyes. "You're a wolf, too, aren't you?"

My eyebrows shoot up. "How did you know?"

She smiles, tapping her nose. "I can smell it on you. Different from our local pack, though."

Before I can respond, a car door slams. Earl Randall backs out of his driveway in a sensible blue sedan. He's heading to the garage, I'm guessing.

"There he goes." Agnes nods in the direction of the retreating car. "If you want that job, now's your chance."

"Right." I hesitate, torn between wanting more information and needing to follow through on my plan. "Thanks for the talk."

"Oh, hey…" Agnes catches my arm as I turn to go. Her eyes widen. Something like fear crosses her face. Her grip tightens, and warmth pulses where her fingers touch my skin, like she's pulling something out of me. "I think… I think you should stop by the apothecary later. I sense you might need my help."

Heat crawls up my neck. "What do you mean?"

"I don't know exactly." She frowns, her eyes unfocused, like she's seeing something beyond me. "But something about you feels… out of place. Wrong, but not bad wrong. Just… wrong. Like you don't belong here. Or maybe you do, but not right now." She shakes her head, frustrated. "Promise me you'll come by?"

"I promise."

She knows something.

She studies my face for a moment longer, then nods and smiles. "Good. Now go get that job before someone else does."

I watch her walk away, red hair glowing in the morning sun. I turn and head toward the garage, mind spinning with everything she told me. Vince is using Everett, hurting him. Not surprising after what I witnessed yesterday. Is Vince the one who gets him killed? The one who leads him to the Concord? I clench my teeth. I definitely need to keep an eye on him.

The garage appears ahead, all three bay doors closed, waiting for the day to start. RANDALL AUTO REPAIR is painted in bold red letters above the entrance. The smell of oil and gasoline hits me as soon as I step inside. I vaguely remember being in here when I was little. My mother and her older brother inherited the place when her parents died. My uncle passed away when I was twelve and my mom sold this place soon after. Two businesses were too much for my parents to manage, and this one was the one to go.

I shake off the memory and take in the quiet space. The office is empty, but I can hear someone moving around in the back. I ring the bell on the counter and wait.

"Be right with you," a voice calls.

A moment later, a man emerges from the back room, wiping his hands on a rag. And just like that, I'm face to face with my great-grandfather.

Earl Randall is younger than I expected, early forties maybe, and almost a dead ringer for Blake. My mother's eyes hit first, blue with little flecks of gold near the pupil. The slope of his nose and the sharp cut of his jaw match Blake's too. Even his broad hands look familiar.

"How can I help you?"

"I… uh…" I swallow hard. "I heard you might need help. I'm good with cars. Just arrived in town. Not sure how long I'll be staying, but I could use the work."

Earl studies me for a moment. His gaze is direct, assessing. "What's your name, son?"

"Calvin… uh… Mitchell."

"You have experience?"

"Yes, sir. Worked in my uncle's shop back in Michigan. I can handle most repairs. Carburetors, transmissions, oil changes, brakes." Everything about that is true except for the Michigan part.

Earl nods. "I was hoping for someone permanent, but I'm so short-staffed right now I can't turn away help."

The back door opens and I look up. Air bottlenecks in my chest.

Everett's blond hair is still damp and combed back off his forehead. He's changed into dark blue coveralls with "Randall Auto" stitched on the pocket. His blue eyes widen when he sees me. He quickly looks away.

"Morning, Mr. Randall," he says, then his gaze shifts back to me. A small smile tugs at the corner of his mouth. "Calvin, right?"

"You two know each other?" Earl looks between us.

"We met briefly last night. At the diner."

"Good timing," Earl says. "Everett, I want you to work with Calvin here on that Cadillac. Carburetor's shot. Let's see what he can do." He turns to me. "You fix that up proper, you've got a job for as long as you're in town."

"Yes, sir," I say, answering without looking away from Everett.

Everett gestures toward the workroom. "I can show you around."

I follow him through the office into the main garage area. Three cars in various states of repair fill the bays, the air thick with oil, metal, and cleaner.

"So." Everett leads me to a workbench where parts are already laid out. "You know your way around a car?"

"I've fixed a rig or two."

Up close, I see how tired he is. Dark circles sleep beneath his eyes like bruises and there's a slight droop to his shoulders. The confident mechanic from yesterday has been swapped out for someone frayed at the edges.

"You know your way around a carburetor?" He nods toward the disassembled parts on the bench.

"I can handle it."

"Good." Everett hands me a wrench.

Our fingers brush. Just the slightest touch. Heat zips up my arm.

Warm skin. Solid flesh. Real.

His eyes widen. For a moment, we just stand there, the wrench suspended between us, our fingers barely touching. Then Everett pulls back, breaking the contact. A flush creeps up his neck. "Sorry. I..."

I offer a crooked grin. "It's okay. I felt it too."

His eyes snap to mine, sharp and questioning. Trying to figure out if he can trust me.

He nods once, barely a movement at all.

It isn't trust. Not yet. But it feels like the start of it.

CHAPTER NINETEEN

Everett

The carburetor sits in pieces between us. I steal glances at Calvin's hands while he works, grease caught in the creases of his knuckles, a small scar along one thumb that disappears every time his fingers curl.

"Hand me that socket wrench?" Calvin asks, his palm already out, waiting.

I drop it into his hand before he even finishes his sentence. We work well together.

His eyes stay fixed on the carburetor. "So. How long have you lived with Mr. Randall?"

I grab a rag, wipe grease from my fingers. "About ten months. He rents me a room."

"You like it here? In Moonridge, I mean."

"It's nice enough. Beats where I came from." My mouth snaps shut.

Calvin looks up, those warm brown eyes catching mine. "Where was that?"

I shrug, suddenly very interested in the grime under my nails. "Small town in Georgia. Not much to tell."

"I thought I recognized a hint of an accent." He smiles and winks. "Family still there?"

I don't meet his gaze, so he won't see my lie. "No family to speak of." More like none that will speak of me.

Calvin's hands still for half a second. "I'm sorry. That was nosy of me."

I pull my mouth into something like a smile. "It's fine. Just not much to tell. Dad and I don't really talk, and Mom died when I was little."

"How did she...?" He clears his throat. "Sorry. Really pushing it now."

"Car accident. I was eleven."

He looks at me like his heart just broke a little. "That's rough."

I pick up a wrench, spin it between my fingers. "Yeah, well. It was my fault, anyway."

"How could it possibly have been your fault?"

I stare at the parts spread in front of us. "We were driving during a bad rainstorm. I was a lonely kid and I'd been begging her for weeks to get a dog. Thought if I pushed hard enough maybe she'd give in." My throat tightens. "And then I shifted. First time ever. Right there in the backseat while she was doing fifty down a country road."

The memory crashes over me. Rain hammering the windshield. My mother's scream. The way the car lurched.

"She wasn't expecting a German Shepherd to suddenly appear where her son had been sitting." I force myself to keep going. "We hit a tree. She died on impact. I shifted back and just... sat there in the wreckage, trying to understand what had happened."

Silence fills the space between us. I wait for him to back away slowly like I'm contagious.

Calvin sets down his tools. Slow. Deliberate. He turns to face me. "You were just a kid. You couldn't control that. It wasn't your fault." His brow pulls tight.

I look up. "Try telling my dad that. He was overseas in the

war when it happened. Came back to find his wife dead and his son a freak."

Calvin's jaw tightens. Something bright and stubborn flashes through his gaze. "You're not a freak. You're a shifter. That's rare and special."

My chest gives a strange, light tug. No one's ever said that. "Tell that to my old man. He wanted a son who played football and joined the army. Someone who used his abilities to be a man." I practically spit the word. "Instead, he got me. I liked music and books. Wanted to write songs and perform."

"You sing?" Calvin's whole face brightens.

I duck my head. "Yeah. Sometimes. Not that good."

"I bet that's not true. I'd love to hear you sometime."

The offer hangs between us. A smile tugs at my lips before I can stop it. "Maybe."

Calvin picks up a different wrench, turns it over in his hands. "I lost my mom in a car accident, too. I was sixteen. Different circumstances, but I know how it hollows you out."

My head snaps up. "Yours, too?"

"Yeah." He studies the wrench like it might erase the pain. "She was driving after having... When she shouldn't have been. She died on impact, they said. Didn't suffer." He lets out a short, empty laugh. "Like that makes it better."

"I'm sorry." The words feel small.

"Me too." He sets down the wrench, meets my eyes. "For you, I mean. For both of us, I guess."

"Hollows you out," I repeat, tasting the words. "That's exactly it. Like someone scooped out all your insides and left just enough to allow you to keep walking around."

"But you keep living," Calvin says. "That's what matters. You survived."

"Did I? Sometimes I'm not sure." Why am I being so vulnerable? And why is he letting me?

"You did. You're here. That counts for something." Calvin

reaches across the workbench. His hand covers mine, warm and solid. My breath stutters. I should pull away. What if someone walks in and sees us? But the gentleness makes me remain still.

"Did you go live with your dad after?" he asks, not moving his hand.

"Grandparents. Until Dad got discharged after the war. They weren't sure what to do with me. My mom was human and they had no magic in their family. My dad took me in when he got back and he wasn't very warm. The war changed him. Made him mean. Or maybe he was always like that. I don't know."

His thumb brushes across my knuckles, a quick sweep of heat and pressure. My heart won't stop pounding.

"What happened? With your dad, I mean. You said you're estranged?"

"Kicked me out. When I was eighteen." I finally pull my hand away, the loss of contact leaving a strange hollow place behind. "He hated that I was a shifter. His father was one as well, and he and his dad had a rough relationship. I think I reminded him too much of who his father was. I didn't have much direction after school. I still lived at home and pumped gas at the local station during the night shift so I had my days free."

I swallow back the memory.

"Then one day, he came home early and found me shifted into my mom. Or… the version of her I remembered." I wince as soon as it's out. This is too weird to hand someone I barely know.

"Sometimes I'd do that when I was lonely."

Calvin just stares at me. He probably thinks I'm a freak show now. Of course he does. Some guy turning into his dead mother? I swallow hard.

"Then what?" he asks.

I shrug. "He threw me out that night. Told me never to come back. Said I was an abomination."

Calvin offers a sympathetic shake of the head. "Jesus, Everett."

I keep my eyes fixed on the table. "So I left Georgia. Bounced around. Ended up here last summer."

Calvin passes me a bolt. Our fingers brush again. "Family's complicated."

"What about yours? Besides your mom, I mean. Any family?"

Something flickers across his face. "It's… complicated."

I recognize the deflection. Respect it. We've both opened enough wounds for one morning.

Calvin clears his throat. "You got a special someone in your life?"

My pulse jumps. Where did that come from? Does he suspect something? Can I trust him? Is he…? "It's complicated."

"Sorry. Didn't mean to pry."

The bolt slips from my fingers, clattering against the workbench. I bend to pick it up. "And you…?"

He shakes his head. "No. Not in a very long time. I'd like to, though."

I reach across to grab a tool and my sleeve rides up. Calvin's eyes lock on the ring of bruises circling my wrist like a bracelet. Purple-black marks where Vince's fingers dug in hard last night.

His eyes widen. He looks at the bruises, then at my face, then back at the bruises.

"What happened?"

I yank my sleeve down. "Nothing. Slammed it in a car door."

He doesn't believe me. His eyes meet mine, questions sitting there like stones.

"Everett—"

"We should finish this." I turn back to the carburetor, fingers unsteady on the metal.

For a long moment, Calvin doesn't move. I feel the weight of his stare, the heat in it. Then, slowly, he picks up his tools.

We work in silence for a while, but it presses down on us in a way it didn't before. Calvin keeps glancing at my wrist. Each time, his jaw tightens. His movements grow sharper, more controlled.

Finally, the carburetor is reassembled, gleaming and ready

for installation. We haul it over and set it in place, passing tools back and forth without looking, reaching for the same bolts at the same time. When Calvin tightens the last one, I jump inside and pump the throttle. The engine roars to life, a deep, satisfied sound.

"Nice work!" Earl calls from across the garage. "You two make a good team."

Calvin grins then winks at me, and something jumps behind my ribs.

"Why don't you two deliver the car and then take the rest of the day off?" Earl offers. "Everything else can wait. It's too nice today to be cooped up inside."

Calvin wipes his hands on a rag. "This wouldn't happen in my time."

I frown. "In your time?"

He goes still, then color hits his cheeks. "I mean, in my hometown. Big city, you know? We don't deliver cars back to customers like you're planning to do and we certainly don't get afternoons off just because it's nice out."

The words stick in my head. What does he mean in his time? "Delivery is a personal touch we offer. Especially for these folks. The Carters' are practically royalty around here."

Calvin's expression twists at the name, like he just bit into something he didn't expect. Recognition flashes across his face and vanishes.

I pull my car keys from my pocket and hold them out. "Here. You can drive my car. Just follow me to the Carter place, and we'll ride back together."

"You'd trust me with your car?"

"You just fixed a carburetor without breaking a sweat. I think you can handle it." I toss him the keys. "Just be careful with her. We just finished rebuilding her engine. She's my pride and joy."

Calvin catches the keys, fingers curling around them like they are something precious. "I promise. I'll take good care of her."

I walk to the office to tell Mr. Randall we're headed out.

Earl looks up from his paperwork. "He done good, huh? Fast worker?"

"The best I've seen."

Earl nods. "Tell him he's hired. For as long as he wants to stay." He glances out the window at the sunny day. "Enjoy the rest of the day."

"Thanks, Mr. Randall."

My mind drifts as I drive. An entire afternoon free. No Vince demanding my time. No shifting into someone else to satisfy his fantasies. Just me and Calvin. Time that actually feels like mine. Maybe I'll see if he wants to go up to Amethyst Beach.

I picture us there. Purple sand smooth and glittering under our feet. Sitting on the rocks and talking. I don't know what it is about him, but he's so easy to talk to, and he seems genuinely interested in me.

I pull up the Carters long driveway. Ancient oaks line both sides, their branches meeting overhead to form a tunnel of green. Sunlight filters through the leaves, dappling the pavement with shifting shadows. The house rises before us. Two stories with a wraparound porch.

I park the Cadillac in front of the garage and hop out, waving Calvin over to park beside me. He climbs out of my car with a strange look on his face, like he's seen a ghost.

"You okay?" I ask.

"Fine." His eyes move over the property, lingering on the house, the garden, the oak tree in the front yard. He stares at that tree for a long moment. "Just… different than I expected."

Mrs. Carter comes out onto the porch, elegant in a floral dress. Her brunette hair is perfectly styled, not a strand out of place, and she holds herself like she knows people are watching.

"Everett, dear! The car sounds wonderful." She claps her hands together. "Earl said you'd have it fixed in no time."

"Yes, ma'am." I hand her the keys. "Actually, Calvin here did most of the work. He's new at the shop."

Mrs. Carter turns her sharp green eyes to Calvin, who goes very still. She studies him for a long moment, her head tilting like she's trying to slide him into place in some old picture in her mind. "Have we met before, young man? You seem... familiar somehow."

Calvin's face loses color. "No, ma'am. I just arrived in Moonridge yesterday."

"Hmm." She keeps looking at him, and I see a sheen of sweat at his hairline. "Strange. I could swear I've seen your face somewhere. You don't have family in Moonridge, do you?"

"No, ma'am. No family anywhere, really."

Her shoulders ease a little. "I'm sorry to hear that. Well, any friend of Everett's is welcome here." She glances between us, a small smile touching her mouth. Her gaze finds its way back to Calvin, brow pinching as that puzzled look returns.

After a few more pleasantries, we escape to my car. I slide into the driver's seat and wait for him to settle in. His hands rest on his thighs, fingers trembling.

"Any plans for your free afternoon?"

He shakes his head. "No. Maybe do some exploring around Moonridge. See what makes the town tick."

"Perfect." I pop the car into reverse. "I want to show you my favorite spot outside of town."

"Where's that?" he asks.

"You'll see." I start the engine. "You know, I haven't had a day off in weeks."

"No?" Calvin turns to look at me, attention sharpening. "That sucks."

A laugh bubbles up. "Sucks? You sure use some funny phrases up in Michigan."

Calvin's face flushes red. "Yeah... sorry. That's too bad you haven't had a day off."

I shrug. "Mr. Randall's been short-staffed. And even when

I'm not working, Vince usually has... plans." The word sours on my tongue.

Calvin's gaze flicks over to me at the mention of Vince, but he keeps his tone easy. "What kind of plans?"

I shrug, not ready to explain how sometimes it feels like Vince uses me. How he promises big things, but it feels like he only wants me when I can fill a void. "Just stuff. Nothing important."

For a few minutes, the car is quiet except for the hum of the engine. Having Calvin beside me feels right. I keep catching myself looking over at him. Sunlight threads through his dark hair, glows across his cheek. His jaw catches the light in a way that makes it hard to look away. His hands rest loose on his thighs now, steadier.

I shouldn't even be entertaining this. I'm with Vince. And Calvin... I don't know him. Not really. For all I know he's just another mistake waiting to happen. I don't even know if he's queer. And yet here I am, hoping.

Again.

At least I know what to expect from Vince.

"So this favorite spot." Calvin breaks the silence. "What makes it special?"

I smile, keeping my eyes on the road. "It's beautiful. Peaceful. You can see for miles. And no one bothers you there. It's where I go when I need to think. Or when I need to feel like myself again."

"Sounds perfect."

"It is. I think you'll like it. The sand around the beach is purple. Someone said it's because these purple rocks, or crystals—amethysts, I guess—got all crushed up and mixed with the sand. That's why they call it Amethyst Beach. The sand catches the light and it's like the whole shore is sparkling. And there's this cliff where you can sit and watch the water. Sometimes I sing there. No one around to hear."

Calvin turns to look at me. "I'd still like to hear you sing."

My cheeks warm. "Maybe. If you're lucky."

"I am lucky." His voice is quiet. "Today, I mean. Getting to spend it with you."

I don't trust my mouth to say anything useful, so I keep driving, letting the road and the possibility of what might transpire at the beach carry us forward.

The thought is barely formed when a familiar white Chrysler pulls up behind us.

The air goes thin. Sweat prickles along my hairline. My grip on the wheel tightens until my fingers ache.

No. Not now.

"Crud." The word scrapes out of my throat.

Calvin follows my gaze to the rearview mirror. "Problem?"

"Vince." My knuckles blanch against the steering wheel. "And Sam Carter's pack."

Vince's horn blares behind me, sharp and insistent.

Damn it.

I pull over, heart hammering against my ribs. Now I'm going to have to deal with this. What's he even doing here in the middle of the afternoon? Shouldn't he be at his daddy's office, pretending to work?

The Chrysler pulls up beside us. Sam is driving and Vince rolls down his window, smiling like he owns the road. "Well, well. Isn't this cozy?" His eyes move from me to Calvin. "Thought you were working today, Ev."

"Mr. Randall gave us the afternoon off." My voice comes out thin.

"Us?" Vince's eyebrows shoot up. His gaze sharpens. "Getting friendly with the new guy already?"

Heat crawls up my throat. "Just being neighborly. Showing Calvin around."

Sam leans across Vince, his handsome face open, more curious than anything. "Where you two headed?"

I should lie. But if they follow us, which they probably will, they'll know. "Thought about taking Calvin up to Amethyst

Beach."

Laughter erupts from the car. Vince's is the loudest. It snaps through me like a broken wire.

"Amethyst Beach?" Jake sticks his head out from the back seat, grinning. "Only witches and women go there, man."

"And guys who want to get with witches," adds the third wolf, Tony Giatti.

Vince's smile vanishes. His eyes go flat. "Come to Skipper Lake with us."

It's not a request. My wrist throbs again, phantom pain mixing with the ache already there.

I glance at Calvin.

"Actually," Calvin starts, "we had plans…"

"Plans change," Vince cuts him off. His voice goes cold. He stares at me, waiting, daring me to argue.

I could say no. Drive away right now. Take Calvin to Amethyst Beach like I planned. Show him the purple sand, sit on the cliff and watch the water. Maybe even sing for him. A nice afternoon that's just mine.

But Vince would follow. He always does. And later, when we're alone, he'd make me pay for it. He knows exactly how to take me apart from the inside out and leave me feeling like nothing.

"Sure." The word scrapes over my tongue. "Skipper Lake sounds great."

Vince's smile snaps back into place. "See you there."

They drive off with a roar, exhaust curling in the air behind them. It mixes with the sour twist in my gut.

"You don't want to go." Calvin's gaze is steady on me.

I stare at the steering wheel. "It's fine. Skipper Lake is nice, too."

"Why do you let him talk to you like that?"

The question lands between us and sits there like an unwelcome guest. Because the answer is complicated. Because I don't like being alone. Because sometimes Vince almost makes me feel wanted.

"It's complicated." My standard answer, weak even to my own ears.

"Doesn't seem complicated to me." Calvin's voice stays gentle. "Seems like he tells you what to do, and you do it."

I flinch. He isn't wrong, but hearing it out loud makes my skin crawl.

"You don't understand. Vince is… connected. It's better not to cross him."

"Better for who?"

I don't have an answer that doesn't make me sound pathetic.

I press down on the accelerator and focus on the road. "He's very lonely. I think that's what draws us to each other. We both have… had… complicated relationships with our fathers. We just get each other. He just needs kindness. I try to give him that because I know how much I could have used it."

Calvin doesn't respond right away. When he does, his words land solid. "No one should make you feel indebted to them."

Something inside me gives, a hairline crack along a wall I have spent years shoring up.

"Maybe not." I admit, my voice rougher than before. "But knowing that doesn't make it any easier to walk away."

"And if you're giving kindness, you should get some in return." His eyes are fixed on me and I'm afraid to turn and look at him.

I nod, changing the subject. "I'm sorry. About Amethyst Beach. It really is beautiful."

Calvin's hand lands briefly on my arm, warm and steady. "We'll go another time."

The promise settles low in my chest. Small. Fragile.

He squeezes my shoulder and smiles, and something shifts inside of me. For the first time in longer than I can remember, someone's looking at me like I matter. Not what I can do. Not what I can become. Just me.

The warmth doesn't last long, but it's there. Real. And maybe that's enough to start believing things could be different.

CHAPTER TWENTY

Calvin

The glint off Skipper Lake throws afternoon sun back in my eyes. I squint as we pull into the gravel parking area, my stomach knotting.

This is where Everett will die in a few days. I've stood on these shores hundreds of times in my own lifetime, but not like this. Not with the clock rewound seventy years. It looks different. Untouched. It feels different, too. Maybe because the guy sitting next to me is still alive, not a ghost chained to the water where his story ends.

In a few days, the police will call it a drowning and the town will turn him into a ghost story. And I'm standing here pretending to enjoy the fucking view. I force myself to breathe. To act normal. To pretend I don't know what's coming.

No. What I'm going to stop from coming.

Vince's white Chrysler roars in behind us. Everett's shoulders curve inward, protective. His jaw clenches so hard I can see the muscle jump.

"Nice spot." I pretend I don't see Everett's whole body tense when Vince's car door slams.

"Yeah. It's a good spot." Everett keeps his gaze on the water.

The lake is beautiful. Familiar, but not. The forest runs thinner, with a strip of charred trees further up the slope. No paddle board rentals. No boat dock. No public restrooms or camping spots. Just wilderness. Quiet and peaceful.

Sam and the other two wolves explode from Vince's car like they've been freed from prison. Their laughter echoes across the water as they race toward the shore.

"Last one in's a rotten egg!" Sam yells, already pulling his shirt over his head.

In ten seconds flat, all three are buck naked, cannonballing into the lake. Water erupts upward, catching sunlight, showering back down like liquid diamonds. Their whoops and hollers bounce off the tree line.

Everett watches them with his arms wrapped tight around himself, eyes fixed on the churning water like he's on the wrong side of the glass.

Then I notice Vince. He stands apart, still fully dressed, his eyes locked on one specific wolf.

Sam.

Vince watches him like a starving man eyes a steak. Hunger radiates from every line of his body. Longing. Unmistakable want. His eyes track every movement Sam makes in the water—every laugh, every splash, every flex of muscle.

My gut goes cold.

Vince is in love with him.

I glance at Everett. He's watching Vince watch Sam, mouth pressed into a thin line. He looks like a guy who knows exactly who his boyfriend wants, and it's not him. He knows he's just a placeholder.

"Hey, new guy!" Sam calls from the water, interrupting my thoughts. "You coming in or what? Time to show us what Michigan wolves are made of!"

One of the other wolves—Jake, I think—whoops in agreement. "First test to join the pack, buddy! Get those clothes off!"

I hesitate, looking at Everett. He pulls his mouth into something that tries to be a smile. "Go ahead. Have fun."

"You sure?"

Everett nods, eyes flicking toward Vince. "Go. Please. I'm fine right here."

I strip down quickly. Growing up werewolf, nudity is no big deal. But halfway through pulling off my pants, I realize Everett is staring. His face flushes pink. He looks away, but not before I catch the look in his eyes, that quick flare of want that hits me right in the ego.

Suddenly I'm very aware of my own skin. I've been naked around dozens of people, but Everett's gaze rewires something. My dick starts to perk up at exactly the wrong time.

Before he can notice, I run and dive into the lake. The cold shocks through me. Thank God. Nothing kills an inconvenient boner like cold lake water. I surface with a gasp, shaking water from my hair.

"There he is!" Jake swims over and dunks me immediately. I come up sputtering as the others laugh.

I'm swept into wolf play. Splashing, dunking, chasing each other around the lake. It feels good to let loose. To not think about why I'm really here.

But I can't let my guard down.

I glance back at the shore where Everett and Vince still stand. Vince lights a cigarette, eyes narrowed against the sun. Everett leans against the car, focused on his fingers. Sam treads water beside me, snapping my thoughts back to him. "So what was your pack like back in Michigan? Why'd you leave?"

I keep my head above water and scramble for a story. "Small pack. Maybe fifteen wolves. I wasn't really involved with them. Territory disputes with another pack got ugly. Didn't want to get caught in the middle."

"Territorial bastards, huh?" The third wolf, Tony or Jake (I really need to lock that down), nods knowingly.

"Yeah. Alpha was strict, too. Everything by the rules. No shifting outside full moons unless he said so. Got tired of being told when I could let my wolf out."

Sam laughs. "Sounds like my old man. He'd have a fit if he knew we were shifting just for fun. That why you left? Looking for a pack that's not so uptight?"

I nod, water dripping into my eyes. "Something like that. Just want to find a place where I fit, you know?"

Sam slaps the water, sending a spray over all of us. "Hey! We should go for a run. Right now."

"Hell yes!" Jake agrees immediately.

"You up for it, Michigan?" Sam grins at me, eyes bright with challenge.

"Always up for a run."

Sam's mouth hooks at one corner. "How about a race? You make it to the top of that cliff before me, you're one of us."

"You're on." I might not know every rock and tree in this version of Moonridge, but I've hiked these woods my entire life. The bones of the place can't be that different.

We swim to shore and shake off like the wolves we are. Sam shifts and takes off running toward the tree line, the others following close behind.

I glance back, looking for Everett, but he's not by the car anymore. Neither is Vince.

Where are they?

A prickle starts between my shoulder blades. Shit. Where did they go? But there's no time. If I want to win this race and gain the wolves' trust, I need to move now.

I sprint for the trees, already feeling my wolf rise inside me, eager for the run. As I hit the shadows of the forest, my body begins to change. Bones shift, muscles stretch, fur sprouts across my skin.

I drop to all fours, fully wolf now, and take off through the familiar-unfamiliar woods. Even as I run, my thoughts snag on Everett and whatever Vince might be doing to him.

My paws skim the ground as I race through the trees. I know these woods better than Sam realizes; the slopes and ridges live in my body. While Sam and the others take the main trail that winds around the lake, I cut straight into a narrow ravine most people never notice. It's steeper and rougher than I remember, brambles catching at my fur, but it slices minutes off the climb.

I burst into the clearing at the cliff top. Alone. Not a wolf in sight. I shift back to human form and stretch out on a sun-warmed rock, grinning.

Skipper Lake glitters below, ringed by forest all the way to the horizon. No towers, no power lines, no sprawl. Just water and trees and pure nature.

Underbrush rustles. Sam appears at the edge of the clearing, still in wolf form, his sandy fur catching the sunlight. He freezes when he sees me lounging on the rock. His eyes go wide, and he shifts back to human form in one smooth motion.

"What the... how did you get up here so fast?" He's breathing hard, sweat gleaming on his skin.

"I'm a good climber." I lift a shoulder.

"But I know these woods better than anyone." Sam narrows his eyes, studying me. "You cheated."

"I took a shortcut. You didn't say which route we had to take."

Sam stares at me for a moment longer, then bursts out laughing. "Sneaky bastard. I like it." He walks over and sits beside me. It blows my mind that this is my grandfather. Young. Alive. Sitting right next to me with our dongs hanging out.

He pats me on the back. "Guess we'll let you run with the pack now."

"Thanks. Nice view up here."

"Best in Moonridge." Sam runs a hand through his hair. Blake does that same thing when he's thinking. "The pack comes up here all the time. Great place to howl at the moon." He stands up, stretching his arms overhead. "Want to keep running? Jake and the others are probably halfway to Miller's Creek by now."

I lean back on my elbows like I don't have a care in the world. "Think I'll hang here for a bit. Enjoy the view."

"Suit yourself." Sam shifts his weight, glances down at his naked body, then smirks. "Just don't fall asleep. You'll get one hell of a sunburn on your dick. Trust me. I speak from experience."

With that sage advice, he shifts back to wolf form and takes off running again, this time following the ridge that eventually circles back to the lake. I wait until he's well out of sight before standing up.

The noise of his paws fades, leaving a softer hush behind it. The breeze dies down. Birds fall quiet. Bit by bit, the clearing settles into something too still.

A slow crawl of dread works under my skin. Everett and Vince slipped off right before we shifted. What are they up to? Where did Vince take him?

I walk the perimeter of the clearing looking out over the lake below. That's when I notice it, carved into the trunk of a massive pine off to my left. A symbol. A spiral wrapped around itself in an endless loop, with strange marks radiating outward like sunbeams. It's fresh. The exposed wood still oozes sap, glistening in the afternoon light.

Cold spills through my chest.

I've seen this mark before. It's the same symbol they carve into Everett's skin before they bleed him dry and bind him to them. They're already here, staking out their altar.

I shift back to wolf form, nose to the ground, searching out Everett's unmistakable scent of summer rain and motor oil. Eventually I catch a faint whiff and it's like a neon sign pointing the way. I follow it through the trees, moving silently now, my paws finding the quiet spots between fallen leaves and twigs. I glance up and directly across from me is another tree with the same Concord mark carved into it.

The scent grows stronger. I slow down, creeping forward until voices filter through the underbrush.

"Vince, someone will see us."

That's Everett's voice, but something is wrong. The pitch runs deeper. I edge closer, peering through a gap in the bushes.

Sam stands with his back against a tree, Vince pressing against him, mouth on his neck, hands roaming over his chest.

Wait. I just saw Sam run off in the opposite direction. Unless...

"We need to be careful. If Sam catches us..."

Vince cuts him off with a rough kiss.

My stomach lurches. That's Everett in Sam's skin. So that's what he does. Vince makes him wear Sam's face, Sam's body. Turns him into the man Vince actually wants.

I watch Everett-as-Sam try to pull away, but Vince holds him in place. Even though I know it's Everett underneath, my brain can't process it. I have to fight to keep from shifting back to human form and tearing Vince apart with my bare hands.

Vince runs his hand down not-Sam's chest, possessive and demanding. "No one's around. The guys will be running for hours."

Everett-as-Sam shifts his weight. "You said you came here to get something."

That gets Vince's attention. He steps back, shoulders tightening. "Right. I was told to pick something up."

"What is it?" Everett asks.

He hesitates. "A box... It contains something that'll... uh... help map out our future."

Everett folds his arms. "What's in it?"

"Potential." Vince toys with the word.

"That's not an answer."

I can't see Vince's face from where I'm crouched, but I hear the change in his tone. "Come on, Ev, you know how it is for me. My friends are all wolves. And me? I'm just the unlit tagalong."

Everett doesn't respond. His silence says enough.

"This will change that," Vince goes on.

"How?" Everett asks, brow furrowing.

"It will make me stronger. Someone deserving of respect. I'll finally be someone who can stand with you. Not behind you." Vince steps closer. Leaves rustle under his shoes. "They said they can give me strength. Enough to break free of my father. Enough to build a future with you without anyone holding us back."

Unease spikes in my gut.

Everett lets out a shaky breath. "You think you need to have abilities to be with me?"

"I know I do." Vince's words tumble out in a rush. "You think I'm weak. I see it. I know I'm not enough for you. You deserve someone who can protect you. Someone who won't be the weak link."

"That's not true."

"I'm tired of being powerless," Vince says. "Tired of pretending it doesn't eat at me. These people I met... they'll fix that. I just need to find this box and deliver it to them. Then we can leave Moonridge. Start over somewhere that isn't choking both of us."

Everett's skepticism shows in the pinch of his mouth. "Why would they leave a box in the woods? That doesn't make sense."

"It had to be buried in consecrated land under the moon for a certain amount of time... look, you wouldn't understand. Just help me find it."

A familiar cold hum starts under my skin. It's part of the ritual.

"It's buried beneath a tree with an insignia on it," Vince says.

My gaze snaps to the tree directly across from the bushes I'm hiding in. Half-covered by brush is a wooden box.

I should grab it. Run. Get it before Vince can. But before I can move, footsteps crunch on the opposite side of the trunk.

Vince circles the tree, close enough to touch.

I flatten myself into the bush, pressing my wolf body tight against the dirt. A twig shifts under my paw. The sound cracks through the clearing.

Vince's head jerks up, eyes scanning the underbrush. I hold my breath, pulse loud in my ears. My muscles brace, ready to run or fight. Every part of me wants to bolt, but movement will give me away. So I stay, trusting fur and shadow to hide me.

"Vince?" Everett calls, coming around the tree from the other direction. He's back in his own form now, blonde hair catching the dappled sunlight. My breathing slows a fraction at the sight of him as himself again. "Did you find it?"

Vince's attention shifts. "Yeah." He kneels down, reaching under the bush just inches from where I'm hiding. His legs are so close I could bite them. I want to. His hand closes around the box, pulling it free. "Got it right here."

He turns to face Everett. "Hey, before we go, we need to talk about something."

Everett shifts his weight. "Okay."

"It's about that new guy." Vince shifts the box from one hand to the other.

"What about him?"

"I saw how you looked at him. Earlier." Vince's grip tightens on the box. "And I saw how he looked at you."

Everett shifts slightly. "It's nothing. He's a nice guy. I work with him. He's new in town and I'm trying to make him feel comfortable."

"I know you, Ev. I know when you're interested in someone. When he got naked? You looked at him the same way you looked at me when we first met." Vince's voice cracks. "And I get it. I do. He's new. Exciting. He's big and tall and handsome. Strong. But he doesn't know all your baggage."

"That's not—"

"Please. Just let me finish." Vince places the box in his pocket and wraps his arms around himself. "I'm not trying to control you. I'm just... I'm scared, okay? There's something off about him."

From my hiding spot, I see Everett's jaw loosen, the anger in his expression shifting to something more complicated.

"Off how?"

"I don't know. I can't put my finger on it." Vince shakes his head, playing the part of the confused, insecure boyfriend. "The way he showed up out of nowhere. How he watches you." He pauses, letting the words sink in. "It feels... calculated. Like he's got an agenda."

"You're being paranoid."

"Am I?" Vince steps closer. He leans in. "You're fragile, Everett. What if he's dangerous? What if he hurts you and I can't protect you?"

Everett's jaw tightens. "Not everyone is out to use me. And Calvin doesn't seem dangerous."

"Neither did your father. Or the guys in Texas who almost killed you. Or the guy in New York who robbed you and left you with nothing but a pair of shoes. You trust too easily."

The words land like a punch; Everett flinches.

"You're weak, Ev. You're needy, and people like him can smell that from a mile away. Once he knows the truth..."

Wow. Vince knows exactly where to strike.

"That's not fair."

"I didn't mean that in a negative way. I just... I worry about you. I know how fragile you are." Vince pulls Everett into his arms. "I'm sorry. I'm just scared of losing you. I want to protect you. You're all I have. You know that, right? If you left me, I'd have nothing."

Everett doesn't pull away from the embrace, but he doesn't return it either. "I'm not leaving you for Calvin. I barely know him."

"But you want to know him." It's not a question.

Silence.

"Just..." Vince pulls back, cups Everett's face in his hands, looks him directly in the eyes. "Just be careful around him. Please. For me. I don't trust him. I don't know what he wants. And until I do, I need you to keep your distance."

"Vince—"

"I'm not telling you what to do. I'm asking." Vince's thumb brushes across Everett's cheekbone, possessive in a way that makes my teeth itch. "If you care about me at all, if you care about us, just... don't let him get too close. Not yet. Not until we know what he's really doing here."

Everett closes his eyes. "Fine."

"You promise?"

"I promise I'll be careful."

"Thank you." Vince kisses Everett's forehead. "That's all I'm asking. Just be careful. Just remember who was there for you when you had nothing. Who will still be there after Calvin moves on to whatever his next stop is."

He kisses Everett one more time. "I love you. I need you to know that."

Everett offers a small smile and Vince kisses him again. "Come on. Let's get back to the cars before the guys get back and start looking for us."

Everett nods and they walk away, Vince's hand heavy on the small of his back.

I stay frozen in the bushes, every muscle buzzing.

I gotta hand it to Vince. He is a master of manipulation. Turning me into a problem. A threat. Really?

Just before they're out of earshot, I hear Vince say, "I'll be out of town tonight. I have to deliver this and then I have meetings in Boston tomorrow morning. You'll be a good boy while I'm gone?"

Their voices fade along the path. I wait until their footsteps fade completely before shifting back to human form. I glance down at the spot where the box was buried.

I should have grabbed it. Taken it and destroyed it.

But maybe it's not too late. Vince is leaving tonight. Maybe I can get Everett alone. Warn him. Make him see what's really happening before Vince comes back and unleashes whatever hell that box contains.

CHAPTER TWENTY-ONE

Calvin

The drive back is too quiet, and not the comfortable kind. Everett keeps his eyes on the road, jaw working like he's chewing on words he won't let out. When he does answer, it's with short grunts that barely qualify as a response. Our easy banter from earlier has vanished. Whatever Vince whispered at the lake is lodged in Everett's head like a burr, and it's doing exactly what Vince wanted.

I try again. A light question. A quick joke. Anything to get Everett to look at me.

I get nothing more than a polite smile in response.

By the time we reach the B&B, the silence has carved a whole new distance between us. Everett barely mutters a goodbye. His hands stay on the wheel and his eyes stay on the road ahead. I step out, and the car rolls away before I even close the door.

Inside, Mrs. Fredericks peeks over the top of her book and gives me a warm little wave, oblivious to the storm sitting in my chest. I lift a hand in return, but it feels half-hearted even to me. I need a shower. Need to wash off the heaviness that I brought back with me and figure out next steps.

I strip off everything and step under steaming water until the heat burns. All I see behind my eyes is that box under the tree and Vince whispering bullshit about me. I brace my hands against the tile and drag in a breath. Agnes told me to come by the apothecary. Said she sensed I needed help. She was right. I need someone who knows what the hell to do next, because right now I'm running on fear and panic and that's a shit plan. I need someone on my side.

I step outside just as the sun drops below the tree line. Everything looks normal. Too normal.

I take a few slow steps down the sidewalk, letting the town settle around me. People chat on porches. Someone sweeps their sidewalk. A screen door bangs shut across the street. All perfectly normal. Kids bike past. Couples stroll with ice cream. Sprinklers click in front lawns. Everyone is completely blind to what's brewing in the shadows.

I head past the barbershop, then the post office, just trying to clear my head. Then I see it. Vince's Chrysler, half a block ahead, sitting outside the community bank.

My steps falter, a jolt shooting through me. I thought he said he was leaving town.

I slow my pace, hands in pockets. Casual. Just a guy out for an evening stroll. My eyes dart from storefront to storefront. Is he in the bank? Or maybe the diner up the street?

I draw even with the car and every muscle goes tight. The passenger window is rolled down. And there, on the seat, sits the wooden box with the spiral symbol. Just sitting there. Unguarded.

Whatever's inside connects to Everett's murder. To the Concord's plan. To everything I came here to stop.

I glance around. The street remains busy but no one's watching. A woman pushes a baby stroller across the street, but doesn't even acknowledge me. A man exits the drugstore, keys jingling. No sign of Vince.

I could just take it.

The thought lands heavy, ugly and tempting. I shouldn't. I'm not a thief. Okay, I stole that twenty from Dad's wallet when I was twelve, but that was different. I came here to save Everett, not steal shit. But I'm pretty sure that box is connected to his death. Knowing what's inside could be the key to saving him.

My hand hovers near the window. Every second I stand here increases the risk. Someone will see. Vince will come back. I'll get caught.

But Everett will die if I don't.

I shift closer to the car as if I am checking out the paint job. Another glance around. Still clear.

I lift the box off the seat and tuck it inside my jacket in one practiced sweep, like I've done this a hundred times.

Got it.

I walk away. Don't run. Don't look suspicious. Just walk. Normal. Casual.

But there's nothing normal about the weight in my pocket. Or the way my chest fizzles like someone lit a fuse under my ribs.

Sweat beads along my forehead and slips down into my eyes. Every footstep sounds too loud, breath short and sharp. Someone probably saw me. Someone's going to grab my shoulder and demand to know what I took.

I turn onto Briarwood, putting distance between me and the car.

What have I done? What if Vince notices it's missing and blames Everett?

Too late now.

Whatever's inside better be worth the risk.

The apothecary rises ahead, cheerful in the golden light. Flowers spill from window boxes, sweet in the cooling air. The sign creaks in the breeze. This is the right move. Agnes will know what to do.

The moment my boots hit the bottom step, something pulses

beneath my feet, a slow heartbeat thrumming up through the sidewalk into my legs. It's like the apothecary itself just noticed me. It's like it knows I don't belong to this year and wraps that awareness around my chest like it's holding me in place while it decides what to do with me. I shake out my leg, trying to shrug it off, and nearly collide with someone coming down the steps.

Ravena.

My fingers curl into fists.

"Oh! Sorry about that." Her smile is bright and friendly, so polished it belongs in a toothpaste commercial. "Michigan, right?"

I keep my voice casual even though she creeps me the fuck out. "That's right."

"Settling in okay?" She adjusts her glasses, studying me. Her gaze lingers on my face, then drops to my jacket pocket where the box sits. Does she see the outline? Can she sense something?

"So far, so good. Got a job at the garage."

"That's swell." She glances past me toward the apothecary door. Something flickers across her face. "Are you visiting the apothecary?"

There's something in her tone, too interested, too sharp. Is she suspicious already?

"Yeah, I was looking for something to help me sleep. New place, strange bed. You know how it is."

"Rachel has a remedy for everything." The way she says "remedy" makes it sound like an insult. "This family has acted as the town's healers for generations. Very talented."

"Lucky for me." I step aside to let her pass, eager to end this. My heart hasn't stopped racing since I saw her face. "I should get inside before they close. Nice to see you again."

"Likewise." She starts down the steps, then pauses. Turns back. Her smile is all teeth now. "Good night."

"Thank you. You, too."

That warmth in my chest lingers as the pulse under my boots fades. I still can't tell if the apothecary just welcomed me or tagged me.

The bell chimes as I push open the apothecary door. The smell embraces me. Warm wood, dancing dust motes in early evening light. Dried herbs, candle wax, something sweet I can't name. Behind the counter, Agnes grinds something in a mortar, humming under her breath.

That tune. It hooks into me. Hazel's song. The one she'll hum seventy years from now while mixing potions in this same space.

Agnes looks up, smile brightening the room. "Hello there, Michigan. I was wondering when you'd stop by."

I approach the counter. Casual. The box feels heavier with each step. "You asked me to come. Remember?"

"So I did." She taps the pestle three times against the mortar. "How was your first full day in our little town? Getting settled?"

"It's been interesting. Got the job at the garage. Met some of the local… characters."

"Like who?" Her eyes light with curiosity.

Before I can respond, a high-pitched voice chirps from a nearby shelf. "Ooooh, who is that?"

I spin around, nearly knocking over a display. Three ceramic cats sit in a row on a shelf, painted in bright colors with atomic starburst patterns. I blink hard, convinced I imagined the voice.

"Did that cat just…?"

"Talk? Yes, she certainly did."

The middle cat's mouth moves, her voice dripping with sarcasm. "What gave it away, genius? The moving lips or the sound coming out?"

Agnes sighs. "Calvin, meet the Atomic Cats. My mother is allergic to real cats, so she enchanted them to be her companions, but they've developed personalities of their own. That's Velma in the middle, always charming as you can tell."

"I'm Trixie!" The first cat bounces slightly, painted blue eyes wide and unblinking. "Are you really from Michigan? I don't know where that is. Is it nice there? Do they have cats?"

"And I'm Lucy." The third cat stretches, impossibly flexible for ceramic. "And you are one tall drink of water. Love a man with broad shoulders. Bet those hands are good for all sorts of things. Come and give me a rub big guy."

Talking cats. And horny at that. This is new, even for someone who grew up surrounded by magic.

"Don't mind Lucy," Agnes says, shooting the cat a stern look. "She flirts with anything that moves."

"And some things that don't." Velma rolls her painted eyes.

"Only the cute ones." Lucy winks at me.

I step closer, fascinated despite myself. "How do they…?"

"Magic, dummy." Velma looks bored. "Were you expecting science?"

Trixie bounces again. "Ooooh, magic is so fun! It makes the world sparkly!"

"I could make your world sparkly, big boy." Lucy's ceramic tail swishes in a slow, lazy S-curve.

"That's quite enough." Agnes claps her hands and the cats freeze, still grinning but silent. She turns back to me, expression shifting to something more serious. "Something's bothering you."

The box feels heavy in my pocket. "Yeah."

Agnes meets my gaze. She reaches across the counter and takes my hand. The moment her skin touches mine, her eyes widen. She inhales sharply. "You're not from here, are you?"

"I told you, I'm from Michigan—"

She shakes her head. "No. You're not from this time. I sensed something earlier, but it's clearer now. Your signature is off. Your energy has a different vibration. It's more electric, and… I can see you and your friends in the future." Her voice drops even lower. "You know someone in the Morehouse line. And I think you have a connection with one of my descendants."

She knows. How much does she see? Can I trust her?

The cats come back to life, all speaking at once.

"Wait, what?" Trixie spins in a circle.

"Time travel? Now it gets interesting." Velma leans forward, studying me like she's reading my aura.

"Future boy? Even better." Lucy purrs. "I bet they have interesting positions in the future."

"I... that's not... I can't..." The words stumble out in useless fragments.

"You don't completely trust me." Agnes says it like she's naming the color of the sky. She goes back to grinding herbs, then adds them to a small pot of simmering liquid. "I understand. Say no more."

I stare at her, dumbfounded. The box in my pocket feels radioactive, like it's announcing itself to everyone in the room.

She holds a small cord in her hand, murmuring words I can't make out. "While I prepare this, tell me about the symbols you found today."

"Symbols?"

"You saw a mark today that upset you, didn't you? I sensed that, too, when I touched you."

I knew Agnes had power, but I didn't know it was that strong. I pull out a scrap of paper and draw the spiral with its radiating lines. "This one. I saw it in the woods, carved into trees. What does it mean?"

Agnes's hands freeze. Her freckles stand out sharper as the blood leaves her cheeks. "That symbol is ancient." She pins me with a stare. "Where exactly did you see it?"

"In the woods near Skipper Lake. It's hard to explain, but lives are in danger."

"How deliciously mysterious," Velma comments, but her tone has lost its sarcasm. She sounds almost worried.

"Is it a bad symbol? It looks pretty." Trixie tilts her ceramic head, concern creeping into her voice.

"I like a man with secrets." Lucy winks again, but even she seems subdued.

I pull out the small rectangular box and place it on the

counter.

"I...uh... found this under the tree with the symbol carved on it." A little lie won't hurt anyone.

Agnes's eyes widen. She doesn't reach for it immediately. Instead, she circles around the counter, studying it from different angles like it might spring to life.

"May I?" Her hand hovers over it.

"Yeah. I brought it here because I figured you might know what it is."

She takes the box carefully, as if it might bite, and holds it up to the light. The wood is dark, almost black, but the grain catches the lamplight in strange ways. Swirling patterns seem to move when I'm not looking directly at them.

"The wood itself has been treated with something," Agnes murmurs. She brings it closer to her face, inhaling. "Nightshade oil and... Blood?"

She traces the spiral carved into the top of the box with her finger and it glows faintly, a sickly greenish light. The symbol is similar to the one I saw on the tree, but instead of radiating clock-like lines, this one has three slashes cutting through the middle of it.

All three cats lean forward, their bodies rigid. Their painted eyes somehow convey pure horror.

"That's bad mojo," Velma whispers, her previously analytical tone replaced with genuine fear.

"I don't like it," Trixie says, her cheerfulness completely gone. "It feels... wrong. Like something died to make it."

"Nothing sexy about that," Lucy adds, shrinking back. "That's pure evil."

Agnes sets the box down on the counter, her hands trembling slightly. She closes her eyes for a moment, her lips moving in what might be a prayer or a protection spell. When she opens them again, her expression is grim.

"It's filled with old magic. Dark magic." She takes a breath.

"Are you sure you want me to open this?"

I nod, even though part of me wants to burn it.

She lifts the lid slowly, as if something might jump out. Inside, nestled on black velvet that seems to absorb the light around it, lies a braided red leather cord. It's darkened in places—dried blood, maybe—and woven into the center is a small black amulet bearing the same slashed symbol.

"Dear gods," Agnes breathes. She doesn't touch the contents, just stares. "This looks like a binding tool. They must have been charging it using the magic from the ley line that runs beneath the lake." She looks up at me, her face pale. "Do you understand what this means? This isn't just dark magic. This is sacrifice magic. Blood magic. The kind that requires a life."

She closes the box quickly, like she can't stand to look at it anymore.

"Leave this with me. I'll examine it with my mother. She'll know more about how to handle something like this."

"Will you be able to dispose of it if it's dangerous?"

"Of course." She wraps the box in a cloth and tucks it beneath the counter. The moment it's out of sight, the cats stop leaning forward and sit back on their haunches again.

"I have so many questions for you about this and the future, but I need time to examine this with my mother first." She moves to a shelf behind the counter and selects a smooth black stone about the size of a quarter. "Black onyx. For protection." She presses it into my palm and closes my fingers around it. "Keep this with you."

The stone is warm against my skin, almost alive.

"Come back tomorrow. And Calvin?" Her expression turns serious. "Be careful."

"Careful is boring," Lucy purrs from her perch.

"So is being dead," Velma mutters.

I slip the stone into my pocket, and the moment it settles there, my anxiety lessens. Warmth spreads through me. Moonridge recognizing me again. Accepting me.

"Thank you, Agnes."

As I turn to leave, Agnes calls after me. "And Calvin? Whatever you're here to do… Just remember that some things are meant to be. Not all paths can be diverted."

Her words settle like stones in my stomach. Some things are meant to be? Not Everett's death. Not if I can help it.

"Thank you, but I have to try."

"Yes." Her smile thins at the edges. "I suppose that's why you're here."

The door closes behind me. I take one step down the worn wooden stairs and that pulse hits me again, a warm thrum through my chest that feels half welcome, half warning.

Moonridge stretches before me, shops closing for the night. A woman flips the sign on the bakery. A man sweeps the sidewalk in front of the barbershop.

I turn the corner, and there it is again.

Vince's Chrysler is parked under a streetlight across from the diner. And behind the wheel, staring straight at me, sits Vince.

Our gazes catch. I offer a smile and a wave. It's not returned. Does he know I took the box? And if so, what is he going to do about it?

I keep walking. I don't run. Don't look back. The onyx in my pocket seems to pulse out a warning.

What will he do? Go after Everett? Hunt me down? Report back to the Concord that their plans are compromised?

I round another corner, finally out of his sightline. Only then do I let myself breathe. Consider what I've done. I've stolen from a dangerous man working with an even more dangerous organization. I've put myself on their radar. Maybe put Everett in even more danger.

But I've also taken the first real step toward stopping them. Toward saving Everett.

Checkmate.

CHAPTER TWENTY-TWO

Everett

I lie back on the bed and stare at the ceiling until the plaster turns into vague shapes. Vince is right. Calvin is new to town. I don't really know him. I should listen because Vince has been in my life, in my mess, longer than Calvin has.

Vince says I'm too quick to trust people. That guys like Calvin show up, smile pretty, and ruin everything. He might be right. I've fallen for sweet voices and soft looks before, only to be taken advantage of and left behind.

But Calvin doesn't feel like the others. He talks to me like I matter. When he looks at me, it lands somewhere deep, like he's seeing past the surface instead of skimming it. My skin buzzes every time I think about it.

Why do I keep finding myself here?

Still, part of me wants Calvin to be exactly who I think he is. Someone who would take all the jagged parts of me and stay anyway.

Is it worth the risk? And what would that do to Vince? He said he loved me earlier today. He's never said that before. He can be controlling, and he pushes me around, but I know how sad he is. How hollow he feels when he thinks no one is looking, how scared he is of his father. He drags that fear around like a packed suitcase he never puts down.

Maybe it's better if I don't let myself imagine a world where someone like Calvin Mitchell falls for someone like me. Safer to enjoy the way he makes me feel from a distance and let the rest go before it turns into heartbreak. At least with Vince I know what to expect.

Footsteps creak in the hallway. Mr. Randall's voice carries through the thin walls. "Everett? You got a visitor."

I jolt upright. A visitor?

I step into the hallway. Vince stands in the open doorway, leather jacket catching the evening light. For a second, my chest drops like I missed a step on the stairs.

What is Vince doing here? He's supposed to be out of town tonight. He leans against the doorframe, hands loose at his sides. "Hey, Ev."

"Hey." I glance at Mr. Randall, who hovers near the kitchen door. "I thought you were leaving town tonight."

"Had a little setback I needed to deal with first." Something flicks across his face that looks a lot like anger. Or frustration. "Could we talk outside? Won't take long."

Outside, the evening air cools the back of my neck. Vince leads me to his car and leans against the hood. He glances around to make sure no one is watching, then his hand finds mine, light and careful. Nothing like the bruising grip from last night.

"I'm sorry." His gaze drops to our joined hands. "I've been impatient with you lately. Taking out my frustrations on you. Making you shift into Sam. It's not fair to you."

I wait, the muscles in my neck pulling tight.

"It's not you, Ev." His fingers trace the center of my palm in slow circles. "It's my issues with Sam. He acts so high and mighty. Carter royalty, you know? Treats me like I'm nothing because I'm human. I'm getting tired of his snide remarks. He's done this for years. I just… I let it get to me."

This version of Vince, the one who speaks his insecurities instead of acts on them, is the one I met last fall. My loneliness recognized his and reached for it. *This* is the dark-eyed, olive-skinned boy who showed me his vulnerability and didn't flinch when I said the messy stuff. This is the Vince I fell for.

"I took it out on you." He looks up now, eyes bright with regret. "I made you be Sam so I could feel like I had some control over him. It was wrong. And then that Calvin guy showed up and I see how he looks at you… I know I said it earlier, but I'm afraid of losing you."

"Vince, I…"

"No, let me finish." His grip tightens, then eases. "I love you, Everett. More than I've loved anything in my life. I felt something special between us when we first met and it's still there. I wouldn't know what to do if you ever left me."

The world shrinks to those three words. I love you. Twice in one day.

I want to believe him. I want to believe this version of him is the real one and the rest was noise. But there's a thin, shaking voice in the back of my head that calls this a trick. I shove it down and nod.

I should accept him. He's the only constant I have.

"I promise things will be different." He reaches into the car and pulls out a long case. "Starting with this."

The guitar case gleams in the evening light. My fingers tremble as I take it from him.

"Open it," he says.

Inside lies a Gibson acoustic, the wood honey-gold and perfect. The sight actually knocks the air out of me. I have wanted a guitar for years, ever since my grandpa taught me basic chords on his old junker when I was a kid. My fingers trace the curves of the body, the neat line of the frets, the clean strings.

This is more than I ever thought anyone would hand to me.

Maybe I've been wrong. Maybe Vince *does* love me. Maybe the times he hurt me were him drowning in his own mess and dragging me under without meaning to. People screw up when they're hurting.

I cling to that. To him.

"Vince, this is..." Words tangle on my tongue. "How did you...?"

"You said you wanted to write songs." He shrugs, like it's nothing. "Now you can."

Before my brain can catch up, he pulls out a small box. "One more thing."

The necklace inside is simple. A small neck chain. It matches the one he wears tucked under his shirt.

"Now we match," he says, stepping closer. He reaches around to fasten it at the back of my neck. His fingers brush my skin. "My commitment to you. Rings are too obvious. But this you can wear and think of me."

The moment the chain touches my skin, warmth gathers behind my sternum and spreads across my chest in a slow tide. The heat branches outward, thin and deliberate, like lines drawn just under the skin.

I run my fingers over it. The surface feels smooth but somehow organic. Like bone that has been polished to a shine.

"I'm going to make all our dreams come true, Ev." His voice drops low, close to my ear. "Everything we've talked about. Your music. Us living free, being ourselves. It's all coming. I promise."

His hand finds mine and he gives it a squeeze. I want to lean in and kiss him, to press my mouth to his and hang onto this softer version of him. Maybe if we stay in this sweet pocket of time, nothing else will bleed through and everything *will* be okay.

As if he can read it on my face, he says, "I'd kiss you, but we're kind of in a fishbowl here. I don't want us to get caught and then get locked up in Hollow Glen Asylum."

I huff out a small laugh. He's right. We're basically on display and I'm not in the mood for a lobotomy.

"I have to go," he says, eyes lingering on me. "I have to get to Boston. But I'll be back tomorrow."

He climbs into his car and drives away, leaving me in the yard with a guitar case and the faint heat of the new chain pressed to my chest.

I start toward the house and catch my reflection in my car's side mirror. It looks like me. Same mop of hair. Same tired eyes.

Then the world around the glass crumples.

The air shivers like ripples spreading across still water. I lean closer, breath fogging the mirror.

My face flickers. Just for a blink.

Half me. Half something else.

The other face wears my features, but wrong. The eyes are empty sockets of shadow, a hollow where a person should be. The skin looks drained of color. The mouth hangs open, slack and lifeless, like someone took a photo of me in the middle of a breath.

I stagger back from the car and reach for the side of it to steady myself.

What *was* that?

I force myself to look again.

Just me. Normal me. Or as normal as I can be.

My fingers skim my cheeks, my jaw, the line of my mouth. Solid. Warm. Human.

"It's fine," I tell myself quietly. "You're fine."

I grab the guitar case with both hands and head for the porch before my brain can start replaying the vision.

I sit on the steps and remove the guitar, setting the case beside me. The wood of the guitar feels sturdy under my fingertips. The weight of it presses me back into my body. I test a few chords, adjusting the tuning until the notes fall into place. The sound is rich and warm, filling the small yard.

A melody finds me. Simple, a little sad. It threads through my fingers and climbs out of my throat before I can overthink it. Words trail after, soft and low, until I'm singing into the thickening dusk.

"That was beautiful."

The string bites into my fingertip when I freeze mid-chord. I look up.

Calvin stands at the end of the sidewalk, hands in his pockets, twilight making his dark hair look even darker.

"I was just messing around." My voice comes out rough. I place the guitar back in its case and wipe my palms on my jeans.

"Everything okay?" He steps closer, scanning my face. "You were really quiet on the way back from the lake, and I wanted to make sure I hadn't stepped in anything."

Stepped in anything? His choice of words confuses me sometimes, but I ignore it.

"Got a lot on my mind," I say, watching the last streaks of daylight fade over the neighboring rooftops.

"I can imagine." He lowers himself onto the step beside me, leaving a polite amount of space. The air between us still buzzes like it has opinions. "Just had dinner at the diner. Thought I would walk off the pie." He pats his stomach.

My fingers drift to the chain resting beneath my T-shirt. The metal feels warmer than it did a few minutes ago, like someone turned up a dial.

"Nice evening for a walk," I say.

"Want to join me?" He tips his head toward the street.

My mind scrambles for all the reasons I should say no. Vince's apology. Vince's gifts. Vince's I love you.

But it's just a walk with a co-worker. A new friend. Nothing more.

"Yeah," I say. The word surprises me. "I would like that."

We head down Maple Street, past houses with glowing windows and the smell of dinner still clinging to the air. Calvin keeps pace beside me, hands shoved into his pockets. Not brushing against me, but close enough that warmth radiates off him.

The sidewalk clicks under our shoes. Somewhere, a dog barks. Curtains twitch. The chain under my shirt gathers more heat with each block, like it's slowly waking up.

"Can I ask you something?" I finally say.

"Anything."

"Why are you being so nice to me?" I stare straight ahead. "Most folks don't give me a second look. And I gotta be honest. It felt like you were looking for me last night when I met you at the diner."

Calvin slows a little and turns his head toward me. "Is it so hard to believe someone would just like being around you?"

"Yeah, actually, it is." I nudge a pebble along with the toe of my shoe. "I tend to fade into the background. People tend to only notice me when they want something, then they take it and move on. You barely know me. So what is it you want?"

"Maybe I just want to know you." His words land without any fancy dressing. "The real you. Not what you can do for me."

My chest pulls tight. The chain burns hotter, heat pooling right over my heart, like it wants to drag me backward.

"I should tell you something." The sentence tumbles out. My tongue feels clumsy. "I'm queer. Me and Vince, we are… I dunno. A thing I guess?"

I fix my gaze on the cracks in the sidewalk and wait for the impact. Anger. A slur. Him walking away.

Calvin's hand settles on my shoulder, steady and firm. When I finally look up, he looks at me with his brows drawn together, expression open.

"I already figured that out," he says. "And you have nothing to be ashamed of, Everett."

"You're not…" I swallow against the dry patch in my throat. "Bothered?"

He shakes his head, the corners of his mouth tipping up. The streetlight catches in his eyes. "I'm gay too. I thought you knew."

I did. I just wanted confirmation.

And it would be so much easier if he wasn't.

"Is that why you're on the run?" I ask. The heat across my chest sinks deeper, a tight band around my ribs. "Because of who you are?"

We pass the town square, now mostly empty except for a few bugs circling the streetlights. Calvin looks ahead, jaw working.

"I'm not so much on the run as looking for something that's been missing," he says after a beat. "Happiness. Peace. Maybe, eventually, love."

He says it the way someone might talk about a grocery list. Clear. Simple.

The chain flares hotter, like it heard that word and took offense.

"Love isn't easy to find," I say. I tug at the neckline of my shirt, trying to get a bit of cool air between the metal and my skin. "Not for people like us."

"Not always. But then sometimes it happens unexpectedly." He meets my eyes, gaze steady. "Sometimes it's right in front of you."

At some point we stopped walking. We stand under a streetlight that bathes his face in gold. His features soften in the glow, all sharp edges blurred.

His hand reaches for mine, fingertips brushing my palm.

Heat races up my arm. My body leans toward his without checking in with my brain. His face is close enough that I can feel his breath against my mouth, warm and sweet.

I glance around. We're out of the residential stretch and stand in front of the hardware store. All of the businesses are closed. If he kisses me, no one will see. No one will come after us. No one will tell Vince.

The chain against my chest flares, a sharp, biting heat that makes me suck in a breath. Vince's voice floods my head, loud and clear. *I love you, Everett. More than anything. I wouldn't know what to do if you ever left me.*

The guitar. The necklace. His promises. All piled on my heart.

I jerk back a step, breaking the almost-kiss. It takes more effort than it should, like I'm pulling against a current.

"I'm sorry," I say. "I can't. I'm with Vince."

"I understand." His shoulders drop a fraction. The disappointment is right there, but he doesn't reach for me again. "I shouldn't have pushed."

"It's not that I don't..." The rest of the sentence tangles and dies. There's no good way to explain that part of me wants to let my lips meet his and forget everything else in my life. To chase this and see where it takes us.

Calvin's focus snaps past me. His whole body goes still.

"What is it?" I follow his gaze.

A figure in a dark cloak walks down the sidewalk across the street. At first glance, it's nothing. People in Moonridge like their dramatic outerwear. But Calvin stares like the ground just opened.

"Calvin?"

The figure turns into an alley that dead ends behind the hardware store. Calvin moves before I can say more, cutting across the road with a sharp, purposeful stride that feels nothing like his easy walk from a minute ago.

"Hey, wait up!" I hurry after him. "That alley is a dead end. It just leads to an old storage shed."

He doesn't answer. The set of his shoulders looks carved from stone.

When we reach the alley entrance, the cloaked figure is gone.

Brick walls rise around us, soaking up what little light filters in from the street. Shadows collect in the corners, thick enough that my eyes have trouble sorting what's real.

"They couldn't have just vanished," Calvin mutters. He moves deeper into the alley, eyes combing every doorway and stack of crates. He flexes his fingers like he's trying to shake something off.

"Maybe they went into one of the buildings?" I ask. My breath ghosts in front of my face. The air feels colder here. "Do you know that person?"

He still doesn't answer. He walks straight to the shed at the end of the alley like something is pulling him there. The shed is old, paint peeling away in strips. Calvin takes the doorknob and tries to turn it. The metal rattles. The door holds.

"It's locked," I say, wrapping my arms around myself. "Like I said, Mr. Wilson just keeps extra stock in there."

Calvin's face drains of color. His knuckles stand out white against the dark metal. A fine tremor runs through his arms, all the way to his shoulders. He looks like someone bracing for a hit no one else can see.

"Calvin?" I step closer. "Talk to me. What's going on? It's just a shed."

"No." The word scrapes its way out of him. "It's not."

"What do you mean?" I rest my hand on his forearm. His skin feels taut under my fingers.

He finally drags his gaze away from the door and looks at me. The expression there sends a chill straight down my spine. It's like he's watching two timelines at once, this alley in front of us and something layered over it that I can't see.

"I can't explain," he says. His voice is rough around the edges. "Not yet. But that shed…"

"It's nothing, unless you're looking for a spare toaster or a sewing machine," I say, trying to lighten my tone.

Calvin shakes his head. "I think we should go."

He lets go of the knob, but his eyes keep hooking back to it as we retrace our steps toward the street, like he expects the door to swing open on its own.

Back on the sidewalk, the normal world seeps in again. The occasional car. Distant voices. The glow of shop windows.

As we walk, one thought keeps circling.

Calvin Mitchell didn't just drift into Moonridge looking for work. He came here chasing something. And whatever it is, it sits behind that locked shed door.

CHAPTER TWENTY-THREE

Calvin

I stumble away from the shed. The door is locked. My escape back to my timeline is gone.

My legs tremble with each step. Questions slam into me. Does the Concord know I'm here? Did they lock me out on purpose? Is La'Tasha okay?

I drag in a breath that feels too thin.

"Calvin? Are you okay?" Everett catches up, his hand hovering near my elbow like he's afraid I'll collapse.

"I'm fine." The lie tastes like ass. "Just... that shed reminds me of one back home. Bad memories."

"What kind of memories?"

I scramble for something believable. "One time I accidentally locked myself in a shed when I was a kid and no one knew where I was." I stop, swallow. "Nothing major. Just a weird flashback."

Everett's brows crease. Another lie on top of all the others.

"I'm sorry that happened to you." His hand brushes my arm, gentle and comforting. The touch settles in my stomach; I almost lean into it.

I breathe deep as my thoughts spin, refusing to line up. If I can't get back through that door, I'm stuck here forever. If the Concord knows what I'm doing, Everett is in even more danger. I need help. Fast.

"I'll be okay, really," I say, waving it off. "Just the locked door triggered something. Don't worry about it."

But Everett isn't buying it. His eyes stay fixed on my face, too sharp.

I should drop the bullshit and tell him everything. Right now.

The speech lines up in my head.

But then what? He still doesn't fully trust me. Why would he believe I've met his ghost? That the Concord will use him as part of their fucked up ritual and he has Vince to thank for it? And he sure as hell won't believe I'm a time traveler from the future.

No. I need Agnes and her mother. They'll know what to do about the door. I need to figure out how to get it open and then I can figure out how to tell Everett.

"Sorry to cut our walk short," I say, rolling my shoulders back. "I should probably head back to my room. Get some rest before work tomorrow."

"You sure you're okay?" Everett steps closer. Twilight catches in his eyes, all worry.

"Yeah. Just tired." I manage a smile. "Thanks for coming with me. And for trusting me with your truth. And your story."

He nods, shoving his hands in his pockets. "I know what you're thinking. But it's not that simple with Vince."

"No. You don't have to explain." I want to say more. Want to tell him he deserves better, but I keep it buried. For now. "Relationships are hard."

"Sounds like you know from experience."

Jace flashes briefly through my mind.

"Let's just say I've watched people I care about go through similar stuff." I force a smile.

We walk back toward his place. Silence stretches between us, thick with everything I'm not saying. The locked door. The cloaked figure. I match my steps to his, count the passing cars, anything to keep from cracking open.

When we reach his street, I stop. "Thanks again for the walk. See you tomorrow at the garage?"

"Sure thing." His fingers touch his sternum again. He hesitates, like he wants to say more. Then simply, "Goodnight, Calvin."

"Night, Everett."

I watch him walk up to his house. He climbs the steps, his hand trailing along the railing. At the door, he pauses, looks back, raises his hand in a small wave. Then disappears inside.

I stand there a moment longer, watching the living room window. No lights flick on. No curtains move. Everett's not watching me leave. I turn and head back toward the apothecary. Guilt twists through me. He thinks I'm calling it a night, but I need answers about that portal, and I need them now. If Agnes and her mom can't help me, I might be stuck here for good.

My steps echo across mostly empty streets. Moonridge feels different at night. Quieter. Every porch light seems to track me as I cut through two blocks, past the diner and the barber shop, toward the apothecary. Agnes and her mother have to be there. They have to help.

By the time the shop comes into view, my jog has cooled to a walk. I pull in a steady breath and step closer.

Through the front window, I can see movement inside. Candlelight flickers, casting dancing shadows on the walls. Two figures hunch over something on the workbench. I step closer to the glass. Agnes and a middle-aged woman stare intently at a small object between them. Is that the box I brought?

I rap my knuckles against the window, harder than I mean to. Both women jump, heads whipping toward the sound. Agnes's eyes widen when she sees me, and she hurries to unlock the door.

"Michigan!" She pulls me inside quickly, glancing up and

down the street before shutting the door behind me. "What's wrong? You look like the devil himself is chasing you."

The older woman straightens, wiping her hands on her apron. Her eyes narrow as they scan me from head to toe.

The floor seems to slide sideways for a second. I grab the edge of the counter to steady myself.

It's Hazel's face. But not Hazel. The bone structure is similar. The same high cheekbones, the same straight nose, the same stubborn set to her jaw. But Rachel's hair is dark brunette streaked with silver instead of auburn, and her green eyes are harder, more calculating than Hazel's playful gaze.

"Mother, this is Calvin Mitchell. The one I told you about." Agnes gestures between us. "Calvin, this is my mother, Rachel Thornton."

Rachel doesn't offer her hand. Instead, she steps closer, her gaze intense. "So you're the one."

"The one?" My voice cracks.

"The one who doesn't belong here." Her words cut straight through my panic. "I've felt a disturbance in Moonridge's energy for the last day or two. Something wrong. It's you."

"Michigan, huh?" Velma speaks from the shelf, making Agnes jump. "More like Michigan by way of the future, I'd guess."

"Velma!" Rachel snaps. "Hold your tongue or I'll turn you back into a paperweight."

"Can't blame a cat for being curious," Trixie pipes up. "He's practically sparkling with future energy!"

"And looking mighty fine while doing it," adds Lucy. "The future must have excellent genetics."

"Enough!" Rachel claps her hands and the cats freeze mid-sentence. She turns back to me. "What brings you here at this hour? What's happened?"

I grip the counter. "The door. My way home. It's locked. I just saw someone in a cloak go through it but I couldn't follow and now it's locked and I'm stuck here and everything's falling apart and I need your help."

Agnes gasps, but Rachel's face stays carved from stone. Something shifts behind her eyes.

"Show me." Her voice turns brisk. She picks up the box from the counter and tucks it carefully underneath, out of sight. "This door. Take us there now."

Rachel doesn't speak as she exits the shop. Agnes follows close behind, her footsteps quick and light on the pavement.

The alley behind the hardware store looks even more ominous now. The shadows pool deeper in the corners, thick and viscous like spilled ink. Rachel steps forward, motioning for Agnes and me to stay behind her.

"Stand back," she commands, pulling a small bottle from her bag. She uncorks it and sprinkles oil in front of the door, murmuring words under her breath.

The air around us shifts, grows heavy. The hair on my arms stands up. Rachel places her palms against the wood of the door and closes her eyes. The words she speaks aren't English. They sound ancient, powerful, like they're pulling energy directly from the earth beneath our feet.

Slowly, the door begins to glow. Not the whole door, but certain parts of it, like veins of light running through the wood. Teal light. Symbols appear in the air around it, floating sigils and letters from a language I've never seen.

Rachel traces them with her fingers, still chanting. Agnes steps closer, her eyes round, breathing sharp.

"Wait. That says...," she whispers.

"I said stay back." Rachel's voice cracks like a whip. Agnes immediately ducks her head and retreats, shrinking under her mother's glare. Only when Agnes has backed up several steps does Rachel return to studying the door.

"This is definitely a time portal. It's still active," she says. "But it's in use."

"In use?" My stomach gives a slow, sick lurch. "What does

that mean?"

"Someone else is traveling through it right now." Rachel brushes dust from her hands. "Using its pathway."

"So I just wait for them to finish?"

Rachel's mouth flattens. "It's not that simple. This door can lead to multiple times, not just your own. I think the lock is a safeguard. The door prevents anyone else from entering when it's in use. Let's hope, for your sake, they return soon."

I step forward. "So I can still use it when they're done, right? It'll open again?"

"Who helped you come through this doorway?" Rachel asks, ignoring my question. "This is ancient magic. Few can manage it."

I hesitate. "I stumbled upon the doorway one day. I tried using it, but it only took me back to my childhood. It seemed to be memory based. A witch named La'Tasha Morehouse helped me feed it information from 1958 so I could travel here."

Rachel's gaze sharpens at the name. "Morehouse." Her nostrils flare like she smelled a fart. "I see."

She turns toward the door again, and in the teal light her face seems to have lost what little color it had. "And why are you here? What are you trying to change?"

"I'm trying to save someone. Someone who dies soon. Someone the Concord sacrifices."

Rachel whips around so fast her skirt flares. "How do you know of the Concord?"

"They're active in my time. They're trying to take over the world." I glance at Agnes, who has gone very still, her freckles stark against her skin.

"So they finally found their thirteen," Rachel mutters, and I can't tell if that's fear or grim respect in her voice.

"I came back to stop them from killing someone important and to weaken them."

Agnes stands frozen in place, her gaze sharp and analytical as she processes everything. Rachel beckons urgently, already backing toward the entrance. "We must go. Now. Before whoever entered that doorway comes back." She turns to Agnes. "Get back to the house."

"But Mother…"

"Now, Agnes." She yanks us both away from the door, her movements quick and jerky. Her head swivels, scanning the alley like she expects the Concord to ooze out of the shadows.

Back at the apothecary, Rachel locks the door behind us and draws the blinds. The match scrapes twice before it catches; she lights candles and sets them at the cardinal points of the room. Her face looks carved and tight in the flickering light.

"You need to leave this timeline," she tells me. "As soon as that door opens again, you must go through it."

"I can't leave without Everett," I protest. "He's the one I came to save."

Rachel's expression hardens, jaw clenching. "You cannot take someone from their proper time. The consequences…"

"The consequence of leaving him is death," I argue. "He's going to be murdered. And the Concord will have all of their members. My friends and family could die."

"Mother," Agnes interjects, "if someone is going to die…"

"No." Rachel cuts her off. "Interfering with someone's fate can cause ripples we cannot predict." She turns to me. "I will monitor the door. When it opens, Agnes will fetch you and you'll return to wherever you came from." She pushes Agnes toward the stairs. "Go to your room."

Agnes catches my eye and nods before disappearing up the stairs, leaving me alone with Rachel.

"You need to leave," Rachel says to me. "It's not safe."

I start to protest.

"Out. Now."

The door behind me flies open and something yanks at me, like the room itself is spitting me out. I stumble out onto the porch and the door slams in my face.

I head back toward the B&B. Rachel's warning drums in my skull, but it changes nothing. I'm taking Everett back with me. Timeline fallout or not. I refuse to watch him die when I can stop it. I'll pack my things, wait for Agnes to tell me the door is open, then force Everett to come with me. Simple.

Except for every single part of that plan. That would be kidnapping.

I need to convince him to come with me. His life is on the line. And Rachel can talk all she wants about timelines and consequences, but she doesn't understand. She doesn't know that his murder powers the Concord for decades.

Sorry, Rachel. I'm taking him with me.

"Calvin!"

I spin around, a jolt punching through my chest.

Agnes hurries toward me, her skirt swishing around her knees. She keeps glancing over her shoulder.

"What are you doing here?" I ask when she catches up. "I thought your mother wanted you upstairs."

She catches her breath, cheeks flushed. "I told her I was going to bed. Waited until she was busy in her room, then climbed down the trellis."

"The trellis?"

"Not my first escape." She grins. "But we don't have much time. Mother will check on me eventually."

"Why risk it? What's so important?"

Her smile fades. "The box. We opened it before you arrived. You need to know what was inside."

"But we saw what was in the box yesterday. It was a braided bracelet."

"But there were other things in the compartment beneath it."

Something cold slithers down my spine. "Tell me."

She pauses. Takes a breath. I can see her gathering herself to say something terrible.

"First," she says slowly, "a piece of vellum."

"Vellum?" I step closer.

"Old. Very old. With symbols written on it." She swallows hard. "Written in blood."

My tongue feels thick. "What kind of symbols?"

"I don't know yet. Mother said she couldn't identify them. But the blood…" She trails off, looking sick. "It's still fresh. Still red. Like it was written yesterday. But the vellum itself is ancient."

"What else?"

"A lock of hair." Her eyes meet mine. "Blonde hair."

The street wobbles in my vision. I grab her arm to steady myself. "Blonde."

"Tied with black thread. Knotted seven times." She touches my hand gently. "And the third thing. A black stone about the size of a walnut. Smooth. Polished. With veins of red running through it."

"Veins?"

"They pulse. Like a heartbeat. Like the stone is alive." Her fingers twist in the fabric of her skirt. "Mother said it's old work. The kind they don't teach anymore because it's too dangerous. Too dark."

Cold spreads through my chest, down into my stomach. "What does it do?"

"It binds a life to a specific death." She leans in, voice thin. "The hair belongs to the target. The blood symbols name the time and place of death. The stone holds it all together, makes it unbreakable."

Even though I expected all of this I still feel unsteady on my feet.

"The stone was still pulsing," Agnes continues, studying my face. "That means the ritual isn't complete yet. The death hasn't happened. Obviously." She steps closer. "It's Everett's hair, isn't it?"

I nod and force the word out. "Yes."

"The moment I saw you look at him, I felt something. A connection. Like you were here for him." She touches my arm gently. "He's going to die, isn't he?"

I swallow hard. "He is."

A rustle comes from behind a tree and we both freeze. Still jumpy after everything that happened tonight. Agnes gestures for me to follow her back the way we came.

"You care about him, don't you?"

I nod. "He's suffering in my time. I want to save him from that."

Agnes squeezes my hand. Doesn't say anything. Just walks beside me while I try to breathe through the enormity of everything that happened tonight.

I care for him. I'm going to save him, even if he never feels the same or hates me for dragging him out of this timeline.

"Then we need to hurry." Agnes's voice pulls me back. She glances behind us. "Mother said she wants no part of this. She believes the Concord is too dangerous to cross."

"She's not wrong," I admit. "But I can't just let Everett die."

"I know." She squeezes my arm. "That's why I'm helping you. But we need to understand what's on that vellum. The symbols aren't like any I've seen before. Not standard witch runes. Something older."

"Can your mother translate them?"

"She said no, but I think she can. She just won't." Agnes starts walking, pulling me along. "We need someone else. Someone I haven't spoken to in years. Someone my mother forbids me to see."

"Who?"

"A… friend." Agnes's voice goes flat. "Or something like that. You mentioned one of their ancestors from the future. The Morehouses."

"Where do we find them?"

"The far side of town." She picks up her pace. "The Morehouses and the Thorntons had a falling out years ago. Mother says they dabble in magic that is too dangerous. I, personally, think it's a control thing, but Mother forbids me from engaging with them."

"Dangerous magic?"

"Old magic." Agnes's mouth is a hard line in the moonlight. "The kind that my family doesn't work with or understand. Since it's different and more powerful, Mother seems to think it's wrong."

"And you think they'll help us?"

"If anyone can read those symbols, it's Esther Morehouse." She glances at me. "But I have to warn you, her daughter, Bea, doesn't like me and I have... history with Bea's brother, Ronald."

"Okay..."

"I just need you to understand that the divide is deep and they might refuse to help." She stops walking, turns to face me fully. "I want to set your expectations that this might not go our way, but we can try."

I nod.

"It's too late to go over there now, but how about I meet you after work tomorrow? We'll figure out what's on this paper and then get you out of here before anything bad happens."

"And Everett," I say.

"Yes, and Everett." We walk up the path together. Side by side. Partners in whatever comes next.

I watch her scramble back up the trellis next to the apothecary and then head back to the B&B.

At least I have a partner in crime now. All I need is a plan that doesn't end with both of us dead.

CHAPTER TWENTY-FOUR

Everett

I press my back against the oak tree, bark biting through my shirt. I hold myself still and small in the dark, willing them not to notice. They can't know I'm here.

Calvin's voice carries through the night air, and I hear my name fall from his lips. What the hell is he doing out here with Agnes Thornton at this hour? And why are they talking about me?

I'd gone inside after our walk, still thinking about the way Calvin looked at that storage shed like it had personally attacked him. Still thinking about how close we came to kissing under that streetlight, and how badly I wanted it, even though I knew better.

Then I glanced out my bedroom window while unbuttoning my shirt and saw him still standing on the sidewalk, looking at my house like he was memorizing it. That was weird enough. Then he turned and walked back toward Main Street instead of heading back to the inn.

Something in my gut twisted. An instinct I should have listened to days ago.

I slipped out the back door, careful not to let the screen door slam. The night air felt cooler than before; or maybe that was just me. I kept to the shadows, following Calvin's silhouette. He walked with purpose. Not the casual stroll of someone heading home. This was different. Tight. Focused.

When he turned onto Main Street, I had to hang back farther. Too many streetlights. Too many windows. Too much chance of being seen. My whole body buzzed, part of me screaming to turn back, the other part needing to know.

Now I'm pressed against rough bark, eavesdropping on a conversation I was never meant to hear.

Calvin says something about the Concord. Agnes answers, but my focus keeps snagging on single words instead of sentences. I catch "vellum" without the context. Then Agnes says something about symbols and blood, and my brain finally snaps into gear.

Wait. Go back. Did she say blood?

"The hair belongs to the target," Agnes says. Her voice is clearer now. Or maybe I'm just listening harder. "The blood symbols name the time and place of death."

Time and place of death.

"The stone holds it all together, makes it unbreakable."

I miss the next few words. My palms grind into the tree. When did I start gripping it so hard?

"It's Everett's hair, isn't it?" Agnes asks, her voice soft but steady in the quiet night.

A cold rush skates over my scalp. *My* hair?

"Yes." Calvin's voice sounds rough, like he swallowed gravel.

"He's going to die, isn't he?" Agnes asks.

"Yes, he is."

The world tilts and my knees buckle. Their voices sink under a heavy pounding in my ears. *My* death. This isn't happening. It can't be happening. I thought Calvin was just some random guy passing through town. Is he here to kill me?

Why?

My thoughts jump to the shed. The locked door. Calvin's haunted stare. The way his fingers dug into the knob. What is he hiding in there?

I should step out from behind this tree. Confront them. Ask what the hell is going on. Demand answers.

Instead I stay planted, lungs burning. If Calvin is planning to hurt me, letting him know I overheard this feels like volunteering myself as a sacrifice.

Their conversation fades. Footsteps move off down the street. Only when I'm sure they're gone do I peel myself away from the tree. My legs feel hollow, like they might give at any second.

The walk home is a blur of dark windows and streetlights. I jump at the scrape of a loose branch, at the rattle of a passing car. My fingers find the chain resting on my chest, and it grows hotter with each step, a steady burn against my skin.

By the time I reach the Randalls' house, my grip on the key is slick. Metal scrapes metal, too loud in the quiet night. The lock finally catches and I stumble inside and down the hall to my room.

I lean my forehead against the door for a second. Thin wood between me and whatever I just witnessed. Between me and Calvin.

I fall onto my bed fully clothed, shoes and all.

This is just further proof that trust is a luxury I can't afford. I feel like everything inside me is trying to curl in on itself, smaller and smaller, until there's nothing left anyone can touch. I try to push it away, but the ache in my chest gets worse. Like someone shoved a rock under my ribs.

Sleep doesn't come. How could it? Every time I close my eyes, I see Calvin's face. Hear his voice saying my name. Feel the ghost of his almost-kiss under that streetlight.

All of it a lie.

All of it leading to something I don't understand. Something that involves my death.

The sky outside my window starts to lighten. Gray dawn seeps into the room. Another day. Eight hours with Calvin, pretending everything is normal.

I have no idea how I'm supposed to look at him and act like I don't know. Like I didn't hear him talking about my death.

But I'll figure it out. I always do. Vince will be back tonight. I'll focus on our future. I'll shove Calvin into the same mental junk drawer as every other mistake.

And hope he leaves soon.

I drag myself out of bed and strip off yesterday's clothes. After my shower, I stand in front of the mirror and practice my face. Neutral. Calm.

Except I look like hell. Dark circles under my eyes. Skin washed out.

"You're fine," I tell my reflection. "You're fine. You're fine."

The words sound thin, but I keep saying them anyway.

Sitting here staring at myself won't fix anything. Thinking sure as hell won't. So I head to the garage because at least a broken-down car doesn't lie to my face.

***

I focus on the stubborn gearbox in front of me, trying to lose myself in the familiar puzzle of metal parts. The Ford has been giving Earl trouble for weeks, and now it's my problem. Good. I need a problem I can actually fix. Not the mess that crawled under my skin last night.

The garage door opens and my shoulders pull tight.

"Good morning," Calvin says.

"Mornin'." I don't look up. Can't look up. If I see his face, I'll either break down or start screaming, and neither option is acceptable.

I see him in my peripheral vision. He leans against the doorframe, coffee in hand, smile in place, like this is any other morning. But there are smudges under his eyes, like he spent the night arguing with his own thoughts.

Or planning my murder.

My fingers move automatically, loosening bolts. I've taken apart hundreds of these. I could do it blindfolded.

Calvin lingers a few feet away. His attention lands on my hands, on the engine, then back on me. It prickles between my shoulder blades.

"Need any help with that?"

"I've got it." The words come out clipped. "Earl needs someone to watch the gas pumps and change the oil on the Stevenson car. Keys are on the hook."

He hesitates. The pause stretches. "You sure? That box looks pretty corroded."

"I said I've got it." My voice comes out rough, and guilt punches me in the gut. I hate snapping at people. Still... Calvin appeared two days ago and zeroed in on me like he already knew where to look. After what I heard last night, that doesn't feel like chance. It feels planned. Vince was right. I can't trust him.

"Okay. Just let me know if you change your mind."

He walks away, and I tell myself the tightness in my chest is relief, not guilt for being rude. My fingers slip on the wrench. I adjust my grip and keep working.

For the next hour, I bury myself in the job. The clutch and gearbox are even more of a mess than they looked, but that's fine. The more complicated the problem, the less room my brain has for prophecies of my death.

Calvin checks on me. Once. Twice. Three times. Each attempt hits the wall I've built. Short answers. No eye contact.

I can't risk meeting his gaze.

The fourth time he approaches, I sense him before I see him, a shift in the air beside me.

"That oil change is done," he says, wiping his hands on a rag. "Want me to take a look at the radiator on the Miller truck?"

"If you want."

He steps closer. Too close. Soap and sweat and wolf crowd my space. My hands still. Every muscle pulls tight.

"Everett." His voice softens. "Did I do something wrong? You're obviously upset."

A hysterical laugh claws at my throat. Did he do something wrong? Only meet with someone in the middle of the night and talk about my death like it was just another item on his to-do list.

"I'm fine," I say. "Just... busy."

"You know you can talk to me, right? About anything."

I make the mistake of looking up. His eyes latch onto mine. Warm. Concerned.

Liar.

"Can I?" I ask. The edge in my voice surprises even me. "Just feels like you're hiding something."

Color pulls out of his face in one quick sweep. His mouth tightens before he smooths it away. "What do you mean? I thought we talked about this last night."

"Forget it." I turn back to the gearbox and snag a smaller wrench, more for something to hold than anything else. "Just forget it."

He hovers a moment longer. I can feel him standing there, ready to push, to pry.

Please leave.

He retreats. Footsteps carry him across the concrete, and some of the tension leaks out of me.

The next stretch of time drags. The garage fills with the usual sounds: metal clanking, the hiss of pneumatic tools, Calvin moving between cars. Everything sounds normal. None of it is.

I hear Calvin talking to Earl near the office. Something about the Miller truck. A part that needs ordering.

I reach for a socket wrench, mind once again chewing on last night instead of paying attention.

My hand slips.

Metal slices clean and deep. Heat blooms across my palm a

beat later. I jerk my hand back. Blood spills over my fingers and onto the engine block, bright against the grime.

"Crap."

I grab for a rag and clamp it over the cut. The fabric goes dark almost immediately, warm and slick against my skin. My knees feel loose. I hate blood.

"Everett?" Calvin's voice cuts through the fuzz. Footsteps slam toward me. Then he's there, one hand steadying my wrist. "Jesus, what happened?"

He peels the rag back carefully, like he's afraid to hurt me more. His touch is gentle, sure, and it somehow makes everything inside my chest pull tight.

"Let me see," he murmurs, turning my palm toward the light.

The cut gapes open. Blood wells up in a steady rhythm. I stare at it, caught between morbid curiosity and the urge to throw up.

"This needs stitches." Calvin's face is close to mine now. Too close. I can see gold flecks in his brown irises.

I should not be noticing that.

He turns toward the office. "Mr. Randall! Everett cut his hand. I need to take him to the hospital."

"I can drive myself," I say, or try to. It comes out thin and unconvincing. Calvin ignores it. His arm goes around my shoulders, solid and warm, steering me toward my car.

My body leans before my brain can stop it. Of course it does. My brain, on the other hand, lights up with alarms. *Do not trust him. Do not forget what you heard last night.*

"Not with your hand bleeding like that," Calvin says. "Give me the keys."

Before I can argue, Earl appears from the office, face creased with worry. "What happened?"

"Cut myself on the Ford," I say, lifting the rag-wrapped hand. "Not too bad."

"Looks plenty bad to me," Earl says. "Calvin's right. You need stitches. Go on."

And just like that, I'm in the passenger seat of my own car, hand wrapped in a towel, Calvin behind the wheel, heading toward the hospital.

I slump against the seat and watch him drive.

He navigates the streets like he grew up here. Takes the first turn without hesitation, left onto Maple, then right onto Oak. No pause at the intersection. No glance at street signs.

My stomach goes tight.

"How do you know where the hospital is?" I ask, suspicion cutting through the haze. "You've been in town less than two days."

Calvin's hands tighten on the wheel for a beat. "Mr. Randall told me when I first came to work," he says. "Said it was important I know in case of emergencies."

Another turn, onto Sycamore. Still no hesitation. He moves through town like he's lived here his entire life.

His excuse sounds plausible. Almost. But Mr. Randall isn't exactly Mr. Safety Briefing.

"Right," I say.

I file it away. One more thing on the growing list that doesn't add up.

He parks, and helps me inside. A nurse with a bright, practiced smile appears and takes me straight to the back, leaving Calvin standing in the waiting room. I half expect him to push to come along. He doesn't. He just nods and watches us walk away, worry pinching his features.

The doctor is efficient. One tetanus shot, five neat stitches, a firm wrap of gauze and instructions to keep it clean and dry. My hand throbs under the bandage, a steady reminder of my own stupidity.

Ninety minutes later, I step back into the waiting room. Calvin is there, hunched over a magazine he clearly isn't reading. His shoulders drop in relief when he spots me, and he sets the magazine aside.

"All patched up?"

I lift my bandaged hand. "Good as new. Almost." The skin around the gauze already feels tight and sore.

"Great." He shifts his weight like he's not sure what to do with his hands. "I went back to the garage while you were getting stitched up. Earl said you should take the rest of the day off."

There's a gentleness in his tone that nudges at something low in my chest. I ignore it.

He holds up a paper bag. "And, I brought sandwiches from the diner. Figured you might be hungry."

My empty stomach answers for me, growling loud enough to be embarrassing. Skipping breakfast was apparently a poor choice.

"And I thought maybe we could take that drive up to Amethyst Beach," he adds. His voice goes careful. "If you're feeling up to it."

Part of me surges toward yes. Wants to sit on the sand with him and watch the water, pretend we're just two guys on a normal day. The want hits so hard I actually lean a fraction closer.

But I can't. I will not be a fool again. For all I know he plans to take me up there and drown me.

"No, thank you," I say, each word like biting down on tinfoil. "I'm tired. I'd rather go home. And don't you need to go back to work?"

His expression tightens. For a heartbeat, everything on his face is bare: hurt, hope, confusion. Then it smooths into something calmer. "Sure. Home it is."

The drive back to the Randalls' is quiet. I stare out the window. I can feel Calvin beside me, steady at the wheel, and that stupid, traitorous part of me keeps stubbornly insisting I'm safe here. Even while my thoughts replay last night on a loop.

Mrs. Randall is outside watering her flowers when we arrive. "Everett! Earl called. How's your hand?"

"Fine, ma'am. Just a few stitches." The bandage tugs when I flex my fingers. Not nothing.

She fusses over me for a minute, then invites Calvin in for iced tea.

He declines politely and lifts the paper bag instead. "Sandwich?"

I take the bag with my good hand. The injured one throbs in protest as I shift its position. "Thanks."

The word feels small compared to everything running through my head. *Thanks for the food, and also, why were you talking about my death last night?*

I start toward the house. I get three steps before Calvin's voice stops me.

"Everett." There's a raw edge to it. "What's wrong? Talk to me. Something's up."

Something inside my chest snaps loose. All the questions, all the replayed words from the night before, pile up and spill over.

I spin back toward him. "I saw you last night," I blurt. "After our walk. I saw you head back toward town, not toward the inn, after telling me you needed to go back to your room."

Calvin goes still. "I can explain..."

"Can you? Because it sure sounded like you were plotting something with Agnes. Something that involves me."

"No, that's not..." He steps forward, reaches for me. I step back. His hand falls to his side. "It's the opposite. I'm trying to help you."

"Help me how? It didn't sound like you wanted to help me."

"It's complicated," Calvin says. His voice frays around the word. "But I swear I'd never hurt you. Ever."

"I don't even know who you are," I say. The fight in me feels thin and worn. "You show up out of nowhere. You act like you know me. You're talking about my death with Agnes Thornton in the middle of the night. And worse, you were talking like you knew me well. None of it makes sense."

"I know." He drags a hand over his face. "And I wish I could explain everything right now, but it would sound crazy."

"Try me." I cross my arms. The motion pulls at my stitches and sends a sting through my hand. I ignore it. "I can handle crazy."

He opens his mouth. Closes it. Tries again. Nothing. He looks lost, like he's searching for a door that isn't there.

"I can't," he finally says. "Not yet. But please, Everett. Trust me a little longer."

"Trust you?" The laugh that breaks out of me is sharp and ugly. "I don't think I can do that."

"You have to." He steps closer, and this time I let him. I'm too worn out to move. "You may not know me yet, but you will... Everything I told you last night was true. I... I care about you."

His gaze locks on mine. Brown and warm and so painfully earnest it stings somewhere under my ribs.

I want to believe him. God, I do. I want to close the distance between us, let him explain, let that warmth be real.

But every bad lesson of my life shouts over the wanting.

"I think you should go," I say instead, my voice rough from everything I'm not saying. "Thanks for driving me to the hospital."

"Everett..."

"Please." I hold out my good hand for my keys. The bandaged one curls close to my chest. "Just go."

He presses the keys into my palm. His shoulders dip, like something heavy settled on them, and for a second he just stands there, studying my face. Memorizing it.

Then he nods once and walks away. I watch him until he disappears around the corner.

I go inside, set the untouched sandwich bag on my dresser, and drop onto my bed. Pride and regret tangle inside my chest. I finally stood up for myself. Drew a line.

So why does it feel like I just set something important on fire?

I close my eyes and Calvin's face fills the darkness. The hurt I saw when I pushed him away.

How I feel about you is real.

Maybe it is. Maybe it isn't. Maybe I'll never know.
And not knowing settles over me heavier than anything else.

CHAPTER TWENTY-FIVE

Calvin

My chest aches with this weird, shitty mix of heavy and empty. Last night we were almost kissing under a streetlight, and now he's treating me like a turd that won't flush.

I kick at a loose stone, watching it skitter across the pavement and disappear into the gutter.

I've fucked this up so completely I don't know where to begin fixing it. And the worst part? I don't have time to wallow. Everett is running out of time. He's going to die if I don't get him out of here.

Part of me thinks I should have just told him the truth. But yeah, "I'm from the future" sounds way more insane than "I was locked in a shed as a kid." I need a better plan. One that doesn't end with him thinking I'm completely out of my mind.

The garage looms ahead, gray and silent in the afternoon light. Earl's sedan is still parked out front. I guess I'll see if there's anything he needs help with even though he did give me the rest of the day off. Maybe if I give Everett some time to cool down, he'll be open to hearing me out later.

Earl steps out of the office as I walk in. "How's Everett doing?"

"His hand's all stitched up. He's resting at home."

Earl nods. Some of the tightness around his eyes eases. "Good, good." He studies my face. "You okay? Look like you lost your best friend."

I blink. "Just worried about him."

"He's tougher than he looks." Earl claps me on the shoulder. "What are you doing back here? I thought I told you to take the rest of the day off."

"Figured I'd finish up the Miller radiator before the weekend. Still a few hours before five."

Earl nods. "Good thinking."

I attack the radiator, grateful for something to focus on besides the hurt in Everett's eyes. It's a mess, corroded and clogged. Perfect. I can pour myself into scraping and flushing and pretend I'm not falling apart.

Somewhere between draining the coolant and removing the upper hose, a plan starts to form. Tonight, I'll talk to Agnes. Maybe she can help me figure out how to explain things to Everett without making it worse. Tomorrow morning I'll try again and give him enough of the truth that he understands I'm trying to help him, not hurt him.

If he still refuses to come with me, I'm screwed. I can't drag him through that portal against his will, and I can't stand here and watch history march him toward a murder I already know is coming.

Just as I'm finishing the radiator, the door behind me creaks open and I snap back to the present, half hoping to see Everett. It's Earl.

"Quittin' time," he says, checking the radiator. "Looks good. You've got a real knack for this. You sure you don't wanna stick around Moonridge? You'd have a job here."

The bell over the door jingles, interrupting us. Agnes bursts through, breathless. She scans the garage, eyes lighting when she spots me.

"Hey there, Earl!" She sounds practically fizzed up on soda and magic.

Earl smiles. "Hello to you, too. We're about to close up."

"Oh, I know. I just need to talk to Calvin for a bit." Agnes flashes her most charming smile.

He locks the cash register, pockets the key, and gives me a nod. "Lock up when you leave. See you Monday. Enjoy your weekend."

The moment Earl's sedan pulls away, Agnes grabs my arm. "You won't believe what we found!"

"What?" I shut the lights off and flip the sign, barely getting the door locked before she's tugging me toward the street.

"Ravena and I charted the energy around the shed today." She talks so fast she barely pauses to breathe. "It's the most fascinating thing I've ever seen!"

"Wait, slow down."

"It's an intentional time weave, something ancient and incredibly complex." She squeezes my arm tighter. "Even more strange, it's like someone built safety rails into the passage itself."

I stop walking, turn to face her. "What does that mean, exactly?"

"It means the portal was designed to prevent paradoxes." Her eyes light up. "It's not just a random tear between times. Someone built it to do something very specific."

La'Tasha and Penny had pretty much figured that out back in my time, but it's still nice to have a second opinion. "Good to know."

"So you know what that means, right?" She bounces on her toes. "You can take Everett back with you without causing catastrophic damage. Mother was wrong. The weave stabilizes the timeline, allows for small changes while preventing anything huge. It's brilliant work, really."

"That's... that's good news." I already assumed that, but okay. "What about the door? Is it still locked?"

Her smile thins. "Yes. But we're working on that part."

I tune out as Agnes rambles about energy signatures and temporal anchors. I want to listen. Really. But all I can think about is that she worked through all this with Ravena. The same Ravena who'll one day try to wipe out Moonridge.

"Agnes," I cut in, "can we really trust Ravena with all this?"

She stops walking, brows pulling together. "Of course. Why wouldn't we? She's my best friend. She's the most talented witch in our coven besides my mother."

I search for the right words, reminding myself this isn't my Ravena. Not yet.

"Just..." I scrub a hand over my face. "Are you sure she's only interested in the academic side of this?"

"Absolutely." Agnes frowns, studying me. "What aren't you telling me? Do you know something about Ravena from the future?"

I know what Ravena becomes. Know the choices she'll make and the pain she'll cause. But this Ravena hasn't done those things yet. Can I hold someone accountable for sins they haven't committed yet? Should I?

"It's complicated."

She arches an eyebrow and starts walking again. "Well, Ravena is the real deal. I trust her. She's brilliant, dedicated, and she's never let me down."

The words scrape at me. Her "trustworthy" best friend will one day become her worst enemy. No point lighting that fuse right now. I need to focus on proving to Everett that I'm not here to kill him.

"There's something else," I say finally. "Something I need to tell you."

Agnes glances at me, concern edging out her excitement.

"What's wrong?"

I take a breath. Let it out slowly. "Everett overheard us last night. He followed me when I went to your place."

Agnes stops. "How much did he hear?"

"Not enough to understand the full conversation," I say. "But enough to think I'm the one who's planning to hurt him. He confronted me today." I shove my hands deep in my pockets. "I tried to explain, but it didn't go well."

"Oh no." She reaches for my arm and squeezes gently. "I'm so sorry. What are you going to do?"

"I don't know." The words come out defeated. "I tried to explain, but how do you tell someone 'I'm from the future and I know you're going to die, and it's your boyfriend and a coven of magical assholes who are going to do it'?"

She chews her bottom lip. "I could talk to him with you. Sometimes hearing things from more than one person helps."

"Maybe, but he knows you were the one I was talking to. He probably won't trust you any more than he trusts me." I sigh. "Right now, I think he needs space. And I need help getting that door open."

Agnes nods, decisive. "Deal. Maybe we ask the Morehouses after we find out what's on that vellum. There's only one person in this town that's more powerful than my mother and that's Esther Morehouse. Just don't tell my mother I said that."

"You mentioned your mother discouraged you from speaking to them," I point out, remembering our earlier conversation.

Agnes flushes as she stops in front of a blue house with a yellow door. "Well, it's not exactly forbidden. More... strongly discouraged."

Before I can respond, the front door opens.

A young man in his early twenties steps out onto the porch. He's tall and lean, with close-cropped hair and warm brown skin that catches the fading sunlight. Rolled-up sleeves reveal solid forearms. His movement is confident without being cocky. When he sees Agnes, something shifts in his face. There's history there.

He leans against the porch column, one hand in his pocket. Relaxed posture, eyes locked on Agnes.

"Agnes Thornton." His deep voice carries a thread of amusement, and something rough underneath. "Been a while since you came 'round."

Agnes goes still beside me. Her breathing tightens, and her fingers bunch fabric at her sides.

"Hello, Ronald." She squares herself. "Is your mother home?"

Ronald's gaze flicks to me, curious more than anything. "She might be. Depends on who's asking." His attention slides back to Agnes and lingers there. "You look good, Aggie. That new lipstick? Suits you."

Her cheeks flare pink. She keeps her eyes on a spot near his shoulder. "It's not... I mean... Don't call me Aggie. You know I hate that."

She sounds more flustered than angry.

"Who's your friend?" Ronald nods toward me. He steps off the porch and offers a hand. "Ronald Morehouse."

"Calvin Mitchell." We shake. His grip is firm, confident. The kind of handshake that says he knows who he is.

"Calvin's visiting from Michigan," Agnes adds quickly. "I need to speak with your mother. It's important."

Ronald straightens, the lazy pose falling away. "Important enough to break the great Thornton-Morehouse standoff? Your mama know you're here?"

Before Agnes can answer, another figure appears in the doorway.

A young woman, maybe eighteen or nineteen, hair pulled back with a colorful scarf tied around her ponytail. She wears a simple yellow dress that looks like it belongs on a magazine cover. Her eyes narrow when she spots Agnes.

"Girl, what are you doing on our property?"

The resemblance stops me cold.

It's La'Tasha without glasses. Not exactly, but close enough that my brain short-circuits. Same high cheekbones. Same arch to the eyebrows. Same proud tilt of the chin. Same stance that says she owns the ground under her feet and dares anyone to argue.

Grandmother, maybe? My sense of time wobbles. That face belongs in my Moonridge, not here.

Time travel is a mindfuck.

"Hello, Bea." Agnes's voice tightens. "I need to speak with your mother, please."

Bea crosses her arms. "And you brought a white man for what? Protection? Think you need it in our neighborhood or something? Because we're so dangerous over here?"

"It's not like that," Agnes protests. "Calvin is a friend. He needs help."

Bea looks me over slowly, taking her time, eyes sharp. I see even more of La'Tasha in that look. The part that sees through excuses.

"And why should we help you?"

Ronald sighs. "Bea, come on. Be civil."

"Civil?" Bea raises an eyebrow as she moves down the steps toward us. "Like when she stopped talking to us because her mama calls us dark magic wielders? Like how everyone crosses the street to avoid us in town because of them? That kind of civil?"

Agnes flinches. "That's not fair."

"Life rarely is."

The air between them pulls tight. I get the distinct impression I've walked into a disagreement that started years ago and never really stopped.

"This isn't about me and Ronald. It's not even about the issues between our families," Agnes says. Her voice comes out thin but steady.

"Isn't it?" Bea stands beside her brother, arms crossed. "Because from where I'm standing, it looks like you broke my brother's heart, decided we weren't good enough for you anymore, and now you're back because you need something."

Ronald shifts. "Bea, that's enough."

"No, it's not." She rounds on him, putting herself slightly in front of him like a shield. "You don't get to defend her. Not after what she did to you. And not after everything her family has done to ours for years."

Ronald reaches for his sister's arm. "Bea, please."

Silence stretches. The front yard might as well be a battlefield.

I stand there, witness to this pain. This isn't just about them breaking up. It's about everything else—families, race, the whole fucked-up mindset of the entire country in 1958. In my time, Agnes and Ronald could have dated openly, maybe built a life together if they wanted.

But this is 1958. Those choices aren't on the table. Not for them. And definitely not for Everett and me.

Before Agnes can respond, another figure appears in the doorway and the hairs on my arms lift.

An older woman steps out onto the porch, and everyone shifts in her direction. Silver threads through her dark hair. Her kind eyes land on each of us in turn, measuring, taking stock. She moves with a quiet, grounded grace that says she's used to being the one people look to for answers.

"What is all this fuss about?" Her voice fills the space, rich and controlled.

"Mama, Agnes Thornton is here," Bea says, still glaring at Agnes. "Wants to talk to you."

Esther Morehouse steps forward, gaze sliding over Agnes, thoughtful and wary. "Does your mother know you're here, child?"

Agnes lifts her chin. "No, Mrs. Morehouse. And she can't find out. But it's important."

Esther studies her. "Important enough to risk her wrath?"

"Yes, ma'am." Agnes doesn't look away. "Life or death important."

"And him?" Esther nods toward me. "Who's this?"

Before Agnes can answer, Bea steps closer. Her eyes drop to my chest, to the spot where La'Tasha's amulet rests under my shirt.

Her whole focus changes. Anger drains from her face, replaced by sharp, startled attention.

"Wait." She moves in, staring at my chest like she can see through the fabric. "Where did you get that? Why the hell are you wearing Morehouse magic?"

The question hangs between us. Esther's gaze snaps to me. Agnes looks between us, lost.

Slowly, I tug the cord from beneath my shirt. The small amulet catches the fading light, simple and solid.

Bea stares in disbelief at the tether that binds me to La'Tasha in my time. Her hand lifts like she wants to touch it, then stops halfway. Her eyes meet mine, wide.

"That's not possible." Her voice drops to a whisper. "It's not just Morehouse magic. It's Morehouse magic that reaches across time."

How the hell can she tell that? But I guess that's a powerful witch for you. They feel things the rest of us walk right past.

Esther steps forward, close enough that I can see the fine lines at the corners of her eyes. Her fingers hover near the amulet, tracing shapes in the air. The charm warms against my chest, responding to her.

"An artifact from a future that we don't know yet." Her gaze hooks into mine. "Who are you, really? What are you?"

My tongue feels thick. "It's complicated."

"I imagine it is." Esther turns and beckons for us to follow her. "You'd better come inside. All of you."

The Morehouse living room is warm and lived-in, books stacked and shelved wherever they fit. Family photos cover the walls, faces watching from different decades, each one carrying that same sense of strength. The air smells like cinnamon and something earthy that might be sage.

Esther gestures to an orange couch, so Agnes and I sit. She

takes the high-backed chair across from us, turning it into a throne without trying. Bea stays near the wall. Ronald hovers by the doorway, keeping an eye on everything.

"Now," Esther says, "explain."

Agnes removes the vellum from her pocket, wrapped in cloth. "We found this. We need help understanding what the writing on it means."

Esther takes it and unwraps it. Her inhale stutters when she sees the symbols. Her shoulders lock. "Where did you get this?"

"I took it," I say. "From someone working with the Concord."

The name lands in the room and everything tightens around it. Esther straightens. Bea uncrosses her arms. Ronald pushes away from the wall.

"The Concord." Esther says it like something foul. "And why would you know about them?"

I breathe in, slow. "I'm from the future. I came back to save someone who means a lot to me. They're going to murder him and use him to help channel their magic."

The room goes quiet. Bea and Ronald trade a look, but Esther's expression hardly shifts at all.

"Go on," she says.

"The amulet was given to me by your descendant. La'Tasha Morehouse." I touch the pendant, and it warms under my fingers. "She used it to tether me to my timeline and to help protect me while I'm here."

Something unreadable passes through Esther's eyes, too quick to read.

"The Concord is still active in my time," I continue. "They're planning something big, something that could destroy everything. I came back to stop them from killing someone important to me. A man named Everett Bradshaw."

"The shifter who works at the garage?" Ronald asks.

I nod. "In my time, he's a ghost. They killed and bound him, forced him to help with their rituals. His murder adds to their numbers and feeds whatever they're building. I came back to save him, to take him out of this timeline before they can kill him."

"And this?" Esther holds up the vellum, careful not to brush the ink.

"Part of their ritual," Agnes says. "I believe it's a binding spell to trap his soul. There was also a braided bracelet, a lock of his hair and a black stone that were used to activate the spell."

"And where is the box? The rest of the contents?"

"My mother took it. I—I don't know what she did with it."

Esther studies the symbols. Magic hums around her hands, prickling over my skin. "This is old work. Very old. Dangerous."

"That's what Agnes's mother said," I confirm.

"Rachel would know." Esther's mouth twists. "These symbols bind a specific death to a specific time and place." Her finger traces one intricate rune without touching it. "This one keeps the soul pinned, unable to pass on. It ties the death into the story itself. His future is already written."

My gut knots. "Can you stop it? Help us get Everett out of here before they complete the ritual?"

Esther sits back, considering. "The ritual can be broken, yes. Since it hasn't been completed yet, there is room to move. But taking someone—a Concord sacrifice no less—from their proper time through a Concord-created portal..." She shakes her head. "Are you sure that's a good idea?"

"There's a weave in the portal, something that stabilizes the timeline against paradoxes," I say. "Agnes and Ravena mapped it."

"The door is locked, though," Agnes adds. "We can't get through."

Esther meets Bea's eyes. They share a look I can't quite read.

"I'm not worried about the timeline. That can be healed. And I believe I can help open the door," Esther says at last. "But understand this. The Concord will know the moment we touch it. They created it. They watch their work. I'm surprised they let you through in the first place."

Cold creeps up my spine. "So they know I'm here."

"I have no doubt." Esther leans forward. "There's something else you should know. The blood on this vellum has a very specific signature. One I've seen before."

"What kind of signature?" Agnes asks.

"It belongs to one of the oldest members of the Concord." Esther's gaze fixes on me. "One who calls himself The Scribe."

Something in the room changes. A stillness. A warning. Something in my gut tells me I need to pay attention. "The Scribe?"

"A record keeper, but more than that." Esther stands, walks to the window, and draws the curtains. "The Scribe doesn't just document history. He can rewrite it."

A chill crawls along my skin. "What does that mean?"

"He was a monk once," Esther says. "A scholar. He devoted his life to preserving history, recording events in careful detail. Then he found old magic, forbidden magic, that let him do more than record. He could alter. Erase. Rewrite."

"How do you know all this?" Agnes asks.

"My family founded Moonridge. We've kept records of everything that has happened in this town. The Concord appears in those records again and again."

I think of how none of us had ever even heard of the Concord until a few months ago. Somewhere along the line, someone buried this history deep. This information no longer exists in my version of Moonridge.

"My mother has never mentioned them." Agnes frowns.

"Your mother is selective with her information," Esther replies. "The Concord has haunted Moonridge for generations. They killed and bound one of my ancestors. Trust me. I know them well."

Like they're planning to do with Everett.

"And The Scribe is involved in what's happening with Everett?" The thought sits heavy in my stomach.

"Yes. And you must be very careful." Esther points to the

vellum. "The Scribe works with personal effects. If he gets anything of yours, hair, blood, clothing, even a written signature, he could use it against you."

My skin crawls. "What would happen?"

"He could completely change your story or even erase you." Bea speaks from the wall, voice flat, like she's reading facts from a book. "Not kill you. Erase you. Make it so you never existed at all."

Every part of me goes cold. "How? Technically I don't even exist yet. I'm not born until years from now. Wouldn't I just be born like normal in the future?"

"No. Your birth would be unmade," Esther says, and somehow her tone softens around the horror. "He can write you out of history and keep you from ever being created."

Ronald shifts against the wall. "That's worse than death."

"Much worse." Esther takes her seat again. "Death leaves a mark. Leaves memories. Leaves a space where you used to be. Erasure leaves nothing. You will just never exist."

My thoughts skid. "How do we stop him?"

"You don't." Esther's answer is quiet and absolute. "You avoid him. Complete your task and return to your time before he realizes what you're doing."

"We need to act fast," Agnes says. "We need to get that door open."

Esther nods, already working through something in her head. "I can help with that. But while I do," she says to me, eyes steady and sharp, "you need to convince your friend to come with you. No small task, asking someone to leave their whole life behind."

"I know."

She moves toward the door. "You need to go now. The less time you spend here, the less likely the Concord will connect us. We'll get started tonight," Esther decides. "Bea will help me gather what we need. Ronald, see them out and make sure we don't have any unwanted visitors."

I stand and offer her my hand. "Thank you. How can I ever repay you?"

"You're a friend of my future granddaughter. You must mean something to her if she was willing to help you do this. I'm just helping her finish what she started."

She pats my shoulder and slips into the kitchen. Bea follows, glancing back long enough to offer a small, reluctant smile.

Outside, the evening air cools the heat in my face. The sky has deepened to purple, stars pricking through. Ronald shakes my hand and gives Agnes a quick wink before heading off to check the yard.

"Thank you," Agnes says softly as he goes. "For helping."

Ronald turns back to her. "Anytime, Aggie."

The way he uses his special nickname tells me everything. He's not over her.

Agnes watches until he's out of sight, her hand pressed against her heart like she's trying to steady something inside it. All her walls drop for a second. She looks like someone who's still hurting. We head back toward the apothecary in silence.

"Do I sense some history there?" I finally ask.

"He never knew why." Her voice frays at the edges. "I never got to explain. Never got to tell him I didn't stop seeing him because I didn't care. That it was never about him not being enough."

"What happened?" I ask, even though I already have a pretty good guess.

"My mother found out. Said she'd disown me if I kept seeing him. Cut me off completely. No family. No home. No inheritance." Her words get smaller. "It was four years ago. I was only fifteen. Scared. I didn't know what to do. Didn't know how to choose between what I wanted and what I thought I had to choose."

"So you chose the latter."

"I chose wrong." She swipes at her eyes before the tears can fall. "I should have chosen him. Should have fought for us. But I was too scared of losing everything. Mother can be... tough."

"And yet you still lost," I say quietly. "Just not the way you expected."

She nods, one tear escaping anyway.

I'd like to believe she might get a second chance with him. Part of me wants to tell her to hold on, that someday the timing will finally line up. But I can't. Hazel's grandfather wasn't Ronald, and giving Agnes false hope could shift things I have no right to touch. I know the portal is supposed to be built to keep timelines from breaking, but I'm not about to chance it.

We continue in silence and I think about Everett. About love that lands in the wrong time, the wrong place, with all the odds stacked against it. And how far you'll go to make it work.

We stop a block from the apothecary to say goodbye. Agnes's gaze shifts across the street, and I follow it. Everett stands there watching us, and something fierce kicks awake in my chest. Time to fix this. I'm not losing him. Not to fear. Not to the Concord.

Not to anyone.

CHAPTER TWENTY-SIX

Everett

My bandaged hand throbs with a dull, persistent ache that seems to sync up with my pulse. What a day. Five stitches and one very confusing, utterly exhausting afternoon that ended with me telling Calvin to get lost. I should feel good about myself. For once I'm finally thinking with my brain instead of my dick.

So why am I still stuck on him?

Every instinct I have twitches when I think about Calvin. I want to trust him, but there's something coiled around him that feels wrong. It's big and dark and dangerous. I should be scared and done with him. Instead, I keep rewinding the fight, wondering if I pushed too hard.

No. It's done.

I should focus on Vince. I know Vince. I can read him. He loves me.

But Calvin looks at me like I'm a mystery he wants to solve. And Vince... Vince looks at me like a prize he already won.

No. That's not fair. Vince bought me a guitar. An expensive, beautiful guitar. He gave me this necklace. He's trying. He's changing.

The chain sits heavy against my throat. I press my hand over it through my shirt. The metal pulses under my palm. One-two. One-two. Just off from my heartbeat, steady in its own rhythm until mine starts chasing it.

That's... that's not normal, is it?

The thought flickers and then it's gone. Lost in the fog filling my head.

I sit up and swing my legs over the side of the bed. My clock reads 8:27 PM. My hand complains as I push off the mattress, a deep, hot ache along the stitches.

I should stay here. I feel wrung out, but my skin feels too tight. The room presses in. I need air. Space to think. And maybe a milkshake, because honestly, when has a milkshake ever made anything worse?

I tell myself I'm just going to the diner. Just getting some air.

I pull on jeans and a T-shirt, easing my bandaged hand through the sleeve. I haven't heard from Vince, so he must still be in Boston. I could use another night alone to figure out what the hell I'm doing.

The Randalls are watching television, so I toss them a quick hello and slip out the front door. Warm evening settles around me. Crickets buzz. The scent of cut grass hangs in the air. The moon is barely a sliver in the sky. Almost the new moon. A time for wolves to reset.

Great. Now I'm thinking about Calvin again.

I decide to walk instead of taking my car. The movement might rattle my thoughts into some kind of order, and the diner is only ten minutes away on foot.

Main Street is quiet at this hour, just a few cars parked outside the Howling Moon Tavern where the older couples hang out. Music drifts from the open windows, something slow and bluesy that belongs in a smoky room with cheap whiskey and bad decisions.

Halfway to the diner, I spot two figures walking ahead of me. My chest tightens when I recognize Calvin's shoulders, the way he moves. He's with Agnes again.

Is there something between them? He said he was queer too, but maybe that was another lie.

I slow, instinct tugging me toward the shadows. I cross the street and hang back, giving them space.

They reach the intersection between Main and Gibbous. Agnes hugs herself like she's cold and Calvin touches her arm, gentle. She tips her head up and her eyes find me. Even from here I feel pinned.

She says something. Calvin turns.

Our eyes lock across the street.

Everything narrows.

I duck my head and walk faster, my shoes slapping the pavement.

He saw me. He knows I saw him. And I bailed.

The diner's neon sign glows ahead, buzzing against the dark. I shove the door open harder than I mean to. The bell over it goes wild. The smell of coffee and fried food rolls over me, thick and familiar.

It doesn't calm me like it usually does.

The place is quiet for a Friday, but then I realize it's still relatively early. Two truckers occupy the counter, and old Mr. Jenkins sits in his corner booth with a newspaper that looks like it came out of the trash. Most folks are probably still at the drive-in movie. It'll get busy later.

I slide into the farthest booth, and angle myself so my back faces the door. If Calvin comes in, maybe he'll miss me. Maybe he'll think I kept walking. Maybe he won't come in at all.

Florence Bailey bustles over, coffee pot in one hand and worn order pad in the other. Her bright red hair is piled on top of her head in a style that somehow defies gravity. Her cat-eye glasses hang from a beaded chain around her neck. She moves like someone who could run this place in her sleep, shoes squeaking on the checkered floor.

"Evenin', sugar," she says, her fake Texas drawl thick as honey. "I don't usually see you in here this late. You okay?"

"Fine, thanks," I lie, sliding the laminated menu from between the salt and pepper shakers even though I already know what I want. "Can I get a strawberry milkshake and an order of fries, please, Flo?"

"Course you can." She tucks her pencil behind her ear and studies my face like she's flipping through my pages. "Extra whipped cream for that hand of yours. Looks like it hurts something fierce."

"It's not so bad," I lie. It throbs under the bandage, but I'm not in the mood to be fussed over.

"Mmhmm." She gives me that look that says she's not buying a word of it and chooses to let it slide anyway. "One strawberry milkshake and an order of fries coming right up."

The bell over the door jingles again as she walks away.

I don't turn around. I don't need to. My spine goes stiff, and the booth feels way too small. The air behind me changes, prickling along the back of my neck.

Footsteps approach. Two sets. Then Calvin's voice, right behind me.

"Everett."

I pull in a breath and make myself turn.

Calvin stands there with his hands jammed into his pockets, shadows under his eyes, hair a mess. Agnes hovers just behind him, worry tightening her mouth.

"Mind if we join you?" Calvin asks. His voice is careful at the edges.

I should tell him no. Tell him to find another booth.

The diner's too quiet, though, and the idea of a scene in front of Flo and Mr. Jenkins makes my skin itch.

"Free country," I mutter, sinking deeper into the seat.

Calvin slips in across from me, Agnes next to him.

We sit there in a stiff, tangled pause.

"How's your hand?" Calvin asks at last, nodding toward the bandage.

"Still attached."

His shoulders twitch. Good. Let him feel it.

Flo arrives with my milkshake, a ridiculous mountain of whipped cream on top, and lifts an eyebrow at my new crowd. "Can I get you two anything?"

"Just coffee, please," Agnes says with a polite smile.

"Same," Calvin adds.

Once Flo drifts back toward the counter, he leans in. "We need to talk."

"So talk."

"Not here. Too many ears."

"Then why are you here?" I ask, wrapping both hands around the cold glass. The chill bites through the bandage and settles into the ache in my palm.

"Because you're in danger, Everett." Calvin's eyes lock onto mine, sharp and unblinking. "Someone is planning to hurt you. Soon."

"Keep your voice down," Agnes whispers, flicking a look toward the truckers.

"Someone wants to hurt me?" I repeat, quieter. "Who? Why?"

"That's what we're trying to figure out," Calvin says. His fingers flatten against the tabletop like he's stopping himself from reaching for me. "But we know it's serious. We know you're the target."

"How do you know this?" My mouth dries out. I lick my lips, but it doesn't help. "And why would anyone want to hurt me? I'm no one."

Calvin's expression shifts. The way he looks at me knocks my next question right out of my throat. "That's where you're wrong. I wish you could see that."

My cheeks burn. The way he says it sinks in deep, too sure to shrug off as a line.

"Who?" I ask again. "Who wants to hurt me?"

Agnes and Calvin trade a look I can't quite decode.

"We're not entirely sure of all the players," Agnes says slowly. "But there's a group. They've been watching you. We think Vince is involved."

The necklace flares against my throat. *They're lying.*

"What group?" My voice spikes anyway. "What does this have to do with Vince?"

"Please," Calvin reaches across the table like he's about to take my hand, then halts halfway. "Just trust us. Meet us tomorrow at the park at noon. We'll explain everything. All of it. Promise me you'll leave here and go straight home. It's not safe."

"Not safe?" I glance around the diner. Mr. Jenkins with his newspaper. The truckers with their coffee. Flo behind the counter topping off mugs. "It's a diner. How's it not safe?"

"Not here. Out there," Agnes murmurs.

Flo appears again and sets a plate of fries down with a clatter, then tops off their coffee. I grab a fry, drag it through the whipped cream, and pop it into my mouth like this is any other night. Like I'm not vibrating apart inside.

The bell over the door jingles, this time with a rush of noise. Laughter spills into the diner, loud and cocky. The quiet frays.

Four guys in leather jackets swagger in like they're walking onto a stage. Sam Carter leads, all muscle and swagger. Jake and Tony follow, still arguing about something. Bringing up the rear, leather jacket gleaming under the fluorescent lights, is Vince.

Shit.

Heat crawls up my throat. I'm not ready to see Vince. Not with Calvin across from me and my brain full of warnings. Vince is going to take one look at this setup and spiral. I don't have the energy for that.

Vince spots me right away. His eyes light up and his whole

face brightens, like the rest of the diner drops out of focus. A little spark fires in my chest despite everything. He heads straight for our booth, ignoring Calvin and Agnes, and slides in beside me so his thigh presses against mine, warm and solid.

"Hey, beautiful," he murmurs against my ear, breath hot on my skin. It should melt me into the seat. All I can think about is Calvin watching from across the table.

Sam leans over our booth, bracing his arms on the table. The move looks loose, but there's a weight to it. "What happened to your hand, Ev?"

"Cut it on a gearbox at work," I say, lifting my bandaged hand. The skin underneath throbs like it heard me. "Five stitches."

Sam winces. Then he clocks Agnes, and the easy look on his face hardens. "What's she doing here?"

"We were just talking," Calvin says. His voice stays even, but there's a sharper note under it now.

"Wolves and witches don't mix," Sam says, flat and loud enough that the truckers glance over. Mr. Jenkins lowers his paper. "Or did I forget to mention that? I don't know what it's like in Michigan, but it's not that way here. You run with this pack, you follow our rules."

Agnes straightens, chin tipping up. "I was under the impression that Moonridge valued tolerance, Sam Carter. Or is that just something you say for the tourists?"

"Tolerance is one thing." Sam's voice cools another few degrees. "Having you witches messing with our pack is another. You should leave."

The diner goes very still. Forks pause halfway to mouths. Sam's hands curl on the table. Calvin sits so still it makes my skin itch.

"Last time I checked, the diner wasn't pack territory," Agnes fires back. Her voice holds steady, but her fingers curl tight around her coffee cup. She's scared, but she doesn't back off.

Brave? Or reckless? Hard to tell.

"Everything in Moonridge is pack territory when we say it is," Sam answers. He steps back a fraction, like a concession. "You should go. Or do I need to tell your mommy you were out after your bedtime?"

Agnes slides out of the booth. "I'm not a child." Her back stays straight as she walks past Sam. Her shoulders are rigid, but she doesn't look away. She flicks one last look at Calvin. Whatever passes between them puts me on edge. It's private and quick and it makes something in my chest twist.

Am I jealous? At the obvious connection they have? The way they don't need words to communicate?

This is stupid. I barely know Calvin. He's nothing to me. Why would I care about… whatever that was.

Jake and Tony start bickering about some girl they both like, voices climbing over each other. Sam flags Flo for coffee and pulls out a cigarette, settling in like he owns the place.

"I have some news," Vince whispers against my ear.

"What news?" I ask, eyes flicking between Sam and Calvin as they talk. Calvin keeps glancing over, tracking me and Vince like he can't help it.

"Everything we've ever dreamed of and then some is about to come true." Vince's voice stays low, buzzing with excitement. "I was in Boston… work meetings… you know…"

I nod.

"On my way back I stopped for a bite to eat. I started talking to this guy at the restaurant. Turns out he's a big shot in the music business. He's looking for new talent. Someone he can mentor into a star. I told him about you, and, well…"

My pulse stutters. For a second, real excitement burns through the mess. "Really? Who was he?"

"A producer. From Chicago. Just passing through on business." Vince's hand finds mine under the table, careful of the bandage. His thumb skims my knuckles.

Hope flares sharp in my chest. A producer from Chicago.

Since Grandpa first put a guitar in my hands, this has been the dream. To be more than the weird shifter kid nobody wanted. To be someone people listen to. Someone people turn up the radio for.

This could change everything.

Calvin's voice cuts across the fantasy in my head. *You're in danger. Someone is planning to hurt you. Vince is involved.*

The bright feeling dims. Confusion creeps back in and fear sidles up beside it. What if saying yes to this puts me in the crosshairs Calvin keeps warning me about? What if this is tied to whatever nightmare he and Agnes are tangled in?

But how could it be? A music producer from Chicago has nothing to do with death rituals.

Right?

"That's amazing," I say, and I mean it. I need this to be simple and good. The chain at my throat warms at the thought. A smooth calm washes through me, like someone turned down the volume on every worry.

"We're heading up to Skipper Lake," I hear Sam tell Calvin. "The new moon is coming up, so we're going to do one last run before the reset. You in?"

Calvin hesitates. His gaze flicks to me. Holds for a second that stretches way too long. Then he looks away and something in my chest sinks.

"Sure," he says. "Sounds good."

Vince's arm slides around my waist. It feels more like he's staking a claim than offering comfort. His grip relaxes a little, though, and his smile looks easier than usual.

"Are you going up to the lake with them?" I ask.

"No. I'll stay with you for a while. I missed you."

I want to believe him.

"It's okay. If you want to go with them, I mean."

"Forget about them," he smiles, eyes never leaving mine. "This is about us. About our future."

I nod and try to pull my focus back to him instead of the churn in my head. I should be thrilled he chose me over going with the pack. His thumb traces slow circles on my hip, and I lean into him on reflex.

"Want me to drive you home after you finish your shake?" Vince asks, stealing a spoonful of whipped cream.

"That'd be nice," I say. Thoughts collide and everything gets jumbled in my head. Warnings. Calvin's face. Vince's promises. None of it lines up.

The wolves hang around for another twenty minutes while I work on my milkshake and fries. Eventually Sam tosses money on the table and they stand to leave. All except Vince, who stays planted next to me.

I feel Calvin's gaze cutting into me. When I glance up, our eyes lock. His expression is unreadable, but there's something there that makes my chest tight. I break the connection and stare down at my plate, refusing to look up again until he's left.

After a few more minutes, Vince says he's tired and ready to call it a night. On the walk to his car, he seems lighter than I've seen him in weeks. Like the future he keeps talking about is already here.

As soon as I shut the car door, he leans over and kisses me. "I love you so much."

I should say it back.

"And I'm not even bothered that you were with that wolf tonight." He turns and smiles, and there's a flash in his eyes that sends a cold shiver across my shoulders. The chain at my throat heats, slow and steady, and the unease melts away.

The drive to the Randalls' is quiet. Some new rock and roll station out of New York crackles through the speakers. The songs are bright and fast, but they barely register. My thoughts keep drifting to Calvin. To danger. To a park bench at noon and answers I'm not sure I want.

When we pull up in front of the house, the porch light glows soft and yellow. The place looks warm and ordinary.

I suddenly don't want the night to end. I don't want to lie awake alone while every ugly thought in my head takes a turn.

"Can I stay at your place tonight?" The words fall out before I can snatch them back.

Vince's face shifts. He reaches over and cups my cheek. "I don't think that's a good idea, Ev. Not tonight. My dad's in town this week. You know how he gets."

"Okay." The word scrapes out. I hear the hurt in it and hate that I can't smooth it away.

"Chin up, beautiful." He takes my good hand and gives it a gentle squeeze. "In a couple of days we'll have everything we ever wanted. We'll never have to be apart again. I promise. I'll close my business deal, and then we'll get out of here and move to Chicago so you can start your career. Just imagine. Soon you could be making records. Touring. Living the dream." His eyes are serious, almost glowing. "And I'll be right there with you. Every step of the way."

I want to believe every word. I lean in when he kisses me, soft and careful. No push. No grab. Just lips and warmth and the kind of sweetness that makes my chest ache.

When he pulls back, he studies my face. "Do you trust me?"

The question sits between us, heavy as a stone.

"Of course," I say. The response is more of a reflex than an honest answer.

"Good." He reaches into his pocket and pulls out something that catches the streetlight. "I got you something else."

He holds it up. A braided red leather bracelet with a shiny black stone in the center. The stone gleams and I see symbols etched in it. For a second the symbols seem to rearrange themselves in the shifting light, like they're alive.

I blink. They settle back into place. Must be a trick of the light.

"It's nice," I breathe. It's delicate but not flimsy. "What is it?"

"My commitment to you." He takes my wrist, the one without the bandage. His fingers are gentle as he fastens it. "You're mine now. Forever."

The braided rope settles against my skin, already warm, like it has soaked up hours of sun. The warmth crawls up my arm and into my chest, a slow, pleasant tide that loosens every knot in my shoulders. My bandaged hand, resting in my lap, throbs once and then eases as if the heat has seeped that far too.

My laugh comes out thin and uneven. "That's quite a promise."

"One I intend to keep." His fingers linger on my wrist, tracing the black stone. "Don't take it off, okay? It'll remind you of me when we're apart."

Heat pours through me, stronger now. All the confusion from earlier fades like a radio station going out of range. Calvin fades with it. Danger. Warnings. They all drift to the back of my mind until they're just faint shapes.

What stays is Vince. Vince and this bracelet and the picture he keeps painting of our future.

He looks unreal in the dim light. He really is a beautiful fella. How did I ever doubt him? How did I even think to question what he wants for us? He loves me. He's going to make all of our dreams come true. That's what matters.

Way in the back of my mind, a small voice mutters that this is wrong. That this feeling climbed too fast. Hit too hard. That it's not mine.

The thought dissolves before I can grab it. Washed away by the warmth drifting through my veins. By the lazy contentment settling over my thoughts like a blanket.

I can't stop staring at the way the symbols on the stone catch the light. They seem to shift again, rearranging into patterns that pull at my eyes. The world goes soft and blurry. I'm safe.

"I'll never take it off," I whisper.

"Good." Vince kisses me again, deeper this time. His hand cups the back of my neck and holds me there. When he pulls back, his eyes are dark with something that looks a lot like satisfaction. "I should let you get some sleep. Tomorrow's a big day."

Is it? Tomorrow's Saturday. I feel like there was something I was supposed to remember about it. Something important. The thought won't land. It drifts out of reach and disappears.

"Okay," I hear myself say. My voice sounds far away. "Goodnight, Vince. Thank you for the bracelet."

"Sweet dreams, Ev."

I slide out of the car, moving slowly, like I'm walking through water. Everything feels cushioned. Soft. Safe. As I walk up the path, the bracelet pulses against my wrist, a faint beat that matches the chain at my throat. Each throb sends another wave of warmth through me.

Calvin's warning brushes the edge of my mind.

The park. Noon tomorrow.

It's hard to care. Hard to focus on any of it.

Right now it's just me and Vince and the life we're going to build. Music. Success. Love. Nothing else seems important.

I creep down the hall to my room, light on my feet despite the weight in my limbs. The bracelet catches the hallway light and throws warped shadows up the wall.

For a second, a face swims in those shadows. Hollow eyes. Empty expression. The same face I saw in the car mirror when Vince first put the small chain around my neck.

I blink and it's gone. Just shadows playing tricks.

I stumble into my room. I don't bother with the light. Don't bother changing. I just drop onto the bed, mentally and physically strung out.

I study my wrist. The bracelet glows faintly in the dark. The symbols on it seem to move, sliding around like tiny eyes turning to stare.

Watching.

Waiting.

The idea should terrify me. Instead it makes me feel looked

after. Guarded.

My eyes drift closed. Sleep tugs at me, warm and soft and inviting, but something inside me won't let go. Calvin's face flashes through my mind. The urgency in his voice. The park. Tomorrow. Danger.

I try to hold onto it, but the warmth from the bracelet spreads deeper, wrapping around that thought like cotton. Muffling it. Not erasing it, just... softening the edges until it doesn't feel urgent anymore.

But that small part of me, the part that remembers Calvin's warning, sits trapped beneath the surface of comfort. Pushing. Prodding.

Unable to break through.

CHAPTER TWENTY-SEVEN

Calvin

The radio blares from the dashboard, too sharp for my frayed nerves. The car's engine rumbles through the seat while my thoughts chew on everything I left behind at the diner.

I should've stayed. Followed Everett and Vince. Forced Everett to hear me out. But he wouldn't have. Not tonight. At least out here, I can sneak away and do some recon work. Scope out the ritual site. Maybe fuck it up real good so it's unusable. If anything, that would buy Everett some more time.

"I almost like the final run before the reset better than the run during the full moon." Sam glances over, his eyes catching the streetlights as we pull away from the diner.

I nod, digging my fingers into my thighs. The new moon is the one night each month where wolves lose access to their shifting powers completely. A mandatory reset. Most packs try to get one last run in before it hits. A final release of energy.

"Yeah. The reset is always nice. Especially running with a

full pack." I glance out the window at the thin crescent hanging in the sky. We still have a couple of days before it goes dark completely. Hopefully, I'll be long gone by then.

"Well, you're in for a treat." Sam cranks down his window. Fresh air rushes in, carrying pine and distant water and a hundred other scents my sharpening senses grab onto.

Jake and Tony sit crammed in the back seat, shoving each other with the kind of boisterous energy that only young werewolves can muster. Their shoulders collide against the car's interior walls, and their laughter bounces chaotically around the cab. It's infectious and a smile sneaks up on me before I can stop it. The way they mess with each other makes it hard not to laugh. The wolf inside me perks up at the sound, restless and eager. It's practically vibrating with the need to run.

But my human brain won't shut up about Everett. It knows that he's sitting on borrowed time. Somewhere out in these woods, in some clearing I haven't found yet, is the place where they're going to kill him. I need to figure out how to derail whatever's coming before it's too late.

"So, do the female wolves join us at the lake?" I ask. In my time, we all run together. The question feels wrong in my mouth.

Sam turns to look at me so fast I worry he might drive us into a ditch. His eyebrows shoot up. "Female wolves? Running with us?"

Jake leans forward from the back seat, breath hot on my neck. "What kind of wild pack you running with, Michigan?"

"They just... run with us," I say, suddenly aware I've stepped in something. "Is that not normal here?"

All three of them lose it. Tony laughs the loudest. He slaps the back of my seat hard enough to jolt my spine. "Man, your pack must be crazy. Women running with men? That's asking for trouble."

"The women have their own run," Sam says, still chuckling. "Over at Amethyst Beach. They do their thing, we do ours. Been that way forever. Even on full moons. Keeps things... appropriate."

Appropriate. Right. Because God forbid the ladies see the boys get weird.

"That's... one word for it," I say.

"You looking to score with a female wolf while you're in town?" Sam waggles his brows. "Because I gotta tell you, the Moonridge ladies are particular. Especially the wolf gals."

Wolf gals.

"No, I'm not looking to score with anyone." That part's easy. I already know who I want. I just need to keep him breathing long enough to get him seventy years forward.

"Good, because Marie Daniels would eat you alive." Jake snorts. "Literally. She bit my shoulder so hard last spring I couldn't shift for a week."

"Woman's got a temper," Tony says. "But damn she's got a nice rack."

They launch into stories about Marie's speed and temper and breasts like they're items on a menu. I tune in and out, catching enough to know she's fast, scary, and turned into a collection of parts instead of a person. In my time, she'd likely be second in command to Blake. But not here. Not in this time.

How much of this crap is instinct and how much is habit no one bothered to question? And how much of it soaked into my dad while he grew up here, listening to this?

"Why didn't Vince come tonight?" I ask when the Marie topic finally loses steam. "And Everett? I thought they might join us."

That gets another round of laughter, sharper this time. The hair at the back of my neck prickles.

"Vince?" Sam snorts. "He's unlit."

That word again.

"We only keep him around because he's got money. And he's desperate to be one of us."

Jake leans in. "His grandfather was a wolf, so he's convinced the gene is just... dormant or something. Been hanging around us since we were kids, hoping it would rub off."

"Like being a wolf is contagious," Tony says, and they all crack up.

"Remember when we were freshman and he was a senior and we convinced him drinking that nasty concoction would help 'awaken his inner wolf'?" Sam slaps the steering wheel. "What was in that again?"

"Beer, raw eggs, tabasco, and I think Jake pissed in it," Tony says, already laughing.

"And the time we told him if he howled at the moon every night for a month, his inner wolf would wake up?" Jake wheezes. "The neighbors called the cops twice."

"He stood outside in the snow in the middle of January. In his underwear. Howling like a maniac." Tony wipes his eyes. "Funniest damn thing I ever saw."

My gut twists. Vince, standing in the snow, begging the universe to turn him into something else while these assholes watched from a warm window.

The Concord must've taken one look at that kind of hunger and seen a tool. Someone who'll do anything to stop feeling like the punchline. Someone they can manipulate to fill their numbers.

"So he's like... the pack's pet human?" I ask.

"More like our lapdog," Sam says with a smirk. "Always eager to please. Always trying to prove he belongs."

"Makes him useful, though," Tony adds. "He'll do pretty much anything if you tell him it'll make him more like a wolf."

Wow. Why does part of me feel bad for him?

"But what about Everett?" I ask. "He's a shifter, right?"

Sam's expression tightens. The humor drops out. "He's nice enough, but shifters aren't wolves. They're... something else. Don't belong with us."

"Different," Jake says. "Unnatural."

"Wolves are born, not made," Sam adds, like he's quoting a sermon. "Shifters choose their forms. Play at being animals. It's not the same thing."

Of course. Hierarchy. Someone always has to be at the bottom.

Does Sam ever grow out of this? Does something knock it out of him before my dad is born, or does my father have to claw his way to better on his own? He had his prejudices, but he was never this bad. Was he?

The car bumps along a dirt road. Trees pull in close on either side. The smell of lake water thickens, tangled with the musk of a hundred past runs. My wolf surges forward in my chest, restless and bright. He doesn't care about Sam's opinions or Concord politics. He just wants the last of the moon and the run.

When Sam finally parks, we're at the edge of a clearing that leads down to Skipper Lake. Silver water stretches under the moon, still as glass. Trucks and cars ring the shoreline. The rest of Moonridge's wolves, waiting.

"Looks like we're the last ones here," Sam says, jumping out.

He starts stripping immediately, zero shame. Jacket, shirt, boots, jeans. Clothes hit the ground in a trail until he's naked in the moonlight, grinning like a kid who just found the gift stash.

Jake and Tony follow, tossing clothes toward the truck in loose piles.

I hesitate only a second, then peel off my own and stack them on the hood, neat on instinct. The night air skims over my skin, cool against the heat building under it. The sliver of moon tugs at something deep in me, steady and loud. My worries fade as the wolf takes over.

Bones crack. Sound snaps off the trees. My spine arches and resets. Joints twist, pop, and find new grooves. Fur ripples across my body.

The world tightens into focus. Shadows hold detail instead of emptiness. I can pick out the individual needles on a pine tree across the clearing. Smell Jake's excitement, Tony's easy contentment, the sharp alertness rolling off Sam. Tiny creatures rustle in the brush, hearts ticking fast.

In seconds, four wolves stand where four men were.

Sam's wolf is big and sandy, a white patch bright on his chest. He moves like the ground belongs to him. Future alpha written in the way he plants his paws.

Jake and Tony look nearly black in the moonlight. They circle and nip, mock-fighting, teeth clicking against fur and skin without malice.

I'm somewhere in the middle, dark brown with a dusting of white around my muzzle.

Sam tips his head back and howls. The sound rolls out over the lake and rebounds. Wild, clear, familiar.

Jake and Tony add their voices, one higher, one low and solid. I slip my own note into the mix, weaving between them until it settles into something that feels like a song we've known forever. More wolves around the lake join in, a rough chorus under the four of us.

For a second, I remember what it's like to just... be.

Then we run.

Wolves explode into motion, paws hitting earth, bodies threading through trees. Moonlight cuts through the trees, all silver and shadow. The rhythm of it loosens the tightness in my chest.

My muscles protest at first, then settle into the stretch and push. Sam leads, of course, carving the path. Jake and Tony flank him, jostling. I stay a little behind, letting them set the pace, letting the land rise and fall under my feet.

When we reach the highest point overlooking the lake, we howl again. Our voices carry, then return to us softer. For a moment, it feels like the town I know is answering back.

Sam peels off first when the roughhousing kicks in, shaking out his coat and trotting toward the trees. Restless. Already done with the pile forming near the cliff. He disappears into the dark, leaving Jake and Tony wrestling in a tangle of fur.

Eventually the rough play slows. Most of the pack sinks into a loose pile. A few peel off for a second wind, pounding into the trees again.

I hang back, watching the stragglers crash together. They nip, lick, and then settle into piles of fur and contentment. Wolves who'd puff their chests and keep distance in daylight curl around each other now, noses tucked into shoulders, paws thrown over ribs. Tony licks Jake's ears in steady strokes while another wolf uses Jake as a pillow.

Leo and I have done this plenty of times. Run until we're exhausted, then collapse together. Sometimes as wolves, sometimes as humans still riding the high of the run. Sometimes it goes further than just sleeping.

Out here, after a run, nobody cares that these men curl up together, showing affection. Nobody makes it weird.

But back in town? In human form when others are around? They'd never let themselves be this open or soft with each other. Someone might see. Might talk. Might make them feel like there's something wrong with being affectionate toward another man.

Wolves don't care about the stupid rules men invent. Maybe that's the real reason these runs stay split by gender. Not to protect the females from anything. To keep them from seeing the men all vulnerable and affectionate and curled up together without shame. Because if they saw, it might make the men feel less strong. Less male. Or maybe it would just bring up uncomfortable questions about why this closeness between men feels so natural when they're wolves. Why it's only shameful when they're human and can put words to it.

My brain creeps back to why I came up here in the first place. Everett. The ritual. The ticking clock.

I ease away from the group, paws light on the forest floor. Jake lifts his head to watch me go, then sets his chin back down, content to snooze under the stars for a while.

The forest glows in silver bands. Trunks rise like walls on either side of the trail. The trees are younger than the ones I know, but the bones of the place match.

I stop.

A symbol is carved into a nearby trunk. Fresh. Sap beads along the cut, sticky and pale.

A spiral with three lines. Cut clean and hard.

It's different from the others I saw yesterday, but the Concord spiral is still evident.

I step back, scanning. Another mark waits on a tree ten feet away. Then another. The shapes ring this stretch of woods in a rough circle, seven branded trees enclosing a patch of ground.

They claimed this place tonight. Recently.

Is this where they plan to kill Everett? Have they already laid everything out, waiting for him to walk into position?

Smoke threads into my nose. Wood, not cigarettes.

Voices drift through the trees, too low for human ears, clear for mine.

My body drops into a stalk without waiting for permission. Belly low, paws quiet, I move toward higher ground. The slope ahead forms a shallow overhang with a view of the clearing below.

I climb, claws scraping stone and root. Muscles pull and tighten. I slow myself by instinct, placing each paw where it won't send pebbles skittering.

I ease my head over the edge.

Five hooded figures stand around a fire in the small clearing below.

Flames throw light up under their hoods, twisting their shadows. They speak words my brain doesn't recognize. Power hums through the clearing, spikes, then settles as the fire jumps and steadies.

Whatever they were doing, they just finished it.

The chanting dies. Silence wraps around the clearing.

The first figure pushes their hood back.

Vince.

His features sharpen in the firelight. No needy smile. No

eager nodding. Just focus. Purpose. The weak guy the wolves described is gone.

The second hood drops. Dark hair, cat-eye glasses, sharp face. Ravena.

Of course she's here. I knew she'd end up deep in this muck, but seeing it this early still crawls under my skin. I'm not surprised. Not really. I know what she becomes in my time.

Something snarls softly nearby. I look to the ground below. A cougar crouches at the treeline, yellow eyes fixed on the scene in front of it. It sniffs, gives a warning rumble, then slinks off. Fine by me. I've got bigger problems than a pissed-off cat.

The third hood falls back. A man's face catches the light. High cheekbones. Watchful eyes. Thin mouth pressed into a line. I don't know him, but the air around him feels off. Like the world has to stretch a little to fit him inside it.

Every nerve I have tells me to back away.

The fourth figure steps forward and raises their hands. Pulls their hood back.

Sam.

My grandfather.

No.

That can't be Sam.

For a second, the clearing tilts. He was wrestling with Jake and Tony not that long ago, fur flying, laughing. Now he stands robed beside a Concord fire like he's always belonged here.

My father's father. Concord.

The realization slams through me.

Did my dad know? Did he grow up under this roof with this secret at the kitchen table? Or did Sam play the good alpha at home and sneak off to serve something rotten when no one was looking?

My jaw tightens. I lock my paws against the rock and keep watching.

"The preparations are complete," Sam says. His voice is flat, formal. Not the guy who teased me about wolf girls in the truck. "The trees are marked. The sacrifice site is ready."

"And the shifter?" the unknown man asks. His accent curls around the words. "He wears the binding charms?"

"Both of them," Vince says. His chest lifts a little. "The chain and the bracelet. He's completely under our influence."

Everett. Wearing two of their traps.

"Good." The man nods. "Your work has been exemplary, Vincent. The Concord will reward you for your service."

Vince's whole posture changes. Shoulders back. Eyes bright. A kid finally getting picked first.

The fifth figure speaks from beneath their hood. My claws slip a fraction on the rock.

"And what of the wolf?"

Female. Cool. Familiar.

Rachel Thornton.

"The time traveler?" the unknown man asks.

"Yes. Calvin Mitchell."

The hood comes back and confirms it. Agnes's mother. Sharp features, red hair catching the fire. The woman who warned me about the Concord. The one who acted scared of them. It was all a ruse.

"He needs to be stopped before he becomes a problem," Rachel says. Her tone stays even, like stating a fact she just read in a newspaper. "I plan to reopen the portal so we can send him back to his timeline as soon as tomorrow. But we should be prepared for resistance. He has a strange attachment to our subject."

So that was the plan. Ship me home, call it kindness, and get me out of the way.

The unknown man nods. "I'm more than prepared for such contingencies. I can write him out if necessary."

My throat goes tight.

He's the Scribe.

The one who can erase people like lines on a page. Standing

there talking about me like I'm a typo.

Rachel continues. "We're too close to bringing the Concord to full power. The shifter is who the elders have requested, and we will not fail them. The ritual must be completed. The sacrifice must happen tomorrow night at the solstice as planned."

Heat roars through me. I want to launch myself off this rock and go for their throats. Tear robes and faces and stop this before Everett ever gets near the lake.

Five Concord members. One of me. One of them can wipe me from existence with a flick of his wrist.

I stay where I am.

"I'll make sure Calvin gets back to Moonridge tonight," Sam says. "And I'll get something personal of his. Hair, blood, anything the Scribe needs. Just in case we need to… address the situation permanently."

My thoughts spin so fast they blur. Sam is not on my side. And Agnes. Did she know? Is she part of this circle, or does her mother work in the shadows? Was the apothecary ever safe, or just another link in the Concord chain?

The Morehouses are the only ones I can trust. I cling to the memory of Esther's voice when she talked about the Concord. The disgust. The fear. That felt real. It has to be. Because if it's not, I've got no one in this time who's actually on my side. I'm just trapped in another time with a group of people who wants Everett dead and me erased.

The meeting breaks up. Final instructions trade hands.

Sam heads back toward the cliffs, toward the path we ran. No doubt already thinking about what of mine he can lift without me noticing.

Rachel, Ravena, and Vince move toward the road. The Scribe lingers a moment by the fire. He whispers something and it goes out before he slips into the trees, swallowed by shadow.

I don't move until the last footstep fades. Until the smoke thins and their scents stretch out, heading away from the lake.

Only then do I back down, paws careful on the rock. My wolf body feels too tight, like a skin that isn't mine.

I need to get to Moonridge. I need to get Everett's charms off him and keep my own stuff glued to my person. No loose hairs. No convenient shirt left on a chair for Sam to pocket.

I lope back toward the clearing where we stripped, keep low to stay out of sight of any stragglers. The cars wait where we left them. I spot my clothes on the hood of Sam's car, grab them carefully in my teeth, and head for the cover of the trees. Old habit from too many naked walks home.

Then I run.

Fast, threading between trunks, paws slamming earth and stone. Branches whip past my ears. My lungs pull hard, my muscles burning from the effort, but I push through it.

I don't slow.

The forest blurs into streaks of dark and silver. My body knows the work. Distance, speed, survival. I'm already planning. Break the chain and bracelet. Get Everett out. Find a way back through the portal.

By the time the shapes of town start to form through the trees, I know what I have to do. I shift back to human form behind the B&B, sheltered in shadow. Bones crack, skin prickles, fur pulls back, and then I'm on two feet again, shivering as I yank my clothes on. My fingers are clumsy and tired but I move fast. Every joint complains, but the urgency buzzing under my skin wins.

I head for the back entrance of the B&B. One thought hammers through my head with every step.

I've got hours. Maybe less.

CHAPTER TWENTY-EIGHT

Everett

Calvin stands at the lake's edge, naked, water dripping off his skin. Moonlight makes him glow like he's lit from within. He's just shifted back, and I can't look away. My breath catches and heat pools low in my stomach.

The moon hangs huge in the sky, too big to be real. Stars blaze so bright they almost hurt to look at.

He turns and smiles at me. "Coming in?"

I walk toward him, night air cool against my flushed skin. My heart pounds. The want I have for him is sharper than anything I ever felt with Vince. It's clearer and more urgent.

We stand together at the water's edge. Our reflections stare back at us from the dark surface. We look good together. Right.

"We make a handsome couple, don't we?" Calvin's voice drops low and intimate.

I nod, unable to find words.

Then my reflection begins to change.

My face begins to shift. The skin pulls tight across my bones until it splits. My eyes go black, empty holes with nothing behind them. No me left inside. My mouth opens wider than it should, stretching wrong, a silent scream with only darkness inside trying to swallow everything.

I try to look away, but I can't. It's me, but not. A twisted, melted version.

"Swim with me!" Calvin jumps into the lake and the splash shatters our reflection. The horrible face disappears, leaving only rippling water.

"Come on!" He laughs, splashing around like a kid. "The water's perfect!"

I stand frozen at the edge, skin crawling. I'm not built like Calvin. Not as strong, not as tall. But he's looking at me with heat in his gaze, so I start to undress.

I pull off my shirt. Kick off my shoes. Step out of my pants.

When I look up, everything has changed.

Calvin stares at me but the warmth is gone from his eyes. They look cold now. Hard. He throws his head back and laughs, the sound bouncing off the water all wrong and sharp.

"What's wrong with you? Look at you."

Heat floods my face and shame burns across my skin. I reach for my clothes but they've vanished. I try to cover myself, but there's too much to hide, nowhere to put my hands.

Footsteps sound behind me. Branches crack in the woods.

I turn to see Sam, Tony, and Jake stepping out of the trees. All human. All naked. All moving toward me with purpose.

They're laughing.

"Well, well, well." Sam draws the words out, slow and mean. "What do we have here? A little shifter who thinks he belongs with the wolves?"

"Pathetic." Jake moves closer and I can smell his breath, hot and rancid.

"Disgusting," Tony agrees, circling around behind me.

They close in like predators. I try to run, but my legs won't obey, like my feet have grown roots into the earth.

"Please." My voice comes out as barely a whisper. "Leave

me alone."

"You don't belong here." Sam's smile shows too many teeth. "You're an abomination."

He shoves me hard.

I stumble backward into someone's arms. A solid grip catches me, holds me upright. For a moment I think I'm safe.

Then I look up and see Calvin's face twisted into something that isn't quite him anymore. Every line looks sharp and cruel. His eyes are black holes, empty like my reflection was.

He's holding a knife.

The blade catches the moonlight, long and thin with something dark and crusted along the edge.

"You don't belong on this earth." The voice coming from his mouth isn't his. It's deeper, distorted and fundamentally wrong. "You belong to us."

The knife comes down.

I jerk awake.

Sheets twist around my legs. My T-shirt clings to my back, damp with sweat. A tremor crawls through my arms and settles in my bandaged hand, grounding me.

My room swims into focus. Ceiling. Window. The familiar mess on my nightstand.

I'm safe.

It was just another nightmare.

The chain around my neck pulses, warm against my skin. A slow, steady thrum. The bracelet on my wrist answers in the same rhythm. Heat gathers where it meets skin, then seeps outward in measured waves.

My breathing eases. Muscles unknot one by one. Thoughts that were clawing at the inside of my skull lose their edge.

You're safe.

The words drift through my mind. Not my voice. Not my thought. Still, they slide into place like they belong there. Quieting. Smoothing.

Warmth settles over me, heavy and pleasant, smudging the terror at the edges.

It was just a dream. My brain chewing on yesterday.

Just a dream.

Except that isn't completely true. Part of it was real. Not the naked Calvin part. Not the knife. Not the wolves closing in.

But I really did go to Skipper Lake last night.

The memory creeps back in.

I couldn't sleep after everything that happened yesterday. My thoughts kept piling up until my head felt too full. Every time I closed my eyes, I saw Calvin and his warnings of danger. The room felt small and suffocating.

I needed space. Needed to be near the water.

Water helps me think.

I got dressed in the dark, snuck out to my car, and drove through the sleeping town. I wanted Amethyst Beach, my usual spot. The place I go when everything gets too loud in my head. But I knew the female wolves would be running there, and I didn't want to be that creep lurking around while they were shifting.

So Skipper Lake it was.

I parked farther up the road where no one would notice my car. The engine ticked as it cooled while I sat there trying to decide if I'd made the right choice. Had I come up here to relax, or had I come hoping to see Calvin?

Then I saw another car parked even farther up. Vince's car. That shiny white paint and the white tire rims stood out even in the dark.

My gut twisted.

Vince said he was tired after his trip. Said he needed a night alone. Said he'd see me tomorrow. But there he was, up at Skipper Lake the same night Sam and the others were supposed to be there.

Why?

Was it to see Sam?

I started the car again and rolled it farther up the road, tucking it behind a curve where Vince wouldn't spot it if he left first. Then I killed the engine, locked up, and slipped into the trees.

Better to shift. Safer. Wolves don't like peeping toms, especially when they're vulnerable. They'd be a lot less likely to mess with another predator.

I stripped behind a tree, folded my clothes, and stuffed them into a hollow log. The change came easy. Skin rippled, bones rearranged, the world sharpening until every sound and scent landed with perfect clarity.

Cougar. Big enough to earn respect. Fast enough to bail if things went sideways. My favorite skin for a reason.

I padded through the underbrush on silent paws, keeping downwind, following Vince's familiar mix of exhaust and cologne.

Smoke found me first. A thin gray thread rising between the branches ahead.

I dropped lower, belly brushing the leaves, ears swiveling to catch every sound. The crackle of fire. Voices murmuring in a rhythm that wasn't quite talk and wasn't quite song. Old words. Wrong words. My fur lifted along my spine.

I crept around a boulder and into shadow.

A small clearing. A fire. Five hooded figures spaced around the flames. The robes looked black as hell, eating the light. The way the fire moved made them look like shadows instead of people.

Two of them pushed back their hoods.

Ravena. Sharp cheekbones, dark hair, that snakeish look she always wears.

And Vince.

My Vince. Standing there wrapped in ritual robes like it was perfectly normal.

Something inside me went very still.

The fire snapped and spit. Their voices threaded over it, most of the words lost in the noise, but a few slipped through.

"...the wolf is getting in the way..."

"...need to deal with him before..."

The wolf. A wolf they needed to deal with.

Calvin? Who else could it be?

Suddenly Vince's warnings slotted into place. *Calvin is dangerous. Stay away from him.* Vince wasn't trying to control me. He was handling it. Protecting me. Cleaning up the mess so I wouldn't have to.

That had to be it.

Movement drew my eye to the ridge above the clearing. A wolf crawled along the top, body low, watching the ritual like I was. It turned, and for a heartbeat our eyes met.

Everything in me said to leave now.

I backed away, one paw at a time, careful not to snap a twig. Once the trees swallowed the clearing, I turned and ran.

Branches whipped past. Leaves crackled under my weight. I didn't stop until the lake and the fire were far behind.

I shifted back behind my tree, dragged on my clothes with clumsy human fingers, and stumbled to my car. The drive home blurred into headlights and dark road, my thoughts circling the same impossible picture of Vince by that fire.

Vince is protecting me. That's what this was. He knows Calvin is dangerous and he's dealing with it. That's all.

The story sounded thin even in my own head, but I clung to it anyway.

I snuck back into my room and lay there, staring at the ceiling until sleep finally dragged me under.

And now I'm awake again, the nightmare still tangled up with the memory of Skipper Lake, the two sliding over each other until I'm not sure where one stops and the other begins.

I take a slow breath.

The bracelet and pendant keep their steady rhythm. Calming. Soothing.

Vince is protecting you. Vince loves you. Vince would never hurt you.

The thoughts slide in smooth. The jewelry hums agreement, warm and approving against my skin.

Deep down, something curls away from it, telling me this is all wrong.

I shove myself out of bed and unhook the chain and bracelet. They land on my dresser with a soft clink. I flip on the radio and head for the shower.

Hot water drums over my shoulders and neck. Steam fills the bathroom, fogging the mirror. I scrub carefully around my stitched hand, work shampoo through my hair, let the spray beat against the back of my skull until my thoughts dull to a low buzz.

It's Saturday. No work. The garage is closed on weekends. Only the gas station side stays open, and some high school kid usually handles that.

I turn off the water, towel off, and pull on clean clothes. The unease stays lodged under my ribs.

Maybe it's time to get out of town.

The thought drops into place out of nowhere.

I could leave. Pack a bag, take my car, drive until the map changes and no one knows my name. Vince is hiding something. Calvin is trouble. Maybe I should cut my losses and go. Start over somewhere new.

Again.

I picture heading west. I've never seen the Pacific. California always sounds like this glittering place where nobody cares if you're weird, where small-town gossip doesn't stick to your skin.

I could be someone new. Someone who doesn't have to explain what he is or who he wants or why he doesn't fit.

I could just go. Today. Take my car and keep driving until Moonridge shrinks in the mirror.

For a second, I can almost taste freedom.

My eyes land on the bracelet and chain lying on the dresser.

Stay.

The word drops into my head, a quiet command that isn't

mine. Not my voice. Not my thought.

Stay for Vince. He needs you. He loves you. You can't leave him. You promised.

I shake my head. The words cloud my thoughts.

Whose promises are those?

My reflection stares back at me from the mirror. Purple smudges sit under my eyes. My mouth pulls tight, like it forgot how to relax.

I need to walk. Move. Get air and distance and some kind of answer.

But as I step outside into the morning sunlight, I already know where my feet are going. To the park. Where Calvin told me to meet him at noon.

I take the long route, hoping the walk will clear my head.

It doesn't.

Every street feels too bright, too normal, like the town is pretending it doesn't hide monsters.

Monsters that have it out for me.

My decision is made. I'll hear Calvin out and close this chapter. Then I'll pack my car and get out of Moonridge for good.

The park bench is warm under my hands. Sunlight comes through the leaves, making patterns on the path. I've been here almost an hour, watching kids pump their legs on the swings and couples wander past, fingers linked.

Normal people. Normal lives.

Must be nice.

"Everett."

I look up.

Calvin stands in front of me, breathing hard. He looks wrecked. Same clothes as yesterday, wrinkled and stained with sweat and dirt. His hair sticks up in wild tufts, and shadows sink under his eyes.

He's got two bags. A duffel and a backpack, both stuffed and bulky, like he grabbed everything and ran.

Something twists in my chest at the sight. Why should it matter if he leaves? He's just some guy who walked into town two days ago and announced I'm about to be murdered.

Some guy whose attention flips my insides every time it lands on me.

I rub my wrist and realize my bracelet is still on the dresser at home. A cold jolt hits. Vince will lose it if he finds out I left without it.

"We really need to talk, please?" Calvin says. His voice comes out rough and worn.

"You look terrible," I say, because it's true and because anything else feels too revealing. I'm not ready to admit I'm worried. "What happened?"

"Haven't slept." He swallows. "Listen, I know you don't trust me right now, but you're in serious danger. Someone wants to sacrifice you, and I need to get you out of here."

"Sacrifice me?" The word crawls over my skin. "What are you talking about?"

"There's a group called the Concord." Calvin drops down on the bench beside me. Close enough our knees almost bump. I catch the scent of sweat and fear and the faint, wild edge of wolf. "They practice dark magic. Blood magic. And they plan to make you join them. Your soul will be bound to Skipper Lake and they'll use your soul to fuel their magic."

I laugh, but it comes out thin and wrong to my own ears. "That's insane."

"Is it?" Calvin digs into his pocket and pulls out a folded, worn piece of paper. He smooths it over his knee.

A symbol stares up at me. Ink-black spiral with three lines cutting through it. The lines slice in a way that makes my skin crawl.

"This is one of their sigils," Calvin says. "I found it carved into trees at Skipper Lake."

Every muscle in my body goes rigid.

I saw those marks. While I prowled through the trees last night, trying to figure out what Vince was doing. Cuts in the bark, sap bleeding out like the trees were wounded.

"Vince is working with them," Calvin says quietly. His gaze pins me, intent and raw. "He's trying to sacrifice you to gain power of his own."

"No." The word leaps out on reflex. "There's no way Vince would do that. We've had our issues, but he's not a monster."

"He's not doing it because he's crazy," Calvin says. His tone softens, careful, like he's inching toward a skittish animal. "He's doing it because he's desperate. They've promised him something he wants more than anything. More than you. You're payment. That's all."

My lungs forget how to work. I don't want to believe him, but part of me does. Because it fits.

I know how badly Vince wants power of his own. How much he resents Sam and the other wolves. The hate he carries for the witches of Moonridge. He hates being unlit.

I know how he hangs around Sam and the pack, waiting for scraps of attention. I know the way his whole face lights up when they let him tag along.

I know. I've always known. I just didn't want to look at it too closely.

"No," I whisper, but it sounds flimsy. Less like an argument, more like a wish. What's left of my trust crumbling.

Calvin opens his duffel. He pulls out several pieces of paper, folded and creased from too many reads.

"See the date?" he asks, pointing to the top of one.

"What are these?" It looks like it came from a newspaper, but it's not the same type of paper I'm used to seeing articles printed on.

"It's a copy of a newspaper article. Just read the date."

I lean closer.

June 25th, 1958.

Four days from now.

"How?" My fingers tighten on the paper. The park tilts, like the world can't quite level out. "How is that even possible?"

"I'm from the future," Calvin says. His voice sharpens with urgency. "Read the headline."

I force my eyes to the bold print. The letters blur for a second, but the words still land.

"Local Man Missing," I read.

Below the headline sits a black and white photo.

My car.

My car, parked at Skipper Lake. The driver's door hanging open. Top down.

The paper rattles in my hands.

"Keep reading," Calvin says.

Everett Bradshaw was reported missing by his employer and landlord, Earl Randall, two days ago. Bradshaw's vehicle was discovered abandoned at Skipper Lake. Authorities are investigating but have few leads. Anyone with information should contact the Moonridge Sheriff's Department.

The sentences string together, but my brain refuses to accept them.

That's my car. My name. From days that haven't happened yet.

Before I can wrap my mind around it, running footsteps slap against the path. Someone calls Calvin's name.

Agnes Thornton races toward us, waving. Her face is flushed, hair coming loose from its ponytail in wild strands.

"Calvin!" she shouts. "The door. It's open. We need to go!"

Calvin jumps up and yanks me with him. His hand closes around mine, grip warm and solid. It steadies me more than it should.

"Please, Everett. Don't you see?" He looks right at me, brown eyes wide and frantic. "Come with me. I met your ghost in the future. Vince and the Concord sacrifice you and bind you. I came back to stop it. You have to believe me."

For a second, the world narrows to his face and the paper in my hand.

This can't be real. Time travel, sacrifice, cults. It sounds like something out of a monster movie.

"Come on! We need to get you out of here while we can," Agnes says, gripping Calvin's arm and tugging us both into motion.

I stumble between them, half dragged down Main Street toward the hardware store. My thoughts run in tight, panicked circles. Stay. Run. Believe him. Don't.

How is any of this possible?

We cut down the alley behind the hardware store. I glance at the stack of articles in my grip and the next headline catches my eye.

Missing Man Found Drowned at Skipper Lake.

My knees almost give out. Calvin catches my elbow and pulls me along. I stumble behind him, my eyes fixed to the paper. The words smear at the edges, but the message lands clean and I stop dead in my tracks barely able to breathe.

Everett Bradshaw, 27, was reported missing two weeks ago when his car was found abandoned at Skipper Lake. His body was discovered yesterday when it washed ashore. Authorities ruled the death an accidental drowning, though questions remain about why Bradshaw was at the lake alone. His friend, Vince Franelli, told authorities that Bradshaw had been depressed lately and he assumed he had skipped town. "I never thought he'd do something like this," Franelli said. "I wish I'd known he was hurting so bad."

Dead.

My body dragged from the lake. Bloated and pale. My life boiled down to a sad quote from Vince.

I stare at my own smiling face in the grainy photo.

I'm going to die. And Vince will tell everyone I was depressed. That I did it to myself. He'll stand there, playing the grieving friend, while he's the one who—

Calvin darts back, grabs my arm, and pulls me down the last stretch of alley.

The door to the storage shed stands open. Blue light spills out onto the pavement. It doesn't shine like normal light; it pulses like something alive. Waiting. The air around it shimmers, bending the alley out of shape. The sight makes the hair on my arms rise. My skin prickles, every nerve suddenly alert.

Something on the other side of that door isn't right. It hums with power that doesn't belong here.

Rachel Thornton stands beside the doorway. Her expression is carved into hard, cold lines. No trace of warmth. No hint of the woman who runs the apothecary with tidy shelves and polite small talk.

"Calvin, you need to go. Now," she says. Her voice leaves no room for argument. "But you must go alone. Everett must stay."

"No." Calvin's grip tightens on my hand. "I'm not leaving without him."

Agnes steps between us and her mother. "Mother, he isn't safe. We have proof." She snatches the piece of paper from my hand and thrusts it forward. "Look. Calvin was telling the truth."

Rachel studies the paper for a heartbeat. Her eyes narrow. Then she flicks her fingers in a small, bored gesture.

Flame races across the page.

I jerk back. Heat blasts my face. The paper blackens in Agnes's grip, curling in on itself before drifting away as gray ash.

Agnes doesn't even flinch.

"Lies," Rachel says. Her voice could frost glass. "Just like everything else he's told you." She turns to me. For a second, her eyes look almost kind. "Agnes was working with Calvin to betray you. I'm very disappointed in her. She'll be punished for dabbling in such dark, dangerous magic."

My thoughts reel. I can't tell which way is up anymore.

"Run, Everett," Rachel says. Now her tone softens, pitched

low and soothing. "Find Vince. He'll keep you safe. He'll help you. Believe me. He's the only one you can trust."

Calvin grabs my arm again. His fingers bite into my skin. "Don't listen to her! She's Concord, too. I saw her at the lake last night with Vince and the others. They're planning to kill you tonight! She's lying. She's trying to—"

Something flashes across Rachel's face. Anger. Pure and sharp. She lifts her hand.

Calvin slams back into the brick wall behind us, his body hitting with a sick crack that makes my stomach lurch. For a second he hangs there, stunned. Then his feet leave the ground entirely. He claws at his throat, fingers trying to pry away the invisible grip.

Agnes screams at her mother to let him go. Calvin's legs kick, searching for anything to stand on. His skin reddens, then darkens toward purple. His mouth opens and closes around nothing. Only a ragged wheeze escapes.

He's dying. Right here in front of me. Rachel is killing him, and I'm frozen.

"I'm trying to help you, Everett. Go now!" Rachel shouts at me. Her hand stays extended toward Calvin. His body jerks in the air, like some invisible fist is wrapped around his neck. Her expression doesn't change. Calm. Focused. Like she's lifting groceries, not a grown man. "I said go! Find Vince. He's waiting for you. He's the only one who can help you."

Agnes throws herself at her mother's arm, trying to drag it down. "Mother, stop! You're killing him! Please!"

"He's dangerous," Rachel says, eyes locked on Calvin's choking form. "He's trying to destroy everything. Trying to ruin the future. He has to be stopped. Everett. Get out of here!"

My head fills with soft webs and a gentle voice telling me to run to Vince. *Vince will help. Vince will fix it. Vince will keep you safe.*

My legs start moving. Not from any decision I make. It's like someone hooked invisible strings into my knees.

One step back. Another.

Then my feet slam against the pavement in a full run. The alley blurs. The shed, the light, Calvin's dangling body, Agnes screaming. All of it smears into streaks of color.

My eyes sting, the world going watery as I bolt around the corner. Air saws in and out of my lungs, but I can't slow down. Can't think over the compulsion pressing me forward.

Somewhere deep inside, buried under the fear and the fog and the borrowed thoughts, another version of me claws for control and yells for help.

CHAPTER TWENTY-NINE

Calvin

I'm pinned to the wall, lungs clawing for air. Rachel's magic cinches around my throat, invisible but crushing. My feet dangle inches above the ground, toes scraping brick. I try to speak, to beg, to scream, but nothing comes out.

The alley blurs at the edges. Heat tears through my chest. This is bad. Very bad.

Faces flicker in and out. Friends and family I'll never see again. Copper floods my tongue.

So this is how it ends.

Agnes stands between her mother and the glowing doorway, her face flushed. "Mother! What are you doing?" Her hands ball into fists.

"Teaching a lesson." Rachel doesn't even look at me, like I'm a bug under her shoe. "To both of you."

"Let him go!" Agnes steps toward her.

I manage to turn my head just enough to see Everett sprinting away down the alley. Away from me. Away from the truth.

Rachel lifts her free hand, fingers spreading in warning. "Stay where you are. How many times do I have to tell you to stop meddling in affairs beyond your understanding?"

"You're hurting him!"

"That's rather the point."

The invisible pressure tightens. A dull thud drums somewhere deep in my skull. *Thump. Thump.* The space between each beat stretches. The light around Agnes dims, narrowing to a bright point.

"You should be more like Ravena." Rachel finally looks at her daughter. "She knows her place. She follows instructions. Doesn't question."

"Ravena is weak," Agnes spits. "She craves acceptance."

"The world has no place for strong-willed women, Agnes." For a second, something tired creeps into Rachel's voice. Then the thorny edge snaps back in place. "You'll learn that sooner or later. The Thornton legacy requires a certain way, and you will obey it."

"I will never be like you." Agnes's words land steady, even with tears shining in her eyes. "Ever."

The door still hangs open behind Rachel, spilling otherworldly light across the pavement. Our way out of here.

So close.

"You disappoint me, Agnes." Rachel sighs. "So much potential, wasted on sentiment. On weakness. You are not the daughter I deserve. If bloodlines weren't required to pass down our power, I would have traded you for a more dignified successor."

Agnes lifts her hands, lips moving. A spell?

"I will never agree just to seem pleasant." Her next words slice through the alley. "But that doesn't make me weak."

She thrusts her hands forward. Golden light explodes from her palms and slams into her mother's chest. Rachel flies backward, skirts tangling as she hits the ground. Her focus snaps, and the invisible grip on my throat vanishes.

I drop like a cut puppet. Knees hit first, then shoulder. Pain rattles through bone. Air saws into my lungs in one ugly, scraping gulp, then another. The alley swims in and out of focus.

Agnes runs to me and grabs my arm. "Get up!" She hauls me upright and shoves my duffel and backpack into my hands. "You know where to go. Now."

Rachel is already pushing herself up, fury twisting her features. "How dare you!" Black tendrils coil between her fingers.

"Go!" Agnes shoves me toward the street. "Don't stop until you get there."

"What about you?" My voice scrapes its way out, raw and thin.

"I'll be fine. She can't hurt me." Agnes's mouth twitches, a lie we both hear. "Just go." She turns to face her mother, hands raised. "I'll hold her off."

I run.

Not my proudest moment. My bags slam against my side with each step while magic cracks the air behind me like live wires.

What have I done? I left Agnes to fight off Rachel.

My foot clips a broken edge of pavement and I slam into a lamppost. Pain spikes through my shoulder. I drag in air, torn between sprinting back and sprinting away. Going back means Rachel finishes what she started. I can barely stay upright as it is. I'd only get us both killed.

Cold fear races through me. The timeline. If something happens to Agnes, what happens to Hazel? Does she vanish? Do I go back to a future where she never existed?

I brace my palms on my thighs and fight for air that suddenly feels thinner. Someone I know, someone I care about, could be erased like they were never here, and it would be on me. For coming. For dragging Agnes into this. For not being strong enough to stop Rachel.

"Move along, son." An older man in overalls slows, eyes narrowed. "You okay?"

"I'm fine." I straighten, swipe my mouth with the back of

my hand. "Sorry."

I force myself forward. I have to trust the portal rules, that the timeline has its own guardrails. Major paradoxes tear reality apart. Would this count as major? In my mind it would. Unless the universe decides one witch doesn't matter.

I push harder.

Storefronts flash past in streaks of color. Signs and faces blur together as I tear down Main Street. People stare at the sweaty stranger charging past, but I don't slow until the shops give way to quiet neighborhood blocks.

The residential streets all look the same. White houses. Picket fences. Perfect lawns. I turn down a side street and there, at the end of the block, stands the small blue house with the yellow door. My lungs finally suck in a full breath.

I drag myself up the front steps and slam my fist against the door.

It swings open. Bea fills the doorway, eyebrows already climbing.

"Well, if it isn't the time traveler." Her voice comes out bone-dry. "Looking like something the cat dropped in a puddle, then dragged back out again. What's wrong with you?"

I open my mouth to respond, but only a wheeze escapes. My knees buckle and I pitch forward into the house.

Bea catches me, bracing under my weight. "Whoa there, Future Boy. No fainting on the welcome mat."

She steers me to a sofa in the living room, where I collapse in an ungraceful heap.

The room holds steady around me for the first time since the alley. Tremors run across my fingers. Air rasps in and out in short bursts.

"What on earth?" Esther hurries in. Ronald fills the doorway behind her, broad and solid.

"Agnes," I manage. Each word costs me. "She's in trouble. Rachel. Magic."

"Slow down." Esther kneels beside me and presses a cool hand to my forehead. A quiet steadiness spreads through me, slowing my breathing. "Breathe first. Then talk."

I match my inhale to the gentle pressure of her hand until the shaking eases.

Bea shoves a mug toward me, steam curling from the rim. "Drink. It'll help."

I wrap my fingers around it. The tea is warm and faintly sweet, something herbal I can't name, but it steadies my lungs and untangles the tight knot in my chest.

"Rachel attacked me." I finally manage whole sentences. "She used magic to choke me against the wall. Agnes fought her and bought me time to run. She told me to come here."

Lines deepen around Esther's mouth. "Where are they now?"

"Behind the hardware store. By the portal." I push myself upright, muscles protesting. "We need to help Agnes. Rachel was furious."

"Start from the beginning," Ronald says. His voice stays even, but his shoulders are a wall of tension. "Everything that happened."

I tell them about the portal being open. How I told Everett everything. How we were almost through. About Rachel stepping out of the shadows and stopping us. About the invisible fist around my throat and Agnes throwing herself between us. Everett bolting. Then I tell them what I saw at Skipper Lake the night before: Rachel in Concord robes, Sam too, standing with Ravena and Vince and The Scribe.

With every detail, Esther's expression hardens. Ronald starts pacing the small living room, boots thumping against the floor.

"Wolves and witches," he mutters. "Working with the Concord. This is worse than we thought."

Bea barks out a laugh. "But are you surprised?"

My eyebrows raise. What does she know?

"You look surprised, Future Boy." She laughs and shakes her

head. "I love watching white people learn they're not always the hero. Especially when it comes to realizing their own families have some stink on them."

My jaw tightens. The first urge that hits is to defend myself. *I'm* not like that. *My* family isn't like that. We're different.

But I can't say that because she's not wrong. My family is smack-dab in the middle of all this shit. Seeing Sam at the lake last night was proof of that. The Carters have been in Moonridge since the beginning. Who knows what they signed on for back then.

Esther cuts her a look. "Beatrice. That's not helpful right now."

"But it's true." Bea folds her arms. "All these old families with their perfect reputations. The mighty Carters. The powerful, respected Thorntons. Turns out they're neck-deep in dark magic. Meanwhile, we're the ones everyone in town crosses the street to avoid."

Gran always talked about the Carter legacy like it was something pure and noble. But clearly it wasn't. Either there were things she never knew, or worse, things she chose not to share.

I drop my gaze, heat buzzing low in my gut. Bea's right. Of course she's right.

"We're here to help Calvin," Esther says, voice firm. "Not tear him apart."

Bea rolls her eyes but lets it go.

"This isn't entirely surprising." Esther turns back to me. "Rachel is doing what she and her family have always done. The Thorntons have a long, ugly history with power."

Ronald stops pacing. "Debating Rachel's morals can wait. Agnes can't."

He's right. The thought of Agnes alone with Rachel twists in my gut.

"We need to help her," he says, already moving toward the hall. "I'll go see what I can do."

"I'm coming too." Bea pushes off the doorframe. Her face

goes hard with determination. "I can cloak us."

I turn toward them. "But I thought she hates you. If she sees you coming to save Agnes…"

"Rachel may be powerful," Esther says, a small smile touching her lips, "but she's not as powerful as a Morehouse. They know what they're doing."

Ronald grabs his jacket and a few items from a cabinet. Bea snags a couple of small jars and a bundle of herbs. Ronald tucks a knife into his belt.

"We also need to stop Everett from going to the lake," I say. Agnes is important, but Everett is the reason I'm here. If the ritual happens, everything else is pointless. "They're planning something with him tonight."

Ronald nods. "We'll keep our eyes open for him. We'll help Agnes, and then we'll search for Everett. You stay here, out of sight."

"Are you sure?" I get to my feet, light-headed. "I should come."

"You'd only slow us down." Bea's bluntness has lost some of its sting. "No offense, but you look like death warmed over. Twice. And they're looking for you. You'd probably cause more harm than good."

She's not wrong. My legs feel unsteady, and my throat still burns from Rachel's grip. I'd be dead weight.

"You're right," I say, even though it hurts to admit.

They slip out the door, and the house goes quiet except for the tick of a clock and the distant bark of a dog.

Esther gestures back to the sofa. "Sit. While they handle that, we need to talk about your return. And about why my family is tangled up in all of this."

I sink into the cushions. "You found something?"

"I was able to do some readings around the portal." She settles into a chair across from me. "The magic itself is basic once you understand the structure."

"So I can get back?" A new kind of tightness pulls at my

chest, this one closer to hope. Finally, a way home that doesn't rely on Rachel.

"Yes, but you can't use the portal you entered through." Esther's expression goes flat and serious. "That doorway in the shed was built with Concord magic. Magic they stole from an ancestor of mine generations ago. They can sense anyone who passes through it. If you try to bring Everett back through their portal, they'll know immediately. And lord knows what they would do to you."

My stomach drops. "Then how am I supposed to get us back to my time?"

"I've created my own doorway. One the Concord can't touch." She says it like it's simple.

"But in my time the witches said this magic shouldn't be possible."

"It's not. At least not to just anyone. I've customized this portal specifically for you—it will take you exactly where you need to go."

"But what about Everett?" I lean forward. "He doesn't belong in my time. Won't your portal reject him or... I don't know, leave him behind?"

Esther's gaze drops to the pendant resting against my chest. "That pendant is bound to my descendant. Bound to your timeline. As long as Everett is wearing it when you go through, the portal will recognize him as belonging. It will pull him through right along with you."

"It's that simple?"

"Magic usually is, when you understand how it works." She meets my eyes. "Just make sure he's wearing it when you cross back through. Don't let him take it off."

The pendant pulses, a soft warmth against my skin, like it heard her.

"But before you go, there's more you need to understand." Esther pushes herself up and crosses to a bookshelf crammed with mismatched volumes. "About my family. About the Concord. About why they care so much about this town."

She runs a finger along the spines, then pulls down a thick leather-bound book. The cover is worn and dark, symbols pressed into the surface so deeply they look carved.

"I want you to take this back with you."

She lays it in my hands. The book is heavy, but not like normal weight. The leather holds a faint warmth, like it's been sitting in sunlight. A low hum tingles under my palms. Like the thing is awake and paying attention.

"Seraphine Lafayette put most of this together," Esther says. "She was one of my ancestors. An escaped slave with the gift of sight. She saw spirits, heard ancestral voices in dreams, even bent time when she had to. She used those gifts to guide people along the Underground Railroad."

I blink down at the book. "Wow. A time mage and an abolitionist."

A hint of pride softens Esther's face. "But before we talk about Seraphine, you need to understand the history of Moonridge. The real history."

She settles into her chair.

"None of what's happening is surprising. Rachel is just continuing her family's legacy." Something ancient sits behind her eyes. "The Thorntons have a… complicated history in Moonridge."

"What do you mean?" I lean forward, desperate for an explanation.

Esther sighs. The afternoon light shifts slightly, stretching the shadows across the floor.

"It's a long story," she begins. "One that goes back to the founding of Moonridge. The Morehouse family, the Blackwood family, and the Carter family were among the original settlers in the late 1700s. Plus a few others, but those three were the most prominent."

I place the book on the table next to me, focused intently

on her words.

"The Blackwoods always felt they held some sort of divine rule over the land," Esther continues. "They were often a thorn in the side of the other families. When they allowed the Thorntons to settle here in the early 1800s, there was quite an uproar."

"Why?" I ask.

"The Thornton line was rumored to have an evil mark on their name." Esther's hands move as she talks, painting pictures in the air. "Rumors of dark magic swirled wherever they went. They'd been chased out of Europe, then out of Salem, then out of Pennsylvania."

"But they settled here without problems?"

"For a time, yes. Things were mostly peaceful. But then, during the Civil War, something changed." Esther leans forward. "Seraphine Lafayette arrived in Moonridge."

I lean back in my chair, taking it all in.

"Seraphine was very powerful," Esther continues, her voice becoming fierce and reverent. "She decided to stay and she fell madly in love with a Morehouse man. Typically, the most powerful in a family keeps their surname and passes it on. That's why you don't hear of many Thornton, Morehouse, or Blackwood men these days. Magical, powerful women keep their surnames. There's magic in a name."

"But Seraphine took the Morehouse name?" I guess.

Esther nods. "The Morehouse name already held a lot of power. And in doing so, she caused... shall we say... insecurities in some of the other magical families."

"What kind of insecurities?"

"They were afraid we held too much power." Esther watches me with sharp eyes. "They wanted us out."

"Why? What did they mean by 'too much power?'"

"Who can say. There was already tension brewing between the Carters and Blackwoods," Esther says. "Which eventually turned into an all-out war between witches and wolves."

"That's right," I say, remembering stories of Moonridge history. "Was that when the Pact was created?"

"Not yet." Esther shakes her head. "First, Seraphine created the Wolfsbane amulet, which harnessed powers of both wolves and witches. It bound them together, creating balance and, to an extent, bringing peace between all families of Moonridge. That work eventually led to the Accords of 1902. Magical balance became the foundation of Moonridge."

"And the Concord noticed," I say.

"They always notice power." Esther's mouth tightens. "They saw a threat and an opportunity in Seraphine. They bound her to them. Sacrificed her. Just like they're planning to do with your friend Everett."

My stomach flips.

"So the Morehouses have a personal score to settle with the Concord."

"That's one way to put it." Esther crosses her legs and folds her hands in her lap.

"And the Thorntons?" I ask. "You said Rachel was continuing the pattern."

"There have been rumors for generations that the Thorntons helped found the Concord Thirteen," Esther says. "They were chased out of Europe for the same kind of work. Dark rituals. Deals with whatever lives beyond our veil."

I think of Hazel, bright and stubborn behind the apothecary counter. "This doesn't fit. In my time, Hazel Thornton fights the Concord. She's one of the good ones. She runs the Blue Moon Apothecary. Her best friend is La'Tasha Morehouse. Your descendant. They've been working together to protect Moonridge."

Esther's brows rise. "Agnes's granddaughter and my descendant. Joined at the hip?"

"Pretty much," I say. "They're inseparable. If the Thorntons started the Concord, how does Hazel end up on the other side of it?"

"Agnes," Esther leans forward. "I knew there was something different about that girl. If Agnes walks a different path, the legacy shifts with her."

Which means everything happening right now matters even more than I thought.

"We still have to keep her alive long enough to do that," I say. "And stop Everett from being turned into their next sacrifice."

"We'll do what we can." Esther's gaze sharpens. "And I need you to focus on what comes after once you return. The Concord might be weak, but they will still be active and I need you to help ensure La'Tasha has every advantage she can to defeat them once and for all."

"How so?"

She taps the cover of the book she'd given me. "Seraphine came to me in a dream and showed me a fire. The Concord destroys this book in the near future. It holds spells and records that guided my family for centuries, including work on time portals. If the Concord wants it gone, that means it's a threat to them, otherwise they wouldn't wipe it out. La'Tasha will need it."

I tighten my grip on the leather. "This is even bigger than saving Everett."

"Yes and no," she says gently. "He matters. So does Agnes. The Concord plays a long game. But so do we."

"I don't..." My throat knots. "What if I screw this up? What if I lose it?"

"La'Tasha is my family, and she trusts you." Esther steps closer until the book is bracketed between us. "If she trusts you enough to send you back here, then I trust you to carry this back to her."

The responsibility settles over me, thick and heavy.

"I'll keep it safe," I say, and I mean it. "Whatever it takes."

I ease the book into my bag, careful, like I'm tucking in something alive. Seraphine's work. The Morehouse legacy. The information La'Tasha might need to save all of us.

CHAPTER THIRTY

Calvin

I can't sit still. I pace the length of Esther's living room, legs refusing to quit. The clock on the wall ticks loud and sharp. Is Agnes okay? Did they find Everett? I need to know they're safe, and then we need to get out of here.

"Calvin." Esther's voice snaps me out of it. "You're going to wear a path in my floor."

"Sorry." I stop, but my fingers tap a frantic rhythm against my thigh. "I just need to do something."

"You are doing something." She stands from where she's been gathering supplies. "You're driving me to distraction with all that pacing."

I crack a smile. "Fair point."

"Come." She gestures toward the back door. "The portal will be ready soon. You can help me finish setting up."

I follow her through the kitchen and out the back door. The late afternoon sun slants across a small, neat garden, turning everything golden. The herby scent of rosemary, thyme, and sage fills the air. Flowers bloom purple, pink and gold. The yard looks calm. Too calm for my anxiety-ridden ass.

At the very back of the yard sits a small shed with a round door and a slanted roof. It's cute and unassuming. Throw some pink paint on it and a white woman in the future would turn it into a she-shed.

"This is where we'll open the portal?"

"Did you expect something more dramatic?" Esther unlocks the shed with an old brass key.

"I don't know. Maybe?" The one I came through was in a storage room behind a hardware store. Apparently time travel loves a storage shed.

"I needed someplace away from the house that was private. This was it. Besides, magic doesn't care about the packaging." She pushes the door open, and I follow.

The shed is bigger inside than it looked from outside. Tools hang neatly on one wall. Shelves line another, holding jars of dried plants, bundles of herbs, and small boxes labeled in neat handwriting.

My skin prickles. The pendant around my neck warms against my chest.

"How are you able to do this so quickly?" I watch as she clears a space in the center of the floor.

"I'm tapping into the power of my ancestors." Esther kneels and runs her hands over symbols that have been drawn on the wooden floor with chalk. "Specifically, Seraphine. She could open portals without preparation or tools. Pure will and magic."

I watch the symbols take shape. They remind me of the ones on La'Tasha's amulet, and I curl my fingers into my palms to keep from reaching out, to keep from smudging the chalk.

"She used that skill during the Civil War," Esther continues, chalk scraping against wood. "She helped enslaved people escape. She could open doorways between places that should have been days apart by travel."

"That's amazing."

"It's why the Concord wanted her so badly." Esther pauses, checking her work. "She was too valuable to kill. So they bound her to their service instead."

The hairs on my arms lift. That's what they want to do to Everett. Bind him. Use him. Turn his power into a weapon for their twisted rituals.

"Fortunately for us," Esther says, "before she was taken, she documented all of her methods. Created spells her descendants could use if needed." She stands, dusting chalk from her hands. "I can't conjure a portal from thin air like she could, but with the right preparation, I can make it work."

"And it'll take us back to my time?"

"It should, yes." She moves to one of the shelves, selecting jars and packets without looking, like her hands already know the order. "I've enchanted the portal to respond to where you belong. Your natural place in the timeline. So long as you don't will it to send you somewhere else, you'll be fine."

I fidget with La'Tasha's amulet around my neck. It pulses warm, like a heartbeat. "How do I make sure I return to the exact place and time I left from? I need to find La'Tasha right away."

"That tether my descendant gave you will pull you back to her." Esther nods to the pendant. "Like a homing beacon across time. But even without it, the portal would return you to your timeline; it's where you belong. Focus on home, on your friends, and the portal will take you there."

Home. I left it a few days ago, but it already feels distant.

"So I just click my heels together three times?"

Esther laughs. "Something like that, Dorothy. Though I think your ruby slippers could use a polish."

I look down at my dirty, scuffed boots and have to laugh too. I'm a mess. Every part of me. But at least I have a way home now. A way to bring Everett back with me.

If I can save him.

No. *When* I save him.

Esther puts down the items she's been gathering and studies me. "You might want to wash up before your journey. There's a bathroom upstairs. First door on the left."

Heat crawls up my neck. I can smell myself now that she mentions it. Sweat and fear and too many hours without a shower.

"Clean towels are in the cabinet," she adds gently. "Take your time."

I nod, grateful, and head back inside.

Upstairs, I shower real quick then try to make myself look less like someone who's been strangled and chased through time. Dark marks bloom along my throat. Shadows hang under my eyes. I barely recognize the guy staring back.

When I come back downstairs, my bags still sit where I left them in the living room. I check the book of spells, making sure it's secure in the center of my duffel. Wrapped in a shirt, protected. I zip the bag all the way and press my palm over it.

The clock on the mantle reads 4:47. Nearly five o'clock. They should be back by now. What if something went wrong? What if Agnes was hurt?

What if they found Everett and he's already—

No. I can't think like that.

"Something's wrong." I press my forehead against the cool glass of the window. The street outside looks ordinary. A group of boys toss a football. A woman waters her garden. "They should be back by now."

Esther looks up from the book she's been reading. "I would feel it if they were in danger."

"Are you sure?" I turn. "Like, absolutely positive?"

"Calvin." She closes her book. "I am connected to my children by blood and magic. If something was truly wrong, I would know."

I want to believe her. I really do. But worry sits low and sharp in my gut.

"Besides," she adds, "Agnes is far more resourceful than her mother realizes."

An engine growls down the quiet street. A car turns the corner, sunlight glinting off its chrome bumper.

Ronald's Chevy.

I rush back to the window. The car pulls up to the curb. Agnes climbs out of the back seat, her hair wild and her clothes rumpled. Her shoulders sag, and the spark in her eyes looks dimmed.

Bea and Ronald follow. Neither of them looks any better.

No Everett.

The back of my throat goes dry. Whatever hope I had thins to a thread.

The front door opens, and the three of them file in. Agnes looks wrecked. A scrape marks her cheek. Her gaze, though, is still sharp.

"What happened?" The words burst out of me. "Did you find him?"

"We found him." Ronald says it from just inside the doorway. "He wouldn't come with us."

Relief flickers and dies. For a second, I can't get my mouth to work. "What? Why not?"

"We told him everything." Bea drops into an armchair and lets out a heavy sigh. "He didn't believe us. Or he couldn't. Those charms they have on him are powerful."

No, no, no. This can't be happening.

"He looked right through us," Agnes says quietly. She slumps onto the sofa. "Like we were strangers."

The sound of her voice hits me right in the chest.

"The charms," I manage. "Can't we just… remove them? Break the spell?"

"Not without getting close enough to touch him." Bea's mouth flattens. "And he ran the moment Ronald tried."

I sink into a chair before my legs forget how to work. All of this, and Everett still won't come. Still thinks Vince is the good guy.

It's like watching someone you love stroll toward a cliff while they rave about the view.

"My mother dragged me back to the apothecary and locked me in my room after you left." Agnes touches the scrape on her cheek. "She warded the door and windows shut. Said I'd stay there until I learned my place."

"How did you escape?" Esther asks, brows drawn as she studies her.

A quick, fierce smile flashes across Agnes's face. "What Mother doesn't know is that I've spent my entire life learning to counter her spells."

"Counter them?"

"You can't be a rebellious witch with a controlling mother and not learn how to undo everything she does to you." Agnes shrugs. "It's basic survival. Self-preservation magic."

For a heartbeat, she looks like the older Agnes I knew. The one who'd stare down a poltergeist and tell it to mind its manners.

"So you just… dispelled her magic?"

Agnes leans forward. Dark circles shadow her eyes, but she's intent now. "Yes, but first I used an Animam Transitus. A whisperwalk spell."

I blink at her. "A what now?"

"It lets you extend your consciousness to other areas." She sweeps her hand through the air. "Your body stays put, but your mind can travel and observe undetected."

"Like astral projection?"

"Similar, yes." Agnes nods. "I heard my mother talking to someone. The ritual is happening tonight. At Skipper Lake, just after sunset."

My whole body leans toward her words.

"It's Summer Solstice, the longest day of the year, so we have a little more time."

Some of the tension in my shoulders loosens.

"And I learned something else." Agnes takes a deep breath.

"My mother is the anchor to the Concord. The member who binds all the others together. Without her, the whole power structure stops working."

Esther's mouth pulls tight. "That makes sense. Rumor has it the Thorntons founded the Concord 13. It would have to be a Thornton who acts as the anchor."

Agnes's mouth falls open. "The Thorntons founded..." She shakes her head. "No. *My* family?"

"I'm afraid so." Esther's voice is steady. "Your family has a long history with the Concord. Going back generations."

Agnes stares at her hands. "No wonder she'd get so mad when I questioned her motives or teachings." Her jaw clenches. "She was training me."

Training her to join the Concord. To continue the legacy.

"I had no idea." Agnes looks up, and there are tears in her eyes.

"You have the power to fix generations of darkness," Esther says. "To be the one who breaks the chain."

Agnes stares ahead, nodding once.

"Agnes—" I start, but she cuts me off.

"There's more." She turns to me. "I overheard my mother telling someone they have to 'erase the wolf.' They meant you, Calvin."

Cold rushes through me. "The Scribe."

"Yes." Agnes nods. "They need something that belongs to you. A personal item. My mother said she has it in a sealed box. They plan to erase you before they sacrifice Everett."

The room blurs for a second. Erase me. Remove me from existence. Like I never was.

"If they erase you..." Bea glances at her mother.

"It's okay." Agnes puts a hand on my arm. Her touch steadies me. "Let me finish. Yes, my mother sealed that box. But what she doesn't know is that I tampered with it."

"You what?"

"I cleansed it." Agnes's smile turns sharp and pleased. "I

removed your hair and any trace of you—skin cells, energy residue—anything they could use, and then I burned it with witch fire. Then I scrubbed the box clean of your essence. What's in there now is just decoy material. It won't erase you."

Air rushes into my lungs like I forgot how to breathe until now. "Agnes, you're incredible."

"What did you replace his effects with?" Esther asks.

"That's not important." Agnes waves the question away. "What matters is that Everett thinks he's joining Vince at Skipper Lake in a few hours for a romantic date. We need to intervene before the ritual begins."

"We need a plan." Ronald speaks from where he's been leaning against the wall, arms crossed.

For the next half hour, we hammer out details. One wrong move and Everett dies. One mistake and the Concord wins.

Bea, Ronald, and Agnes will come with me to the lake. Bea can cloak us so we won't be detected, but the spell has limits.

"We can't get too close or stay hidden for long," she warns. "And the more people I'm cloaking, the weaker it becomes. We'll have maybe fifteen minutes. Twenty if we're lucky."

"I'll shield Calvin," Ronald says. "You focus on keeping us hidden."

"Sam is a wolf," Bea adds. "And you may need to fight him."

The idea of facing Sam, young and strong and loyal to the Concord, curdles in my stomach. But I'd do it for Everett. I'd do anything for Everett.

Even fight family.

"Vince has no real power," Agnes says. "He's a puppet. He's not much of a threat."

"What about Rachel and Ravena?" I ask. I've felt Rachel's power. Seen what she can do.

"I've trained with both of them since I was a child." Agnes meets my eyes, gaze steady. "I know every spell they'll use and exactly how to counter them."

"They can't match Ronald's and my power," Bea chimes in. "And if things get crazy, I can mess with the weather. Create distractions. And Ronald can make pretty convincing hallucinations."

"Hallucinations?" I ask.

"I can make people see things that aren't there," Ronald says. "Or not see things that are."

"And I'll wait here," Esther says. "Ready to open the portal the moment you return."

It's not a perfect plan. Too many variables, too many powerful enemies, but it's all we've got.

"We should leave soon," Ronald says, checking his watch. "Get in position before dark. The ritual won't start until after sunset, but we need to be ready."

I nod and pull in a long breath, forcing my shoulders back. "Okay."

The Chevy sits at the curb, chrome catching the last of the sun. I climb into the back seat beside Agnes. Bea takes the passenger side. Ronald slides behind the wheel, and the engine rumbles to life.

As we pull away from the house, I watch it shrink in the rear window. The setting sun reflects off the windows. Inside the car, no one speaks. The quiet settles over us.

I stare out the window as familiar streets roll past, my mind already at the lake.

"Everett'll come around." Agnes speaks beside me. "Once he sees us fighting for him. Once he understands the truth."

"What if he doesn't?" I ask. "What if the charms are too strong?"

"Then we break them." Her chin lifts. "Bea, Ronald, and I combined are more powerful than my mother and Ravena."

I want to believe her confidence. Want to feel that same certainty, but fear continues to needle at me.

"Thank you," I say. "For helping. For fighting your own

mother."

"Thank you for showing me the truth." She meets my eyes. "Even if it hurts."

Bea shifts in the front seat. "If you two are done with the emotional bonding, we're about five minutes out. We should go over the plan one more time."

Ronald takes a turn onto a dirt road. Trees press close on both sides, branches overhead. The light shines green and gold through the leaves.

"We'll park a quarter mile from the lake," Ronald says. "Approach on foot. Bea will cloak us once we're close."

"I'll scout ahead first," Bea adds. "See who's already there and where they're positioned."

"Once we know the layout, we move in fast," Agnes says. "We have to get to Everett before the ritual starts."

"And if it's already started?" I ask.

Silence.

"Then we interrupt it," Ronald says. "Whatever it takes. If he's not dead, then we still have time."

The car slows, then stops. We've reached the end of the drivable road. Through the trees ahead, I can make out the glimmer of water.

Heat prickles along my arms. This is it. No more planning. No more waiting.

Ronald kills the engine. The sudden quiet presses in.

"Ready?" he asks, turning to look at us.

I open the car door. "Let's go."

We move through the trees like ghosts. Bea's cloaking spell wraps around us, and the world feels muted, like we're watching it on TV rather than experiencing it.

The lake appears through the trees, reflecting the sky, all pink and orange as the sun drops. It's beautiful and peaceful and completely wrong for what's about to happen.

Bea raises a hand, signaling us to stop. She creeps forward

alone, scouting.

I crouch behind a tree, my legs trembling. Agnes is beside me, her hands glowing with gathered magic. Ronald stands like a sentinel, watching and waiting.

Bea returns, her mouth tight. "They're here. All of them. Rachel, Ravena, Sam, the Scribe. They're setting up the ritual circle on the north shore."

"Vince and Everett?" His name scrapes out of my throat.

"Not yet. But Sam keeps checking his watch. They'll be here soon."

We creep closer. I can feel the strain on Bea's spell, feel the air hum with all that gathered magic.

An engine rumbles in the distance. The robed figures melt back into the trees as Everett's car pulls up to the lake.

It's time.

CHAPTER THIRTY-ONE

Everett

The bracelet throbs against my wrist, pulsing in time with the chain around my neck. Like they're trading signals, testing my skin. Whenever I try to think about that alley, about Calvin choking and Agnes fighting her mother, my thoughts scatter and refuse to settle.

Nothing to worry about. Everything is fine now.

"Everett? Honey?" Mrs. Randall's voice filters through the door. "Are you alright in there?"

"Fine." The word lands flat, even to me. "Just... tired."

"You don't sound fine." Her voice comes closer. "Can I come in?"

I stare at the doorknob. Part of me leans toward telling her everything. About Calvin and his warnings. About Rachel Thornton trying to kill him with invisible hands. About Calvin's stories of some cult that wants to sacrifice me.

But the last thing she needs is blood rituals and magical murder plots on her mind.

"Really, I'm okay. Just having an off day."

A pause. "Earl and I are going out for dinner. It's our anniversary."

"That's great." I nudge my voice lighter. "Have fun."

"There's meatloaf in the fridge if you get hungry. We'll be back around eleven."

"Thanks, Mrs. Randall."

"You sure you're okay?"

No. Not even a little bit.

"Positive. You guys have a good time."

Her footsteps retreat down the hall, slow and reluctant. I wait by the window until I see their car pull out of the driveway, taillights fading around the corner.

Alone. For now.

I should follow my instincts. Pack a bag. Get in my car. Drive until Moonridge is just a dot in my rearview mirror. The thought surges up, bright and sharp.

The bracelet warms against my skin.

No. Stay. Trust Vince. Vince loves you.

The thought is not mine. It slides into place like someone setting a book on the wrong shelf. The jewelry hums approval as it sinks in, warmth spreading through my ribs.

A knock at the front door snaps through me.

My heart jumps. The Morehouses. It has to be them. They found me earlier on my walk, Bea and Ronald with Agnes in the backseat, all of them trying to convince me to get in their car. The way they looked at me—like they knew something I didn't—sent me running. What if they've come back?

I creep to my bedroom window and peek through the curtains. Relief floods through me when I see it's not the Morehouses at all.

Vince stands on the porch, holding a picnic basket. His dark hair is slicked back with a careful pomade curl hanging over his forehead. He really is a handsome fella. He looks up, catches me watching. Waves.

My feet move before I decide to use them. The bracelet and

chain around my neck pulse faster, bright little taps under my skin.

Vince loves you. Vince wants you. Vince will take care of you.

The thoughts drift through my head like someone else is whispering in the next room.

I open the door. Vince grins and lifts the basket. Something metal clinks inside.

"Surprise!"

"What's this?" My voice comes out lighter, dreamier than intended.

"Our celebration." He steps inside, kisses my cheek. "I've got something special planned. Get your shoes on. Grab a jacket and a blanket."

"Where are we going?"

"Skipper Lake. Just the two of us. Romantic picnic by the water to celebrate our future."

The lake.

Something tugs at my memory. *Calvin said... Calvin warned...*

The chain burns against my neck and the bracelet tightens, sending waves of heat up my arm. The memory slips away, like I tried to grab it with numb fingers.

"Sounds perfect," I hear myself say. My tongue drags in my mouth. Vince doesn't seem to notice.

I grab a blanket from the closet, find my shoes, get my keys, and follow him outside to my car, ignoring the voice shoved deep in my head yelling that this is exactly what Calvin warned me about.

"I'll drive," I offer, and Vince doesn't argue. He just slides into the passenger seat with the picnic basket on his lap, one hand resting on the lid.

The drive breaks into pieces in my mind. Vince talks the whole way, words washing over me. Something about opportunities. About our future together. About dreams coming true. I nod. Smile. Make the right noises. Inside, my thoughts drag, slow and syrupy, like my brain is trying to move through glue.

The sky blazes orange and pink as we reach Skipper Lake. No other cars in the parking area. Just us.

Just Vince and me and the stars. Just like it should be.

We walk to the edge of the water. I spread the blanket on the ground while Vince unpacks the basket. Cheese. Crackers. Strawberries. And a bottle of red wine.

"Wine?" I raise my eyebrows. "That's new for you."

Vince has always been a beer guy.

"Special occasion calls for special drinks." He pours two glasses, hands me one.

The bracelet pulses again, faster now. Expectant.

I take a sip. The wine tastes off. Too sweet and bitter at the same time. The aftertaste sticks, clingy and unpleasant, settling in my stomach with a slow twist.

"Good, right?" Vince watches me. His gaze sticks to my face, unblinking.

"Yeah." I take another sip. "Good."

The sun begins to dip below the trees. The lake shore blurs at the edges. Colors smear together. Vince's voice stretches, syllables dragging out.

Heat crawls under my skin. My clothes feel too tight.

I shrug off my leather jacket. The chain against my bare skin sears. The bracelet feels welded to my wrist.

"You feeling okay?" Vince asks, but his words wobble, like they're coming through a bad radio station.

"It's hot," I manage.

He nods, says something else, but it might as well be static.

My vision doubles. Then triples. The trees shift when I blink, rearranging themselves like a deck of cards being shuffled. The lake water flashes blue, then red, then silver.

Shapes move at the edge of my vision. Hoods. Dark fabric. Faces swim.

Sam?

Ravena's profile, sharp and amused.

Why are they here?

Why can't I draw a full breath?

My entire body burns and voices fill my head. I can't breathe. Wrong. This is wrong.

With clumsy fingers, I grab the chain around my throat and yank. It snaps against my palm.

Cool air rushes into my lungs. The fog thins. Not gone, but thinner. Enough for me to feel how wrong the bracelet is.

It scorches. The skin beneath it blisters and smokes, carving patterns in my wrist.

I claw at it, panic flaring. The rope cinches tighter, digging in like it's trying to burrow into my bones. I grind my nails under the edge and rip. Flesh tears. The bracelet gives. I wrench it free and fling it into the grass.

The pressure in my head loosens. The warmth inside the jewelry snaps away like a cut wire. Whatever had a hold of me has finally let go.

I can still taste the drugged wine, but without the jewelry feeding it into me, the worst of it drains off. Thoughts slot back into place. Sharp. Horrible.

There's a mark on my inner wrist where the bracelet sat. A symbol burned into my skin like a fresh brand: a spiral with three lines cutting through it.

Calvin showed me this symbol this morning. The Concord sigil.

Calvin…

Oh God. Calvin wasn't lying.

Stomach acid fills my throat. I lean over and retch into the grass. The wine comes up.

I push to stand, but my legs buckle. My balance wobbles, like the ground dipped underneath me.

Vince watches me. Whatever soft thing used to live in his eyes is gone. His gaze is flat, measuring. Behind him, two more figures in dark robes step out of the trees. Now there are four of them.

Sam. His jaw set, lips pressed thin.

Ravena. Smiling like she's been waiting years for this.

Rachel Thornton. Her expression carved tight, eyes dry.

A man I don't know, Asian, his stare so cool it makes the hairs on my arms rise.

Vince gets up, takes something from Sam, and turns back to me.

A knife. Long and curved. The blade catches the dying sunlight in a sharp line.

They begin to chant. The words grate against my ears. The air gets thick, hard to breathe. My skin buzzes.

Vince walks toward me, knife raised. His mouth pinches. His eyes shine.

"I'm sorry, Ev." His voice cracks over the word. "But they promised. They promised I'd be powerful. That I'd be special too."

The sun slides below the horizon. Shadows crawl across the lake, across Vince's face. The tip of the blade points at my chest.

I cry out.

A roar answers. It tears through the clearing so loud it shudders in my teeth, rattling the ground. Something massive slams into Vince from the side. The impact sounds like a wreck: weight and speed and pain colliding. Vince flies, shouting, his body rolling across the dirt. The knife spins from his hand, flashing in the last light before tumbling across the ground.

A wolf stands where Vince was. Huge, with dark brown fur and white around its muzzle, easily four feet at the shoulder. More bear than dog. Its lips curl away from teeth the size of my fingers.

Calvin. Somehow, impossibly, Calvin found me.

The wolf dips his head, grabs the knife by the hilt between his teeth, and flings it toward the lake with a sharp twist of his neck.

The robed figures scatter. Sam rips off his ceremonial garment with a snarl, buttons snapping, fabric ripping. His face contorts.

"Not tonight, Michigan!" His voice comes out strangled,

halfway between human and animal. Then his body convulses. Bones pop loud as firecrackers. His spine bows. Skin ripples. Fur bursts across him in clumps.

In seconds, a wolf stands where Sam was. He launches himself at Calvin, teeth bared, claws gouging furrows in the dirt.

The wolves collide midair with a sound like thunder. They crash down in a tangle of fur and teeth. The snarls that tear out of them sound ancient and feral.

They roll across the clearing, ripping up grass. Calvin's jaws clamp onto Sam's shoulder. Blood sprays. Sam yelps, twists, sinks his teeth into Calvin's flank. They tear apart, circle, hackles up. Calvin drops low, then surges under Sam's guard. His jaws close around Sam's throat.

Not enough to kill. Enough to pin.

Sam thrashes, claws tearing grooves in the dirt, but Calvin's grip holds. He drives Sam down until the sandy wolf's belly hits the ground.

"The box!" Rachel screeches, her voice slicing across the chaos. "Scribe! Now! Get rid of the wolf!"

The Asian man steps forward. His hands move in quick, practiced shapes as he accepts a small wooden box from Rachel. No bigger than a jewelry case, symbols carved into the lid.

His eyes shift. Silver floods them, reflective and impossible.

He opens the box. Pulls out a single strand of dark hair.

The Scribe starts writing in the air, his finger cutting lines into nothing. Silver symbols appear where he moves, hanging in front of him. They glow on their own, throwing strange shadows.

Old letters. Words I'd never understand.

Rachel and Ravena move to either side of him. Their voices braid through his, building something dense and patterned. The air presses down. Static crawls over my skin. Sparks snap between my fingertips.

"Stop!" I try to get up, legs still unsteady from the wine and whatever was in it. My vision wavers. "Leave him alone!"

No one looks at me. The magic swells until it feels like a living thing, crowding the clearing. My ears pop.

The symbols in the air pulse. The light jumps faster and faster, like a strobe.

Then Rachel screams.

Not furious. Afraid. High and sharp and terrified.

Her edges blur. Her whole outline ripples. She looks like wet ink being dragged across the page. She grabs at her chest, face warping.

Her mouth opens. "What... what's happening to me?"

Her fingers begin to break apart. Bits of her flake away, drifting off her hands and wrists. The pieces shine, then thin out, vanishing as they float like ashes in the breeze.

"No!" She claws at herself, trying to hold on. Her hands pass through her own arms like there's nothing solid to catch. "No, no, no..."

Her arms hollow next. Then her torso. She's unraveling from the outside in, her body falling away in glowing scraps. Each shard flashes once before going dark and winking out.

Her face goes last. Her features warp into something raw and terrified as the final pieces lift away and dissolve.

Then she's gone. No body. No ash. Just empty air and the echo of her scream.

The Scribe stares at the space where Rachel stood, his silver eyes wide. The wooden box slips from his fingers and hits the ground. The symbols hanging in the air stutter and go out.

"Goodbye, Mother."

I whip around to see Agnes Thornton standing at the edge of the clearing. Dirt streaks her cheeks. Her jaw is tight. Her eyes shine, but the tears stay put.

Her fingers twitch. Her shoulders tremble once, then set.

"What did you do?" Ravena shrieks, breaking away from the ritual. She rounds on Agnes, features sharpened by fury.

"The Scribe's spell worked perfectly... just not on who you

thought." Agnes steps forward. Light gathers along her knuckles. It grows, gold and steady.

Ravena screams, pure rage. She flings a bolt of crimson energy at Agnes. It hisses through the air, burning the grass in a line. Agnes snaps her arm up. A golden shield blooms in front of her, round and bright. The red bolt slams into it and bursts into sparks. The shield holds.

Agnes answers with her own spell. Words tumble from her mouth, low and sure. Golden light pours from her palms, splitting into three separate streaks. They curve in the air like they each have their own target. Ravena dives aside. One bolt clips her shoulder. Her robe catches fire. She shrieks, rips it off, and stands in a black dress, hair wild.

The clearing erupts.

Magic crashes back and forth. Red and gold light slam together. The air between them turns purple and ugly. Trees at the edge of the clearing catch fire. Bark blasts outward. Splinters rain down. Agnes and Ravena circle, trading hits.

Ravena sends a red wave racing along the ground. Agnes vaults over it, lands in a crouch, and hurls a golden spear that rips through Ravena's shield.

Ravena snarls, clutching her side where the spear burned. Dark blood oozes between her fingers.

She's not done.

She lifts both hands. The ground shudders. Cracks split open. Tree roots burst upward, thick and grasping, lunging toward Agnes.

Agnes says a single word, and the roots crumble to ash mid-reach.

Behind them, Calvin and Sam are still fighting. Sam has wriggled free of Calvin's throat hold. They face off again, both limping, both bleeding, both too stubborn to quit.

I drag myself across the ground, trying to get clear. Dirt grinds into my palms. My limbs lag like they're half a beat behind my brain.

A hand clamps around my arm and yanks me upright. Fingers bite into my bicep.

Vince.

Blood smears his face, his nose obviously broken from Calvin's hit. His eyes have gone wild, pupils blown wide.

In his other hand, he holds a gun. A small black revolver. So that was the weight in the basket.

He jams the barrel against my temple. The metal shocks my skin.

"I'm sorry," he whispers. His breath hits my ear, sour with wine and copper and fear. "I'm so, so sorry. But they promised if you die..."

His finger tightens. I feel the pull on the trigger.

I close my eyes.

I'm sorry, Calvin. I should have believed you.

The gun fires. The sound shatters the world, a white-hot crack right beside my head. My ears ring, high and shrill.

But nothing hits me.

I open my eyes.

Vince's arm points straight up. The shot went into the sky, lost in the dark.

I follow his arm.

A man floats above the clearing, suspended about ten feet up. Tall. Dark-skinned. Ronald Morehouse. His eyes go pure white. No iris, no pupil. Just white light.

With a small turn of his wrist, everything shifts.

Copies of me pop into existence around the clearing. Dozens of Everetts. Some sprinting, some stumbling, some standing still. Each one solid, each one wearing my face.

I wrench free and stumble toward the trees. My legs finally listen, unsteady but working.

Vince's head jerks around as he tries to track all of us. "What... which..."

A sharp yelp cuts through the roar of magic.

Sam's wolf body shoots sideways through the air, as if a giant hand swatted him. His legs flail, useless. He hits a tree so hard the trunk shivers and leaves dump down on top of him. He crumples at the base.

Ronald lowers his hand. Air ripples around his fingers.

The Scribe looks from Sam's crumpled form to the empty space where Rachel vanished and then to the battle still raging. His silver eyes dull back to brown.

He runs.

The last scraps of silver writing drift apart, leaving the smell of ozone behind.

Ravena and Agnes keep going. Their spells come slower now. Shoulders sag. Hands shake between attacks, but neither of them gives.

Agnes sends a sheet of golden fire. Ravena blocks with a wall of ice. Steam blasts up where they meet, filling the clearing with heat and fog.

Through the haze, I see Ravena pull power into herself. Both hands raised. Red light gathers between her fingers, spinning tighter and tighter. It hums with violent promise.

She's about to drop that on Agnes.

Agnes sees it too. Her eyes flare. She lifts her hands, but her movements drag. She's half a second behind.

And then lightning splits the sky.

Not from above. From off to my right.

A young Black woman steps out from behind a tree, close enough that I can see the determination in the line of her mouth. She lifts her arms. White flashes through her eyes. Somewhere above us, clouds that were just hanging there a moment ago roll in on themselves.

Bea Morehouse.

Thunder cracks loud enough to hurt.

Lightning rips out from her fingertips, a jagged branch of

white. It slams into the ground at Ravena's feet and explodes. Ravena flies backward, hits the dirt hard. Smoke curls off her hair. The hem of her dress ignites.

Ravena scrambles up, spinning. She looks from Agnes, swaying but still upright, to the man floating with glowing eyes, to the woman walking forward with hands still humming with leftover charge, to Sam bleeding in the dirt.

She retreats.

"This isn't over!" she shrieks. She's already backing toward the trees. "We're not finished!"

She turns and bolts into the forest. Branches whip her dress as she disappears.

Vince still stands near the picnic blanket, gun in hand. He whirls in place, tracking fake Everetts. He fires. Once. Twice. Three times. Bullets slice through illusions that don't bleed.

Bea raises her hands and murmurs something. Fog rolls in off the lake, thick and low, moving against the natural wind. It folds around Vince, swallowing him. Gunshots pop blindly from inside the mist.

"Come on!" Agnes grabs my arm. Her palm is hot; her fingers shake against my skin. "While they're distracted!"

I look for Calvin. Find him near the tree line. Sam lies at his feet, still in wolf form, still unconscious. Calvin's body shrinks and reshapes. Fur recedes. Bone shifts. In seconds, he's standing human again, wounds healing themselves.

Every incredible bare inch of him gleams with sweat and blood in the fading light. His breathing roughens his chest. Cuts and scratches stripe his arms and ribs. He scans the clearing, trying to pick me out from Ronald's copies.

"Calvin!" I shout, my voice scraping my throat. "I'm here!"

His head snaps to me. Our eyes meet.

His face cracks and then he moves, sprinting toward me, muscles tight and sure, body doing things I should not be admiring right now.

I run to meet him, finally doing what I should have done days ago.

He latches onto me and his arms fold around me hard, pulling me in. Heat and strength and the sharp smell of sweat and dirt and wolf fill my nose. He pulls my head to his furry chest, cradling me.

"I've got you," he mutters against my hair.

I hang on like letting go would be the end of me.

"Do you believe me now?" he asks. His voice comes out raw.

I answer by kissing him.

The kiss is messy and frantic and overdue. It fits. His body is solid against mine, and for once in my life, something lines up exactly how it should. I cup his face, his stubble scraping my palms. His arms tighten, hauling me up so my toes barely skim the ground.

For one second, everything else disappears. The thunder. The lightning. The yelling.

There's just this. Calvin and me and the truth. Nothing else matters.

A gunshot snaps the moment in half.

We break apart.

Vince stands about twenty feet away, gun raised. His face has gone tight and ugly. The fog has thinned. The illusions are fading. He can see us. And he's not happy.

"You're mine!" he screams.

He swings the gun toward us. His grip wobbles.

Lightning slams down again, closer this time. Heat brushes my face. The strike hits a nearby tree. Wood explodes. The trunk splits, sending burning shards across the clearing. Vince throws his arms up, yelping, the gun tumbling from his hand.

"Run!" Agnes yells. "Now!"

Ronald glides down, feet touching the dirt, his eyes dimming back to normal. The last of the extra Everetts blink out. Bea jogs toward us, breathing hard.

We race toward a car waiting at the clearing's edge. Calvin pushes me into the backseat and piles in after me, Agnes scrambling in from the other side. His arm comes around me, pulling me close. I feel his ribs rising and falling against me, fast and uneven but steady. Alive.

"Go, go, go!" Bea shouts.

Ronald is already behind the wheel. The engine roars. Tires spit dirt as we lurch backward away from the chaos.

Through the windshield, I watch Vince claw his way free of the splintered tree. He staggers toward us, empty hands reaching, his face twisted with rage and defeat.

He grabs the gun off the ground and fires. The shot rings out just as we hit the dirt road, the car fishtailing before Ronald straightens us out and floors it. We careen forward, leaving Vince and the ritual and my almost-death shrinking behind us.

I press my face into Calvin's shoulder.

I'm alive.

CHAPTER THIRTY-TWO

Everett

I sit in the back of Ronald's car, mind racing. I can't get my muscles to calm down. The mark on my wrist burns. I trace the spiral symbol branded into my skin. The flesh is hot, raw and angry red, like the burn went deep into bone.

Next to me, Calvin sits completely naked. His skin glows pale in the moonlight leaking through the car windows. Blood and dirt streak his chest, his arms, his thighs. I should look away, give him privacy, but my gaze keeps sliding back.

My savior. My wolf.

My... what? What is he to me now?

"Are you okay?" Bea turns around from the front passenger seat.

I nod, throat tight. What do you say after your boyfriend tries to murder you as part of a magical ritual? After you realize the man you thought you couldn't trust ended up being the one to save you?

"We need to get rid of that mark when we get to the house." She points at my wrist. "The Concord can track you with it. Even across time. Even in the future."

The future.

Calvin said something about taking me to the future. To his time. Away from here. Away from everything I've ever known.

Cold slides through me.

"And you." Bea shifts her attention to Calvin. "Really should have put your clothes on. I'm seeing way more of you than I ever wanted to."

I glance over again. Of course I do. Calvin is completely exposed, muscular thighs pressed against the leather seat, relaxed like this is no big deal. Heat prickles along my skin, low and insistent.

Calvin laughs. The sound is rich and warm, cutting through the tight, wired quiet in the car. "I didn't exactly have time to gather my clothes while trying not to get shot in the ass."

"You could have at least grabbed your drawers," Bea grumbles, though her mouth twitches.

"I have more clothes back at Esther's," Calvin says.

Ronald keeps his eyes fixed on the road, his hands locked on the steering wheel. The car speeds through the night, headlights cutting through the dark. Moonridge comes into view and then slides past in a blur of quiet porches and dark windows.

"How did you know?" I ask Calvin. My voice comes out rough, scraped raw. Maybe from yelling? Whatever it is, my throat feels like I swallowed glass.

His hand finds mine, his skin fever-hot against my cold fingers. "The short version is, I met your ghost in the future."

"My ghost?" The words scrape out.

He nods, holding my gaze. "In my time, the Concord sacrificed you. They bound your spirit and were using you as one of their members. They sent you to retrieve one of my friends for a ritual. They were going to use her as a key to rip open the veil between worlds. When I met you, you appeared human. We went on a few dates. I started to fall for you. And then I learned who you were and it gutted me."

Something sour creeps up the back of my tongue. That would have been my fate tonight. If Calvin hadn't found me. If Agnes and the others hadn't stepped in. I'd be dead and working for the people who killed me.

"But then we reconnected and I learned the truth. About what had happened to you," Calvin continues, squeezing my hand. "And when I found a way to travel back in time, I took it. I came back to save you."

"But why?" My voice barely makes it out. "You didn't know me. Not really."

His smile is soft. Sad. "I knew enough to care about you. And I couldn't stand the thought of you suffering forever. Plus, saving you means weakening the Concord in my time. Two birds, one stone."

"So practical," I say, aiming for a joke, trying to lean toward humor instead of panic. "Rescue the damsel in distress and screw over the evil cult at the same time."

"You're hardly a damsel." His eyebrows rise as he looks me up and down.

"But definitely in distress."

"Not anymore." His voice drops low. "Not while I'm around."

The car goes quiet as he leans over and kisses me again.

He sits back and exhales. "We saved you. They'll be down one member in the future. We weakened them."

"No." Agnes speaks up. Her voice is steady but thin, like it had to fight its way out. She's been so quiet I nearly forgot she was there. "They'll be down two members."

Silence pulls tight over the car.

"Your mother," Ronald says quietly, his deep voice rumbling from the front seat.

Agnes nods. Her profile is sharp against the passing streetlights, her chin tipped up. "She's gone. Written out of history."

My brain trips over the thought. Rachel Thornton, who I watched dissolve into nothing right in front of me, erased like she never existed. By her own daughter.

"Any regrets?" Bea asks. There is a strange respect in her voice.

"She was an awful woman. The things she would say and do to me... the abuse... ever since my father died it just kept getting worse." Agnes says it like she's reading a list. "When I learned what she really was, I knew she had to be stopped. I replaced Calvin's hair with hers in the box. The Concord doesn't have a Thornton anchor now. They're weak. And I'm not about to join them."

The car feels smaller. Tighter. The simple words hit like stones, one after another.

Ronald shifts his weight. "Wait. If Rachel was erased from history, how are you still here?" His brow furrows. "Shouldn't you have been erased too since you're her offspring?"

Agnes meets his eyes. "I thought of that. I assumed she would be written out from today forward and I would be fine, but just to be sure, I performed a binding spell before you rescued me." Her voice drops. "I tied my essence to an object that's buried beneath the apothecary's foundation. That building has been part of Moonridge longer than any of us. By anchoring myself to it, to the land itself, I made a connection the Scribe's magic couldn't erase. My existence is woven into Moonridge's history now, separate from my mother's. I needed Moonridge to hold a piece of me on this plane. Something that would keep me here even if my mother's entire existence was taken out of the timeline."

"Impressive," Bea murmurs.

"Were you certain it would work?" I ask.

Agnes gives a small, tired smile. "No. But I'm still here, so I suppose it did."

Ronald pulls the car up to the Morehouse home. The blue paint looks almost black in the dark, the yellow door a slice of warm color waiting for us. We climb out, stretching cramped limbs. My legs wobble, like they forgot how to hold my weight.

I move toward Agnes as she steps out of the car. My arm

goes around her shoulders. She goes rigid for a second, then eases into the half-embrace.

"Thank you," I whisper. "Not just for saving me. For all of it."

She gave up more than any of us. She doesn't answer. She gives a single sharp nod, but her hand comes up and squeezes mine where it rests on her shoulder.

We walk toward the house. Ronald leads. Bea just behind him. Agnes and me side by side, arms linked. Calvin, still bare-assed, brings up the rear. The porch light flickers as we step closer, throwing shadows across the boards.

I pull in a long breath as Ronald opens the door. This is me walking toward whatever comes next. Away from the only life I've known. Toward a future with Calvin in a place I can't picture yet.

Inside, the warm light feels wrong and comforting at the same time. In here, everything looks normal. A clock ticks on the mantel. The house smells like herbs and old wood and something sweet. Cinnamon. Apple. My stomach growls, a sharp reminder that I haven't eaten since... hell, sometime before everything went to shit. The day already feels stretched and warped.

Bea moves first, crossing the room in three quick strides. She throws her arms around Agnes in a fierce hug that nearly knocks her off her feet.

"Thank you," she whispers, her voice rough. "What you did... your mother... I know what it cost you."

Agnes stays stiff for a breath. Then her posture eases and she hugs Bea back. Her hands slide up and grip Bea's shoulders.

"She would have killed us all eventually," Agnes says quietly. "It was the only way. I'm sorry for how awful she always was to you. To all of you."

They stay like that for a long moment.

Calvin clears his throat. Still gloriously, completely naked in the middle of the living room. "I hate to interrupt, but I need to get to my bags and..."

"Lord have mercy." Bea laughs. She swipes under her eyes

and steps back. "Boy, go put some clothes on before my mother comes in and catches you with your ding-a-ling out."

Calvin grins and squeezes past, which gives me a full, unobstructed view of his backside. I take my time appreciating the scenery.

"You made it. All of you." Esther appears in the doorway from the kitchen. Her gaze passes over each of us, sharp and quick, like she's counting heads. "The portal is ready when you are."

When she says portal, something inside me jolts. This is real. This is happening. I'm about to leave 1958 and never come back.

Forever stretches in my head, huge and hollow. I'll probably never see these people again.

Everything I know is about to turn into history.

Literally.

Calvin comes back a few minutes later, dressed in jeans and a T-shirt that hugs his chest in a way that shouldn't be legal. He carries a duffel bag and a small backpack slung over one shoulder.

"The portal won't stay open long," Esther warns. Her face is set. Serious. "The energy required is immense, especially with the Concord's magic still active in the area. The magical balance of Moonridge is shifting. I can feel it. Once we get you two out of here, we have some work to do."

"How long do we have?" Calvin asks.

"Twenty minutes. Maybe thirty if we're lucky," Esther says. She presses a hand flat over her sternum, like she's centering herself. "Not more than that."

"Are you sure you're ready?" Agnes turns to me, her expression soft, almost motherly.

"I… I don't know," I admit.

"With my mother gone, the Concord is weakened. You might be safe here if you want to stay," Agnes says.

The idea hits sideways. Stay?

I hadn't even put that on the table. I've been so focused on escape that I never stopped to think about anything else.

"They're still out there," Esther says. Always practical. "And they know where Everett lives, works, everything. Rachel is gone, but the Concord is not finished. They'll keep trying to fill their ranks. You wouldn't be safe if you stayed."

She's right. I can still see Vince's face, warped with rage and betrayal as he aimed that gun at us. He wouldn't stop. He would hunt me down. Finish what he started.

"The mark," Agnes says, nodding toward my wrist. "We need to heal you before you go. Remove it so they can't find you again."

I look down at the spiral burned into my skin. A small ring of scarred flesh that nearly ended everything.

Esther comes over and takes my hand, examining my wrist. She holds her palm above the mark and murmurs under her breath. She lifts her other hand and Bea passes her a vial without needing to be told. Mother and daughter slot into place like they have done this a thousand times. Ronald starts to hum, a low, steady baritone that vibrates in my chest. Esther rubs oil into my skin, still chanting. The scent is sharp and herbal. She hands the vial back and Bea passes her an egg.

I have no idea why an egg is involved, but at this point, why not?

Esther runs the egg across my body from head to toe, voice rising and falling while Ronald hums and Bea joins him. The air thickens. The whole house seems to buzz. A strange lightness rolls through my limbs, as if something heavy I've been dragging finally slid off my shoulders.

Esther takes the egg into the bathroom. I hear the crack, then the flush.

"You're clear," Bea says.

I look at my wrist. Smooth skin. No spiral. No angry red edges. No mark at all.

Esther steps back into the room. "We need to move if you're going to leave tonight. It'll take me another day or two to form a new one after it closes."

I hesitate. This really is it.

"What's it like?" I ask Calvin. "The future, I mean."

His smile is gentle, knowing. "Different. Better in some ways. Music is louder. People are freer to be themselves. Technology is going to blow your mind."

Freer to be themselves.

I think about hiding. About the constant calculation. About watching every word, every glance, because one wrong move could get me arrested, beaten, killed.

"And you'll be there," I say. It's not a question.

"Every step of the way." His eyes hold mine. "For as long as you want me to be."

That settles something inside me. What do I really have here? A room at the Randalls'. A job at a garage. No family. No real friends except the people in this room, and I barely know them. Vince was all I had, and that turned out to be smoke and lies.

Images flicker through my mind anyway. The diner. Florence's bad Texas accent and the extra whipped cream she piles on my milkshakes. Earl's face lighting up whenever he talks engines and radios. Little pieces of a life that never fully fit but still managed to root in me.

Leaving means turning my back on all of that. On the only time I've ever known.

Staying means spending the rest of my life watching doors and shadows, waiting for the Concord to find me. Even if I left Moonridge, I'd never really be safe.

"I'll go," I say. My voice comes out steady. "There's nothing for me here that's worth dying for."

"You'll need to wear this." Calvin removes a pendant from around his neck. "I can get back because I'm tied to that timeline. It's where I belong. But you need a key."

He hands it to me and I can't help but balk. Another magical necklace? It looks ancient, the metal worn smooth. Strange symbols twist along its surface.

A knot tightens low in my gut. Not this again.

"It's safe. This is the key," he explains. "My friend La'Tasha gave it to me. It's a tether. It will ensure you can come back to my time."

I stare at the little disk and cord that's supposed to drag me into the future.

My fingers close around it. The metal feels warm and steady against my skin, like it remembers where it's supposed to take me.

A way forward.

"Put it on," he says. "And hold my hand. It will get us back safely."

I slip it over my head and let it settle against my chest. It's not exactly heavy, but I feel the weight of it anyway.

Calvin picks up his duffel bag and hands it to me. "Can you carry this? I'll take the backpack."

I nod and take the bag from him. The solid weight is almost comforting. Something I can hold onto.

Then I take his hand. Our fingers lace together, like they were always meant to fit this way.

"I guess this is goodbye," Agnes says. She stands near the fireplace, hands clasped like she's not sure what to do with them.

"Thank you," I tell her. The words are small compared to what she's done. "For everything. For believing him when I didn't. For helping save me."

Her smile is small but real. "Just be happy in the future, okay? That's how you can thank me."

"I will," I promise. I hope I'm not lying.

Calvin hugs Bea, who rolls her eyes but wraps him up anyway. Then Ronald pulls him into a hug that lifts Calvin off his feet. Esther kisses his cheek like she is sending her kid off to a new life.

"Be sure to give La'Tasha that book. Your future may depend on it."

Calvin nods, eyes tearing up. "It's right in there." He points to the bag I carry.

I watch them, throat aching. All these people bent their lives around mine tonight.

Me.

Someone they barely know. Someone who has always felt like an afterthought. For the first time in my life, I feel like I matter.

And then the window behind us explodes.

Glass blasts inward, a spray of glittering knives. I throw my arms over my head as shards slice into my skin. A ball of fire punches through the gap and slams onto the living room rug.

Flames roar to life in an instant, racing up the curtains like they already knew the path. The couch catches. The heat punches at my face.

"Out! Now!" Ronald bellows, shoving us toward the back door.

We run. Smoke pours through the house at an impossible speed, thick and black and choking. It sears my lungs, scorches my eyes. Shapes blur. The air tastes like poison. A hand clamps around my arm and drags me forward.

This fire feels wrong. Too fast, too hungry, like something alive is feeding it.

We burst out the back door into the yard. Cool air rushes over my face. I cough and drag in greedy breaths. Tears blur everything.

"Hello, Everett."

Everything inside me goes still.

Calvin and I turn. Vince stands at the edge of the yard, the fire casting his face in streaks of orange and shadow. The Scribe stands at his side, Ravena and Sam drifting behind them like smoke.

Vince holds something in his hand. A white shirt.

"You should have grabbed your clothes before you left, Wolf. This is your last chance," Vince says. His tone is calm, almost casual. "Everett can leave with me now and the wolf stays safe. If not, the Scribe has what he needs to erase him."

The Scribe's eyes flash silver as he looks at the shirt. Even worn fabric holds traces. Essence. Calvin's life smeared into the seams.

Calvin steps in front of me, body shielding mine. "He's not going anywhere with you."

Behind us, the house is a solid wall of fire. Flames pour from every window and crawl up the roof. The heat shoves at my back. Wood pops and snaps. Glass shatters. Esther's home is turning into ash.

"Go!" Esther shouts. Her voice cuts through the chaos. "Now! The portal won't last!"

The shed waits at the back of the yard. Its door hangs open. Blue light spills out, bright and wrong and alive.

Bea lifts her hands. Her eyes flare white. Thunder crashes overhead, even though the sky is empty. The air shrieks. Lightning spears the ground a few feet from Vince.

The world detonates there. Dirt and grass erupt into the air. The blast throws me off my feet.

Vince doesn't flinch. He raises his gun at Calvin's chest.

For a heartbeat, Ronald's eyes meet Calvin's. Something passes between them. Understanding. Then Ronald moves, faster than I knew he could. He throws himself between Calvin and the gun just as Vince fires. The bullet slams into him. Dark spreads across his shirt, soaking the fabric.

He crumples to the ground.

"Ronald!" Bea's scream rips out of her, ragged and wailing. She drops to her knees beside him. "No, no, no..."

He doesn't move. Blood gathers under him, seeping into the grass.

He can't be gone.

Magic surges around us. Gold light flares from Agnes. Blue from Esther. Crimson from Ravena. And a bright glow emanates around the Scribe, whose eyes shine silver as he begins to write in the air.

Symbols appear, hanging there, pulsing. The same kind that tore Rachel apart.

He's going to erase Calvin.

"Run!" Esther yells. "Get to the portal. We'll hold them off!"

Agnes sends a streak of golden energy at Vince. It hits the ground where he stood a second ago, leaving scorched earth. He's already moving, trying to line up another shot.

Esther throws a shimmering shield over Ronald's body. Blue light hums, crackling with power.

The Scribe keeps writing. The symbols multiply, spreading through the air like a sickness.

"Calvin!" I grab his hand. "We have to go!"

He looks at Ronald's body. At Bea, sobbing over him. At Esther and Agnes standing their ground.

"We can't leave them—"

Another gunshot. Something hot snaps past my ear.

"Go!" Agnes screams. Sweat runs down her face. Blood trails from her nose.

We run.

We tear across the yard toward the shed. Calvin's duffel bag slams against my hip. Gunshots crack behind us. Lightning answers. The night turns into noise and light and heat.

The house groans, then caves in on itself with a deafening crash. Sparks spray into the sky, scattering like wild embers.

The shed door gapes ahead. Blue light churns inside, bright and terrible and beautiful.

Vince shouts behind us. Footsteps pound over the grass.

I reach the doorway first and turn to make sure Calvin is there. He's right behind me, hand reaching for mine.

The Scribe's silver symbols litter the air now, crowding in, swelling with power.

"Go!" Calvin shouts. "I'm right behind you!"

A gun fires as I step through.

The world drops away.

I fall and spin. Everything and nothing all at once. My insides lurch. My skin feels flayed and slapped back into place.

Heat flashes over me, then a deep, aching cold.

Colors that shouldn't exist smear together. Sounds scrape against my bones. Something pulls me thin as paper, then crushes me into a single point.

Time hooks into me and yanks.

Solid ground slams into my feet.

I stagger, almost go down. The duffel bag drags along the ground. My legs wobble. The room tilts.

What the hell?

I'm in someone's living room. But it's like no living room I've ever seen. An orange couch sits across from a purple chair with a blue footstool covered in patterns. Pillows everywhere. Plants hang from the ceiling in pots. Crystals line the windowsill, catching light that comes from the portal I just stepped through.

Where am I?

A hallway opens to my left. Footsteps pound toward me.

A Black woman bursts into the room wearing rumpled pajamas, sleep mask askew on top of her head. She's barefoot and brandishing a baseball bat. "I don't know who the hell you think you are, but you picked the wrong—"

She stops mid-charge, the words dying on her lips. Her eyes dart from me to the glowing wall behind me.

Bea? No. Not Bea, but she looks just like her. This must be La'Tasha.

"Everett?"

I nod and spin back around. The wall glows blue, pulsing with that same light from the doorway. The surface ripples like water.

"Come on," I whisper to it. "Where are you?"

Any second. He was right behind me. Any second.

"Oh my God, it's really you." Her voice climbs with excitement. The baseball bat hits the floor with a clatter. "You made it!"

Footsteps rush toward me. She throws her arms around me from behind, squeezing tight. "I can't believe it worked. Calvin did it. He actually brought you back. Where is he?"

"He was right behind me." I pull free, stepping toward the portal. The blue light pulses, waiting. "He should be here by now."

She moves to stand beside me, staring at the glowing wall.

Seconds crawl past.

The blue light flickers.

It thins. Pulls inward. The edges of the doorway curl in on themselves.

"No." I lunge toward it, but La'Tasha grabs me. Her grip clamps down like iron.

"Don't. You could get trapped between times."

The doorway keeps shrinking. The blue fades to violet, then to a bruised purple.

Then it's gone.

Nothing but a solid wall. Cold. Unmoving.

"Calvin?" My voice comes out wrecked. "Where's Calvin?"

La'Tasha shakes her head. "Was he with you when you left?"

"Yes. He was right behind me. There were gunshots and…" My voice climbs. I don't bother to pull it back. "Where is he?"

"I don't know," she says.

Did Vince's bullet hit him? Did the Scribe finish that spell? Has Calvin been wiped out of history? Out of everything?

My legs give out and I drop to the floor. The duffel bag lands with a dull thunk. The pendant at my chest turns ice-cold.

I made it.

Calvin didn't.

And there's no way back.

SOMEWHERE IN TIME

CHAPTER THIRTY-THREE

Calvin

I slam into the floor and the air blasts out of my lungs. Pain roars through my abdomen. I roll onto my back, pulling in shallow, hitching breaths.

Where's Everett?

The blue light of the portal is gone. Instead, warm yellow light from antique lamps fills the room. The smell of dried herbs curls through the air. Sharp. Earthy. Familiar, but... off. Like something that doesn't belong was added to the recipe.

The world refuses to hold still. Colors smear. Shapes bend at the edges. I reach for a thought and it slides away before I can catch it.

"Well, well, well. Look what the cosmic winds blew in."

I know that voice.

Impossible.

"Is he dead? He looks a bit dead around the edges."

Another voice. Higher, curious.

"Don't be stupid, Trixie. Dead things don't bleed, and he's

making quite the mess on our nice clean floor."

I force my eyes open. Three cats sit in a row on a wooden counter, staring down at me with expressions far too judgmental for the state I'm in.

The Atomic Cats. Trixie, Velma, and Lucy from the Blue Moon Apothecary.

Why am I at the apothecary?

Esther said I would make it back through the portal. I must've landed here instead of with La'Tasha. That has to be what happened. Everett probably ended up wherever she is because the pendant was tethered to her. I landed here because of my anchor to…

My brother? Blake does spend half his life in this place. Maybe the magic knows that?

I try to sit up. Pain flares through my middle and I drop back, breath ripping free, somewhere between an exhale and a groan.

"Yeah, I wouldn't do that if I were you," Velma comments, licking one paw with maddening calm. "You've got quite the hole where holes shouldn't be."

Hole.

I lift my head just enough to see my stomach. Blood soaks my shirt, spreading in a dark circle from a wound on the left side of my abdomen. Too dark. Too wide.

Fuck. That's a lot of blood. My head drops back to the floor.

"I've been shot," I say. My voice sounds wrong, distant, like it belongs to someone in another room.

"Give the man a prize," Velma drawls. "Such powers of observation."

"He's in shock," Trixie notes. "Humans get very slow when they're leaking."

"Want me to lick your wounds, handsome?" Lucy asks.

Music drifts from somewhere nearby. Synthesizers. Drum machines. A woman's voice, bright and hopeful.

The song snags in my foggy brain. It's from the 80s.

That makes zero sense. Hazel hates any music from before the early 2000s. Says it's "criminally overrated nostalgia bait."

I turn my head, taking in the room. The layout matches the Blue Moon Apothecary I know. Same counter. Same shelves hugging the walls. Same doorway to the back room.

But little details are off. A rotary phone sits on the counter where Hazel's laptop usually lives, and a boombox sits on a shelf above the register.

A cold jolt hits my gut.

"What year is it?" I ask, already bracing for a bad answer.

"What year do you think it is?" Velma counters, whiskers twitching.

"Not helpful." I press my hand against my wound. Heat slicks my palm as blood seeps between my fingers. My vision wavers, edges softening. "Just tell me. Please."

"He's going to pass out," Trixie observes with clinical detachment. "Then he'll die. Very inconvenient timing."

"Should we get Agnes?" Velma asks, kneading the countertop. "She'd be upset if we let him die on the floor."

Agnes. Not Hazel.

Oh God. How far off am I?

The cats keep arguing over whether to let me bleed out on the floor. Their voices fade in and out like a radio that can't quite find the station.

"If he dies, who's going to clean up the mess?" Lucy points out.

"Fair point," says Velma. "And Agnes has been waiting for him. She'd be quite cross if we let him expire after all this time."

Waiting for me?

My brain can't hold onto anything. I went through the portal after Everett. Or I tried to. The Scribe was trying to erase me. Vince had a gun. There was fire and shouting and magic crackling through the air.

Ronald got shot. He went down. Didn't move.

Is he dead? Did Ronald die?

My lungs forget how to work for a second.

Footsteps approach from the back room. Light and quick.

"Mom! MOM!" A girl's voice rings out, high with panic. "There's a man bleeding on our floor!"

A teenage girl stands in the doorway, eyes wide as saucers. She can't be more than fifteen or sixteen, and she's dressed like she stepped out of an 80s music video—lace top over a neon yellow tank, tulle skirt billowing around her knees, leg warmers bunched at her ankles. Her bangs are shellacked into place with enough hairspray to punch a hole in the ozone.

For a second, I think it's Hazel. Same heart-shaped face, same scatter of freckles across her nose. But her hair is darker. And she's too young. Hazel is in her late twenties in my time.

"Mom! Hurry!" The girl doesn't come closer, just stays rooted in the doorway.

More footsteps, faster and heavier. A woman bursts into the room, slightly out of breath.

"Fiona, what are you yelling about? I was on the phone with—"

She stops when she sees me. Her hand flies to her mouth.

"Oh. Oh my Goddess." Her voice cracks. "It worked. Oh my heavens, you're bleeding."

She's maybe forty, wearing black leggings and an oversized "Frankie Says Relax" T-shirt, her auburn hair pulled back in a scrunchie.

I know her face. She's older now. Lines bracket her eyes and mouth, but it *is* her.

"Agnes?" The name scrapes out of me.

Her smile is instant. Warm. The same one she gave me when I first met her.

"Calvin!" She crosses the room in three quick strides, kneeling beside me. "It's about time."

The girl stares at me like I stepped off a spaceship. "You know this guy?"

"I've been waiting for him for about twenty-five years," Agnes says. She presses her hands against my wound, and I hiss through my teeth as pain spikes bright and sharp. "Sorry. I need to stop the bleeding."

Twenty-five years?

"By the way, this is my daughter, Fiona," Agnes adds. The girl gives me a nervous little wave. "My husband Barry is at work. We need to get you fixed up before he gets home. He's sensitive about blood."

Daughter. Husband. Agnes has a whole life now. A family. My brain struggles to stack that on top of the girl in the yellow dress who wrote her mother out of existence just a few hours ago.

"Where am I?" I ask, though the answer is mostly obvious. "When am I?"

"Blue Moon Apothecary, but you already know that," she answers. Her hands are warm and steady over my skin. "1983. August fifteenth, to be exact."

"1983." I repeat the year like it might rearrange itself if I say it enough. "I'm in 1983."

The weight of it crashes over me. I'm not just displaced. I'm stranded.

Assuming he made it, I'm more than forty years away from Everett. He's probably with La'Tasha right now, thinking I died or was written out of existence. I said I was right behind him.

I lied to him. Again.

Will he be okay? He has no one to help him adjust. He's probably terrified.

"I have so many questions," I say. My voice sounds thin to my own ears.

"I'm sure you do." Agnes's tone is calm. The same gentle authority she had as a younger woman, now layered with years I missed. "But first, let's stop you from bleeding to death on my nice clean floor."

"That's what I said," Velma comments from her perch.

"Not now," Agnes says without looking up. To Fiona, she adds, "Get my blue bag from the back room. The one with the silver clasp. And bring clean towels."

Fiona spins and vanishes, clearly relieved to have something to do that doesn't involve the bleeding stranger in front of her.

"How did I get here?" I ask, clinging to the sound of my own voice to stay conscious. Every breath pulls at the wound. "I was supposed to go back to my time. With Everett."

Agnes exhales slowly. Her hands never stop moving as she checks the wound, adjusts pressure, evaluates the mess Vince left me in. "The night everything went down, Ravena threw a fireball through the Morehouse window. The house burned to the ground."

What was years ago to her happened mere minutes ago for me. I can still feel the heat. See the glass raining down, flames racing across the room.

"Ronald was shot," she continues, her voice softening.

"Did he…" I can't make myself say the word.

"Oh, he's fine. Shot him in the hip. He has a nasty limp now, but it doesn't slow him down much."

Relief comes so fast my eyes sting. I don't think I could live with knowing La'Tasha's great-uncle died for me.

"What about Everett?" I finally manage. "Did he make it through? Is he okay?"

Please. Please let him be okay.

"He made it through the portal," Agnes says.

The tension in my shoulders drops so fast my body feels loose. I choke on a breath that wants to turn into a sob.

"Bea confirmed it with a tracking spell," she adds. "But where or when he ended up…" She shakes her head. "We can only hope he made it to your time."

I have to think he made it. I can't think that he, too, could have been thrown into another time where I'll never be able to find him.

Fiona returns with a blue velvet bag and an armful of towels. Agnes takes them, already shifting into full healer mode.

"The Scribe tried to rewrite your existence," Agnes says as she works, opening the bag and pulling out bottles and packets of herbs. "Vince shot you right as you stepped up to the shed. You fell before you could make it through."

Yes. The crack of the gun. Heat blooming in my gut. Hitting the ground as reality split open.

"I had thrown magic at the Scribe," Agnes says, mixing something in a small bowl. "Esther intervened with his writing. Disrupted the spell. She managed to burn your T-shirt."

The mixture she's grinding smells sharp and medicinal. The scent pricks at my nose.

"I had no idea what year you were from," she admits. "You never told us. Just said 'the future.' So when I saw what was happening, I used magic to push you through and shouted '1983' as loud as I could. I needed you far enough ahead that the Concord's grip would weaken."

She speaks like someone who has replayed that moment a thousand times.

"Why 1983 specifically?" I ask as she spreads the mixture over the wound. It burns hot for a heartbeat, then the edge of the pain starts to sink away.

"I panicked," she admits. "1983 seemed a long ways off. A safe distance. When I pushed you, that was the year I anchored you to."

"You're more than forty years off," I tell her as the pain settles into something I can breathe through.

Agnes's face tightens. "I know that now. I'm so sorry."

"You saved my life," I say. "You don't need to apologize for that."

She smiles and pats my shoulder. "We need to get you fixed up and then over to see Bea. She's been waiting for you, too."

Something warm stirs in my chest. For the first time since

I landed here, I feel the shape of hope.

"Esther?" I ask. "Is she…"

"Very much alive." Agnes's voice turns fond. "And very eager to see you. She and Bea have been waiting. They're ready to help."

"So you all knew I'd show up?"

Agnes nods. "We didn't know when you'd get here exactly, or how bad it would be when you arrived. Just that you were going to show up sometime this year if my spell had worked."

"What's going to happen if I'm still here in nine years? That's when I'm supposed to be born. Will my birth not happen, or will there be two of me?"

She helps me sit up. The floor seems to roll once under me, and I grab her arm until everything evens out.

"We need to get you back home before then," she says. Her eyes are serious now, all humor gone. "The universe doesn't like paradoxes. Two versions of the same person in the same timeline for more than a few days can tear holes in things we really don't want torn."

The bleeding has slowed to almost nothing thanks to whatever she smeared on me. The pain settles into a steady throb in my side. Manageable. Survivable.

"So let's go see Bea and Esther," I say, as I peel myself off the floor. My legs are steadier now, and the pain in my abdomen has eased, the magic paste doing its thing. "If anyone can help me get back to my own time, it's them. They can open a new portal."

Agnes winces and I know I'm not going to like what she's about to say.

"Yeah, so, we thought about that. But then we remembered that Everett was carrying the bag with the Morehouse spell book in it. It had the spell for creating a new portal."

I drop my head back and fight the urge to scream.

"But we'll figure it out," Agnes says. She lifts my arms and starts winding bandages around my torso in practiced loops. "You need to focus on healing. And we need to plan how to keep you safe until we can get you out of here. The Concord isn't gone. They're still out there. Waiting."

Her words send a chill through me that has nothing to do with blood loss.

"What happened to them? After that night?"

"Without my mother as their anchor, they splintered," Agnes says. "They went into hiding. But they didn't stop. They never stop."

"What about Vince?" I ask. My fingers twitch at the memory of the gun in his hand. "And Ravena?"

"Vince disappeared," Agnes says, securing the last bandage. "No idea what happened to him. His father filed a missing person's report, but no one saw him again after that night. He just vanished."

"And Ravena?"

A small, sharp smile flickers across Agnes's face. "Let's just say she won't be back in Moonridge anytime soon. She's been banished."

"What did you do?"

"I stripped her of most of her power," Agnes says, like it's the most ordinary thing in the world. "Bound it. Scattered it across Moonridge so she couldn't gather it back. She left town with barely enough magic to light a candle."

Until she comes back after you die, I think. But that's a problem for another decade.

I look down at my blood-soaked shirt and grimace. "Everett has my duffel bag. The one with my spare clothes."

"Right." Agnes stands. "Let me grab you something to wear. I'll be right back."

She disappears down the hallway and returns a minute later with a blue T-shirt. "It's my husband's. Should work for now."

I peel off the ruined shirt and pull on the blue one. Or try to. The fabric stretches tight across my chest and shoulders, stopping a good three inches above my waistband. I look down at myself. It's basically a crop top.

"Uh…"

Agnes presses her lips together, clearly fighting a smile. "You're a bit taller and broader than Barry."

"Just a bit." I tug at the hem, which doesn't budge. My stomach is completely exposed.

"We'll stop by the store and get you some proper clothes," she says, grabbing her purse from the counter. "Can't have you walking around Moonridge looking like that."

"Appreciated."

"Can I come?" Fiona asks, brightening.

"Not this time," Agnes tells her. "You need to watch the shop. And if your father gets home before I do, tell him I went to visit Aunt Bea and I'll be back for dinner."

Fiona rolls her eyes and moves to the counter, snapping her fingers as she goes. The blood vanishes from the floor like someone erased it with a cloth.

Agnes grabs her keys and a light jacket. "Ready?"

I nod, then look at the cats, who have watched all of this like it's mildly interesting television.

"Thanks for the warm welcome, guys."

"Try not to die before you get back to your time," Lucy says, stretching. "It would be such a waste after all this waiting."

"He'll be fine," Trixie insists. "He's got a destiny to fulfill."

"Destiny is just another word for 'inevitable suffering,'" Velma grumbles.

Their commentary trails after us as we step out into the bright August sunlight. People move along the sidewalk in clothes that will end up on Halloween racks in my time. High-waisted jeans. Shoulder pads. Loud prints. Hair teased and sprayed into shapes that should not survive gravity.

Agnes leads me to a station wagon parked at the curb. It's powder blue with wood paneling along the sides.

"Nice ride," I say, trying for levity.

"Barry's very proud of it," Agnes says, unlocking the doors. "He calls it the Family Cruiser."

I ease into the passenger seat, wincing when the movement tugs at my bandages. The interior smells like vinyl and artificial pine. A tiny tree dangles from the rearview mirror.

Agnes starts the car, and the radio crackles to life.

"Buckle up," she says, checking the mirrors. "We've got a future to save."

Acknowledgments

If the acknowledgments in this book sound familiar, it's because writing these gives me a ton of anxiety. I'm so afraid I'm going to leave someone or something out, so I tend to just copy and paste from book to book and then make edits as needed.

Ally, Susie, and Carter your editing wisdom, sharp eyes, and design skills are unmatched. This book is cleaner, tighter, and far more readable because of your generous help and occasional tough love. Thanks for keeping me on my toes with the time travel rules and for asking me the tough questions that I needed to have asked. It made it all so much cleaner. Extra special shout out to Susie who had the idea for the atomic cats. I love them so much!

To my beta and sensitivity readers: Corey, Deidre, and Mel. I'm so grateful for your honest, thoughtful, and often hilariously blunt feedback. Thanks for traveling through time with me.

To my friends not directly mentioned here (there are many), thank you for letting me disappear for hours and sometimes days without too many questions or interruptions. This is what I was doing when I turned down dinners, canceled plans and left texts unanswered. Your patience with me and my quirks means more than I can say. I often wonder what I did to deserve you all.

And finally, to you, the reader. Thank you for taking a chance on an indie author, and for coming back for another Moonridge adventure. I hope you love these weird and wonderful characters as much as I do. I can't wait for you to see what happens next!

About the Author

Avery Arujo is the pen name of a socially anxious, awkward, and proudly introverted author of the paranormal mystery/romance series Welcome to Moonridge. Avery lives in the northern U.S., where the scenery is beautiful, the weather perfect, and the food divine. When not writing, you'll find Avery watching a horror movie or trashy reality TV or reading under a blanket with a cup of coffee, and the world's sweetest dog trying to prove that they are more interesting than any old book.

For more information about the *Welcome to Moonridge* series, or to sign up for the newsletter, visit welcometomoonridge.com.

COMING SOON

Will Calvin make it back to present-day Moonridge?

Keep an eye out for the next book in the *Welcome to Moonridge* series, planned for release in the Fall of 2026. For updates, sneak peeks, and early news, visit welcometomoonridge.com and sign up for the newsletter.

www.ingramcontent.com/pod-product-compliance
Lightning Source LLC
LaVergne TN
LVHW032007070526
838202LV00059B/6329